Her Father's Name

by

Florence Marryat

edited with an introduction and notes by Greta Depledge

Victorian Secrets 2009

Published by

Victorian Secrets Limited
32 Hanover Terrace
Brighton BN2 9SN

www.victoriansecrets.co.uk

Her Father's Name by Florence Marryat
First published in 1876
This Victorian Secrets edition 2009

Introduction and notes © 2009 by Greta Depledge
This edition © 2009 by Victorian Secrets

Composition and design by Catherine Pope
Cover photo © iStockphoto.com/andipantz

All rights reserved. The use of any part of this publication reproduced, transmitted in any form or by any means, electronic, mechanical, photocopying, recording, or otherwise, or stored in a retrieval system, without prior consent of the publisher, constitutes an infringement of the copyright law.

A catalogue record for this book is available from the British Library.

ISBN 978-1-906469-14-6

CONTENTS

Introduction	i
The life and work of Florence Marryat	i
Her Father's Name: Cross-dressing, detection and hysteria	x
Female cross-dressing in nineteenth-century literature	xi
The female detective and *Her Father's Name*	xxi
The nineteenth-century hysteric	xxvii
A note on the text	xxxiii
Further reading	xxxiv
Her Father's Name	1
Appendix A – Extract from Maria Edgeworth's *Belinda*	325
Appendix B – Extract from Sarah Grand's *The Heavenly Twins*	329
Appendix C – Hysteria	335
Appendix D – Contemporary reviews of *Her Father's Name*	338

Acknowledgements

I am grateful to Catherine Pope for her enterprise and ingenuity in setting up Victorian Secrets publishing house and thereby making the works of neglected and forgotten writers increasingly available to the modern reader. It is a wonderful enterprise and it is a pleasure to be involved.

I would like to dedicate this edition to my own little Florence.

Greta Depledge, 2009

Introduction

1. The life and work of Florence Marryat

The life of Florence Marryat contains all the intrigue of one of her sensation fictions – marriage, adultery, separation, numerous children, bereavement, notoriety, fame and success. A glimpse of Marryat's life can, perhaps, be gained from her 1892 novel *The Nobler Sex* which is generally perceived as being her most autobiographical work. It tells the story of a most eventful and dramatic life with a heroine who is admirable and infuriating in equal measure, but whose life is far from dull. The central protagonist of the novel is an unhappily (twice) married, successful author who converts to Catholicism and who finds comfort in spiritualism.

A book by Harry Furniss who was a regular contributor to the *London Society* journal during Marryat's reign as editor contains the following anecdote about Marryat's eventful life:

> Known as Mrs Ross Church when I first met her, she decided to marry someone else, and discarded her husband, who I think was in the army. Anyway, she sent all her friends and acquaintances, myself included, a statement in cold printers ink, informing us that she was not divorced, but that in future she wished to be known as Mrs Lean. This little piece of eccentricity fell into her husband's solicitor's hands and thus ended the Church business.[1]

Hardly surprising then that a woman so doggedly determined to follow her own path has left us with a collected works full of independent, strong-minded female characters.

That this prolific novelist, editor, journalist, actress and spiritualist is finally receiving critical interest is no surprise. What is perhaps surprising is that it has taken so long for academic attention to bring to light her long-neglected work. Florence Marryat was immensely popular with the reading public throughout her long and

---

[1] Harry Furniss, *Some Victorian Women: Good, Bad and Indifferent* (London: John Lane, The Bodley Head Ltd, 1923), p. 11.

prolific career. Furniss in his book on Victorian women writers describes her as "a prolific writer, but not a great one."[2]

However, her popularity and success cannot be ignored. It is, perhaps, only with hindsight that we can really assess the place her work had in the nineteenth century. She regularly wrote about characters that challenged and transgressed social mores and that her novels sold in such vast numbers makes the content of her work of interest. Now, as Marryat's novels, and appraisals of them, are becoming increasingly available her work can be reassessed.

Whilst names like Mary Elizabeth Braddon, Marie Corelli, and Rhoda Broughton are now quite familiar, it is likely that many readers of nineteenth-century fiction will not have heard of Marryat despite her prominent place in Victorian literary circles. Marryat's contribution to the 1892 collaborative novel *The Fate of Fenella* alongside such writers as Frances Eleanor Trollope, Arthur Conan Doyle, Bram Stoker, and many others does give us a clear indication of her literary standing at this time.[3] In fact, Marryat was familiar with literary circles from a young age. For example, her father's friendships with his leading literary contemporaries meant that Marryat was able to approach Charles Dickens for advice early in her career. The Marryat archive at Yale contains a letter from Dickens to Marryat with his detailed comments on her 1867 novel *The Confessions of Gerald Estcourt.*

Marryat's 1897 gothic tale *The Blood of the Vampire,* one of the few works by Marryat to have received some critical attention, was published the same year as Bram Stoker's *Dracula,* and whilst *Dracula* has achieved the status of being probably the most regularly listed novel of all undergraduate English Literature degree programmes, Marryat's novel of that same year is barely known - although I would suggest that the central female figure of this novel, Harriet Brandt, is as worthy of academic interest as her fictional vampiric sister, Lucy Westenra. All this builds a somewhat confusing frame of reference to our under-standing of Marryat's prominence and then obscurity in the history of English literature.

---

[2] Furniss, *Women*, p. 10.
[3] This collaborative work has recently been reprinted – see *The Fate of Fenella,* ed. by Andrew Maunder (Kansas City: Valancourt Books, 2008).

Introduction

An obituary published in the *Academy* perhaps sums up the dichotomy that was Marryat's career – her popularity coupled with her inability to please the literary elite.

> Miss Florence Marryat, who has died in Bayswater this week, bore a name that has been adored by successive generations of schoolboys. Captain Marryat, R.N., C.B (his titles are lost in his fame as a story-teller), had a large family; and his daughter Florence was only sixteen, and therefore much too young, when she became the wife of Captain Ross Church. When nursing her children through a fever she wrote her first novel – her first of some seventy novels! That they had a certain vogue their number suggests: that half their names are all known to any single individual it would be rash to aver.[4]

It could perhaps be argued that Marryat initially established her career on the coat-tails of her successful father. Marryat, apparently, showed an interest in becoming a writer at the age of 11, when she wrote a novel which she illustrated with her own pen and ink drawings.[5] Captain Marryat's sea-faring novels were hugely successful and Marryat's devotion to, and reverence of, her father is abundantly clear in her 1872 *Life and Letters of Captain Marryat*.

Furthermore, despite having been married a number of years before her first novel was published Marryat chose to publish in her maiden name. In an interview given in 1891 to Frederick Dolman for *Myra's Journal: The Lady's Monthly Magazine* when discussing her decision to try and get her first work, *Love's Conflict*, published by her father's publishers Bentley's she said "Mr Bentley, probably glad to have the name Marryat again on his books if they had any merit at all, sent me a cheque within a very short time."[6] Clearly it was an astute business decision to use her father's name and reputation to get her own career off the ground. Marryat's pride in her father's legacy and the influence he had on her is evident throughout her life and career. In this 1891 interview Dolman describes the

---

[4] Unsigned obituary, *Academy* 57 (1899: July/Dec) p. 519.
[5] Unsigned obituary, *The New York Times* 28 October 1899, p 13.
[6] Frederick Dolman, 'Miss Florence Marryat at Home', *Myra's Journal: The Lady's Monthly Magazine* vol XVII, no. 5, (1891), pp. 1-2.

memorabilia related to her father that Marryat kept in her study, he writes: "with these and many other things to keep alive the memory of her gallant father, it was not strange that at the close of our conversation the novelist should be speaking of him rather than of her own varied and interesting career."[7]

However, the *Athenaeum,* regularly quite critical of Marryat's fictional output, was notably disappointed with Marryat's work on her father's life:

> It would have been well had Mrs. Church taken counsel before putting together, in the same volumes, the materials of her father's life, and materials which have little or nothing to do with it. What the public wanted was a reproduction of the living man, not of dead, dull documents, official and non-official, which refer to his professional deeds and duties. All that his daughter has told us of the sailor and novelist is worth reading. We only wish further details of his doings had been allowed to take the place of very ordinary letters, and still more ordinary documents. Mrs. Church complains that she has been able to collect but few letters; we regret that she has not collected fewer, and told more of what remains untold.[8]

Nevertheless, Marryat's popularity and reputation were soon established and her literary talents came to be recognised in their own right. Her novels were regularly reviewed in many of the leading journals, and whilst some of the reviews appear somewhat double-edged, and sometimes very negative, her ability to write a readable story that some readers would respond well to was regularly commented on. The very tone of the reviews of her work that regularly appeared in journals like the *Athenaeum* and the *Academy* indicate, I think, how troubling Marryat was to the literary establishment. They regularly delight in finding fault, inevitably compare her less favourably to other writers, regularly condemn her on moral grounds, and begrudgingly acknowledge when they think she has done something well, or at least not too badly. It seems the

---

[7] Dolman, 'Marryat', *Myra's Journal: The Lady's Monthly Magazine* vol XVII, no. 5, (1891), pp. 1-2.
[8] Unsigned review, *Athenaeum*, 2346, Oct. 12, 1872, p.455.

reviewers struggle to understand the popularity of her work, but yet, at the same time, cannot ignore her. The review given to *Her Father's Name* in the *Academy*, is representative of how much of the work of this writer was received:

> Mrs. Ross Church has gone to Brazil for the opening scenes of her new book, and a very elaborate picture of Brazilian scenery she presents us with, a picture which serves as background to a young woman of fabulous beauty, who is attended by a goat, like Esmeralda, by a 'rhamphastos' (so called by Mrs. Ross Church, and by gods doubtless, but by men usually denominated a toucan), and by an old mule. It is rather odd that, after all this elaborate scene-painting in the beginning, we are never treated again to a single piece of description, or indeed, of careful writing of any kind. ... However, the reader of easy faith and unfastidious taste will perhaps be able to pass his hour with *Her Father's Name* as well as with most of its companions.[9]

Marryat was, from the very beginning of her career, a very canny literary professional. She displayed an excellent astuteness for working her contemporary marketplace. This talent and her ensuing popularity, whilst clearly clamoured for by many, were lamented too. In his London Literary Letter for the *New York Times* in 1898 W. L. Alden deplores the mass of Marryat novels, and those of other women writers in the same vein, in the Tauchnitz catalogue and held by libraries generally, compared to the much smaller number of works available by writers such as Kipling and Stevenson.[10]

There is no obvious answer why a successful novelist like Marryat should have disappeared from the history of Victorian fiction in the way that she has. Andrew Maunder, in his excellent introduction to *Love's Conflict* for Pickering and Chatto's *Varieties of Women's Sensation Fiction* series, suggests that Marryat was aware of the 'ephemerality' of her own work and certainly that she has been,

---

[9] Signed review by George Saintsbury, *The Academy*, 11 (1877: Jan/June), p. 6.
[10] W. L. Alden, 'London Literary Letter,' *New York Times*, September 10, 1898, p. 24.

until now, largely out of print would support this assessment.[11] The *Athenaeum*, usually critical of her novels in their reviews, wrote in their obituary of her that she was 'author of some seventy novels, too hurriedly written, unfortunately, to prove of enduring value.'[12]

However, Marryat's novels of the 1860s such as *The Confessions of Gerald Estcourt, Love's Conflict, For Ever and Ever* and *Nelly Brooke* are typical of the sensation fiction that was so popular at that time and for which writers such as Mary Elizabeth Braddon became well-known. Marryat's books sold equally well, although Maunder's research has revealed that Marryat, in her early career, regularly felt that she was not paid as handsomely as many of her contemporaries.[13] So why Marryat is so far behind Braddon in terms of revival is curious. As Maunder rightly points out Marryat was one of the most prolific writers of her time and her works were translated into a number of languages giving her international fame.[14] Clearly Marryat's style of writing would have become increasingly unfashionable as the modernist period developed in the early decades of the twentieth century. However, appreciation of her work is certainly due for a revival and is very relevant to the current academic trend for revisiting forgotten and neglected Victorian popular novelists.

Whilst the novels which make up the greater part of Marryat's oeuvre do deal with classic sensation themes – adultery, bigamy, murder, seduction, madness – there is, throughout Marryat's writing, a strong vein of interesting and complex female characters. Unsurprisingly, given her own experiences of married life, raising and financially supporting her family, Marryat wrote about strong women but also about the vulnerability of women in the nineteenth-century marriage market. Her lurid themes regularly led reviewers to condemn her on grounds of morality. A review in the *Academy* of her 1892 novel *The Nobler Sex* reads: "Indeed, the whole story is an odious account of the ways of people whom nobody would wish to know, and it is as undesirable to make their acquaintance in a novel

---

[11] Andrew Maunder (ed) *Love's Conflict,* in *Varieties of Women's Sensation Fiction 1855 – 1890,* (London: Pickering and Chatto, 2004), vol 2, p. vii.
[12] Unsigned obituary, *Athenaeum* 3758, Nov. 4, 1899, p. 622.
[13] Maunder, *Love's Conflict,* p. x.
[14] Maunder, *Love's Conflict,* p. vii.

Introduction

as it would be in actual life. Books of this sort are repellent at best."[15] The main subject matter of *The Nobler Sex* is divorce and the central protagonist, as mentioned above, is a strong independent woman who refuses to tolerate an unhappy marriage. By condemning "books of this sort" the *Academy* seems to disapprove of novels that deal with, yes unpleasant, but arguably very real situations. If a fictional heroine who divorces her husband can be so thoroughly condemned, one can only admire women, like Marryat, for making similar decisions in their own lives and having to deal with the repercussions.

So, Marryat does, in many of her novels, pay particular attention to the vulnerability of women in marriage but she also depicts the vulnerability of women at the hands of the medical profession and engages with scientific and medical debates throughout her writing. This awareness of contemporary aspects of science and medicine warrants further academic study. Through her presentation of Lucilla in this novel we see an engagement with issues surrounding the treatment of hysteria in women in the nineteenth century – which will be covered in more detail later in this introduction.

Marryat's popularity, professional acumen in the literary marketplace, the range of writing she produced, and her varied career should have guaranteed her an enduring place in the study of Victorian fiction. However, this was not to be the case. As Maunder wrote, quite rightly, in 2004: "The idea that anyone would ever want to write a book solely devoted to this eminent Victorian woman or even republish some of her work has seemed eccentric or at least unnecessary."[16] Thankfully 2009 sees a different picture emerging with Marryat's work appearing regularly on conference programmes, editions of a number of her novels becoming available and at least one book devoted to her life and work being prepared for an academic press.

Marryat's work most certainly warrants further academic interest and the publication of this novel is a welcome addition to the range of works, penned by this writer, which is currently available.

---

[15] Unsigned review, *Academy,* 42 (1892: July/Dec) p.190.
[16] Maunder, *Love's Conflict,* p. viii.

Introduction

A Brief Chronology:

1833 (9th July) Born in Brighton. Parents were the former naval officer turned novelist Captain Frederick Marryat and Catherine (nee Shairp).

1847 Brother, Frederick, drowned at sea.

1854 (13th June) Marryat married Thomas Ross Church, Ensign in the 12th Madras Staff Corps in Penang. She went on to have eight children by Ross Church, of whom seven survived in to adulthood.

1860 Marryat leaves Penang and returns to England pregnant with her fourth child. Ross Church travels regularly to see his family.

1861 Death of Florence Marryat's daughter, Florence, at the age of 10 days, (10th January).

1863 Begins writing *Love's Conflict* whilst nursing her children through scarlet fever.

1865 *Love's Conflict* is published by Bentley and Son. That year also saw the publication of *Too Good for Him* and *Woman Against Woman*.

1868 Publication of *Gup* – sketches of garrison life in India.

1872 Marryat publishes *The Life and Letters of Captain Marryat*.

1872 Begins her time as editor of *London Society*, a position she holds until 1876.

1872 First play *Miss Chester* produced.

1875 *Open! Sesame!* published.

1876 *Her Father's Name* published.

1878 Sued for divorce by her husband Thomas Ross Church who cited his wife's adultery with Colonel Francis Lean.

1879 Married Colonel Francis Lean – 5th June.

1881 *Her World Against a Lie* – Marryat became an actress performing in the above drama which she had written herself. The play was produced in London.

1882 Began touring with the D'Oyly Carte theatre company.

1886 *Tom Tiddler's Ground* published – an account of her travels in the United States of America.

1891 *There is No Death* published.

1892 Publication of *The Nobler Sex*, regarded as Marryat's most autobiographical novel.

1894 *The Spirit World* published.

1895 Marryat becomes very active in the recently formed Society of Authors.

1897 *The Blood of the Vampire* published.

1899 Died on the 27th October aged 66 due to complications from diabetes. Her funeral was held on 2nd November at the Church of Our Lady, St John's Wood. Marryat was buried at Kensal Green Cemetery.

2. *Her Father's Name:* cross-dressing, detection and hysteria

Readers who do not wish to learn details of the plot might want to read the introduction afterwards.

Florence Marryat's 1876 novel *Her Father's Name* combines murder, mystery, cross-dressing, illegitimacy, amateur sleuthing and hysteria. As such it gives us a rich vein of sensation themes and topics in which to revel.

In the first instance it is, perhaps, the title that is worthy of comment. It does, of course, offer a literal meaning in terms of the plot – the central heroine desperately keen to clear her father's name of the murder it is alleged he committed. Further to this, given how, as discussed above, Marryat's very career was founded on making use of the reputation and fame attached to her father's name it would be fair to assume, as well as the literal meaning as it relates to the plot, that a pun is intended, which would be indicative of Marryat's honesty about her early success.

The central heroine of this novel, Leona, like many of Marryat's heroines, yearns for more freedom. That she enacts a rousing Joan of Arc speech very early in the story tells us that we are being introduced to a woman of uncommon valor and one who remains focused on her purpose: "Leona Lacoste was a woman who would *never* give in—until she died."[17]

Leona is determined to follow her own path and, as such, is emblematic of Marryat herself. Leona's journey in the course of this novel is most eventful including risking her life very early on fighting a duel, and whilst she continually challenges gender norms and, arguably, transgresses gender boundaries she does, throughout, remain virtuous. Although the *Athenaeum* review states that there is "too much promiscuous kissing" it does acknowledge that actually there is "no fault to find with *Her Father's Name* on the score of

---

[17] Of course, we also know that Joan of Arc routinely dressed in male costume which also has relevance to the plot developments that we see.

morality."[18]

Marryat has Leona challenge, in an arguably playful way, what was understood to be "womanly" or "feminine." Whilst the sexual and gender politics of twentieth century feminism are a long way from what Marryat is doing, Leona is noticeably more proactive than the male characters, including her father, his brother and their uncle, who never made any attempt to find out who was responsible for the murder of the clerk, Anson. Indeed, Marryat seems to set up some of the male characters in the text as being significantly less courageous than our heroine Leona – Leona's father's suicide indicates his own inability to deal with the accusation surrounding his name becoming known "in the Brazils." Leona challenges ontological constructions of femininity. However, by the end of the novel she does conform to perceived codes of feminine behaviour by acknowledging her love for her childhood sweetheart and agreeing to be his wife – a position she had previously refused.

I am not suggesting that Marryat was at the very vanguard of nineteenth-century feminism. However, by allowing her heroines, such as Leona, to push at the boundaries and restrictions which were placed on women she was able to present, to vast swathes of the female reading population, many of whom would not have accessed more formal and recognized feminism, ideas as to how they might challenge the boundaries in their lives, in ways that had not, necessarily, been available to them before. Whilst Marryat's work received scathing reviews it is the mass appeal of her non-elitist popular fiction that makes novels like *Her Father's Name* worthy of notice.

The rest of this introduction will look at three of the central themes of this novel: cross-dressing, the amateur female sleuth and women and hysteria in the nineteenth century.

2a. Female cross-dressing in nineteenth-century literature

Leona adopts various disguises during the course of this novel in order to attempt to clear her father's name of the murder which was committed on the night he disappeared from England, long before

---

[18] Unsigned review, *The Athenaeum*, No 2563, Dec. 9, '76.

Introduction

she was born. However it is her adoption of a male disguise that creates the potential for the most intrigue in the novel and it is this disguise that is the most challenging in terms of ideal feminine behaviour.

One of Leona's first acts, whilst dressed as a man is to challenge a fellow traveller to a duel; Christobal learns that:

> "But, *caramba!* it was the little one that challenged him. They came to words over some difference of opinion, and d'Acosta gave Guzman the lie to his face. He could not, in honour, have refused to meet him, though I believe he regretted it almost as much as you do. Guzman is not bad at heart."

Now whilst the *Academy* review of this novel might state that "In the way of probability the book will hardly stand examination,"[19] this seemingly unlikely event of Leona being involved in a duel does have historical precedence.

The institution of the duel was well established in the eighteenth century, as Robert Baldick states in his book on the history of dueling: "early historians of the duel were fond of tracing it back to ancient and even Biblical times."[20] Although Baldick does see the importance of making "a distinction between the hot-blooded combat, fought on the spur of the moment, and the duel proper, which is fought in cold blood, before witnesses, with a certain ceremony and in accordance with a strict code of honour."[21] However, by the nineteenth century dueling became increasingly unfashionable. Stories of "real-life" duels became ever scarcer. The duel did, however, become increasingly popular with writers of fiction.

What is being fought in this novel is, of course, a duel of honour. The rules of dueling are clearly well known to the combatants and witnesses here; to refer once more to Baldick:

---

[19] Signed review by George Saintsbury, *The Academy*, 11 (1877: Jan/June), p. 6.
[20] Robert Baldick, *The Duel; A History of Duelling* (London: Chapman & Hall, 1965), p.11.
[21] Baldick, *Duel*, pp. 11-12.

Introduction

> But if the fair fight between two men armed with equal weapons was to become an accepted and established institution, the rules governing it had to be generally understood and stringently enforced. Hence the multiplicity of treatises published all over Europe between the sixteenth and nineteenth centuries attempting to regulate every circumstance of the duel, from the cause of the quarrel through the challenge and the choice of weapons to the fight itself.
>
> The causes of duels varied in both nature and seriousness. For the man imbued with a chivalrous respect for the opposite sex, an injury or insult to a woman to whom he was related or attached was the gravest and most obvious reason for a duel. ... For another man, the slap or the blow was the mortal, unforgivable offence, while yet another considered a slur on fame or reputation a more serious provocation. But most authorities on the subject, at least in the seventeenth century, agreed that 'giving the lie' was the gravest provocation of all.[22]

Arguably Leona's challenge would not have been taken up by Guzman had he known that his challenger was a woman. Baldick gives details of duels held in similar circumstances where a male duelist was challenged and beaten by a woman in disguise such as:

> The next noteworthy duel involving a woman was probably fought by the Comtesse de Saint-Belmont. When her husband, who had been fighting against the King, was taken prisoner, the countess remained on his estates to take care of them. A cavalry officer having taken up his quarters there without invitation, Madame de Saint-Belmont sent him a polite letter of complaint about his discourtesy, which he ignored. Annoyed at this, she resolved that he should give her satisfaction, and sent him a challenge signed: 'Le Chevalier de Saint-Belmont.' The officer promptly accepted the challenge, and went to the appointed place, where Madame de Saint-Belmont met him dressed in male attire. Within a few moments, the countess had disarmed her

---

[22] Baldick, *Duel*, pp. 32-33.

opponent, after which she reduced him to utter shame and confusion by saying: 'You thought, Monsieur, that you were fighting the Chevalier de Saint-Belmont, but you are mistaken. I am Madame de Saint-Belmont. I return you your sword, Monsieur, and politely beg you to pay proper respect to any request made by a lady in future.[23]

Baldick also gives details of duels where both combatants were women:

On January 31, 1772, an even bloodier encounter occurred between Mademoiselle de Guignes and Mademoiselle d'Aiguillon, two ladies of quality who had quarrelled about precedence at a *soirée*. There seem to have been no seconds and very little decorum attending the affair, for the pair fought with knives until both were wounded, the former in the arm and the latter in the neck.[24]

And it would appear from this history of dueling that the act became increasingly more common amongst women in the eighteenth century. Maria Edgeworth gives a wonderfully vivid description of two women dueling in her 1801 novel *Belinda*.[25] In Edgeworth's novel the impropriety of women dressing as men and engaging in armed combat outrages the local population and almost results in them getting a ducking in the village pond.

After Leona seriously wounds Guzman in the duel we read that:

All the woman had come back to her in the idea that she might have killed her antagonist. She grew deadly pale, threw down her pistol on the ground, and crossed over quickly to where the seconds were kneeling by Guzman's side.

Her concern over Guzman even prompts Christobal to rebuke her womanly behaviour:

"Do you want the whole lot of them to know that you're a

---

[23] Baldick, *Duel*, p. 170.
[24] Baldick, *Duel*, p. 173.
[25] See appendices.

woman?" said Christobal, as he went straight up to Leona, and whispered in her ear.

"Christobal, no! What are you dreaming of?" she answered, in the same tone.

"That you betray yourself with every word you speak, that this romantic interest about the man you were resolved, against all advice, to meet, is ridiculous—foolishly and absurdly feminine, and if you do not show a little more reason in the matter, your sex will become apparent to the whole company."

Tobal says all this even though he deplores the fact that Leona ever adopted male disguise. What this exchange makes clear is the essential fragility of Leona's disguise, raising questions as to whether clothes alone can make a man to fool other men? Yet many women have successfully "passed" as men. Bullough and Bullough, in their study of cross-dressing, record many stories of women who donned male garb in order to fight such as Frances Hook (who served as Private Frank Fuller), Elizabeth Compton and Loreta Janet Velazquez who all fought in the American Civil War.[26] Also, they record the story of Dr James Barry (1795 – 1865) who served in the British Army.[27]

As Bullough and Bullough state: "clothing helped determine one's gender,"[28] and whilst "motives for some of the more famous cross dressers remain obscure,"[29] there is no doubting the freedom that many women gained by being believed to be men. And there are many literary examples of cross-dressing on which we can draw. Angelica remonstrates to the Tenor in Sarah Grand's *The Heavenly Twins* (1893), after her disguise as the Boy has been exposed:

'having once assumed the character, I began to love it; it came naturally; and the freedom from restraint, I mean the restraint of our tight uncomfortable clothing was delicious.'[30]

---

[26] Vern. L. Bullough & Bonnie Bullough, *Cross Dressing, Sex and Gender* (Philadelphia: Pennsylvania Press, 1993), p. 157.
[27] Bullough & Bullough, *Cross Dressing*, p. 161.
[28] Bullough & Bullough, *Cross Dressing*, p. 159.
[29] Bullough & Bullough, *Cross Dressing*, p. 160.
[30] Sarah Grand, *The Heavenly Twins* (Michigan: Ann Arbor Paperback, University

Many tales of cross-dressing, true and fictional, are about women who see cross-dressing as a way of life, for them it is a life-style choice enabling them to traverse the boundaries society has imposed on them as women, and as Bullough and Bullough note many female cross-dressers were lesbian.[31] This is where Leona differs, for her it is a means to an end, a way for her to access people and places in order to find out the truth surrounding the murder linked to her father.

However, whilst disguised as a man, there arise several amorous moments for Leona, some of which result in the 'promiscuous kissing' commented on in the *Athenaeum* review.[32]

Without doubt Leona's attractions confuse Guzman:

> "Fine young fellow!" remarked the wounded man, in a weak voice. "I am glad he hasn't killed me. He would have felt it so much."
>
> "Rather clap-trap business to my mind," said Christobal. "I don't admire emotion in a man."
>
> "He is not a man," replied Guzman. "He is but a boy. I wonder if he has any sisters," he continued, with a faint smile; "if he has, I shall tell him he must give me one in return for this."

This idea of the sister of an attractive "boy" being a desirable and acceptable alternative to feelings of love for the boy himself is, of course, seen later in the century in Grand's *The Heavenly Twins* when the Tenor believes Angelica to be the sister of the boy who visits him nightly. The Tenor is greatly attracted to Angelica whilst:

> The Boy was associated in the Tenor's mind with many sweet associations; with the beautiful still night; with the Tenor's far off ideal of all that is gracious and womanly. (p. 405)

---

of Michigan Press, 1992), p. 456.

[31] Bullough & Bullough, *Cross Dressing*, p. 164.

[32] Unsigned review, *The Athenaeum*, No 2563, Dec. 9, 1876. See appendices.

Introduction

As far as Leona and Guzman are concerned, a little later we read how Guzman "regarded her fine face and figure with interest." Even when they go their separate ways, we are told that: "They parted, however, the best of friends, and with many hopes, on Guzman's side at least, of meeting again."

There is, perhaps, a homoerotic reading that could be made here, although that Leona is undoubtedly an effeminate male figure is made clear. Marryat is showing more how ideas and expectations are governed by codes of dress rather than attempting to outrage moral sensibility by transgressing sexual boundaries.

Cross-dressing, which leads to gender confusion, is equally evident in George Meredith's *The Ordeal of Richard Feverel* (1859) when Richard's friend, the disreputable Mrs Mount, regularly dons male attire and becomes "Sir Julius": "What do you think of me? Wasn't it a shame to make a woman of me when I was born to be a man?"[33] Richard revels in Mrs Mount's "Sir Julius" persona, we are told that "Sir Julius … was frequently called for on his evening visits." (p. 424) Even when Mrs Mount ceases to dress up as Sir Julius; "The memory of Sir Julius breathing about her still, doubled the feminine attraction." (p. 426)

The distortion of gender that arises because of disguise provides disquiet in terms of propriety and cultural anxiety but also an added intrigue and allure. Matilda's disguise as the novice monk, Rosario, in Matthew Lewis's *The Monk* (1796) is troublesome for Ambrosio:

> Ambrosio on his side did not feel less attracted towards the youth: with him alone did he lay aside his habitual severity; when he spoke to him, he insensibly assumed a tone milder than was usual to him; and no voice sounded so sweet to him as did Rosario's.[34]

The chemistry between Ambrosio and Rosario culminates, after Rosario reveals himself to be Matilda, into one of the most frenzied love scenes in the novel.

---

[33] George Meredith, *The Ordeal of Richard Feverel* (Oxford: Oxford University Press, 1984), p. 421.
[34] Matthew Gregory Lewis, *The Monk* (New York: Dover Publications, 2003), p.25.

Introduction

As mentioned above, in *The Heavenly Twins* there is definite attraction between the Tenor and the Boy, the Tenor works, and goes without, in order to have food for the Boy on his night-time visits, and there is a moment, when he thinks the Boy has drowned, when he acknowledges exactly the "loss to himself the boy would be." (p. 442) The devastation the Tenor feels when the Boy is revealed to be Angelica, and coupled with the knowledge that Angelica is married, is terrible. It was not cruelty that drove Angelica to perpetrate her fraud but that she wanted to "see the world as men see it, which would be from a new point of view." (p. 451)

There is more amorous complexity and intrigue for Leona when, still disguised as a man, she enters the house of her uncle Henry Evans, and succeeds in making a number of women fall in love with her, including the daughter of the house, Lucilla, who is later revealed to be her half-sister. There is, of course, the possibility of reading lesbian undertones in to the attraction of Leona to Lucilla and the other women who frequent the Evans's household. However, on the surface this attraction is more straightforward as the women are falling for a "man". Leona, herself, is very well aware of the paradoxical situation:

> "The girl Lucilla fancies me, I can see plainly. How strange it is that I, who, in a woman's garb am generally disliked by women, should excite their sympathies directly I assume clothes to which I have no right. All the girls fell in love with me on the stage when I appeared as a boy. Bah, the fools! How short-sighted they must be. But I must not blame them for it now. Their folly may prove my salvation."

Whilst it would be easy to over-complicate these scenes of cross-dressing by trying to determine homoerotic readings to an extent not envisaged by Marryat, the scenes of potential love interest when Leona is disguised as a man are, on the whole, very playful in nature and no real moral outrages are committed. However, "the survival of over a hundred ballads that deal with women cross dressers in the period 1650 to 1850 emphasizes the ubiquity of the phenomenon and public fascination with it."[35]

Leona's ability to "pass" as a man is, of course, the reason for her success on stage in New York.

> She had now been a year upon the stage, and though she had not yet made the fortune prophesied for her by Mr. John Rouse, she was earning sufficient money to keep herself in comfort and respectability, and had also managed to lay aside a few dollars against sickness or any other emergency. She was rapidly gaining favour with the manager of the Memphis from her love of her art and steady application to business; and from having stood on the stage to be admired as the Captain of the Guard, had been promoted to fill all the male parts that could be adequately represented by a woman.

We are reminded of Lucy Snowe's reluctance to dress like a man for the role she needs to take in the school play in Charlotte Brontë's *Villette*. She adapts a costume that maintains the overall garb of a woman and adds things to indicate maleness. Lucy's reluctance to embrace the idea of a male costume is completely in contrast with Leona's enthusiasm to do so. Leona is being given roles as Captains and Chevaliers; as Sara Maitland says in her book on the singer, actress and male impersonator Vesta Tilley: "male-impersonators usually present favourable images of masculinity: the hero – be he soldier, Pantomime prince or dandy; the beautiful young man, whose decadence can even be charming; or the dashing drunk, not the down-at-heel wino."[36] Leona can have pride in the male characters she is playing on stage.

A woman dressing as a man for a stage role is part of theatrical tradition and a tradition that has continued to be seen on screen. We saw Katherine Hepburn dress as a man in *Sylvia Scarlett*, Julie Andrews in *Victor/Victoria*, Barbara Streisand in *Yentl*, all adopting male garb to further their opportunities, as Elizabeth Taylor's character did in *National Velvet*. Whilst many cross-dressers that have been studied in the work of critics such as Bullough and Bullough dressed as men because of a radical lifestyle choice

---

[35] Bullough & Bullough, *Cross Dressing*, p. 167.
[36] Sara Maitland, *Vesta Tilley* (London: Virago Press, 1986), p. 90.

Introduction

whereas Leona, and fictional cross-dressers discussed here, have done so as a means to an end. They have all crossed gender boundaries but not to make a life choice of transvestitism. Leona is happy to divest herself of all disguises – male and female – at the end of the novel when she has cleared her father's name. Marryat's indebtedness to Renaissance tradition is clear here: 'At the close of literally dozens of English Renaissance plays the cross-dressed page doffs her doublet and hose and reveals herself to be a woman – usually a well-born and marriageable woman.'[37] Leona's cross-dressing enables her to access people and places necessary to investigate her father's story. Garber notes that "Cross-dressing is a classic strategy of disappearance in detective fiction."[38] Whilst usually it is the criminal who uses disguise to disappear, seen in detective fiction from Conan Doyle to the present day, in this novel cross-dressing is merely one of the disguises Leona adopts as a cunning amateur detective.

It is important to take a cautious approach to the gender politics of cross-dressing in this novel – Leona is simply using male dress, for a specific purpose, to escape the restrictive role assigned to her as a woman. The romantic trysts she becomes involved in are mere interludes. Of the more notorious fictional and "real" cross-dressers some were not only seeking to battle male prejudice, they were defying codes of dress and behaviour that they saw society imposing on women and were, many of them, living in openly lesbian relationships – we think of Radclyffe Hall, Colette.[39] Sara Maitland again:

> There are…reasons…why women in fiction and myth and history dress up as men…they may do it for disguise: for whatever reason a woman wishes, or needs, to be perceived as, treated as, and believed to be a man. In the vocabulary of transsexualism, she wants to 'pass' in the social world as a member of the other gender: her most important, basic act is to put on men's clothes. For motives ranging from the

---

[37] Marjorie Garber, *Vested Interests: Cross-Dressing and Cultural Anxiety* (New York & London: Routledge, 1992), p. 187.
[38] Garber, *Vested Interests*, p. 186.
[39] Garber, *Vested Interests*, see chapter six.

Introduction

pathological to the pragmatic, women choose to appear as men for anything from a few hours to their whole life span.[40]

2b. The female detective and *Her Father's Name*

Leona's role as "detective" is central to this novel. There is a murder mystery to solve and, it seems, only she is prepared to take on the task. By the end of the nineteenth century the female detective figure was becoming increasingly more common in popular fiction – perhaps one of the best known being Catherine Louisa Pirkis's *The Experiences of Loveday Brooke, Lady Detective* (1894). At the time *Her Father's Name* was published in 1876 there had been few professional detective figures although two did appear in the 1860s, "G" from Andrew Forrester's *The Female Detective* (1864) and Mrs Paschal in the anonymous *Revelations of a Lady Detective* (1864). However amateur female detectives, like Leona, appeared in sensation fiction from the 1860s. Unsurprisingly two of the most well known writers of sensation fiction, Wilkie Collins and Mary Braddon, featured amateur female sleuths in their work: Eleanor Vane in Braddon's 1863 novel *Eleanor's Victory* and Margaret Wentworth in Braddon's 1864 novel *Henry Dunbar*. Like Braddon's female detectives and like Leona in this novel, Collins's female sleuths are women playing at detective in order to unravel the mystery of a domestic drama close to their own hearts. Collins's 1859 novel *The Woman in White* features Marion Halcombe who undertakes detective work to protect and solve the mystery surrounding her sister. Marion is described by Walter Hartright as having a complexion which was "almost swarthy, and the dark down on her upper lip was almost a moustache."[41] Marion's moustache is a distinguishing feature she shares with our heroine Leona:

> She had a dark creamy complexion and skin, under which her warm blood played as it chose. Her mouth was firm and well cut; the lips not full, but scarlet tinted, and upon the

---

[40] Maitland, *Vesta Tilley*, p. 81.
[41] Wilkie Collins, *The Woman in White* (London: Penguin Popular Classics, 1994), p. 24.

upper one the softest, faintest, most delicate down that ever existed on a woman's mouth—the merest shadow of a moustache, that only served to make the lip look more curved and scornful.

Both Marion and Leona's unconventional behaviour is signified by their unconventional physical attractions.

Marion, Leona, Emily Brown from Collins's 1885 novel *I Say No*, Valeria Woodville from his 1875 text *The Law and the Lady* push at the boundaries of the domestic sphere in order to protect, clear the name of, or help someone they love.

Leona perhaps has most in common with Valeria Woodville of Collins's *The Law and the Lady* which was serialised in the *Graphic* between September 1874 and March 1875 before being published by Chatto and Windus in February 1875, in that both heroines are adult women who take up an investigation that men have failed to solve. Like Valeria, Leona is guided by her female intuition and firmly held conviction that her father is innocent of the murder associated with his name. Both Valeria and Leona transgress boundaries of feminine behaviour, in different ways, but both with successful outcomes. As Jenny Bourne Taylor writes in her introduction to the Oxford World Classics edition of *The Law and the Lady*, "Valeria's reopening of the unresolved trial of her husband is prompted both by the desire to clear his name, and by the need to establish her own position as his legitimate wife."[42] Leona needs to clear her father's name and thereby remove any stain from her own. On entering into English society her disguise means that she does not have to be tarnished with the label of daughter of an infamous father. When she finally reveals herself to be George Evans's daughter his name has been cleared.

During the course of her investigations the possibility is raised, temporarily, that she might be illegitimate. Her relief when she discovers this not to be true is palpable. Wilkie Collins's Rosamond from his 1857 novel *The Dead Secret* is not so fortunate, her amateur sleuthing into a family secret reveals her own illegitimacy. In *Her Father's Name* it is Leona's half-sister, Lucilla, who it is revealed is

---

[42] Wilkie Collins, *The Law and the Lady* ed. and intro by Jenny Bourne Taylor (Oxford: Oxford University Press, 1992), p. xiv.

illegitimate. However this information is kept from her, although revealed to her husband-to-be Dr Hastings who believes, because of Lucilla's health (more of which in the next section) that she should be left in ignorance of her true origins. That in Collins's *The Dead Secret* Rosamond's illegitimacy makes little difference in the outcome of the story – she keeps her inherited fortune, and the love of her husband, Lillian Nayder suggests is due to Collins, in this novel, delivering

> an explicit social message – that one's class rank should be a matter of merit rather than birth, since birth is an 'accident' that says little about one's character or value. While Collins appears to retain his faith in class differences, he redefines the grounds of gentility to account for and reward the noble nature of characters like Rosamond.[43]

The difference between the characters of Rosamond and Lucilla from *Her Father's Name* is that Rosamond discovers her illegitimate status and has the strength of character to cope with this revelation whilst, because of her ill-health, or hysteria, Lucilla is deemed unfit to know. Arguably, given the strength of character we have already seen Leona display we presume she would have coped with the stigma of illegitimacy had it proved to be so. The perception of Lucilla as hysteric and unable to deal with such a revelation is used to highlight the differences between these two half-sisters. Further, we might raise the question as to whether Marryat shied away from making her central heroine a bastard because of the way the supposed immorality of some of her works had already been commented on in reviews.

As discussed in the previous section, Leona's cross-dressing is crucial in enabling her to carry out her amateur sleuthing – it is of course slightly ironic that she disguises herself as a man in order to clear her father's name, an investigation her father, his brother, and their uncle all singularly failed to even attempt.

So, Leona's detection is aided by her ability to don a disguise. Her adoption of the disguise of an older woman is also of interest. Her use of glasses in chapter 23: "Leona had taken the extra

---

[43] Lillian Nayder, *Wilkie Collins* (London: Twayne Publishers, 1997), pp. 54-55.

precaution during this interview of shielding her glorious eyes with a pair of spectacles," is reminiscent of Lady Isabel Vane in Mrs Henry Wood's *East Lynne* (1861) who "wears disfiguring green spectacles, or, as they are called, preservers, going round the eyes,"[44] and by doing so manages to live undetected in the house of her husband and children. However, it is the idea of being disguised as an older woman and, therefore, becoming "invisible" and thus able to hear and discover things, that looks toward the amateur and professional female sleuths of later crime fiction. One of Loveday Brooke's greatest assets as a woman was that she could be largely invisible. We read that "She was not tall, she was not short, she was not dark, she was not fair, she was neither handsome nor ugly. Her features were altogether nondescript."[45] Jumping forward to the Golden Age of crime fiction we think of Agatha Christie's Miss Marple, who, as the Vicar says in *The Murder at the Vicarage* (1930) "There is no detective in England equal to a spinster lady of uncertain age with plenty of time on her hands."[46] Miss Climpson, from the Lord Peter Wimsey novels by Dorothy L Sayers, has her superior detecting skills described by Wimsey in *Unnatural Death* (1927) in the following way:

> "Just think, people want questions asked. Whom do they send? A man with large flat feet and a notebook – the sort of man whose private life is conducted by a series of inarticulate grunts. I send a lady with a long, woolly jumper on knitting needles and jingly thinks round her neck. Of course she asks questions – everyone expects it. Nobody is surprised. Nobody is alarmed."[47]

A spinster woman of indeterminate age is neat and prim, seemingly harmless and inoffensive, and the very stereotype society has created for her enables her success. She is, essentially, invisible.

---

[44] Mrs Henry Wood, *East Lynne* (London: Everyman's Library, 1984), p. 397.
[45] Catherine Louise Pirkis, *The Experiences of Loveday Brooke, Lady Detective* (USA: Kessinger Publishing, 2008), p. 4.
[46] Agatha Christie, *The Murder at the Vicarage* (London: Harper Collins, 1997), p. 528.
[47] Dorothy. L. Sayers, *Unnatural Death* (London: Hodder and Stoughton, 1968), p. 35.

Introduction

Whilst Henry Evans might have had his suspicions about Leona when disguised as a middle aged woman because of the links she claims to have with his past, secret, adoption of Lucilla, the people she gleans information from have no reason to suspect her and are happy to talk. So Leona, in this disguise, prefigures these very successful female sleuths of later detective fiction.

I think, given Leona's clear detective agenda we can consider *Her Father's Name* to be classified as a nineteenth-century detective novel like Collins's *The Law and the Lady*, *The Woman in White* and *The Moonstone*. Clearly in this 1876 work Marryat taps in to a genre that was rising in popularity. By the end of the century she further demonstrated her literary canniness and knowledge of the popular market by writing a novel with a professional female detective, *In the Name of Liberty* of 1897. In this novel Jane Farrell is persuaded by an old family friend, Harold Herschel, who is a police inspector, to join the police force: "You have heard that we employ a good many lady detectives in the Force nowadays, haven't you? ... I think you are eminently suited for such work, both physically and mentally..."[48] However, without giving away the plot, despite Jane's success as a detective and aptitude for her job, her loyalty to the force is challenged by the involvement of a loved one in a crime she is detecting.

With the publication now of *Her Father's Name* and, hopefully, at some point in the future, the publication of *In the Name of Liberty*, the idea of Marryat as a contributor to the genre of nineteenth-century detective fiction will come to be more fully acknowledged.

The judgement of the *Athenaeum* review to the idea of *Her Father's Name* as a detective story is somewhat dismissive:

> The story is not very well composed, and the motives, in many cases, inadequate. The heroine finds out that her father has been accused of murder, and contrives to get, under a false name, into the family of his brother in England, whom she quite gratuitously suspects of having been the real murderer. The reader is also led to suspect this, and the various incidents are so combined as to foster the suspicion,

---

[48] Florence Marryat, *In the Name of Liberty* (London: Digby, Long & Co, 1897, 3rd edition), p. 87.

which turns out quite suddenly to be unfounded. So the story has not even the merit which belongs to the ordinary 'detective' novel.[49]

I would suggest that this review fails to appreciate the "red-herring" which Marryat gives us with this part of the plot. Red-herrings in detective fiction are plot devices that have become a classic feature of the genre. Arguably, Leona's suspicions surrounding her uncle are understandable, although based on no firm evidence. Henry Evans had the motivation of money; with his brother's name blackened, coupled with his disappearance and the belief that he must be dead, leaving Henry as the sole inheritor of the family business. Without doubt financial reasons have long been considered adequate motivation for murder.

The *Academy*, in its review of this novel, is also critical of the detection aspect of the story.

> Mrs. Ross Church has not the ingenious patience with which Mr. Wilkie Collins embroils his mysteries and plagues his characters. On the contrary, everybody tells Leona everything she wishes to know in a charmingly obliging and communicative manner. The steps, indeed, are so simple and so clear that the only wonder is why the damsel's uncle, who is represented as equally anxious to clear his brother's name, did not take them himself. In the way of probability the book will hardly stand examination.[50]

However, Leona's intuition, disguise and feminine wiles are, as discussed above, exactly what makes people open up to her.

This novel has a good central mystery and a feisty female protagonist who doggedly pursues the truth. Whilst it might never be ranked alongside the detective novels of Wilkie Collins I would suggest that the plot is no more unbelievable than many of those by Wilkie Collins and Marryat's popularity at the time certainly indicates that many appreciated her ability to produce a good page-turning novel.

---

[49] Unsigned review, *The Athenaeum*, No 2563, Dec. 9, '76.
[50] Signed review by George Saintsbury, *The Academy*, 11 (1877: Jan/June), p. 6.

2c. The nineteenth-century hysteric

Marryat's presentation of Leona's half-sister, Lucilla Evans, in this novel is, I would suggest worthy of a little further discussion. In this secondary character we have an almost text-book case history presentation of the hysteric female so dominant in nineteenth-century literature. Whilst this is not a new literary "type" I do think Marryat's presentation is interesting because of the relationship Lucilla has with her doctor, Dr Hastings. Marryat does not just present a hysterical female character but also depicts the relationship between the hysterical woman and her doctor that withstands detailed cross-referencing to medical journals of the day and which highlights the potentially vulnerable position the female hysteric was in at the hands of the medical profession.

The problem of hysteria in the nineteenth century was perennially troublesome and when aiming to draw conclusions from the wealth of critical readings available on the subject it would seem that two quite challenging readings of the hysteric and her treatment can be made: on the one hand she is the empowered woman seeking to exert some control over her life, on the other hand she is the oppressed victim of male medical control. Arguably we could attach both of these readings to Lucilla. The implication that women were complicit in moulding themselves to the demands of the prevailing social ideology raises interesting questions. Such an interpretation suggests that women were conforming to socially engendered expectations of them as weak individuals prone to all manner of pathological behaviour

The critic Sheryl Burt Ruzek argues "historically, physicians have served the interests of those in power, […] serving as arbiters of morality and agents of social control."[51] First wave feminist historians have been summed up as seeing the hysteric as "a victim, a front-line casualty of the intensified war of men on their womenfolk's aspirations and protests."[52]

However, Jane Ussher, whilst not disagreeing with the idea of

---

[51] Sheryl Burt Ruzek, *The Women's Health Movement: Feminist Alternatives to Medical Control* (London, Sydney & Toronto: Prager Publishers, 1978), p. 67.
[52] Lisa Appignanesi & John Forrester *Freud's Women* (London: Virago, 1993), p. 68.

medicine and its intense focus on female maladies as being prompted by the desire of the medical profession to use "diagnosis and treatment [...] as methods of social control," adds that: "symptoms were in reality a form of protest."[53] Though, Ussher, whilst acknowledging the concept of hysteria as social protest, goes on to argue that a blanket approach, which interprets all women diagnosed with hysteria in the nineteenth century as being a petticoated army who took this form of action in the hope of exercising some control over their lives as a "seductive argument, but [one that is] very simplistic and incomplete."[54]

Other critics dispute the idea that the signs and symptoms of hysteria were at all empowering. Helen Small, in her landmark study, acknowledges that "hysteria and depression have been far from liberating for most of the women who, from the eighteenth century, have made up the majority of patients in mental asylums."[55] Similarly, Elaine Showalter argues that such an interpretation of women's behaviour does imply a "self-destructive form of protest."[56] Indeed, by displaying hysterical characteristics women would, in all probability, be subjected to the controlling measures of the medical profession, which also seems a fairly ineffective form of protest.

That the signs and symptoms were an attempt for sympathy was noted in medical writing of the time: "hysteria as an exaggerated and undue demand for sympathy [...] developed by the unwise and too devoted services of near relatives. The cure must be a self-cure, in which the patient is taught to rely upon her own efforts..."[57]

The complex nature of the male doctor and female patient relationship, and the power struggle this inevitably indicates is crucial to the understanding of the position of women at the hands of the medical profession at this time. Evelyn Ender sees hysteria as a means of putting gender "to the test" in her study of the

---

[53] Jane M Ussher, *Women's Madness: Misogyny or Mental Illness?* (New York & London: Harvester Wheatsheaf, 1991), p. 76.
[54] Ussher, *Women's Madness*, p. 92.
[55] Helen Small, *Love's Madness: Medicine, the novel and Female Insanity 1800 – 1865* (Oxford: Clarendon Press, 1996), p. 27.
[56] Elaine Showalter, *Hystories* (London: Picador, 1998), p. 10.
[57] Anon, *British Medical Journal,* 22 November 1890, p. 1209.

disease in the nineteenth century. Hysteria was essential to the emerging theory of gender in the way that it defined roles for the male doctor and female patient.[58]

It will be clear how this debate about hysteria relates to our reading of Lucilla in this novel. In a lecture on hysteria in 1889, one physician wrote "the hysterical are found chiefly [...] among the pampered, the lazy, the unemployed."[59] Marryat is very quick to give an astute reader a clear indication of Lucilla's disease:

> Lucilla ... had been an invalid for many years past, was unable to do more than follow the lead of her parents. ... She had no organic disease, but she had suffered from a weak spine for many years past, and it prevented her taking any active part in life. And the restraint made her fractious.[60]

Lucilla is clearly over indulged: "Not a wish she ever expressed was left ungratified." Her love/hate relationship with her physician is also made very clear. She revels in his attention but professes to hate his very presence. We also get a sense that Dr Hastings may

---

[58] Evelyn Ender, *Sexing the Mind. Nineteenth Century Fictions of Hysteria* (Ithaca & London: Cornell University Press, 1995), p. 282.

[59] J. M. Duncan, 'Clinical Lecture on Hysteria, Neurasthenia, and Anorexia Nervosa', *Lancet*, 18 May 1889, 973 - 974 (p. 974).

[60] In 1866 Isaac Baker Brown published a book entitled *On the Curability of Certain Forms of Insanity, Epilepsy, Catalepsy and Hysteria in Females* in which he stated that these diseases were, primarily, caused by masturbation and had a very poor prognosis. He saw eight distinct stages:

1. Hysteria
2. *Spinal irritation*
3. Epileptoid fits or hysterical epilepsy
4. Cataleptic fits
5. Epileptic fits
6. Idiotcy
7. Mania
8. Death

Isaac Baker Brown *On the Curability of Certain Forms of Insanity, Epilepsy, Catalepsy and Hysteria in Females* (London: Robert Hardwicke, 1866), p.7.

possibly indulge Lucilla's illness: "He did not consider Lucilla's case hopeless, and constantly cheered her parents and herself with the prospect that another year or two would see her outgrow the constitutional debility."

A study of medical journals and textbooks from the period reveals how debates amongst medical professionals about hysteria were part of a competitive struggle for professional prestige. The material illustrates how the medical profession made use of society's beliefs about women and, to some extent, society's fear of women, to help establish their professional status. Ann Dally, a medical historian and qualified medical doctor who writes with a critical eye about the medical profession and the variety of motives that spur on those who enter in to it states that:

> misleading is the belief that the chief interest of the medical profession is in curing patients, preventing disease or helping people to be healthy. These are the aims of some individual doctors, but the profession as a whole has always existed for itself and for the benefit of those who run it.[61]

If Dally is correct, by treating this recalcitrant group of patients, doctors could be assured of a rise in status and, presumably, income, whilst obtaining the kudos that would come with curing a problem that beset society so widely.

However it would seem that Dr Hastings interest in Lucilla extends beyond the professional and pecuniary – (although there is, of course, her inheritance):

> Dr. Hastings was a very clever and rising surgeon, and deserved all his friends thought or said of him. He was, moreover, a man of the world, and not to be easily deceived. During his town practice, he had visited with all sorts of people, and had his eyes wide open. For this reason there were a few ladies and gentlemen (Madame de Toutlemonde and Sir Sydney Marchant, for example) who both hated and feared Dr. Hastings, and lost no occasion of speaking against him. It was strange, however, that Lucilla Evans should have

---

[61] Ann Dally, *Women Under the Knife. A History of Surgery* (London: Hutchinson Radius, 1991), pp. 36 - 37.

> taken a distaste (it was scarcely to be called a dislike) to the man who had really benefitted her health, and was so constantly attentive to her—strange, that is to say, to anyone who did not know the secret of her heart and his. For the cause lay in the fact that Dr. Hastings was too attentive, and that his attentions bore a deeper meaning than mere interest in her as a patient. He was fond of Lucilla Evans, and she felt the influence without acknowledging it; and not being prepared to return his affection, it worried instead of pleasing her. She was a nervous, sensitive girl, who had been brought up in the country, and unused to be flirted with or dangled after, and she could not bear to see that Dr. Hastings' eyes rested on her longer than was necessary, or that he lowered his voice when he addressed her.

Professional boundaries are clearly being transgressed here, that a doctor has romantic feelings towards a patient who he is currently treating is at odds with regular codes of medical ethics. However, Dr Hastings goes on to be the accepted suitor of Lucilla, once her infatuation with the male-dressed Leona passes. Whilst Lucilla repeatedly professes her disdain for Dr Hastings she is not beyond playing the coquette. The information that

> Dr. Hastings, who has been a friend of our family for many years, and is a man in whom I have implicit confidence, has proposed to me for Lucilla— ... and I think he has every chance of succeeding in his suit. He is thoroughly fond of the girl, and understands the management of her health, so he is by far the best husband she could have. I have told him, of course, whose child she really is, and he has no objection to her on that score, but agrees with me that she had better be left in ignorance of the fact.

does perhaps put readers in mind of Charlotte Perkins Gilman's "heroine" in *The Yellow Wallpaper* whose husband, a physician, colludes with her acknowledged physician to control every aspect of her life. We get the sense that Lucilla will continue to have little or no autonomy but, then, Marryat hardly presents her as a character who would know what to do with it if she had. She is far from being presented as a heroine:

> With Lucilla Evans, any man who paid court to her was the right man; and she would be as happy in the future with Dr. Hastings as she would have been with anybody else. She was a phase of womanhood that made Leona anything but proud of belonging to the sex. But Tom Hastings was content, so no one had a right to be otherwise.

However it is not difficult to see a somewhat sinister edge to the relationship that is played out between this doctor/patient – wife/husband.

> We have constituted ourselves the true guardians of their interests, and in many cases inspite of ourselves, we become the custodians of their honour. We are, in fact, the stronger and they the weaker. They are obliged to believe all that we tell them, they are not in a position to dispute anything that we say to them. We, therefore, may be said to have them at our mercy.[62]

---

[62] Anon, 'Report on the Meeting of the Obstetric Society of London', *Lancet*, 6 April 1867, 429 – 441 (p. 430).

A Note on the Text

Her Father's Name was first serialized in the *Bolton Weekly Journal* from 4th March 1876. The *Bolton Weekly Journal* was owned by William Frederick Tillotson and was started in 1867 (under the title of the *Bolton Evening News*). By 1871 it became the *Bolton Weekly Journal* and began to carve out a name for itself as having a dynamic editorial policy for the publication of popular fiction. Tillotson wrote directly to many authors asking for material and published such writers as Ouida, Charles Reade, and Arthur Conan Doyle. By the 1880s Tillotson had established his "Fiction Bureau" as a major publishing concern with a proliferation of prominent writers on its list.[63]

---

[63] For further information on Tillotson, the *Bolton Weekly Journal* and the Fiction Bureau see Aled Jones, "Tillotson's Fiction Bureau: The Manchester Manuscripts", *Victorian Periodicals Review*, Vol. 17, No. 1 / 2 (Spring – Summer, 1984), pp. 43-49.

Further reading

Vern. L. Bullough & Bonnie Bullough, *Cross Dressing, Sex and Gender* (Philadelphia: Pennsylvania Press, 1993).

Wilkie Collins, *The Law and the Lady* ed. and intro by Jenny Bourne Taylor (Oxford: Oxford University Press, 1992).

Maria Edgeworth, *Belinda* (Oxford: Oxford University Press, 1999).

Evelyn Ender, *Sexing the Mind. Nineteenth Century Fictions of Hysteria* (Ithaca & London: Cornell University Press, 1995).

Marjorie Garber, *Vested Interests: Cross-Dressing and Cultural Anxiety* (New York & London: Routledge, 1992).

Sarah Grand, *The Heavenly Twins* (Michigan: Ann Arbor Paperback, University of Michigan Press, 1992).

Joseph. A. Kestner, *Sherlock's sisters: the British female detective, 1864-1913* (Aldershot: Ashgate, 2003).

George Meredith, *The Ordeal of Richard Feverel* (Oxford: Oxford University Press, 1984).

Sheryl Burt Ruzek, *The Women's Health Movement: Feminist Alternatives to Medical Control* (London, Sydney & Toronto: Prager Publishers, 1978).

Helen Small, *Love's Madness: Medicine, the novel and Female Insanity 1800 – 1865* (Oxford: Clarendon Press, 1996).

Jane M Ussher, *Women's Madness: Misogyny or Mental Illness?* (New York & London: Harvester Wheatsheaf, 1991).

Her Father's Name

by

Florence Marryat

Her Father's Name

– CHAPTER 1 –

LEONA IN THE WOODS

In the far South—beneath a bright blue sky, surrounded by fruitful valleys and dark hills—lies Rio de Janeiro.[*]

Before her stretches out the bay, more beautiful in colours and scenery than can be traced by pen and ink, bearing on its bosom the Ilha das Cobras, the Ilha das Euxadas, and farther on, Long Island and Paquetà,[†] both shady with the leafy mango and cashew tree, and blossoming with myrtle and the olive-like camarà.

But our destination is beyond all these.

Nestled in the long line of mangrove that skirts the shore beyond Paquetà, or prominently set upon the verdure covered hills, or sunk, peaceful and retired, amidst the vegetation of the valleys, are to be seen towns and villages, with houses and villas, forts and churches, to attest their presence. Amongst their residents may be found men of all nations and all callings: merchants, farmers, speculators, and perhaps a few retired gentlemen, French, American, or Portuguese, who do not care, in their old age, to leave the spot where they have toiled all their lives, and the country to which they have become naturalised in thought, manner, and feeling.

It is in one of these small outlying towns of the capital of Rio de Janeiro, perhaps the most sequestered and least conspicuous of them all, that the first scenes of this story will be laid. No sky that ever stretched itself above the heavy atmosphere of our fog-laden and smoky island, even on the brightest and clearest summer morning, could convey the faintest notion of the transparent brilliancy of the hyacinth-tinted firmament that overhung the little town I speak of. White fleecy cloudlets, that seemed to be

---

[*] One of the 26 states of Brazil. The most populous city of the state is the capital of the same name.
[†] All in the state of Rio de Janeiro.

suspended half-way between earth and heaven, floated over it at intervals to shade the eye from resting too long on such an uninterrupted mass of colour, whilst the softest of summer breezes occasionally stirred the leaves of the tall palms and feathery Brazilian cedars, as though the silence were becoming too oppressive and the trees were whispering to each other.

Noonday had fallen. The town itself—which was composed of detached houses built in the style of villas, kiosks, châlets, and cottages (each tenement standing within a garden of its own, gorgeous with tropical plants and flowers)—appeared to be asleep. The windows were shaded with green jalousies,[*] the animals had retired to their respective abiding-places; a few field-labourers composed all the life presented by that beautiful sun-lighted picture. But there was a solitude for those who sought it, within five minutes' walk of the closed portals, and an outdoor life is almost natural to a Brazilian.

The winding road, bordered with plantations and fringed with flowering myrtle hedges, that led from the little town into the country, lured one on with the soft plash and silvery tinkle of falling water, over a carpet of living green, to where the dense forest clothed the base of the frowning mountains, whose stern uncovered peaks, capped with bare rock, stood out strongly defined against the smiling sky.

Here, as the road lost itself in a narrow path that commenced to wind between tall trees of pine and palm and cedar, the dazzling sunlight became more bearable, viewed through a delicate tracery of parasites that swung, from branch to branch, and interwove their tender tendrils until they formed a curtain for the sight. Further on the trees became a perfect botanical garden, for the air plants that nestled in their forks, the lovely ribbon-like ferns that hung pendant from their branches, and the maiden-hair, or feather-leaf, the orchid, and the mimosa that clustered around their stems. Every now and then appeared a break in the dense forest— a grassy knoll so sheltered by surrounding foliage as to be invisible until you reached it—a kind of natural bower diverging from the

---

[*] A blind or a shutter with adjustable horizontal slats which enable the flow of air and light to be regulated.

general path, of which the walls were formed of waving bamboos and velvety stapelias*, the carpet of green and brown mosses, and the seats of every coloured flower.

It is to such a spot, in the very heart of the forest, outlying the little town I write of, that I wish—in imagination—you would come with me.

* * * * * *

To say that the girl who stood on that spot was beautiful, is to say little. There are so many handsome women in the world, and she was connected with a race celebrated for its personal attractions. But she was better than beautiful. She was uncommon-looking. She struck the eye at once, and having struck, she chained it. In the little place where she had been born and bred, she was passed over with the acknowledgment of being the finest woman there, but in any other country her beauty would have been termed remarkable. She was very tall for her sex, five feet seven inches at the least in stature, and her limbs were perfectly moulded in proportion to her height. Her features were large without being masculine; her hair, profusely thick, as is the case with most women in the Brazils, hung down in rippling waves below her waist. But the first thing about her that struck anyone familiar with the characteristics of her country people as strange, was that her hair, instead of being black, was of a deep chestnut colour, and her eyes a rich brown with yellow lights upon them; eyes of burnished bronze, like none but those of Titian's "Fonarina,"† or the eyes of a spotted panther in repose. The rest of her appearance did not so much differ from that of other women in the South. She had a dark creamy complexion and skin, under which her warm blood played as it chose. Her mouth was firm and well cut; the lips not full, but scarlet tinted, and upon the upper one the softest, faintest, most delicate down that ever existed on a woman's mouth—the merest shadow of a moustache, that only served to make the lip look more curved and scornful. Yet she was very young. Although her full

---

* Plant with starfish shaped flowers, native of South Africa.
† See the appendices for the *Athenaeum* review of this novel and commentary on Marryat's art history knowledge.

firm breasts and rounded limbs and lofty carriage might have led a stranger to suppose she had attained the full term of womanhood, her appearance was due to the clime in which she had been bred, and where she had only numbered seventeen years. Her dress was a strange mixture of European and Spanish fashions, for the modern Brazilians have almost entirely discarded the picturesque costume they retained until the commencement of the present century, although they still preserve some parts of it. She wore a white dress, with a long skirt, and loose hanging sleeves, that displayed her glorious arms whenever she raised them. A bright-hued Mexican scarf tied round her waist held a loaded pistol on one side and a long knife on the other, and her Spanish mantilla[*] of black silk and lace was thrown down on the grass beside her. She was not entirely alone—a large dun-coloured goat with a long black beard was lying down close to her, chewing the herbs that grew within his reach with evident satisfaction, and blinking his eyes at every fresh burst of energy on his mistress's part (for the girl was speaking), as though he understood all about it, and it was no use trying to stop her until she had done. Hopping about the trunks of the trees, looking for such insects as his soul loved, but never attempting to go out of sight, was her favourite large-beaked, black-and-orange-throated rhamphastos,[†] a bird peculiar to the country, which, though exceedingly timid and difficult to entrap, is most easily tamed by kindness, and makes an excellent and faithful pet. She herself was leaning with one arm on the neck of a dark-coloured mule, bearing an old-fashioned Spanish saddle with trappings, which, although of silver, presented more the appearance of lead from the effects of age, neglect, and ill-usage.

There was no human creature near her, positively none but those three dumb animals to bear her company, and yet the girl was declaiming aloud and vehemently, as though she had an audience to fill the woods.

"Sire!" she said, with one arm extended as to command attention, "this is no time for argument or for delay. Your army has been routed, your towns pillaged, your women and children

---

[*] Lace or silk scarf worn over the head and shoulders.
[†] A toucan, a South American rainforest bird. See the *Academy* review in the appendices.

massacred by the sword! The soldiers are dispirited, the enemy is triumphant—the country begins to lose her faith in you! In this extremity I throw myself into the breach—willing to die, to be martyred, to shed the last drop of my blood for my country, my people, and my king!

"What do I propose to do, you ask? I propose to lead your army, sire, on to victory, to throw myself into the breach made by your late defeat, to go forward at the head of your troops, and to show these base and cowardly Englishmen the spirit of a woman of France, that they may begin to fear the men! I will ride into the thick of the battle—"

"On a mule of twelve hands laden with an old Spanish saddle twice his own weight! Ha, ha, ha, ha!" roared a voice from the surrounding covert.

The girl started, flushed crimson with anger, and had laid her hand upon the pistol in her belt, when the bushes parted to admit a young man, some three or four years her senior, who carried a gun in his hand, and several brace of birds slung in a hunting-bag across his shoulder.

"Bravo, Leona," he exclaimed jestingly, "three cheers for the Maid of Orleans.[*] I've been listening to you for the last half hour. It's as good as a play."

He was a handsome young fellow, dressed in a Panama hat, large top-boots of unbleached leather, and a striped cotton shirt, and he spoke to the girl in Portuguese. At first she did not answer him.

Her hand had relaxed its hold upon the pistol as soon as she recognised the intruder, but the angry flush had not died out of her countenance, and she beat her foot upon the ground ominously.

"Are you angry that I should have overheard you?" he inquired, presently perceiving her annoyance.

"It is not fair of you, Christobal," she answered. "It is not right

---

[*] Joan of Arc, also called the Maid of Orleans – a patron saint of France and national heroine. In 1429 Joan of Arc led troops to a victory over the English during the Hundred Years war. Captured and sold to the English in 1430, then handed to an ecclesiastical court at Rouen she was tried for witchcraft and heresy and in 1431 was burned at the stake. During her 'trial' much was made of her choice of male clothing.

that you should steal behind people in this way, and listen to what does not concern you!"

"*Caramba!*[*] Who could have helped hearing? Your voice reached me half a mile away. And why should you mind *my* hearing you, Leona?"

"I do mind it! You make me look like a fool to myself! You have spoilt the pleasure of my day."

"But you were doing it so beautifully. I was admiring every word you said long before I spoke! You appear like a born actress to me! You would make your fortune on the stage."

As he said these words the girl's look of annoyance softened. She had made her goat rise, and taken her bird upon her wrist as though intending to leave the spot, but now she hesitated and placed the rhamphastos on the saddle-bow again.

"Who would believe, to hear you, Leona, that the greater part of your education had been acquired through the newspapers? Of course, I know that your father has taught you much, yet in this solitude, where nothing new seems ever to penetrate, it is marvellous you should know what you do, and be able to speak as you do. It is not knowledge, Leona—it is inspiration! Are you still angry with your Tobal, *urpilla chay?*"

He drew nearer to her and laid his hand on hers. She did not repulse him nor shrink from him: on the contrary, she clasped his hand warmly and frankly, then raised it gratefully to her lips.

"We could not be long angry with each other, Tobalito, if we tried. We, who have grown up together since we were little children. But the newspapers you speak of, I would not exchange them for any books. Books speak of the dead. Newspapers of the living. I do not care what people did a hundred years ago. I want to know what they are doing now—this very day—in Paris and New York, and London, and Madrid. Ah! how I envy you, about to set out on your travels and see the world. Would heaven had made me a man, instead of a stay-at-home, do-nothing woman."

"I do not envy myself, Leona," the young man answered, as he regarded her mournfully. "I am content to go out into the world, but I leave too much of my heart behind to go happily. It will not

---

[*] See reviews (Appendix C) for comments on Marryat's 'unusual' use of language.

Her Father's Name

be long before I wish myself back again."

"Bah," she replied contemptuously, "what do you leave here compared to what you will find? Your mother; true, she has been an excellent mother, but what did she rear you for except to part with you?"

"There is yourself, Leona."

"I am nothing, Tobal, except your friend, and the world is full of friends like myself, for a good-looking fellow like you. But think what you will see. The great city of New York—with its thousands of citizens, its marts, its stores, its shipping—above all, Tobal, its theatres. Oh! if I had but wings to fly with you there for one day to see the grand play 'Joan of Arc,' as they have placed it on the stage. It must be glorious."

"You might go with me there altogether, Leona, if you willed it so," said her companion, wistfully. But if she understood his meaning, she did not choose to acknowledge it.

"How thoughtlessly you speak! How could I leave my father?" she answered shortly, as she threw her mantilla over her head and shoulders, wound the mule's bridle about her arm, and calling to her goat, turned into the forest-path. The young man followed her and walked by her side.

"Is your father no better, Leona?"

"I think not. He seems to me to grow weaker and more apprehensive each day. Oh, Tobal, there is some mystery in my father's life that is killing him by slow degrees."

"A mystery, Leona!"

"Yes. I may say so much to you, may I not? You would not betray him or me? You look upon me as a sister."

He drew himself up proudly.

"I am of Spanish descent, Leona. You know that I have no Portuguese blood in my veins, and that, though to our misfortune, my family have been banished to these Brazilian wilds, and I have to accept service at the hands of a New York trader to earn my daily bread, I am the lineal descendant of an hidalgo,[*] and have the right to use the title of 'Don' before my name."

"I know it, Tobalito. And you are as proud of your Spanish as I

---

[*] Spanish nobility

am of my European blood."

"And a Spaniard never betrays his friend, Leona. So that even if I did not regard you as—as—a sister, your father's secret would be safe with me."

"But it is not in my power to tell it to you, Tobal. My only knowledge lies in the fact that he has a secret, and that it is connected with the English. How my father hates the English, or the mere mention of them. He would like to forget even that such a nation exists."

"And yet he has taught you to speak English—and speaks it so well himself too."

"Not better than he speaks French and Portuguese."

"Yes, better; because it is so far more difficult a language for a foreigner to acquire. Had it not been for M. Lacoste's instruction, for which I cannot sufficiently thank you, I should never have procured such an appointment as that I have obtained in New York."

"And for which you leave us next week. Is it not so?"

"For which I must leave you (unfortunately for myself) next week. How I wish your father could be persuaded to leave this place and settle in New York also!"

"Ah! that is hopeless, Christobal! I have entreated him again and again to take me out of this wilderness to some more populated district—even to Rio—but he is steadfast in his refusal. He will not even see strangers when they come here, or make friends with anyone, excepting just the two or three families that he has known for years. Some people attribute this morbid feeling or excessive grief for my mother's death. I do not believe it. That he should lament the loss of a pretty, amiable Brazilian girl, who had been his pleasant companion for a short time, is natural, but not that he should shut himself up from all society for the space of seventeen years. And I can never remember my father different from what he is now, Tobal."

"Neither can I, Leona."

"He always had grey hair from the time I was a child, and he cannot be fifty yet. And he was always nervous and miserable, and subject to fits of depression and melancholy. Tobalito," continued the girl, drawing closer to him and dropping her voice to a whisper,

"I have sometimes even thought that my father was a little—*mad!*"

"No, no, Leona; not that! Don't say that," cried Christobal, hastily.

She had stopped short in the forest-path as she spoke, and was leaning against his shoulder with closed eyes breathing heavily. He turned himself round and folded her in his arms. His frame trembled all over at the contact, but hers remained steadfast as marble. She was thinking only of her father.

"Don't say that—don't think it—my darling," he went on fervently. "It cannot be so bad as that, Leona. If I thought it were, I *could* not leave you here alone with him. I would sacrifice everything to stop by your side and protect you."

She thanked him by raising her head languidly and kissing him upon the cheek. Then they recommenced their walk homeward as before.

"I have often wished of late that you were not going to leave us, Tobal. I shall miss my brother greatly. There is another thing I fear, though I cannot tell you why, and that is the intimacy of my father with Señor Ribeiro."

"But why should you fear that, Leona? It is but natural they should be intimate. M. Lacoste has, I believe, engaged in several speculations with Ribeiro lately,"

"And failed in them, Tobal."

"I am sorry to hear that, because he cannot afford to lose. Is Ribeiro often at your house?"

"Constantly! He is about the only person my father will even admit. And they remain closeted together for hours at a time."

"In all probability they are discussing some means by which they hope to regain the money they have lost."

"Perhaps so; but I distrust Ribeiro, Tobal. He has an evil eye."

"Does he dare to cast it upon you?" exclaimed Don Christobal, fiercely

"Softly, my brother. There is no need of alarm. The daughter of Louis Lacoste is not for Antonio Ribeiro."

"Who is she for, Leona?" he whispered tenderly.

"For no one at present, Tobalito, except her father and herself. And perhaps—by-and-by—in a distance so far off that she cannot now discern it, for the world; but the saints alone know what lies in the future."

As the girl concluded, she drew from the folds of her sash an embroidered pouch of tobacco, a case of cigarette papers, and a box of allumettes. Then nonchalantly rolling up a cigarette, she lighted and placed it between her lips, as though smoking were the most ordinary thing in the world to her—as, indeed, it was.

Christobal sighed, and continued to walk by her in silence. He knew from past experience that he had touched a point on which it was useless to try and sound her. Leona's temperament was warm, her disposition luxurious, her body supple as a cat-o'-mountain's; but her heart remained (as far as appearances went) hard as a rock.

* * * * *

Meanwhile a very different sort of scene was being enacted within the walls of the low-roofed, white tenement that owned M. Lacoste as master. There—in a room from which all the sunlight was carefully excluded—dressed in the loosest and most slovenly of Brazilian costumes, with a cigar in his mouth, and that look upon his face of anxious depression and bodily fear which seemed native to it, sat Louis Lacoste.

It was impossible to look at this man without seeing how handsome he had been. Amidst his thick hair and beard—now almost white from some mysterious cause—could here and there be traced a thread of auburn, to show from whom his daughter had inherited hers. His eyes were brown, his complexion fair, his hands and feet small and slender, in every respect he vastly differed from the companion who sat opposite to him, Señor Antonio Ribeiro. This last-named, a Portuguese of the lowest stamp, was almost repulsive in appearance. It is not generally known, perhaps that the Brazilian is to the Portuguese what the American is to the English, and that the race becomes much more energetic and refined from mixture with Indian blood. Señor Ribeiro had had no such advantages in his composition. He was of pure Portuguese descent, as might be traced by his large thick nose, the yellow white of his eyes, and his ungainly hands and feet. Added to this, he was not a day under forty, and had become more obese than is desirable for the preservation of a graceful carriage. As he lolled

Her Father's Name

back in his chair, keeping his sinister eyes upon the countenance of M. Lacoste, and puffing out clouds of smoke from his thick lips, he looked a very undesirable acquaintance indeed. The conversation had evidently not been of an agreeable nature. Louis Lacoste appeared more than usually anxious, and Señor Ribeiro more than usually unpleasant.

"The failure of that last speculation was entirely due to your carelessness," he said. "If you had gone on board the New York steamer at Rio, as I desired you, and spoken to Joghmann yourself, it would have been all right."

"I told you at the time that I could not go on board the steamer for you," replied M. Lacoste. "The original agreement was that you were to work the Rio speculators and I attend to the up-country merchants."

"What was your objection to be seen in Rio?" demanded Ribeiro, suspiciously.

"That is my affair," replied his companion; but he looked uneasy. "I am out of health, and I have other business to attend to. Anyway it was not part of my contract with you."

"Anyway the money's dropped, and must be accounted for. You don't suppose I intend to pay for your swindling," said Ribeiro, coarsely.

"When men agree to speculate together they stand to fall or rise together. I have lost money on the transaction as well as yourself. We must be content to take the thick with the thin."

"But I'm not content to do so, Lacoste. I sunk good money on that speculation, and if it hadn't been for your confounded negligence it would have turned up trumps. I must stand the loss of what I expected to gain from it—but hang me if I stand the loss of the sum I laid down. It was through your fault it was frittered away, and I look to you to return it me."

"Well! I can't do it; and there's the long and short of it."

"You *must* do it."

"Ribeiro, it's of no use blustering at me, for I haven't got the money."

"Then you must get it."

"And go into debt to pay what I don't owe. I shall do no such thing."

"I'll make you! Do you suppose I'm going to be swindled by a cur like you?"

Lacoste sprung to his feet.

"How dare you apply such a term to me, Ribeiro? You'll have to give me satisfaction for this."

"Give you satisfaction?" laughed the Portuguese. "I'll give you satisfaction by making the story of your life public to the whole country side, my fine fellow."

"What do you mean?"

Lacoste put the question defiantly, but he trembled as he waited for the answer.

"Ah—what do I mean? Why, just this—that you're moving amongst us under false pretences; that your name is no more Lacoste than it is Ribeiro; that you are no more a Frenchman than you are a Portuguese. I've found you out, my friend. *Your real name is George Evans, and you are an Englishman!"*

– CHAPTER 2 –

"YOU ARE IN MY POWER"

At these words M. Lacoste leant on the back of his chair for support, every nerve of his body quivering with suppressed emotion, whilst Ribeiro retained the seat opposite to him, and kept his evil eye fixed upon his victim, as he continued to puff huge volumes of smoke from between his coarse, defiant lips.

"Who told you this?" Lacoste managed at last to articulate.

"What matters it who told me? Ye know it is the truth! I don't walk about New York, and Boston, and Philadelphia with my eyes shut, or my ears either. The firm of Evans and Troubridge is as well known in those towns as it is in Liverpool, *nor is the name of Abraham Anson entirely forgotten either,"* added Ribeiro significantly.

The beads of perspiration stood on Lacoste's forehead, but he attempted to brave it out.

"I don't in the least know what you are alluding to," he said, with a sickly smile.

Her Father's Name

Up to this point, Ribeiro had been coolly insolent, now he became violent.

"Don't you attempt to lie to me," he exclaimed loudly, "or I'll shout the story out from Rio to New York. Once for all, *I know everything*, and can set justice on your track to-morrow if I choose. So if you are wise you will conciliate instead of angering me."

"But it is not true! It was a lie—a calumny. The chain of circumstances by which I was unfortunately surrounded—"

"Does it look like a lie?" interrupts his companion. "For the last twenty years you have lived in this place under an assumed name and nationality, not using it as others do for an occasional retreat or country residence, but as an habitual home, from which you have refused to stir, even as far as the adjoining towns, and in which you have lived the life of a hermit—or a criminal!—shutting yourself up from all society, and brooding on your evil thoughts, until your hair has turned white with fear! But the time is up for concealment, my friend. You are found out, *Mr. George Evans!*"

The scoffing tone in which the English name dropped from the foreigner's lips seemed to strike his companion with mortal dread. His trembling hands wandered in a nervous manner through the masses of his whitened hair, as though he would make excuses for its appearance.

"The climate," he faltered, "the heat—illness—"

"And the remembrance of *murder!*" continued Ribeiro, finishing the sentence for him.

"No! no! Ribeiro! upon my soul!—by all that is holy—it was a mistake—a false accusation—a—"

"Sit down," said the Portuguese roughly, "and don't make a fool of yourself. I'm here to speak to you on this subject as a friend. Send for brandy—anything you like, that will stop that trembling fit of yours, and make you able to listen to what I have to say,"

He sounded a bell that stood upon the table as he spoke, whilst Louis Lacoste dragged himself to, rather than sat down in, the cane chair he had been leaning against. A negress, dressed in a striped blue-and-white cotton dress, with a scarlet and yellow handkerchief tied round her head, answered the summons.

"Here, bring brandy—rum—spirits of any kind," said Ribeiro, "the master is not well."

The negress returned with what was ordered.

Ribeiro made a strong mixture of brandy and water, and forced it down the throat of Lacoste.

"Drink," he said, "and be a man, if you can. It's lucky for you that you have fallen into such hands as mine."

Lacoste drained the glass, and turned to his tormentor.

"What do you want me to do?" he demanded, in a plaintive voice.

"To look at this matter in a proper light. I know your story. I need say no more to convince you of that. Don't speak," he went on, raising his hand to stop the words which were trembling on M. Lacoste's lips, "for it is useless. If the accusation were a thousand times false, it would make no difference to the fact. And you know best whether you wish it made public or not!"

"You will ruin me if you make it so," muttered Lacoste.

"Very good! Then we have arrived at the point in the whole matter. *You are in my power.*"

"What can I do to buy myself out of it? You have your price, Ribeiro, like other men. If it is this money you require—"

"Softly, my friend, softly! We are coming to that presently. The fact I want to establish first is, that you are in my power."

"I am in your power," echoed the unhappy Lacoste, with a look of despair.

"And by merely raising my voice I could bring you—*where?* Eh?" said Ribeiro, with a lengthened intonation that was torture to his listener. "But suppose you put it out of my power! Suppose you unite our interests to that degree that to ruin you is to ruin myself. Suppose—"

"You mean Leona!" interrupted M. Lacoste.

"I mean *Leona!*" repeated Ribeiro, with another sort of light in his evil eyes; "and when I say I mean Leona, I say that I mean to have Leona—or—or—*Mr. George Evans!* Now you know the whole of it." And he assumed another position in his seat, and crossed his legs one over the other, as though the matter were then and there concluded. Louis Lacoste glanced furtively at the ungainly figure— the shock of coarse hair—the greasy complexion—the thick limbs and features—and shuddered—not for himself. But he could not afford to show his feelings on the subject.

"You have always liked Leona," he remarked, aimlessly.

"That is neither here nor there," replied Ribeiro. "The fact is that I mean to marry her. For the same reason I enter upon no question of ways and means. I am not poor, as you know (though you've done your best to impoverish me with your late folly); but if I were the poorest devil in Rio you could not afford to make an objection to me."

"My daughter is very young," said Lacoste.

"Bah! In a country where the girls marry at fourteen! But were she twelve it would make no difference. She is old enough for me."

"But she will require a little preparation. You would prefer her to go to you of her own accord. Leona is very high-spirited."

"I will soon break her spirit."

"But she has never been coerced in her life. She is my only child," said the poor father, trembling at the prospect presented to him by Ribeiro's words.

"Very good," was the sullen answer. "Keep your only child, but I shall have my substitute."

"No! no! Señor! I did not mean that. Leona is deeply attached to me. She will do anything to which I urge her. But women are fanciful at times, you know; the question of marriage suddenly proposed is apt to have rather a startling effect on a young girl. Still, of course, she is aware it must come some day."

"You will be good enough to make her aware that the day will come very soon—next week at latest."

"Next week!" exclaimed Lacoste.

"*Next week*," repeated Ribeiro, rising from his chair. "I have business in Rio de Janeiro next week, Mr.—I mean *Monsieur Lacoste*," with a mockingly deferential bow, "*and I shall wish to take my wife with me in order to keep temptation out of my way! You understand.*"

And with this significant farewell the Portuguese stretched himself, lit a fresh cigar, placed his broad-brimmed straw hat upon his head, and stalked forth into the open air. At the entrance of the garden he encountered Leona and Christobal, who, having completed their homeward stroll, were exchanging a few words in parting. Ribeiro scowled at the young Spaniard, who returned his glance with interest. There was no love lost between the two; nor did Leona look much more pleased than Christobal Valera at the interruption to their interview.

"Good morning, mademoiselle," said Ribeiro, with a leer. "Is it to attend mass that you have left your good father to my company for so many hours?"

"I do not usually take my mule, and my goat, and my bird to mass with me, señor!" she answered indifferently.

"Ah! true. I had overlooked the favourites. You have been riding, perhaps, then, on the high road?"

"By no means. The high road has no attractions for me in a broiling sun. I have been in the woods."

"And unprotected! M. Lacoste is not as careful of so much beauty as he ought to be, mademoiselle. There are often vagrants passing through the forest. You might come to harm."

"I am never unprotected, Señor Ribeiro," replied Leona, as she placed her hand upon her sash. "I have my pistol and my bowie-knife, and if occasion arose I should know how to use them."

"*Madre de Dios!*[*] I would rather encounter your bowie-knife, mademoiselle, than one flash of your beautiful eyes."

"You would repent your choice, señor. Though I can use them too if I choose," she answered, as she turned them angrily upon him, and led her mule through the garden into the court at the back of the châlet.

Valera was about to follow her, when Ribeiro stopped him.

"You are not wanted there," he said, rudely; "mademoiselle has business with her father."

"And who gave you the situation of door-keeper?" retorted Valera, as he pushed past him. "Keep your place, señor, and learn to know where it is."

"Your place is not inside these gates, nor ever shall be," exclaimed Ribeiro, still attempting to block his path.

"What has come to you?" said Christobal, with the purest surprise, as he regarded the other's countenance. Have you been drinking?"

"It has come to me to tell you plainly that I'll have no half-breed hanging about Mademoiselle Lacoste, and that you've paid your last visit to this house," retorted the Portuguese.

---

[*] Mother of God

"Half-breed!" exclaimed Valera, all his Spanish blood rushing into his handsome face at the insult. "Half-breed, you d——d Portuguese, when you know that I would scorn to own the mud that does duty in your veins for blood. *Caramba!* that I should have lived to hear such words from a pig like you. Take that—and that—and that, and learn to know a Don next time you meet him." So saying, he darted at the obese Ribeiro, and with three well-directed blows that would have done credit to an Englishman, rolled him over on the ground; then quietly straightened himself and followed Leona into the courtyard.

The Portuguese picked himself up from the dust into which he had fallen, recovered his Panama hat, shook out his loose linen trousers, and walked away with a scowl and an oath.

"The first time and the last time," he muttered. "By to-morrow mademoiselle will understand what is before her, and we shall have no more insolence from her or her dog of a Spanish cavalier, or Antonio Ribeiro is very much mistaken—very much mistaken indeed."

* * * * * *

Christobal had only followed Leona for the purpose of delivering over her mule to the negro who had the charge of it, which done he was too well aware that it is the custom of the Brazilian ladies to bathe and take a siesta at that hour of the day to intrude upon her presence any longer. Yet he lingered for a moment beneath its creeper-festooned verandah to tell her of his encounter with the Portuguese.

Leona did not smile at the recital; she frowned.

"Had I been there," she said, clasping the handle of her bowie-knife, "he would not have spoken to you in that manner."

"So I am glad you were not there," laughed her companion. "You are too quick with that knife; you will get into mischief with it some day, Leona."

"Then it will as easily take me out of mischief," she answered coolly. "Would you have me *afraid*, Tobal?"

"I would have you nothing but what you are, Leona—a beautiful panther in female form. But be merciful to the poor mouse you have between your paws *urpilla chay*."

"A tigress and a turtle," she laughed quietly. "I must be a strange combination, Tobal. *Adios*, brother, until evening. I go to my father and my midday rest."

She moved away from him as she spoke, and he stood watching the undulation of her white robe till it had disappeared. *"Moving"* is the best term by which to express how Leona walked. There was no light, springy gait about this girl. All her actions were slow and solemn, yet eminently graceful. She reminded one of nothing so much as of that to which Valera had likened her—a panther—a creature of strength and grace and beauty and softness, until it is offended. And even then, though its revenge is quick and its spring fatal, it is still beautiful, perhaps more so in its anger than its play. But when man has at last succeeded in taming one of these apparently untamable creatures, how much more faithful and loving and submissive it becomes than the lesser animal who fawns on everybody.

Leona walked into her father's presence. Lacoste was still sitting where Ribeiro had left him, his hands lying nervelessly upon his knees; his head sunk forward on his breast. At that sight, the finest part of her nature—the woman part—was stirred. She went up to him, and knelt down by his side. As she did so, her waving chestnut hair fell almost to the ground.

"Father, are you ill—worse—has anything happened to disturb you?"

At the sound of her voice he looked up at her affectionately, imploringly. There was something eminently touching in the contrast between these two—the man so feeble, cowed, and fear-stricken; the woman so strong, energetic, and bold.

"I have had a great, a great *shock*, Leona. I want to speak to you, my child."

"I am here, dear father. Tell me all about it."

She was used to see him indulge in fits, not only of terrible depression, but occasionally of unaccountable fear. She only thought now that some dream, or old recollection, or wayward fancy had arisen to disturb him. She had no conception of real danger.

"I don't want to part with you, Leona," he commenced

tremblingly.

"Of course not, father. Neither do I intend ever to part with you. We will cling to each other till death parts us."

"But it may be necessary. Women cannot remain single always. In this country it is a disgrace."

"What do we care for the customs of this country, father? You are French, not Brazilian," she answered proudly.

"But I am not strong, Leona, and death may part us any day; and I could not die happy if I left you without a protector!"

"Without a protector," echoed the girl, "when I have myself, my weapons, and Tobal."

"You do not *love* Christobal, my girl?" demanded Lacoste anxiously.

"I do—dearly! He is the best friend I have, after yourself, father. If Tobal were my brother I could not esteem him more."

"Ah! I did not mean that sort of love, Leona. I meant that love that leads to marriage."

"I love no one in that way," replied his daughter. "I wish to love no one in that way. I have no desire of marriage—no intention of marrying. I have never seen the man to whom I would submit my will, and I never expect to see him."

"But, Leona, whatever your private feelings may be, it is expedient from a public point of view that you should think of marriage. A woman without a husband is thought little of by all nations; in this country she becomes a nonentity—almost a disgrace."

"Then I prefer to be a nonentity and a disgrace."

"But for *my* sake, Leona—to allay my anxiety—to make me happy," he said entreatingly.

The girl rose and stood opposite, looking down upon him. Looking *down* in each sense of the word, for there was contempt in the tone of her answer, though she tried hard not to make it visible.

"How could it increase your happiness to make me miserable, father?"

"How can you be sure it would make you miserable?"

"If I am not sure for myself, no one can be sure for me. I am quite determined, father. I shall never marry. Marriage is slavery, and I was born free. I will never be such a fool as to barter my birthright for any man."

"But I *want* you to marry, Leona," said Lacoste plaintively. "There is a man here, a good man, and a rich man—one who can give you a house in Rio, and a carriage and horses, and every comfort—and one who loves you, Leona, and—"

"Who is he?" she demanded, curiously.

"He is well known and wealthy, my child. You would be envied as his wife, and he would be a friend to me. It is in his power to help me, and—"

"What is his name?" she asked again, in the same tone.

"I know he is not very young, nor perhaps what a girl would call handsome," continued Lacoste, nervous at the prospect of coming to the point, "but he is well known in Rio and New York as a wealthy merchant—"

"*Is it Ribeiro?*"

The question was put in such a tone of complete amazement and disbelief that it was very hard to answer in the affirmative. Her father did so almost more by the action of his head and hand, than by the quavering "yes" that fell from his lips.

"*Ribeiro*," she repeated, incredulously; "and you would throw me—me, Leona Lacoste—into the arms of that pig—that beast—that low-bred, money-getting, swindling Portuguese! *Me!* your *child!* whom you profess to love! Father, if this be true, I shall wish I had never been born!"

"No, no, Leona, don't say that."

"I would not live to see the day on which you so prostituted me. I would take this knife and put an end to my existence before it dawned. The crime would be on your head, father, but it would be merciful of me to leave it there. Better your conscience should be heavy with the murder of my body than the murder of my soul."

"Not murder! Leona—not murder! Oh my God, keep me clear of that!" exclaimed the wretched man as he covered up his face in his hands.

"Then why propose a course that would drive me to it? You know what I am—high-spirited, strong-willed. Afraid of no one—and nothing. Loneliness, poverty, death, have no fears for me; but I will sell myself to no man, above all the world not to that sordid, sensual brute, Ribeiro."

"Say no more, my child, every word you utter goes through me like a sword."

"You will promise never to mention this subject to me again, father?"

"I promise, Leona."

"And you will tell that—that *creature*, who has dared to look at me, what I have said."

"I will tell him."

"And you will command him never to place his foot within these walls again. Ah, I know what you are going to say. We owe him money. Father, we will pay him his money, if I beg in Rio to obtain it; but his presence here would be an insult I could not trust myself not to avenge."

"When he has had his answer he shall not come again!" replied her father in a low voice—low, and so full of despair, that Leona sprung to his side and knelt down as before.

"And you will not hate me, father! You will not be angry with me because I cannot consent to leave you for any other man! Why! what would you do without me? Who could understand all your strange moods and ways, and sympathise with them as I have done? You loved my mother, father! You would not have thrust her from your side against her will. Think that I am she! She only lived with you for eighteen months. I have been your companion since my very birth. Would you part with me more easily than you would have done with her?"

"No, no! child, rest easy! You shall not be the one to go! But if, in years to come, they should ever tell you that your father committed great crimes, don't believe them, Leona. I have led a thoughtless and a dissipated life, but not a criminal one—not a criminal one!"

"Who should dare to tell me so?" said the girl with a look of amazement. "But you are not well to-day, dear father! You are going to have one of those strange fits of depression which leave you so weak and exhausted. Will you not lie down? The sun is very high, and a sleep will do you good—Epiphania shall sling your hammock under the trees in the garden, and I will mix you a sherbet and bring it to you there!"

"No! not in the garden—not in the garden!" said Lacoste, with a look of vague alarm, "lest there should be anyone about to see me. But I *will* lie down, Leona. *I will lie down!*"

He rose as he spoke, and she supported him tenderly. She was used to these wild incoherent speeches on her father's part. They had given birth to some of the misgivings she had communicated to Valera concerning his sanity.

"You will feel better when you have rested," she said soothingly.

"Yes, yes," he muttered. "A long rest! a long rest! But don't believe anything they say against me, Leona. Your father is true; remember that! Foolish—but true!"

"I know he is true," she answered, smiling up into his face.

He took hers between his shaking hands.

"A good face. An honest, brave face. A most beautiful, courageous face. A better face than mine. I am glad Ribeiro will never call it his."

"You may stake your life on that, father," she interposed.

"I will stake my life on that," he murmured. "I will stake thy life on that."

She led him carefully to his room, and saw him laid upon the bed, then, darkening the chamber, brought him a refreshing lemonade.

"You will sleep now, dear father," she said, as she prepared to leave him.

"I shall sleep now," he repeated slowly, "and remember, Leona, that *your father was true!*"

He lifted his eyes wistfully to hers, and she smoothed his hair and kissed his forehead, as though she were soothing a fractious child to rest, then left him to repose.

As she walked away she felt more troubled than usual on his account. If his strange fancies were to take this direction again she might have much difficulty, not only in combating them, but in repelling Ribeiro's insolent advances. At this thought the girl's proud heart began to beat irregularly, and a dark crimson flush stained her olive skin. She called to the negress Epiphania to sling her net hammock beneath the branches of a wide-spreading cedar tree, and as soon as she had taken her noonday bath she ensconced herself at full length in its narrow folds, and swung lazily to and fro in her leafy bower. The warm, soft air played through her unbound tresses, and lifted the diaphanous drapery that enveloped her supple limbs. From where she lay she could watch the gorgeously-painted butterflies, and the tiny humming birds that revelled in the broad sunlight, darting from flower to flower—now burying themselves in the cups of the fuchsias and lilies, or shaking the slender tendrils of the passion flower, and scattering the perfume of the orange blossoms upon the already too-heavily-laden air. Yet Leona could not charm herself to sleep. Her anger had been too powerfully excited; her pride too suddenly alarmed by her father's proposal, to enable her, all at once, to forget and forgive it, even for him.

Unaccountable as were some of M. Lacoste's words, she had never known him attempt before to make her the cat's-paw by which his difficulties were to he solved. And in such a way too! The bare idea caused her strong nature to shudder, her brave face to pale!

What *could* have happened to make her father entertain the notion of such an awful sacrifice, even for a moment? He must be very largely in Ribeiro's debt before he could contemplate offering his child's honour as the price of his own liberation.

How could this debt have been incurred—and for what? She knew only of the failure of the speculation before alluded to, by which both parties had been losers to some extent, but not an irremediable one.

Leona lay in her hammock, trying to work out this problem for herself, until the warm Brazilian breeze and the lively Brazilian insects fanned and hummed her into repose.

How long she slept she had never occasion afterwards to recall—for she was roused from her siesta by the sound of a piercing scream that rung through the rooms of the little chalet, and penetrated the recesses of her leafy bower, recalling her to the affairs of life with a sense of terror.

– CHAPTER 3 –

THE LETTER AND THE RING

Her *father!* That was her first thought. She sprang from her hammock with the agility of a cat, and rushed into the chalet. On the threshold of the door she encountered the negress Epiphania, wringing her hands and screaming.

"Oh, come to the master, missy! Come to the master. He very sick indeed."

She walked past her hurriedly into his chamber. One glance was sufficient. Her father was either dying—or dead.

"Go and fetch Dr. Linton," she exclaimed, mentioning an old English surgeon and naturalist, who had been staying for some months in their town, and lived within a few yards of them.

In a few minutes he was by her side.

"Oh, Dr. Linton!" she cried, "what does all this mean? What has he been doing to himself? Why is there such a smell of almonds in the room?"

M. Lacoste was lying on his bed, apparently as his daughter had left him, but his face had turned livid, his nails were blue, and his fingers clenched together. His eyes were wide open, prominent and glistening, which had led Leona to believe he was in a fit, and about his closed mouth was to be seen a ring of foam. Dr. Linton examined the eyeballs, laid his hand upon the heart, and then looked compassionately at the girl kneeling beside the corpse.

"Is it a fit, Dr. Linton? Should he have a warm bath?"

"It is not a fit, mademoiselle."

"What then? has he gone mad? Oh doctor, don't say that! I have feared it for so long."

"You have no need to fear it; but try and gather up your courage to meet a great shock. Your poor father is dead."

"*Dead!* and in a moment, But how came he dead? What has killed him?"

"I am afraid this has," replied the doctor, as he disengaged a small phial from the stiffened grasp.

"*That! What is that?*" demanded Leona, trembling.

"It is poison, mademoiselle. This bottle has contained prussic acid."[*]

"And you mean that he killed himself with it—that my father committed suicide? That he has left me to go through the world alone."

"Hush! Hush! mademoiselle, be calm, be quieted. Do not faint, I implore you."

"I shall not faint, doctor, I have too much European blood in me for that. But this—I *cannot, cannot* believe it, Oh! will you not try something before you give up all hope. Are there no remedies, no medicines, nothing that might yet save him?"

"My dear young lady, he has been dead for the last two hours! I know it must be hard of belief, but nothing will ever recall your poor father to this world again."

"He might have waited," said the girl in a plaintive voice; "he might have struggled on a little longer for my sake. Was I not here to share his burdens? Why did he not confide in me?"

"He was probably not in a state of mind to understand the depth of your affection. Tell me, mademoiselle, have you had any reason to suppose lately that M. Lacoste contemplated such an act as this?"

"None whatever—at least not more than usual."

"Was he commonly depressed in spirits, then?"

"Very much so at times, and he has often said he wished that he were dead. But I thought little of it. My father's life has not been a happy one."

"Has M. Lacoste had any fresh trouble lately that would have been likely to upset his mind?"

"He experienced some money losses, but I do not think they were heavy."

"And nothing has occurred to-day or yesterday, for instance, to make you suspect he suffered more than ordinary?"

"Nothing except—-Oh Holy Virgin! It could not have been that."

"To what do you allude, mademoiselle?"

"Only a conversation he and I held a few hours since, in which my father urged me on a course I much objected to. He seemed

---

[*] Cyanide.

wounded at my refusal, but he said nothing—nothing—to make me think—to make me fear—" But here Leona's narrative broke down in a fit of weeping.

"Be comforted, mademoiselle, and rest assured that no ordinary disappointment drove your poor father to this rash act. I have observed much peculiarity about him myself, and have little doubt that the seeds of the insanity that took possession of him at the last were sown years and years ago. And now, what can I do for you in this sad extremity?"

"Nothing, doctor, but leave me alone with him."

"But that is not fit for a girl of your years."

"We have been always alone since I can remember, and I wish to share my last duty to him with no one. I must have time to think about it. He was the only thing I loved on earth. I cannot believe all at once—that *he is gone!*"

"Think, dear mademoiselle. Is there no one you would wish to see. No friend—"

"I have no friends! Stay, though, there is Tobal. Yes! Tell Don Christobal Valera that my father is *dead*, and that I want him to come and weep with me."

She turned all her attention then to the corpse, and Doctor Linton, wondering at the fortitude and composure she displayed, left her alone with the body of her father.

He would not have thought so much of her fortitude and composure could he have seen her *when* she was alone. Her first grief was manifested in a wild unchastened cry of despair; but it exhausted itself, as such outbursts will, and then she became quiet and resigned, and dispensed the various orders that were necessary with all a woman's firmness and decision.

In the Brazils (as in all southern climates) interment is conducted as soon as possible after death, and by the same evening poor Lacoste's body, decked with all manner of flowers by his daughter's loving hands, was lying in its coffin, ready for removal at the following sunrise. Her friend Christobal had been of the greatest use to Leona at this juncture, taking all the business part of the matter off her hands; but when the evening fell, and the preparations for the morning were complete, her sick heart wearied even of his sympathy, and she prayed him to leave her once more alone with her sorrow.

So she sat, poor child, taking no heed of the gathering gloom, beside the bed on which her father's coffin rested, with her tired head laid upon the pillows.

Suddenly a shadow darkened the open doorway. She looked up languidly; it was that of Ribeiro. In a moment Leona was on her feet.

"What do you do here, señor?" she demanded coldly. The Portuguese bowed deferentially.

"I come—after a friend's custom—to offer my sincere sympathy to Mademoiselle in the loss she has sustained, and to take a last look at the features of my poor comrade Lacoste."

"You shall not touch him! You shall not even see him!" exclaimed Leona, as she threw a white covering over the face of the corpse. "Your presence here, señor, is an intrusion and an insult, and I command you to leave the house!"

"Gently, gently, mademoiselle," said Ribeiro, "such words are hardly seemly in the presence of the dead."

"In the presence of the dead whom you drove to his death by your diabolical demands!" exclaimed the girl with excitement. "I tell you, señor, that if you were to attempt to touch my father's body with your treacherous hands, it would rise up from its coffin and confront you!"

"*Sacristi!* A modern miracle! I should like to see it performed, mademoiselle. Permit me at least to try my power."

"If you come a step nearer I will run you through the heart!" exclaimed Leona passionately, as she drew her knife.

Ribeiro stepped backward.

"Come, come, mademoiselle, one murder is enough in a day, surely. But I admire your spirit. You inherit it, doubtless, from your father. You are what the English people call 'a chip off the old block.'"

"If my poor father had possessed one half my spirit he would never have had any dealings with such a man as you."

"Better and better. I like a woman who can speak her mind. But your father had clearer views than yourself, mademoiselle. He desired me for a son-in-law."

"It is a lie."

"Your retort is impolite, mademoiselle. It is also untrue. M. Lacoste not only looked on my proposal with favour, but also promised me your hand in marriage."

"I do not believe it; but if he did you must have used some more powerful persuasion than you possess with me."

"Your father's name, perhaps, is of no value to you."

"My father's name, señor, is everything to me. That is one reason why I would never sink it in yours. I will live to guard his name—as he left it me—intact."

"Ha, ha! And you do not even know it."

"What do you mean?"

"I mean that your father's name was not Lacoste— that he was a criminal—in hiding here—under an assumed name. That I discovered his secret, and, under the fear of exposure, as the price of secrecy, he promised me his daughter's hand in marriage."

"It is false—as false as yourself! You are trumping up these base stories now in order to force me to yield to your wishes. But I will die first, and so I told my dear father."

"You told him you would not marry me? Mademoiselle, *his death lies at your door!*"

At these words Leona stared Ribeiro in the face, unable either to deny them or expostulate with him.

"Listen, mademoiselle!" said the Portuguese, advancing a step nearer and lowering his voice; "I love you, and by fair means or foul I intend to have you! Your father there was an Englishman—by name George Evans—and he fled from his native country *to escape the gallows!*"

"*What?*"

"He committed a murder, but before the officers of justice could secure him he had escaped to America, and hid himself in the Brazils. *This* was the reason of his false name, his false nationality, his studied seclusion, his fear of his fellow-men. He was afraid of recognition, detection, arrest! His conscience was his gaoler, and to avoid a public execution he had to live in solitary confinement. Now you know your father's story, Leona Evans."

With the swiftness of lightning her thoughts had darted over the past years, recalling all her poor father's fits of melancholy and fear, and her heart felt like a stone in her bosom at the thought of all he must have suffered. But her indignation was reserved for him who had exposed the dead.

"And *you* dared to make use of this knowledge as a means of frightening him into submission. *You* threatened to expose his misfortune, and claimed his only comfort, his daughter, as the price of secrecy?"

"I did, mademoiselle! More, *I do*. Exposure can no longer harm the poor creature lying there, but it can injure his good name, and through his good name it will injure you. But, as my wife, mademoiselle—"

"*Your wife!*" she repeated, in accents of bitterest contempt. "*Your wife!* you base, lying cowardly Portuguese! I would sooner be the wife of my negro helper! *Your wife!* I will never touch your hands again, unless it be in order to come close enough to you to kill you. I do not believe one word of what you have said. Your story is a fabrication from beginning to end. My father was an honest, honourable gentleman, too good to tread the same ground as a cur like yourself. But if it were true, a thousand times over, I would still say '*Do your worst!*' I shall never be any nearer to you than I am now, when I tell you that I hate, and loathe, and despise you as the meanest creature that crawls upon God's earth."

Her look of scorn was unmistakable. She gathered up her skirts as though she feared they might come in contact with him, and stood gazing down upon him—fearless and defiant—like some grand pythoness of old.

Ribeiro shrunk before her eyes. He knew, to all intents and purposes, that his threats had become harmless. They could no longer hurt the poor unconscious figure lying in the coffin—and if they could not control the daughter's sense of shame in the horror of exposure, they were impotent. Still he could wound her, and he let fly a poisoned shaft as he withdrew.

"Very good, mademoiselle—your compliments shall not be forgotten! At the same time allow me to observe that it is by your obstinacy your father's life has been sacrificed. This morning he offered me his daughter's hand as the price of preserving my faith with him. This afternoon you refuse at any costs to fulfil his contract—you tell him you will die first. Your poor father—with exposure on the one hand, and your unhappiness on the other—

prefers death, and so extricates himself from the dilemma. Your father's death is on your head, mademoiselle. I wish you joy of the reflection. Adieu."

And so Ribeiro left her, with her father's silent, unreproachful body, and her own sad thoughts.

* * * * *

Night, which falls so suddenly in the climates where twilight is unknown, gathered about her. Large dusky moths began to flop against her forehead in the darkness; and bats, with maize-lined breasts and wings, chased each other round the room in eddying circles, uttering shrill cries as they went; still she sat there alone, silent, absorbed, like a figure carved in stone. The scent of the lotus and the neighbouring datura,[*] exhaled by the evening dews, began to make itself perceptible; a sensation of cold and fear passed over Leona; she glanced around the dark room shudderingly, and yet felt as if she had no strength or energy to rise. The dreadful story she had heard struck on her heart like ice. She did not, could not believe it; but she knew Ribeiro's malicious, revengeful temper, and that he would stop at nothing to punish her for the disappointment she had caused him. Her kind, gentle, amiable father, whom—for all his learning and superiority to herself—she had cherished as a child for so many years past, a *murderer!*

It was impossible! She knew it to be a falsehood; yet that his name should have been so cruelly traduced, his weak fears for his own safety worked upon—and by reason of her decision—pierced her inmost soul.

She was too sensible and clear-minded to fall to lamenting the course her actions had taken, because the event had proved contrary to her expectations. She knew that in refusing to marry Ribeiro she had followed the instincts of her better nature, and refused to commit a crime. She felt that could she by such an act even then raise her father in health and strength from the coffin where he lay, it would be impossible to her still. She could only

---

[*] Flowering plant native to South America, the seeds of which are toxic.

weep silently over the weakness of which the dead man had been guilty, and wonder what there had been defective in her conduct towards him that he had never confided to her the fear under which he laboured. For though she rejected with scorn the idea of his guilt, she felt that his failing mind must have been burdened with a sense of great terror before it could have broken down so utterly as it had done. If he had but told her of Ribeiro's threats and presumptuous demands, she would have defied the one and repelled the other till she had exposed the craven through the land. Why could not her poor father have trusted to her—his own child—the nearest relation he possessed, to fight his battle for him and clear his name from all undeserved blame? As Leona thought thus it struck her that amongst M. Lacoste's papers might be found something to throw a light upon the mystery of his life and death. There was one small deed-box which he had always kept in his own room and forbidden her to touch. Once—many years ago—she had found him burning some papers out of this box, and he had spoken sharply to her because she had picked up part of one before it was wholly consumed as though with the intention of examining it.

Leona would never have dreamed of disobeying her father during his lifetime, but she felt now that she owed a higher duty to the dead than to the living.

His secrets—if he had any—were safe with her, but if it lay within the range of possibility she must have wherewithal to refute the cruel slander that Ribeiro had cast upon his name, and which he had threatened to make public property. With this end in view the girl dragged herself slowly up from her recumbent posture, and calling to the negro servants, Epiphania and Daniel, to bring lights into the chamber and close the jalousies of the windows, she set herself to her appointed task. The box—an ordinary deed-case with a Bramah lock[*]—was not difficult to find. It stood in the usual position in M. Lacoste's wardrobe, but for the key that fitted it Leona searched long in vain. It was not in his desk, nor with his other keys, nor in any of his private drawers. At last, as she was

---

[*] Bramah locks were designed in 1784 by Joseph Bramah, with 479,001,600 keys needed to open all its variations.

feeling for it over each separate vestment he had been in the habit of wearing, she suddenly came across something hard in the lining of a coat. In another moment she had ripped it open, and there lay the missing key, enveloped in several folds of cotton. The discovery made her turn sick and cold. The evident desire of secrecy smote her with a sudden fear, for which she bitterly reproached herself. Why should not her father have used caution and secrecy—like all prudent men—in the conduct of his private affairs? What greater need of them than the fact of his being in the daily company of an unscrupulous scoundrel like Antonio Ribeiro, whose character perhaps he knew more of than his daughter had ever suspected? She carried the deed-box to a table, and opened it beneath the lamp-light. It contained a tray with a small partition closed with a sliding lid. Leona's curiosity led her first to examine this. Within were several layers of cotton wool, beneath them a small phial, carefully stopped and tied down, and labelled "Hydrocyanic Acid." It was the exact counterpart of the one Dr. Linton had disengaged from her dead father's hand and carried away with him. There was little doubt of one thing then. He had foreseen the crisis which might arise, and provided against it. The daughter's heart stood still with the terrible doubt this fact excited. She replaced the sliding lid quickly, and turned with a shudder to the examination of the rest of the contents of the deed-box. They consisted chiefly of papers. The first packet she took up was labelled, *"Maraquita's letters. To be given to my daughter Leona, or burned, after my death."* These were a few love-letters that had passed between her pretty girlish mother and himself before their marriage, or during the brief periods of their separation afterwards. Maraquita had only been a wife for eighteen months when a sharp fever carried her out of this world. Her daughter, who, happily for the preservation of her filial respect, had been spared a knowledge of her weak, indolent, exacting southern nature, still cherished the memory of an ideal mother—beautiful, loving, and faithful to her father and herself—and the large tears gathered in her eyes and coursed slowly down her cheeks as she contemplated this frail memento of her brief happiness.

"Poor mother!" she whispered softly, "poor, young, pretty mother! It is as well you left him when you did, for this would surely have broken your heart—unless, indeed, your love had succeeded, where mine has failed, in making him courageous enough to brave the world, and slander, and all things, for the truth's sake."

She raised the faded writing to her lips, and laid the packet on one side to examine at her leisure. She did not expect to find anything in it to aid her search, which appeared destined to be fruitless. Old receipts, cuttings from newspapers, schemes for speculations (by means of which and the little knowledge he had of the trade, M. Lacoste and she had chiefly lived), made up the bulk of the contents of the deed-box.

She could not find a line to throw any light on her father's life before he came to the Brazils; not a word of France or the Lacoste family. If he at any time had preserved such records, he must have destroyed them with the papers she saw him burn. There was a little money at the bottom of the box, a roll of Brazilian notes, amounting, according to English valuation, to about fifty pounds; and a solitary piece of jewellery, a man's signet-ring, which Leona did not remember to have seen before. It was formed of a cornelian,[*] without inscription, and set in the plainest gold. Inside it were engraved, as though they had been scratched with some sharp instrument, the two letters "A. A." Leona regarded them curiously, but indifferently. They conveyed no meaning to her mind. But the ornament pleased her as a memento of her father, and she placed it on her finger. The deed-box, then, contained nothing after all—except that dread witness of the fear by which his sorrowful life had been ended. As she thought of it the girl's strong heart became a well of compassion. She would have liked to kill the man who had driven her father to his death.

"Poor sorrowful spirit!" she exclaimed, as she rose and stood by the coffin; "how you have been startled from your shelter. You were too weak to feel capable of coping with a false accusation that should embroil my good name with yours. Your brain gave way under the impossibility of clearing yourself. You were without friends or family in this country—without money to return to your home. How could you prove to the world that you were really

---

[*] A red form of quartz.

Louis Lacoste, and that this foul charge brought against you was a lie?

"How can I prove it, who would die to clear your memory from such a stain? This man may spread the tale all over Rio, and I can but sit still and deny it.

"But I will live to see your honour cleared, father. I cannot think of any means at present. The way is all dark and uncertain before me. But one thing is sure, that you are innocent, and that I, Leona Lacoste, will live among these people, whom Ribeiro will teach to blame you, until by God's help I have proved you so."

She said the words slowly and solemnly, as if she were taking an oath before high heaven, and as she concluded them she stooped and kissed the dead man's forehead. Then drawing the lamp nearer, she sat down again beside the coffin and proceeded to examine her mother's love-letters. It was the fittest spot, she thought, on which to read them.

"They are together now," said Leona to herself as she untied the packet, "and she is comforting him, perhaps, for all he has gone through. She at least knows his innocence and his suffering. And for the rest—what does it matter? The truth will out."

She read the silly little letters—written in bad Portuguese and worse grammar—one after another, almost without comprehending them, so preoccupied was her mind with the graver matter. But presently, folded inside one of them—evidently left there by accident—she came upon a very different sort of production, written in English, and by a man's straggling hand. It has already been said that Leona Lacoste understood the English language. Her father, who was an accomplished linguist, had taught her both to read and speak it. She had no difficulty, therefore, in comprehending the document that had slipped amongst Maraquita's love-letters.

As she perused it her face grew more and more pale; her eyes seemed to start from her head, as though fascinated by the words they saw; her whole body trembled and swayed backward and forward on her seat. Presently she rose, and looking round the room as if she feared there were spectators to her action, snatched the signet-ring off her finger again, rolled it tightly up in the letter she had been perusing, and thrust it down her bosom. Then she began to walk up and down the room, as though inertion were impossible to her, whilst she tried to think what was best to be done. Once she paused, and, going up to the coffin, took the ring and letter from her bosom and placed them carefully in the folds of the shroud; but on further reflection she drew them forth again and replaced them in their former hiding place.

"What shall I do—what shall I do?" she wailed above the corpse. "I am sure you *never*, never did that of which he accuses you; but how can I deny it with *this* in my bosom? And I cannot stay to hear your name traduced and vilified and yet remain silent. Oh! what *shall* I do—what *shall* I do?"

– CHAPTER 4 –

THE SNOUT OF PEPITA

It was still early morning on the following day when Christobal Valera returned from having seen the body of his friend M. Lacoste lowered into the grave. There had been some little difficulty about the interment. Poor Lacoste had never professed to belong to any religion. It was commonly supposed in the town that he was a free-thinker, and that he had committed suicide was an indisputable fact.

Under these circumstances his corpse was refused burial in consecrated ground; and Valera had taken great trouble to conceal the truth from his daughter. It was certain that sooner or later she must hear it, but he trusted the knowledge would not be so painful when her first grief had abated. Leona therefore sat at home in ignorance of all, save that they had taken her father's body from her, whilst Christobal, with a few other friends, saw the coffin placed in a grave dug on the outskirts of the fence which surrounded the burial-ground. And then he walked slowly back to the little chalet, in hopes of comforting poor solitary Leona.

As he entered the house he could trace the signs of her abandonment everywhere. Epiphania had prepared the breakfast as usual. The chocolate was ready and the table was spread; but the only moving object in the sitting-room was the orange-throated rhamphastos, who was hopping about the matted floor, picking up such insects as were foolish enough to be caught, and uttering his shrill cry of "*tucano! tucano!*" at each fresh capture. Leona's guitar, with its broad blue ribbon, was lying on the ground. The flowers were faded and dying in the vases. A little snow-white Cuba terrier, called "Pepita," which was considered her especial favourite, looked up from the couch and whined as Valera appeared. This change was more remarkable in the home of Leona than it would have been in that of any other woman, for her indomitable spirit, her independent bearing, and free, reckless manners seemed to make anything like desolation or despondency an anomaly to her. Yet when, after Christobal had called her by name three or four times, she appeared before him, he was fain to confess that the alteration in herself was much greater than in her surroundings. Her rippling hair was hanging over her shoulders in a tangled mass, her fiery, golden-brown eyes had become dull and heavy, her proud lip uncurled and drooping. She was but a crushed, sodden likeness of the bold, animated woman who had walked by his side through the forest but yesterday.

"Is it over?" she demanded, in a low voice.

"It is over, dear Leona, and I have come to see what I can do for you."

"You can do nothing for me, Tobal."

"That is not a kind answer, *m'amie*. The shock you have received is a terrible one. No one knows the weight of it better than myself. But you live still, Leona, and whilst you live, I must care for you. Is it not so?"

"Do you care for me very much, Tobal?" she said suddenly, as she placed her hand upon his arm. "More than anything else?"

The young Spaniard's face flushed crimson.

"*Very, very* much," he answered fervently. "More than for my own life, Leona."

"Then take me with you when you go away from here, Tobal. Take me with you to New York. Don't let me stay in this place any longer."

"Will you go?" he cried joyfully.

"Oh, I long to go. I am panting to leave this town behind me. I feel as if I could never breathe in this air again. It chokes me."

"Leona, I should never have dared to propose this to you so soon. But you know it has been in my thoughts for years. The time is short, my dearest; but if you are willing, it cannot be too short for me. I am to start from Rio next week, and we might be married—"

"Married!" echoed the girl sharply. "Who spoke of marriage?"

"Why yourself, Leona. Did you not ask me to take you with me to New York? Don't say you have repented of your goodness already."

"I did ask you. I ask you again. I must leave this place, and I want to travel to New York with you—but married, Tobal! Oh no; I shall never be married."

"But how am I, then, to take you with me, Leona?"

"As you would take anyone else. As you would take me if I were your sister in reality, and not only in name."

"But you are not my sister."

"What difference does that make?"

"None to us; but every difference in the eyes of the world. You would lose your good name, your reputation—"

"I do not care for my reputation."

"But I do—a thousand times more than for my own."

"You refuse to take me, then!"

"I *must not* take you, *m'amie*, under these circumstances."

"Then I shall go alone."

"You cannot do that, Leona," said Valera hastily. "You cannot travel by yourself such a distance. So ignorant as you are of journeying, and so—so—good-looking. All manner of harm might happen to you by the way."

"*Madre purissima!* Am I not able to protect myself? No harm will come to me but of my own free will. But it must be free. I will shackle it with that of no man. Christobal, if you love me, as you say you do, you will never mention the subject of marriage to me again. I hate—despise it."

"Why are you so anxious to leave your home, Leona?" asked the young man, without taking notice of her last remark.

"*My home!* Where is my home? I have none, *without him*. I told you yesterday, Tobal, that I belonged only to my father and myself, and perhaps at some future period—to the world. I little thought then how soon the world would claim me. But to-day I am all alone; I owe duty to no one, and I must go forth and make money for myself."

"How, Leona?"

"On the stage! I mean to be an actress, Tobal."

"But without friends or interest—a stranger in New York—how could you accomplish your design? It requires an education to take up such a profession. You must be trained for it."

"I intend to be trained!"

"And then it is replete with danger to a woman—replete with temptation, with scandal,"

"Bah! how timid you men are! Am I not to live? and how can I live unless I work for my support. I could have travelled with you to New York, but you refuse to take me. Good! then I must look after myself. But my mind's made up. I am going on the stage."

"You will want money for such an undertaking."

"I have money; and I shall dispose of this house and furniture that belonged to my father. Tobal, do not try to shake my resolution," she added in a lower and more hurried voice, "for I cannot stay here any longer. It is too painful to me, and—and"—looking round her nervously—"*I am afraid.*"

"Afraid, Leona! I thought you were never afraid of anything!"

"No!—not of things—but people! I fear Ribeiro! I doubt his friendship to my father—or for me. I dislike him, and he knows it; and I could not live here, all by myself, subject to anything he might do—or—or—*say.*"

"Of course you cannot, Leona, and that is what I came to speak to you about this morning. You cannot continue to live in the châlet alone, it would not be right or safe; but you have known my mother since you were a little child, and when I am gone she will be lonely too. Why not go and live with her, *m'amie*, or let her come and live with you here?"

"Dona Josefa has always been kind to me," said Leona, "but I cannot accept charity from anyone."

"It would not be charity. You would be under no obligation to her, for here she would live rent-free, which would more than cover the expense of keeping you. And the commandant and padre both think it would be the very best thing that you could do."

"You have spoken to them about it?" inquired the girl, with a look of displeasure.

"I have been so anxious about your future," he replied, "particularly as I have to leave you so soon myself. And my mother is quite prepared either to receive you or come here."

"I shall not remain in this place," said Leona, determinedly.

"Neither Ribeiro nor any other scoundrel shall molest you whilst under my mother's protection," continued Valera, earnestly. "Say that you will consent to it, Leona, at least, for the present, and then when I get to New York I will make all the enquiries that are needful, and let you know what chance there is of your succeeding in the project upon which you are bent. I am forced to go to Rio this afternoon, to make some final arrangements for my journey, and you will make me so much happier if you would promise that you will remain with my mother before I go."

"You are going to Rio this afternoon?" she said inquisitively.

"Yes, but only for a few days, and I shall return here to bid you farewell. Be kind, Leona, and set my heart at rest before I start, else—"

"Else what?"

"I must send my mother and the padre to talk you into consenting to our plans."

"No, no! You shall send no one here, Tobal. I am not well enough. I will not see them. But listen: I will think over what you have said to me, and when you return from Rio you shall have my answer. Will that content you, Tobalito?"

The caressing diminutive charmed her listener.

"A thousand thanks, *m'amie*," he exclaimed, as he kissed her hand. Leona calmly raised her head and kissed him in return upon the cheek.

"Thou art a good brother, and I love thee," she said in his own language; but neither the action nor the words brought the least access of colour to her pale face. "And now leave me, Tobal, for my heart is very heavy, and I am in need of rest. But come for your answer as soon as you return from Rio."

Valera left her, full of hopeful anticipation. He thought in her last words that he heard signs of her relenting—not towards living with his mother, Dona Josefa—but himself. For he knew how

Leona's independent spirit would chafe at any coercion on the part of another woman, and how eagerly she had always desired to step outside the prescribed and narrow limits of her native town. And if marriage could be made the watchword of liberty instead of bondage in her eyes, she would consent to he married.

He loved her very dearly, but he knew her very little. He loved her so passionately, with all the strength and fire of his Spanish breeding, that he had given up all other women for her sake, and had no thought or desire for anyone but Leona Lacoste.

And his fervent attachment, which had grown up with him from childhood, the girl had considerably fanned by her complete indifference to every phase of it excepting the innocent childish part. Her Tobalito was her brother, and her playmate, and her friend, and she kissed and caressed him with a freedom that very often nearly drove the young man crazy, whilst if he presumed on her familiarities to speak of a warmer love than her own, she ridiculed, or blamed, or grew angry with him. Still Valera could not help hoping that the day might dawn when Leona would discover that he had become necessary to her, and he dreaded her going out into the world of New York and assuming a position that would bring her uncommon beauty into prominence, and subject it to the admiration of the crowd. He was selfish—like most lovers—and wanted to keep others from even looking at the treasure he had found, and it was with that idea he had proposed that the girl should remain behind in the place she hated under the protection of his stupid old mother, Dona Josefa, who had no ideas in her head beyond garlic and decorum—garlic in her own dishes and decorum in the conduct of her friends. Valera had in fact— especially by mentioning the matter to the commandant and padre—attempted to assume a certain amount of coercion with Leona, which she resented far more strongly than she had shown. Of this, however, he was happily unaware, and, during his compulsory stay in Rio, was wondering what her answer to him would be; and flattering himself that, horrified at the idea of further seclusion and longing to travel to New York under his protection, Leona would throw herself into his arms and say, "Do what you will, my Tobalito, so you take me away with you." Under this pleasing delusion he hurried over his business in Rio, and flew back to his home, where the first question he put to his mother was whether she had seen Leona.

"Seen her!" exclaimed Dona Josefa, whom he had disturbed in the discussion of a mess of meat and garlic which scented the whole house, "I should like to know who *has* seen her—*she's gone!*"

"Gone! Where?"

"The saints preserve us! How can I tell you *where*? The girl has left the châlet and the town. Epiphania came crying to me with the news two days after she went, that's yesterday. They thought nothing of her absence the first day, she's always been so strange in her manners; but when it came to staying two nights from home, they began to think it extraordinary, even for Mademoiselle Leona."

"But has no one followed or looked for her?" demanded Valera, excitedly.

"Great heaven! Do you suppose an old woman like myself can go running after every headstrong, ill-mannered girl that chooses to leave her home, or that the commandment or the police have time to do it? Who, knows even if she went alone."

"Mother, you shall not hint at such a thing, even to me. Heavens! to think that it should have happened and I not here. If grief should have driven her to destroy herself!"

"Bah, Leona is not the girl to cure grief after that fashion, Christobal. She has always been too wilful and independent for a woman. In Spain such conduct would not be tolerated. She would have lost her reputation, her character, her good name," replied Dona Josefa, reapplying herself to the garlic-flavoured mess.

"No lady in Spain, even the very highest, and most carefully guarded, could be purer or more modest than Leona," said Don Christobal, proudly.

"And you call it modest to run away from home within a few days of her father's shameful death, and without leaving a word or sign by which she may be traced or followed!"

"Is it possible that the servants know nothing on the subject?"

"You had better question them yourself. To me they are silent as the grave."

"I will question them at once," cried the young man, as he seized his hat and left the house.

The chålet looked still more desolate than it had done on the occasion of his last visit there. The potted basil, pinks, geraniums, lavender, and sweetherbs, in which all the Brazilian women take so much delight, and which in troughs raised above the reach of the poultry ornamented the front of the house, were drooping for want of water. The little white bantams and guinea fowls, the pigeons and the doves, that had been Leona's care, flocked round him as he passed through the court-yard, as though asking for her; and Epiphania, seated in the blinding sun on the steps of the verandah with her hands folded, was as speaking a sign as any of the double misfortune that had fallen on the household.

"Have you seen the mistress?" she cried, starting into life as Valera appeared.

"No, Epiphania; I wish I had. I have only just returned from Rio, and received the news; and I have come to hear all you can tell me about it."

"There is nothing to tell, sar. On the day poor master was buried the mistress was very sad, and that night she never went to bed, for Daniel and I watched her walking about the room through the jalousies. The next morning she went out riding on her mule, and she never came back again. No word—no news—nothing. All dark—all miserable. Daniel and I cry all day for poor mistress."

"But what has become of the mule?"

"Don't know, sar. Gone with the mistress, I suppose. Mule never came back either."

"But have you searched the house? She must have left a letter, or something, to say where she has gone."

"Daniel and I not look at anything, sar. Know our duty better. Leave that for padre or you to do."

At this information Valera rushed past the woman into the house, but everything was in its usual place. Leona apparently had taken nothing with her. Even the white dress he had last seen her wear was thrown across the bed, as if it had just been taken off.

But presently his eye caught sight of a volume laid conspicuously upon her toilet-table. It was a copy of "Don Quixote,"* a present from himself to her, and which was generally

---

* *Don Quixote* by Miguel de Cervantes, published in two parts in 1605 and 1615.

kept in the sitting-room. In a moment he had opened it. On the flyleaf was written:

"Sell the house and furniture, Tobal; and keep the proceeds till we meet again. You will find the necessary authority in the deed-box, in a letter addressed from my father to me. Do this before you start on your journey—for Leona."

That was all. Not a hint of where she was going, or why she went, or when he might expect again to meet her. He might guess at her intentions or her wishes from the last conversation he had held with her, but he had no proof of them. And meanwhile she had imposed a certain duty on him, which inferred she had no design of returning to her home.

"Did Mademoiselle Leona never see nor speak with anyone before her departure except myself? Did not the padre or the commandant call to see her?" he demanded of Epiphania, thinking perhaps that one or other of those worthies had irritated the girl into leaving home.

"No, sar. Padre not come, commandant not come. Señor Ribeiro, *he* came the same evening and talked a good deal with the mistress—talked very comfortable in loud voice, but it didn't seem to do her any good."

"Ribeiro has been here, has he?"

"For a little time, sar—not long. Mistress called Daniel to bring his mule round, and then the señor went away again."

"*Caramba!* that he should have dared! Well, Epiphania, your mistress is not coming here again."

"Ah! Hoo!—the bad news. And where is mistress going to live, sar! And what is to become of Daniel and me, and the poor animals, and the house, and everything?"

"I will look after all that. You and Daniel must remain quietly here for a few days, and I will see that you are provided for. The animals will be sold, except Pepita. Where is she?"

"Oh, she went with the mistress, sar. The last thing I saw was Pepita's face under the mistress's mantilla."

"And the bird?"

Probably the most well known and revered text in the Spanish literary canon, and considered by many to be the first true novel.

"He's moping on the back of the sofa, sar. He's hardly moved off there since she went away."

Valera re-entered the chalet, took the rhamphastos on his wrist, and with the volume of "Don Quixote" beneath his arm, returned to his mother's house. During the three days that he remained in the town no further news was heard of Leona Lacoste, neither could he elicit any information from her neighbours. No one appeared to have seen her go, or to know more than the fact that she was gone.

Armed with the authority contained in her father's letter to herself, which he found in the deed-box, he religiously carried out the directions she had left him, and having disposed of the house and its contents, lodged the money in a Rio bank in Leona's name. And then, with a very heavy heart and full of miserable forebodings, he took leave of his mother and his friends, and set off on his road to New York.

* * * * * *

The first part of the journey was performed by steamer. Valera had scarcely set his foot on board and lost sight of Rio pier, before he began bitterly to reproach himself that he had not remained longer in his native town, in order to prosecute his search for Leona.

Why had he so readily abandoned himself to the general conclusion that she was perfectly well able to take care of herself, and even permitted one or two jealous doubts to take possession of his mind as to whether she had really had the courage to commence the world alone? What, if she should be at this very moment in need of his assistance—in danger, in distress, in perplexity; and he, her Tobalito, steaming far away in the opposite direction to her? Should he ever hear of or from her again? Would her letters ever reach him in New York? Was their sweet childish friendship dissolved for ever? Valera had no occasion thus to reproach himself, for he had amply done his duty towards Leona, and giving up a journey on which all his future hopes of success depended could in no wise have assisted her. The appointment he was going to New York to take up, that of a foreign correspondent and traveller to the firm of Upjohn and Halliday, had been procured for him more than a year previously, and he had spent all that time in acquiring a knowledge of the duties that would be required of him—an occupation in which poor Lacoste had materially assisted him by his apparently marvellous knowledge of the English language. To have failed in taking up his appointment at the time agreed upon would have been virtually to resign it, and Christobal Valera had his mother as well as himself to think of in the matter. Yet he blamed himself for nothing—as lovers will—and was thoroughly unhinged and low-spirited from the moment of leaving Rio. His first few days on board were spent as usual, more in the seclusion of his cabin than anywhere else, but at the end of that period he felt he had overcome the enemy, and eagerly sought the fresh air of the deck.

It was a lovely evening; the passengers were mostly above stairs, and the deck was crowded. Valera's eyes roved indifferently over the groups of women, children, and nurses who mostly did his handsome face the honour of a prolonged stare, to the further end of the vessel, where a few of his own sex were assembled, smoking. He hardly wished or expected to make the acquaintance of any of them, but one figure attracted his attention so often, that at last, by the sheer force of sympathy, he took a seat behind it. It was that of a young man of, perhaps, eighteen or twenty years of age, who, attired in a loosely-made white suit of clothes, with a broad leaf hat, worn well over his brows, was leaning over the gunwale, smoking a cigarette, with his eyes fixed upon the water. *Why* he experienced a desire to see this youth nearer, Christobal never knew, but he certainly waited with much patience, or pertinacity, until some chance movement should make him turn his head so that he might see his features.

Meanwhile, the only view he could obtain was that of a very youthful-looking throat and a crop of thick chestnut hair that was not long enough to cover it. As he was gazing at the back of the stranger, however, and wondering why he should interest himself in the subject, a slight movement under one of his arms attracted his attention. The next moment two little beady eyes and a tiny black snout were thrust into view.

They were the eyes and snout of Pepita!

– CHAPTER 5 –

QUITE ABLE TO TAKE CARE OF MYSELF

In a moment the truth flashed on Valera, yet he did not dare believe it.

"Pepita," he said nervously.

The dog, who had known him for years, and was an affectionate little brute, wriggled its small body from beneath the arm that held it, and commenced to lick his hand; but the figure of the youth leaning over the gunwale* gave no evidence that he was aware of what was going on behind him.

"Poor little Pepa! So you know me again, do you?" continued Valera, in hopes of attracting the attention of the owner of the dog. Still there was no movement—no sign of recognition.

"*Leona!*" he next ventured to whisper below his breath.

Then she answered, but without turning her head, so afraid was she of the effects of too sudden a confirmation of his suspicion.

"My name is Leon d'Acosta, señor."

"I ask ten thousand pardons, Señor d'Acosta," replied Valera, trembling with the excitement of his discovery, the truth of which her voice had confirmed, "but I think we must have had the pleasure of meeting before. May I offer you a cigar?"

Leona turned and looked him steadily in the face.

"Many thanks, señor. I will throw away mine in recognition of your politeness. Do you speak English?"

At this hint Valera fell into that language, of which they were probably the only students on board.

"Leona, what a delight and a surprise to find you here."

"Please call me Leon, or you will not get used to it. It should not have been a surprise. I told you I could look after myself."

"But in this dress."

She laughed slightly as she looked down at it.

"It doesn't suit me, I know, but it is convenient as a disguise."

"And where is all your beautiful hair?"

"Lying in a ditch ten miles the other side of Rio—at least, that

---

* The uppermost line of planking on the sides of a boat.

is where I left it. But if we wish to talk undisturbed we had better make some excuse to go down to your cabin. Everyone is watching us here."

"Oh! *do* come," said Valera, earnestly. "I am most anxious both to hear your own plans and to tell you what I have done."

As he concluded the sentence Leona caught up Pepita and rose from her seat.

"*Caramba*," she exclaimed, in his own language, using a Spaniard's most ordinary expression, "if you do not believe my word, señor, perhaps you will believe your own eyes. Five hundred ducats to a doubloon that you've never smoked a cigar equal to what I can give you this side of the Equator! You won't take the bet? Right! Neither would I. 'Twould be sheer robbery. But be good enough to accompany me to my cabin, and you shall taste the cigar. *Allons!*"

She commenced to stroll leisurely in the direction of the cabin as she spoke, and as Valera followed her, he could not help wondering at the easy grace with which she filled her part, and the admirable disguise it was, to which, however, the effeminacy of many of the men in those southern climates much assisted her. But the woman was a born actress, and as she sauntered in front of him, with her broad leaf hat slightly tipped to one side, and her cigar between her lips, Christobal could see how much she enjoyed keeping up the little mystification that evidently surrounded her in the eyes of her fellow-passengers.

But when they had reached the cabin he occupied, and the door was closed upon them, her manner changed. She threw herself down upon the first seat that came to hand, with an air of such complete weariness as disarmed any animadversions he might have felt disposed to make upon her conduct.

"And so you left me to take care of myself, Tobal?" she commenced, reproachfully.

"My dear Leona! I would have done anything in the world for you—"

"Except the one thing I asked—that you should take me away from that horrible place!"

"But if I had known that you intended to leave it by yourself—"

"Bah. If you did not know, you should have known. Why will

men never believe that women can mean what they say—and that at once! You proposed instead that I should remain there, on the very spot, under the charge of your mother. You must be a fool, Tobal."

"But most people would have thought it a very desirable arrangement for a young girl like yourself."

"I am not 'most people.' I am Leona Lacoste, and you, who have known me from a little child, should be able to believe I did not make up my mind without necessity. And the end of it is that I am here."

"But why in this disguise?"

"When you returned from Rio, did you not try to discover where I had gone?"

"Of course I did. It was my first thought."

"And how far did you trace me?"

"I could trace you nowhere. From all the nearest villages and towns through which I calculated you must have passed in order to leave home at all, not a scrap of information was to be gained."

"Just so, *mon frère*. But had you asked if they had seen a young man driving a mule—"

"But it never entered my head to ask such a thing, Leona."

"And that is just why it entered mine to assume the dress, Tobalito. And after all it is most convenient for travelling in. No man would have dared to insult me a second time if dressed like a woman. Few will attempt it the first time as I am dressed now."

"You don't look so very formidable an antagonist, after all," said Valera, smiling.

"Let them try it who dare," replied Leona, with a dark flush upon her face. "But tell me now, Tobal, what you have done since I saw you last."

Valera then repeated to her what he had heard from his mother and Epiphania—the trouble he had taken on her behalf, and the money he had realised and placed in the Rio bank for her.

"Good brother!" she said, caressingly, when he had concluded. "And now one word more. *Did you see Ribeiro before you started?*"

She put the question with such evident constraint that it surprised him.

"I did see him, Leona."

"And did he speak to you of—of—my father?"

"Only to demand back his share of the money sunk in that last unlucky speculation of theirs."

"Did you give it him?"

"Not a piastre.* It is not his due. They went partners in the chance of gain—it is only fair they should go partners in the certainty of loss."

"And he did not speak to you of—of—*anything else?*"

"Of nothing else—certainly of nothing of consequence. But why are you so anxious about it, Leona? Why do you fear him?"

She looked around the cabin cautiously before she answered.

"Promise me secrecy, Tobal! Promise that you will never repeat what I am going to tell you, and you shall know. *I hate Ribeiro.* I hate him and I fear him! I wish that he were dead; and if I could kill him without detection I would. But they shan't say it of me too—not of me too."

"Leona!" cried Valera, alarmed at her manner, "how has the brute insulted you? What has he said or done? *Dios!* if you had but told me more before we started!"

"I did not wish to tell you. I had my reasons for concealment. But he *is* a brute, Christobal—a lying, cowardly, unscrupulous brute! And he knew something—he had heard something—that he threatened to use against me; and if I had remained there, *I might*—I might have been *compelled to marry him.*"

She uttered the last words in so low a tone that had Valera not been stooping over her he would hardly have caught them.

"Been compelled to marry him!" he cried aloud in his astonishment. "To marry that low scoundrelly Portuguese! And you, who scorn the idea of marriage with any man! Leona, what horrible secret of yours does this man possess that he should hold so much power over you?"

"Oh! not of mine—not of mine," she said unhesitatingly. "I have no secrets, Tobal, that you do not know."

"Of whose, then?"

"Of my poor father's."

"And that was—"

---

* Unit of currency in many French speaking regions at this time.

"A *lie*, which I will repeat to no one. A lie, Tobal. I am sure of it as I stand here, but one which I have no power of disproving. And I knew that if I remained in my old house that man would never cease to persecute me, until I had given up everything to save my dead father's name from calumny and falsehood; or he would blazon the vile slander, as he threatened to do, amongst the people who have respected us, until every finger would have pointed at me with scorn."

"But are you not afraid that his rage at your departure will produce the same effect?"

"No, for in the first place it would be useless, and in the second it would destroy all chance of his succeeding in his object if we meet again. But we shall never meet again, Tobal—I have taken my oath of that—or, if we do, I shall be so altered he will not know me."

"You have carved out a difficult path for yourself, Leona."

"I know I have. And I have something here," she continued, pressing her hand upon her heart, "which makes it ten times more difficult. But I will struggle through it, even if I fall in the attempt."

"It is a wonder to hear you confess to feeling the least degree of weakness, Leona. And you cannot be brought to believe that a burden shared is only half as heavy, and that my love and sympathy might help to lighten the load you carry."

"I have them both," she answered shortly.

"But not as I would give them to you."

"Bah! Would you make me a woman again just as I'm turned into a man? If you talk to me in that way, Tobal, I will not come into your cabin," said Leona, rising from her seat.

"You will not go so soon," he pleaded.

"I have stayed too long since you have forgotten the warning I gave you last time we met. Your memory is short, Don Christobal."

"The joy of meeting you must be my excuse. I will not offend again. Say adieu to me in the old familiar fashion, Leona."

"I think not, Tobal. We have left the wild woods and are entering upon a more civilised existence. Let us conform to its customs for the future."

"You will not be so cruel."

"It is your own fault if I appear so. But you have overstepped the bounds of friendship lately, and have robbed all our little familiarities of their innocent charm. I am sorry for it, but I have no more pleasure in kissing you, Tobal."

"How I wish I had never spoken," cried the young Spaniard, despondingly, "But it is so hard to be with you and not love you, Leona."

"Listen to me, Tobal. If you do not wish to make it harder by not being with me at all, we must start on a new plan from to-day. We must be friends and nothing more. The days of our childhood are passed. The world is opening before us both; we must attend to our work and let nothing interfere with it. You can be a great help to me if you choose, do not be a hindrance. It will be good for me, a stranger in the great city of New York, to know that you are at hand in case of need; but if you do not promise me to check all such feelings as you have been betrayed into displaying towards me lately, I will not let you even see me."

"Oh, Leona! you are not a true woman—you have no heart!"

The girl's lip slightly quivered, but she as instantly checked the action.

"I know I have not, and I am glad of it. What should I do with such an encumbrance on my present journey? We may not have many opportunities of speaking in private whilst on board, Tobal, so pray remember my caution. I am Leon d'Acosta, a youth whose acquaintance you have picked up on the steamer, and in whose affairs you have but a passing interest. Don't try to interfere with anything I may do or say, or show any unusual familiarity, or you may force me to pretend to take no notice of you."

"Why could you not have confided your plans to me previously, and passed as my brother," said Valera, downcast at the prospect of their divided interests.

"I gave you the option and you refused. We won't revert to that any more, Tobal. You know that I am somewhat of a mimic, and that I have lived amongst men long enough to make their manners sit on me almost as well as these loose suits of my poor father's do. You need have no fear, therefore, of my sex being suspected. And should I disguise myself too well for the ladies' peace of mind," she added, laughing, "why, I'll hand them over to you. Now, let us return to the deck. There is one personage after whose fate you have quite forgotten to inquire, and that is my mule."

"Ah, poor Pedro! What has become of him?"

"*Caramba*, señor," she replied, as, with the little dog tucked under her arm, she left the cabin, and re-assumed the nonchalant air she had dropped whilst there. "You never saw such another animal as that mule. The saints defend us! how he could trot. I trotted him once for a wager ten miles against a beast double his own height, and brought him in eight minutes before the other without a hair turned. And he went at last, saddle, silver trappings, and, by my faith, a suit of woman's clothes into the bargain, for a couple of doubloons! *Sacristi! That* was a beast!"

"The last item sounds suspicious," said Valera, humouring her mood.

"The sound is all you will hear of it, señor. I am not one to tell my lady's secrets," rejoined Leona, as she resumed her old seat by the side of the vessel.

* * * * * *

Yet with all the joy of finding Leona again, the days that followed was a sore trial to Valera. Knowing who she was, and what she was, he became jealous of every man that approached her; and she, with all a woman's innate coquetry, despite her garb and assumption of indifference towards himself, seemed to take the greatest delight in torturing him. Day after day, until the steamer reached its last landing-stage, she slighted his company for that of other men, and he stood apart, gloomy and self-absorbed, whilst she interchanged jokes and saucy remarks with those of his sex who imagined she belonged to theirs, and treated her as men treat an impudent boy with whom it is not worth their while to quarrel. Now and again Valera caught her by herself, reproached her with her unkindness, but she was never without an answer for him.

"Would you have me do things by halves," she would cry indignantly, "assume a garb and then betray that I am unused to wear it? How unreasonable you are, Tobal; but there, you are a man, and what can one expect otherwise. But I am not so weak as to give in to your caprices."

"Do you call it caprice to wish the dearest friend I possess in this world to exhibit some small proof that she cares for me?"

"Certainly I do, when your friend is not a 'she' and to exhibit it would be to betray herself."

"Oh, Leona! you are the veriest 'she' that ever existed."

"Matteo and Guzman do not think so. They are ready enough to accept me for what I appear to be."

"That is what so much enrages me. To see those fellows tapping you on the shoulder and addressing you as familiarly as if you were one of themselves!"

"How strange that what appears to me a compliment you should take as an insult. But I shall have a better opportunity of distinguishing myself in my new character before long. I shall quarrel with Guzman, Christobal."

"Leona! I entreat of you to be careful," said Valera with real alarm. "The man might be dangerous. What has he done to offend you?"

"We do not agree," she answered abruptly.

"Then avoid his company, or the subjects that offend him. You frighten me by your rash way of speaking, *m'amie*."

"I am quite able to take care of myself," said Leona, in her old independent tone.

Valera took her words for a girl's bravado, until, a few days later, he overheard some of the other passengers talking about her.

"He'll get the worst of it, to a certainty," said one man to the other.

"Of course he will. What should such a youth know about duelling? And with such a dead shot like Guzman."

The name rivetted Christobal's attention.

"May I ask to whom you allude?" he said, addressing one of the speakers.

"Certainly, señor. It is no secret. Young d'Acosta has a little affair on this evening with Don Silvester Guzman."

"They have arranged to meet?"

"They have; at the next landing stage which we reach, at eight this evening."

"*Madre di Dios!* And for what reason?"

"That is best known to themselves, señor. They quarrelled over some difference of opinion this morning, and the result is as I have told you. I am sorry for d'Acosta. He is a pretty youth, and Guzman has no pity."

"But it must not be, gentlemen. It *shall* not be. It is a butchery—a slaughter. The lad is too young—too inexperienced," exclaimed Valera with agitation, hardly knowing what he said.

"He is not too young to quarrel, señor. *Sacristi!* You should have heard the two this morning! And Guzman is resolved to give him a lesson. Poor boy! I trust it may not prove his last one."

"The meeting must be prevented at all risks!" cried Valera. "The captain must be spoken to."

"That will be useless, señor. The captain of a steamboat has no authority over his passengers. He will laugh at your interference."

"Then Guzman must be reasoned with himself. If he stains his hand with one drop of that boy's blood, he must answer for it to me."

"*Caramba*, señor, one would imagine you were defending the cause of a woman instead of a man," remarked one of his listeners laughing.

The expression recalled Valera to himself. If he betrayed Leona, she might never forgive him. He resolved to appeal to her own fears, the risk she ran, and the necessity there was for running it. But here he found himself baffled. The girl, evidently aware of, and prepared for, the opposition she would encounter, rigidly avoided all chance of a private interview with him.

He hovered about her all day in an agony of nervous apprehension, but she kept scrupulously on the men's side of the vessel, and refused either to read his appealing looks, or to understand his half-disguised entreaties to be allowed to speak to her alone.

"You have not been below decks once to-day, d'Acosta," he said entreatingly.

"I prefer the fresh air, señor," was her reply.

"Might I ask the favour of a few minutes' conversation with you?"

"I am ready to listen to anything you may have to say."

"But my communication is private."

"I must ask you to postpone it till to-morrow then, señor. I am pledged to play a game of cards with Don Matteo."

"Give up your game, and listen to me," he said imploringly.

"To-morrow, to-morrow, señor," she answered lightly, as she commenced her game.

She guessed the purport of his desired communication, and was determined to defeat it.

"Valera will not persuade young d'Acosta to relinquish his revenge," remarked one of the bystanders. "The youth has mettle. He will go through with it."

"But will never come out of it," was the response. But Valera was not to be put off so easily.

"D'Acosta, I *must* speak to you," he said at last in desperation.

"There is no such word as *must* in my dictionary, señor," she answered.

"But there is in mine. And if you are determined to balk me—"

"If I am determined to balk you," repeated Leona, without looking up from her cards—"*what then?*"

"*I will disclose all I know*," hissed Valera into her ear.

She rose from her seat and confronted him unflinchingly.

"In which case," she said, with a slow and steady emphasis, "I should request you to meet me afterwards, Don Valera."

"Which you know I could never do," he answered energetically.

"Then I should brand you a coward, and drop your acquaintance," she continued as firmly as before.

Their eyes met. Valera's sunk before the fiery flash of hers, which said so plainly, "*Thwart me and you lose me for ever*," and he turned away sick at heart with the dread of what was coming, but unable to see how he could prevent what Leona was determined to carry through.

The steamboat reached its next landing stage at eight that evening. Valera, who had been hovering round Leona all day, anxiously watching for the moment when she should disembark, rushed down stairs for his purse as the side of the boat grated against the end of the rickety landing pier, resolved to accompany her when she went ashore, whether with her will or against it. As he entered the saloon of the steamer, however, he ran up violently against and upset a toddling infant, thereby seriously injuring its tender little frame.

"Oh, my child, you have killed it," screamed the mother, as its loud cries resounded through the vessel. In common humanity Valera could do no less than stop and enquire how much damage had been done. The poor little child's face was covered with blood, and he could feel for nothing but the mother's distress until proper assistance had been rendered, and it was found that the injuries he had inflicted were less alarming than they appeared to be. Then he had leisure to remember his mission, and the time he had wasted in fulfilling it. He sprang on deck again, but only to find that Leona and Guzman had already left the steamer. At that Valera gave vent to an oath of rage and alarm, clapped his sombrero tightly over his eyes, and followed them on shore with all the speed of which he was capable.

– CHAPTER 6 –

LEONA'S STRAIGHT SHOT

Duel is so common a thing in the country where to stick a man in the back with a bowie-knife, or to shoot him across the dinner-table with a revolver, are every-day occurrences, that none of the passengers except the two or three directly interested in the affair had considered it worth their while to follow Guzman and d'Acosta to the place of meeting. It pleased them better to linger on the deck of the steamboat, enjoying the evening air and watching the various scenes that took place on the quay, or to stroll up and down the jetty smoking their cigars until it was time to re-embark, than to meddle in a business which might end very unpleasantly for one or both parties concerned in it. They hardly expected to see both the combatants return to the steamboat, and perhaps they had one or more little bets dependent on the result of their meeting, but—there their interest in the event came—to a standstill. Valera could hardly get an answer to the eager questions that fell from his lips respecting the direction which the duellists had taken, but as he stepped off the pier he fell in with a man bent on the same errand as himself—namely, to watch the issue of the proceedings—and with whom he almost ran to the place of meeting.

"I know the exact spot in that wood yonder," said his new acquaintance, "for I've been in this place before and so has Guzman. Is he your friend?"

"Certainly not," said Valera. "I consider him a coward and a bully to challenge so young a lad as d'Acosta, and have come prepared to tell him so directly this affair is over."

"Then there will be a second meeting?"

"If d'Acosta's pistol spares him, yes! A second meeting, and, I trust, a final one. The sooner the world's rid of such a brute as Guzman the better."

"You speak interestingly, my friend; but do you know the rights of the quarrel?"

"I know nothing except that Guzman has consented to meet a boy half his age and with half his experience. It is not satisfaction—it is murder. If there were any laws in this country such a butchery would be punishable by death."

"But, *caramba!* it was the little one that challenged him. They came to words over some difference of opinion, and d'Acosta gave Guzman the lie to his face. He could not, in honour, have refused to meet him, though I believe he regretted it almost as much as you do. Guzman is not bad at heart."

"Oh, my foolish Leona," sighed Valera to himself. But he openly said "I can accept no excuses, señor. I would as soon meet a woman as a tender lad like that."

"You are much interested in d'Acosta," said his companion, with curiosity.

"I have known him before!" replied Valera.

They had now nearly arrived at the place of meeting. Already they could distinguish the little group of men arranging themselves in position on a grassy plot. Already could Valera's eye detect the suit of white and the broad leaf hat that marked the figure of the creature he loved best in the world, and it made his heart stand still with sickening fear.

As they came up with them the duellists had just taken their places.

"Stop!" cried Valera, authoritatively. Guzman and Leona lowered their weapons, and the latter turned round to him.

"What do you mean by this interruption, señor?" she demanded fiercely.

"Cannot this matter be arranged otherwise?" continued Valera, appealing to Guzman. "You are scarcely a fair match for this youth, señor; and should anything happen to him, you may get into more trouble than you think of."

"I have given Señor d'Acosta the option of an apology," replied Guzman, as he quietly lighted a cigar with which to employ the interval, "and he has refused to take it."

"I have!" said Leona, "and I refuse it again. You insulted me by doubting my word, and I demand satisfaction; more, I will have it. This gentleman," intimating Valera, "has not the slightest authority for interfering in the settlement of my disputes."

"I have not even heard the cause of quarrel," commenced Christobal.

"It is one which you of all men have the best means of settling," replied Guzman.

"Señors," interrupted Leona, haughtily, "I object to any discussion on the cause of quarrel. I refuse to make an apology. I should refuse to accept one, and I demand that the duel proceeds. If Don Valera has any objection to make to my resentment of his unwarrantable interference, I shall be happy to settle our differences afterwards."

The seconds then advanced to place the antagonists in proper position. Valera's alarm amounted to agony. The cold sweat stood on his forehead—he trembled in every limb—he turned his eyes imploringly to Leona.

"*For the love of God, Leon,*" he said earnestly.

At the tenderness which his voice expressed, she could not fail also to feel. She went up to him for one moment and pressed his hand, whilst their eyes met.

"Thanks, my friend," she said with unflinching firmness. "But have no fear for me, I have none for myself."

"Señor!" exclaimed Valera, as he rushed over to the side of Guzman, "if a hair of that lad's head is injured, you will have to answer for it to me."

"Indeed!" was the reply, with shrugged shoulders; "then, if I understand you rightly, I am expected to stand here and be shot at like a target. Sorry to disoblige you, señor, but I prefer the alternative of meeting you afterwards."

"D'Acosta has gone too far! Guzman means mischief," whispered the man who had accompanied Valera to the place of meeting.

"To business, gentlemen," cried the seconds, as they placed Guzman and Leona back to back.

"You are each to take sixteen paces forward as we count them, then turn and fire!"

The seconds commenced to count—the antagonists to walk—One, Two, Three, Four! Every nerve in Valera's body began to quiver; he could only send up a kind of gasping prayer that he might retain his consciousness. Five, Six, Seven, Eight! The perspiration stood in large beads upon his forehead—Leona's figure was growing less distinct to his failing vision. Nine, Ten, Eleven, Twelve! Should he rush between them and receive Guzman's fire in his own heart? Oh! the thought of that tender flesh torn by powder and bullet! Thirteen, Fourteen, Fifteen— "*Mother of God! save her!*" burst in an agonised scream from his lips, but, as he said it, the final number was pronounced, the combatants had turned, and his last words were lost in the sharp cracking reports of two pistols.

"Saints defend us, Guzman's down!" said the man by his side, in a tone of the utmost surprise. The news revived Valera. He rushed up to Leona.

"Are you hurt?" he cried, anxiously.

"No," she said, wildly; "but *he* is."

All the woman had come back to her in the idea that she might have killed her antagonist. She grew deadly pale, threw down her pistol on the ground, and crossed over quickly to where the seconds were kneeling by Guzman's side.

"He is not seriously wounded, gentlemen," she said, anxiously.

"I hope not, señor, but the shot has entered his chest. *Caramba!* but you have a straight aim. The wound bleeds outwardly—that is a good sign; but we should have assistance as soon as possible."

"What do you want? Tell me. I will run and fetch it," cried Leona, "or Valera here will. What is it, gentlemen? Wine—brandy—a doctor? Ah! let me know at once."

All her forced courage and intrepidity had fled. She was shaking like an aspen leaf in her anxiety lest she had done irremediable harm. The wounded man saw her distress, and held out his hand.

"Good lad," he said faintly, "do not alarm yourself. It is a mere bagatelle after all. I admire a steady aim and an unflinching nerve, but I like a tender heart better. We will be friends henceforward, will we not?"

Leona was crying, but she tried hard to keep back her tears.

"If you will permit it, señor; but you are too good—too forgiving. It was all the effect of my bad temper. If I have injured you seriously I shall never forgive myself."

"It is nothing, you will see," replied Guzman; but, as he said the words, he fainted.

"We must have something to carry him back to the boat on," said his second. "And perhaps we had better fetch a doctor to him first, if there is one to be found."

"There must be one in the town!" exclaimed Leona. "At all events we can but ask. Run, Valera," she continued, turning to Christobal, "run as fast as ever you can and inquire for a doctor, and bring back a bed—a hurdle—anything on which to carry him to the steamer."

But Valera, being quit of his own anxiety respecting Leona's safety, was not over-pleased to see hers for that of her rival.

"I should think Don Guzman's friends were the properest people to procure what he may require," he answered, somewhat sullenly. "I have no right to interfere."

"Señor, how can you stand on etiquette at such a moment? Pray lose no time in procuring us assistance; or, if you really will not help us I must go myself. If anything should happen to Don Guzman by reason of this affair I shall die of grief."

"Do you want the whole lot of them to know that you're a woman?" said Christobal, as he went straight up to Leona, and whispered in her ear.

"Christobal, no! What are you dreaming of?" she answered, in the same tone.

"That you betray yourself with every word you speak, that this romantic interest about the man you were resolved, against all advice, to meet, is ridiculous—foolishly and absurdly feminine, and if you do not show a little more reason in the matter, your sex will become apparent to the whole company."

He spoke angrily—jealously—and the woman resented the tone he adopted. It was hard for him, doubtless, who had been suffering so acutely on her account, to find that, as soon as the danger was over, all her sympathies seemed to be enlisted on the side of the man by whose aim she might have been stretched lifeless on the sward at that very moment. But quick, impulsive, emotional, like all her sex who have any claim to the name of woman, Leona only felt that she was safe, and the blood of her enemy might lie on her head, and was as ready now to fall down and administer to Don Guzman's smallest need, as she had been an hour before to shoot him through the heart.

"If none of these gentlemen will take the trouble to fetch a doctor for him, I will go myself," she said, as she turned from them and ran quickly in the direction of the town. Two of the men were at her heels in a minute, but Valera, though he longed to follow too, turned proudly away, and professed to direct his interest towards Guzman, who had revived from his temporary unconsciousness.

"Fine young fellow!" remarked the wounded man, in a weak voice. "I am glad he hasn't killed me. He would have felt it so much."

"Rather clap-trap business to my mind," said Christobal. "I don't admire emotion in a man."

"He is not a man," replied Guzman. "He is but a boy. I wonder if he has any sisters," he continued, with a faint smile; "if he has, I shall tell him he must give me one in return for this."

This remark, innocently as it was made, went to Valera's soul. In a moment his quick, jealous spirit foresaw and dreaded the confidences that might ensue upon a reconciliation between the duellists, and he could almost have found it in his heart to wish that Leona's shot had taken a better effect than it had. He turned away from Guzman's side, and walked apart moodily. In the course of time Leona reappeared, accompanied by her companions, an old Brazilian doctor, and a species of stretcher. Guzman's wound, though serious, was not pronounced dangerous, and he was permitted to proceed on his journey. The bullet was extracted then and there, the sick man placed upon the stretcher, and the little cavalcade took its way back to the place of embarkation—Leona walking by Don Guzman's side, Valera some little way in the rear. The doctor, on extracting the ball, had laid it in Don Guzman's hand, with the jesting advice to keep it in memory of a narrow escape. Guzman now transferred it to that of Leona.

"It is more yours than mine, d'Acosta, and I am glad to have the opportunity of returning it to you. Perhaps you will place it amongst your curiosities as a memento that sometimes courage stands in good place of experience."

"I will preserve it as a holy relic, señor," she answered, as she placed it in her bosom; "and thank our Lady each time I see it that I was prevented taking the life of a good and brave man by my headstrong folly. By rights this bullet should have been in me instead of you."

"Heaven forbid!" said Guzman earnestly, as he regarded her fine face and figure with interest.

Christobal overheard the conversation, and cavilled at it. He felt as angry now with Leona for risking the discovery of her sex as he had done before with her for concealing it.

The party reached the steamboat in safety, and Don Guzman was comfortably disposed in his berth. Still the girl hovered about him, arranging his pillows and offering him refreshment, until the doctor requested that everybody should leave the cabin and give his patient the chance of going to sleep. Valera, who, in his jealousy, could not keep away from Leona, and had also been present at the little scene, followed her into the saloon, intending to remonstrate with her when they should reach the deck, but as she passed his cabin door, which stood open, she staggered, reeled, and finally fell over the travelling-case that stood upon the threshold. Christobal's illusion vanished—he had his arms around her in a moment.

"My darling, what is the matter?" he cried with apprehension. She did not, as usual resent the fond appellation. On the contrary, she permitted him to raise her, and leaned up against his breast as though the shelter it afforded were necessary in her weak condition.

"Leona, are you wounded after all?" continued Valera, unable to comprehend the change which had so suddenly taken place in her.

"Only here, Tobal—only here," she answered, pressing her hand against her heart. "Oh, if I had killed him, what *should* I have done?"

"You seem to have taken an unaccountable fancy to this Guzman," said Christobal, his jealous fears again in the ascendant.

"You are mistaken, Tobal. It is an accountable hatred I have taken to myself. I have only just escaped committing murder. *Have I escaped it?* I had all the will, the desire for revenge. Will my hands ever be clean again?"

"You are overcome, Leona. Notwithstanding your boasted strength, this excitement has been too much for you, or you would not talk such nonsense."

"Oh, don't say so, Tobal. I—I have a double reason for avoiding all such mischances. He will not die, Tobal—tell me he will not die."

"Not from your shot, *m'amie*, though it was directed with all your heart to his. I shall begin to be afraid of quarrelling with you, Leona. I had no idea you could shoot so straight."

"Don't speak so, Tobal. I said hasty words in my anger to you. I was so afraid you would tell them I was a woman; but I did not mean them. I shall never quarrel with you, dear brother—never—*never*. I have had enough of quarrelling," and here the poor girl began to cry, and Christobal to kiss the tears away. It was well for the success of Leona's reputation, as one of the masculine gender, that there were no spectators to their reconcilation.

"And now tell me, *m'amie*," said Valera, when the girl's sobs had somewhat subsided, "what was the cause of the quarrel between Guzman and yourself that led to this result?"

All the Brazilian blood rushed to her cheek as she was reminded of it. Her companion could read at a glance how much the quarrel had agitated her.

"He doubted my word," she said indignantly. "He did more. He gave me the lie to my face. Oh, Tobal, when I think of that I am glad that I met him."

"But on what subject, Leona, did he contradict you?" demanded Valera, with increasing curiosity.

"He denied your Spanish birth, *mon frère*. He said you were only a Portuguese—a half breed."

"*He did, did he?*" said Valera, with set teeth, forgetting all but the greatest insult that could be offered him.

"Yes; and when I attested your parentage—said I had known you almost from your birth—he laughed. *Laughed* at me, Christobal, for a foolish boy who didn't know the difference between a Spanish and Portuguese when I saw them."

"I wish to heaven I had kept to my resolution and challenged him as soon as you had done with him," exclaimed Don Christobal fiercely.

"Ah, no! Tobalito, my brother, my friend, spare him further. He has had his lesson. Surely you can trust your honour with Leona."

The loving tones recalled him to a sense of what he owed her.

"And you did this for me—*for me*," he exclaimed, joyfully. "You risked your precious life for me, Leona, my darling!"

But as he grew warmer she chilled.

"Surely yes, Tobal, as you would risk yours any day for me. *Am I not your sister?*"

"But you should not have run such a risk. You might have perished, and what then would have been the world to me?"

"We must all run risks occasionally," she answered, with a touch of her former intrepidity, "and since it is well over, let us say no more about it. But—but, I hope," with a slight shudder, "the necessity for it will never arise again!"

* * * * * *

Don Guzman's wound progressed favourably. After a few days' nursing, all anxiety ceased to be felt on his account, although he was considered an invalid to the end of the voyage. It was not long before Leona and Christobal had to exchange the steamboat for the train, whilst Don Guzman's destination took him in another direction. They parted, however, the best of friends, and with many hopes, on Guzman's side at least, of meeting again; but though Valera felt easier when Leona had lost sight of her admiring antagonist, he could never quite satisfy himself as to how much or how little she returned his professions of cordiality. For—from the day that her physical weakness had led her into betraying her sentiments in the cabin—she had withdrawn into her former self, and resented any idea that a softer feeling had mingled with her eagerness to avenge the honour of Valera's name. So they travelled on together—excellent company, but no more—the man anxious only to construe each affectionate look or word into something warmer than it was intended to convey—the woman, to repel his advances without wounding his too sensitive love for herself. And ever and anon, a lurking jealousy of Guzman would spring up in the breast of Valera, who was only too ready to interpret each sigh or downcast look, or dreamy reverie on the part of Leona into a regret of her separation from the stranger, whose destinies had been so strangely entangled with her own. At last the weary journey was all but accomplished, and another day would bring them to New York. At the last town at which they slept (by Leona's particular desire) Valera missed her. They had dined together, and after dinner he had strolled out with his cigar, and coming back to the hotel, found that she had left it for a walk.

He sat down to wait quietly for her return, never dreaming that she could be long absent, but hour after hour slipped away and still she had not come back. Valera now grew anxious—he always was anxious when Leona was concerned—and had some idea of going out to seek her—still, the fear of missing her kept him to his post. Just as his anxiety was at its height, and he had made up his mind to follow in her pursuit, one of the hotel servants brought him a card inscribed in a delicate feminine hand—

"DONNA ANITA SILVANO."

"I don't know the Donna. Who is she?" he inquired of the attendant.

"I cannot say, señor. She is a stranger to us, but says she is an old acquaintance of yours."

"She has the advantage of me then. I am just going out on business. I have no time to receive her."

"I told the lady you were going out, señor, and she says she will not detain you a moment."

"Well, I suppose I must admit her then," said Valera, vexed at the delay, and by no means friendlily disposed towards his mysterious visitor. "Show the donna up."

The servant obeyed his orders, and in another minute a female figure, closely veiled and shrouded, stood before him.

– CHAPTER 7 –

DONNA ANITA

The dusk was falling fast, and for a moment Valera could not distinguish whether his visitor was old or young. With chivalrous courtesy he advanced to meet her at the door and lead her to a seat. Then he perceived that the undulations of her figure were not those of an old woman, and his curiosity became piqued to discover who she could possibly be, and what she might want with him at such an hour.

"You are at a loss to account for the meaning of this visit, señor," she said, in a thin piping voice, which instantly disenchanted him, so unlike was it to the rich harmony of Leona's tones.

"I confess, donna, that it is as unexpected as it is flattering," he replied. "You were good enough to say you were acquainted with me. Surely I can never have had the happiness of knowing and yet have forgotten you."

"I should rather have said I was acquainted with your family, señor. I have had the honour of speaking to your mother, Donna Josefa."

"Indeed! That must have been more years ago than I can give you the credit of having counted."

"You have the flattering Spanish tongue, Don Christobal; none who heard you speak could doubt your nationality! But I have heard of you from others than your mother. I come from New York, and am intimately acquainted with some of the principal members of the firm you are about to join in the capacity of foreign correspondent!"

This announcement much interested Valera. He was like an emigrant about to enter on a new world, and anxious to hear all he could concerning it.

"Indeed, donna. I was not aware that the English of New York mixed so intimately in foreign society."

"We have no 'foreigners' in New York, señor. The city is cosmopolitan. We ignore the nationality, and look only to the individual. I cannot say that fortune has thrown me intimately into the society of Mr. Halliday or Mr. Upjohn, but they bear an excellent name for hospitality amongst us. And they are expecting with no small anxiety the arrival of the new member of the firm!"

Christobal coloured with gratification. This was an honour of which he had little dreamed a mere clerk would be invested.

"I am proud to hear you say so, donna; but it is more than I deserve—an unknown, inexperienced youth—"

"Inexperienced perhaps, señor," interrupted the stranger, who still kept herself closely veiled, "but, pardon me, not unknown. The good old name of Valera is a household word in Spain, and your future employers are perfectly aware of its worth, and what may be expected from one who bears it."

"It pleases me more than I can say to hear you acknowledge it," replied Valera; "for my name is the only possession I can boast of. You are also Spanish, Donna Anita?"

"I am also Spanish, Don Christobal, and in that fact lies hid the reason of my visit to you. I am jealous for the honour of our country—of our names."

"You alarm me. What cause have you for fear?" said Valera, tenderly, as he essayed to take the lady's hand.

But she drew it away from him.

"A rumour reached New York before I left it, to the effect that a duel had been fought on board the steamer in which you travelled from Rio Janeiro, and that you had some hand in it."

"Pardon me; that was a mistake. A duel was fought, sorely against my wish, but I was neither principal nor second in the affair."

"But you took a deep interest in some one who was?"

"That I cannot deny, donna."

"And that some one was a woman in disguise?"

"*Caramba!*" exclaimed Valera, startled out of his propriety. "Who can have repeated such a story?"

"Is it true, señor, or not?" demanded the stranger.

"I do not know by what right you put such a question to me, donna. But supposing it were true, how can it affect *my* reputation?"

"Only that the principals of your firm are excessively particular about the conduct of their clerks, and that the report of your being accompanied from Rio by a woman in the disguise of a boy has greatly annoyed and disappointed them."

Donna Anita spoke inquiringly, as though she expected Valera to deny the allegation, instead of which he walked away from her side and stood with his face towards the open balcony, thoughtfully pulling his moustaches.

"You have nothing to advance in your own favour, Don Christobal?" she said, after a pause.

"I do not see any need for my speaking, donna. I am at least not responsible to *you* for any follies of which I may have been guilty."

"That is hardly a grateful speech after the trouble I have taken to warn you, señor. For the sake of your name and the friendship I bore your mother, I seek your presence at the risk of my own reputation, to save yours; and all the reward I get is to incur your displeasure and be subjected to your sarcasm."

"Oh, forgive me, Donna Anita! I acknowledge your goodness and intrepidity in coming to tell me of this, but it has greatly upset me. So long as I perform my public duties conscientiously, what. possible right can my employers have to cavil at my private actions?"

"Every fresh word you utter convinces me that the report they heard is true," said the stranger. "It was an imprudence, señor, to say the least of it—or folly on your part—more than folly on hers."

"You do not know of what you are speaking," returned Christobal, hotly.

"I am quite sure I must be correct in saying that any woman who could so far degrade herself as to appear in the garb of the other sex, must be lost to all sense of female modesty and decorum."

"She is not. She is as pure and discreet as any woman living," cried Valera, blurting out the truth in his anxiety to defend Leona's honour.

"Ah, then your employers have heard rightly that your travelling companion was a lady in disguise. I am afraid it will go hardly with your situation in consequence, señor. Messrs. Upjohn and Halliday are very unlikely to overlook so serious a breach of decorum."

"You wrung the truth from me," answered Valera, biting his lip.

"And if you consider you obtained it by fair means, you must make what use of it you think fit. I am at your mercy. Only this you must believe—that the woman you speak of is as true and pure a woman as ever breathed, and that she assumed her disguise for reasons of her own, and totally apart from any idea of travelling in my company."

"Oh, I really cannot consent to listen to the praises of one whose conduct was so very questionable," said Donna Anita, as she rose from her chair and shook out her skirts. "I suppose you have had your peccadilloes to answer for, the same as other gentlemen, señor, and may not be able to hold yourself entirely blameless of the sin of loving 'not wisely but too well;'* but you should know better than to attempt to palm it off as a virtue on your lady friends. I consider it an insult to my dignity that such a creature as the one I allude to should be mentioned in my presence. Pray let me hear no more of her!"

"But you *must* hear more, madam," exclaimed Valera, as he placed himself across her path. "You have introduced yourself, a perfect stranger, to me, to vilify and traduce one of the noblest and most pure-minded women God ever made; and I cannot let you go until you have heard me deny to the death all you have said against her. She has been my sister and my friend since childhood. I love and honour her above all her sex, and I will lose my promised situation, and throw up every prospect I have in life, sooner than stand by quietly and hear one slur cast upon her character. She is the most courageous, the most generous, the most—"

"Oh! stop! Christobal, stop! I cannot hear one word more. I have heard too much already!" cried Donna Anita Silvano, as she threw off her mantilla, and hood, and veil, and disclosed to his astonished gaze the lightning eyes, and smiling mouth, and milk-white teeth of *Leona Lacoste*.

"*Leona!*" he exclaimed, in real astonishment, as he fell backward and stared at her.

"Yes, truly Leona! and fancy, my brother, that you should know me so little that a veil and a hood have the power to transform me

---

* *Othello*, Act V, scene 2, line 340. Also Rhoda Broughton's 1867 novel *Not Wisely But Too Well*.

into another woman. Pesta! how warm the things have made me! My face is burning from your compliments and the weather. Come! kiss me, Tobal, for the valiant way in which you stood up for Leona behind her back. I thought I would make your Spanish blood rise. Now confess! Did I not play my part well?"

"So well that I am in utter astonishment still. Are you sure that you are Leona, or that Donna Anita is not hidden somewhere in this dusky room? What did you do to your voice—your air—your expression? How did you ever think of making up such a story, and frightening me with the prospect of losing my poor appointment—and all for your sake, you wicked rogue!"

Leona's laugh rang through the apartment.

"Saint Jago! how alarmed you looked. But you have a stout heart, Tobal, and you love me far more than I deserve. Give me some sherbet, for my tongue's parched with so much abuse of myself, and then I will tell you all my history. Ah! how beautifully I deceived you!"

"But who would have dreamt of seeing you in these? Are they your own?" said Valera, as he touched her dress and mantilla.

"My own, of course. Am I in the habit of wearing those of other women? And did you expect I should walk into New York in my poor father's old gardening suit, Tobal? What an idea! But, then, what can one expect from men?"

"You have had your hair curled," remarked Valera, as he passed his hand over the thick crop. "How nice it looks."

"Keep your hands to yourself, Tobal; you will disarrange my *chevelure*. Yes, I went first into a barber's, and had my hair curled, and then I went to a modiste's* and told her I wanted a ready-made dress and mantilla for a masquerade, Tobal, mind you, for a masquerade. *Caramba!* How I laughed!"

"And what did the modiste say?"

"She prophesied I should make a pretty girl enough, and gave me a kiss with her receipt. I changed my clothes in her back room, got her to write my name upon a card, and came back to the hotel to see how far I could impose upon my brother."

"Which you did to any length. You might have left me in the

---

* Fashionable dressmaker or milliner.

same perplexity had it been your will. I was most completely and thoroughly taken in. But then I could not see your eyes, Leona," he added tenderly, "or I should not have been such a fool as to mistake them for those of anybody else."

"I would not have been so cruel as not to undeceive you quickly. But I am glad you were deceived; it was a test of my power. And now that the dread of forfeiting your situation is off your mind, and I am no longer likely to disgrace you by my disguise, let us talk of our plans for to-morrow, Tobal."

"I shall first see you comfortably settled in rooms, Leona, and then go and present myself to the principals of my firm."

"*Après?*"

"Then I must find rooms for myself."

"Will not the same rooms do for both of us?" demanded Leona.

"No, they would not," replied Valera shortly; and he said no more.

"But we are to pass as brother and sister, Tobal; have we not agreed upon that?"

"Certainly, if you wish it," he replied with a sigh. "But how will you manage about your name, *m'amie?*"

"There will be no necessity to speak of it. The world will think that I call myself d'Acosta because I am on the stage."

"You are still determined to be nothing but an actress?"

"What else is there for me to be? I want to make money, Tobal, and the opportunities for a woman to make money are so few. All I have to sell is my beauty. Can I sell it any other way?"

"God forbid!" cried Valera, with a sudden pain. "But why are you so anxious to make money, Leona?"

"Must I not live?" she replied, evasively.

"And when you have made a name for yourself, I suppose you will be going to England, and leaving me all alone."

"*To England?* Ah, no—not to England," exclaimed Leona, with a sudden look of horror.

"Why, *m'amie?* what is there in that word to frighten you?"

But the girl, over-excited and over-tired perhaps, only answered his question with a burst of tears. Christobal was by her side in a moment, but she put him from her impatiently.

"Why do you speak of England? Why do you ever mention the

place, when you know how my father hated it? Oh my poor, poor father! How I wish that I could forget everything in the grave with him."

She sobbed herself into serenity again, like an impulsive child, and Valera, used to see the emotional side of her nature, was waiting quietly until she should be able to resume the conversation, when a loud voice was heard in the corridor exclaiming in English:

"Here—quick—presto! I am nearly starved to death. Bring me stew, ragouts, fowl—anything you've got, so long as there's none of that infernal garlic in it—into the saloon as soon as you can serve it. And beer, man. Look alive and give me beer. By Jove, what weather to travel in, and what a people to travel amongst!"

The saloon in which Leona and Christobal were sitting was a public one, and the owner of the voice entered as he spoke, shaking the dust from the travelling coat he held in his hand. He was a short, stout, red-faced man, of about fifty, of unmistakable British stamp. As he caught sight of Leona be bowed in a rough, off-hand manner, and proceeded to apologise for the fervour with which he had dispensed his orders.

"But with these infernal foreigners—" he commenced.

But here, guessing by their appearance at the nationality of his new acquaintances, he halted and looked foolish.

"Pray don't mind us," replied Valera, in his prettily-accented English, "we can quite sympathise in your difficulties. Can I be of any use in explaining to the waiter what you may want?"

"Much obliged, I'm sure, monsieur. Are you French?"

"No; I am Spanish. But I can speak both languages."

"And madam?" inquired the Englishman, not knowing exactly by what title to designate Leona.

"Mademoiselle is my sister," said Christobal. Leona bowed in her grand, lofty way, and the stranger having jerked a response, acquaintanceship was established between them.

"It's very awkward for a fellow to light upon one of those exclusively foreign hotels," said the Englishman; "and I don't know what the deuce my New York friends meant by giving me this address. I suppose there are English hotels here?"

"I think not. This is but a small town."

"I can manage to *parlez-vous* pretty well, and I *have* made my wants known in German; but hang it all, when it comes to Spanish it's enough to crack a fellow's jaw. And I have just come off the railway, after six hours' travelling, and am as hungry as a hunter."

"Let me give your orders," repeated Valera.

"Thank you, sir! if it's not too much trouble, I shall be obliged to you. I just want a decent dinner, with wine that won't make me ill, and that's all."

"Your name, monsieur?"

"Ah, true! Rouse, my good fellow. John Rouse, bound from New York to Boston. I shall owe you an eternal debt of gratitude, I'm sure."

As Christobal disappeared on his errand of mercy, Mr. Rouse turned to the contemplation of Leona, and thought he saw before him one of the most glorious women his eyes had ever beheld. The sight of him did not strike his fair companion with equal favour. Naturally prejudiced against his country and countrymen, this short, spare, thick-built Englishman did not appear to have much chance of disabusing her mind of a pre-conceived dislike. She turned her back upon him, and looked out of the open window.

"Mademoiselle is also Spanish?" said Mr. John Rouse, wishing to enter into conversation.

"A woman is generally of the same nationality as her brother, monsieur," was the evasive reply.

"Sharp, by Jove!" muttered her companion. "Is mademoiselle also on her travels?"

"We are on our road to New York."

"Ah, I wish you joy of it. The most expensive place to live in of the whole world. You have friends there?"

Leona resented this questioning, yet something led her on to answer it.

"No; we have but ourselves to look to. We are alone in the world, and have to work for our living."

"You are too beautiful to work, mademoiselle," said the Englishman roughly, but not rudely. "You should leave that to the men to do for you. I warrant there'd be no lack of volunteers for the service."

"But I would rather work for myself," replied Leona.

"And may I ask in what direction your work lies?"

"I am going to be an actress," she answered proudly.

"*By Jove!*"

The stranger seemed quite struck by the idea. He slapped his hand on his thigh, and continued to stare at Leona earnestly. Not till Valera returned with the announcement that his dinner would be served within the shortest time possible did Mr. John Rouse find his tongue again.

"Your sister here is an actress, sir."

"She hopes to be so. It is her desire," replied Christobal.

"How strange that I should have fallen in with you. Here am I, journeying down to Boston for the very purpose of superintending the opening of a new theatre there, and on the look-out for members to make up a company as I go."

"Indeed, that *is* curious," said Valera, indifferently.

But Leona was not indifferent. At the mention of a theatre and a company, her eyes sparkled and her cheek flushed, and the commonplace stranger became invested with a halo of romance.

"Yes, yes!" she exclaimed, as she drew nearer to the table at which Mr. Rouse was seated.

"Your sister has the very face and figure for the stage," continued the manager to Valera. "A noble presence and commanding height. I'll guarantee she'll make her fortune on the boards."

"But she has never acted. She has everything to learn," said Christobal.

"I'll warrant she *can* act. I read it in her eye—the trick of her voice—her expression. I do not often pronounce a judgment at first sight, but here I feel I am not mistaken. And such beauty, sir," he continued in a lower tone, intended for Valera's ear alone, "such unusually transcendent beauty! Such a face and figure are worth all the talent in the world. Trust me."

Valera saw the manager's eager look and shuddered. Leona's words about selling her beauty came back like ice upon his heart.

"And you are going to Boston?" said the girl, evidently anxious that the conversation should not be discontinued.

"I am going to Boston, mademoiselle. I have come from England on purpose to put some new pieces on the stage there, and I have visited New York first to see if I could find any ladies to suit my purpose, and been disappointed. But if you will come with me to Boston I will engage to give an appearance there within the month, and as good a salary as a beginner could expect to draw. You must remember you have, as your brother says, everything to learn."

"It is quite impossible!" exclaimed Valera, but Leona interrupted.

"Are you in earnest, monsieur? Will you really give me an engagement without seeing more of me than you have done?"

"I am in earnest. I offer you on the spot fifteen dollars a-week if you will come with me to Boston, and appear on the stage of my new theatre."

"Oh, Tobal, how fortunate I am! This is just what I have been wanting. I shall have no more trouble in the matter. Was ever such luck as mine?"

"But we are going to New York, Leona, and Boston is miles away. We are much obliged to this gentleman for his kindness, but you cannot accept his offer."

"But why not, Tobal? What is to hinder me? Where shall I get such a chance again?"

"Ah! it's no easy matter to get on the stage in New York," said Mr. Rouse. "All the stars over from England; every theatre crammed; and actors and actresses going for a song. If you want a good thing, mademoiselle, you'll take my offer."

"You hear what monsieur says, Christobal. And how am I to live unless I get work?"

"*I will support you,*" replied Valera, falling into his native tongue. "*Do not go with this man, beloved, for the light of my life will go with you.*"

But this was not the way to conciliate Leona. She frowned at the tender message, and ignored its affectionate entreaty.

"What nonsense you talk, Christobal. If we are never to part for a few weeks or months, we may just starve together. I must decide for myself in this matter. Monsieur Rouse, I accept your offer, and I will go with you to Boston."

"That's a fine girl," exclaimed the Englishman, "and you shan't regret it. By George! that face of yours ought to stir them up. We shall have them pulling down the theatre to get at you. Well, that's a bargain then. Strike hands upon it," he continued, slapping his great fist across hers, "and we'll make out the papers and sign them before we sleep to-night."

"I'll be no party to the transaction," said Valera excitedly, as he rushed from the apartment. He was deeply, cruelly hurt to find that Leona was so ready to leave his company and protection for that of another man; but beyond this, a great and appalling fear had come over him at the idea of trusting the beautiful and unsophisticated girl, whom he loved with so true a devotion, to the tender mercies of an utter stranger, and the dangers of a perilous profession, in an unknown place, and at a distance from himself. Horrible visions of all the misadventures that might befall Leona— of how they might never meet again, or meet estranged and with divided interests—floated through his mind until he had worked himself up to a pitch of madness.

He was walking rapidly up and down the garden that surrounded the hotel, brooding on all the unhappy circumstances that had led to this catastrophe, when he was startled by the subject of his reverie flying under cover of the darkness into his very arms.

"Take me away, Tobal," she exclaimed wildly, as her heart beat fast against his arm. "Take me away this very minute. I will not stay in this place another hour."

"What is the matter, *m'amie*? Has that man dared to insult you?"

"No, no; only take me away before he sees either of us again. I cannot stay here any longer."

– CHAPTER 8 –

"THE CAPTAIN OF THE GUARD"

The tone in which Leona spoke—her very words so reminded Valera of that other time when she had clung to him in like manner, and entreated him to take her away from the place in which she had been born, that for the moment he could only suppose that she had again encountered Ribeiro, of whom she seemed to stand so much in awe.

"Tell me your cause of alarm, my dear Leona, and I shall be

better able to help you. What! *you* trembling so much that you cannot stand upright—you, who, apparently without a quiver, put that bullet so straight into Guzman's breast. Where's the brave defender of my honour gone to?"

"I would rather fight twenty duels in succession than go with that man to Boston, Tobal. Oh! don't let me leave you. Let us go on to New York by the night mail, and have no more to say to him."

"My dear Leona! no one could be better pleased to hear your decision than I am. I have been making myself wretched ever since you said you would accept his offer, with the idea of being separated from you. But why have you changed your mind?"

"I don't know. I can't tell you; only that it is changed."

"Is it the distance, the uncertainty, the strange life that frightens you, Leona?"

"Again I say that I cannot tell you. Only I will not go to Boston with Monsieur Rouse."

"Is it the thought of our separation, darling?" whispered Valera, in his tenderest tone. But the rigidity with which the girl immediately disengaged herself from his grasp gave the answer before it was spoken.

"Bah, no!" she exclaimed, with no small degree of irritation. "Why is it that whenever I come to lean on you as a friend, Tobal, and to ask your advice on some important matter, you directly do something to make me angry? What has our separation to do with our work? We are both bound to work, and if our work lies in opposite directions, we are bound to separate. We should look like two fools if we went whining and pining about the world every time we had to part for a few weeks. I tell you plainly that I won't go to Boston, and I want to go to New York, as we first arranged. Is not that sufficient? Why do you directly want to know the reason? But, like all men, you are made up of curiosity."

"I thought I could act better for you if I understood the meaning of your change of feeling."

"Well, then, you won't know it. There is nothing to know. So you must act without it, Tobal."

"I am only too happy to act for you at all. And now what does your imperious majesty wish me to do?"

"Pay the bill, put the baggage on a car, and take me to catch the night mail to New York."

"Without speaking to the Englishman?"

"Why should we speak to him?"

"Common politeness demands it from us; besides which he visits New York, and he might meet you there some day, when your breach of faith with him might injure you in your profession."

This consideration had more weight with Leona than any other. She weighed the consequences.

"Are you sure he will not insist upon my going with him?"

"Quite sure! Why, *m'amie*, this is a free country. Who could insist upon taking you anywhere unless it was your desire to go? And you have signed no papers for him."

"No, he is drawing up the agreement at this moment. Go to him at once, Tobalito, and say I am ill—mad—anything—but I cannot go to Boston."

"I will settle it in a flash of lightning, *m'amie*," said the young man, delighted to be sent on such an errand. "Do you go to bed and rest well, and we will proceed to New York by the first train in the morning."

Pleased as he was at the fact of Leona having changed her mind about going to Boston, Valera still puzzled himself to discover the reason she had done so. His pleasant self-gratulation that it was for his own sake, she had nipped in the bud. And knowing the girl's indomitable will when she had once determined on a certain course of action, and the eagerness with which she had accepted unexpected good fortune that had fallen in her way, he felt that some extraordinary cause must have suddenly arisen to shake her resolution.

He found Mr. John Rouse busy over some sheets of foolscap paper, which he had partly covered with writing. "Look here, monsieur, what's your name?" he commenced as he caught sight of Valera. "It is not always the custom to have a written agreement in these cases, because the ghost walks regularly every week you see, and when there's no money in the till all the agreements in the world won't get it out."

But here (perceiving Don Christobal's look of unmitigated astonishment and mystification) the manager consented to interpret. "Ah, don't understand our lingo, I see. What I mean is, that as mademoiselle will be paid weekly she'll always have the option of cutting if she doesn't get her salary—still, as she's new to the business, and I like things ship-shape, I thought I'd just put it down in a few words of writing, and then there can't be any mistake about the matter."

And here Mr. Rouse began to read over a document commencing "An agreement entered into this twentieth day of May—" etc., etc.

"But stop, monsieur," said Valera, interrupting the manager's flow of eloquence. "My sister is very sorry to have given you this trouble, but she has changed her mind—she cannot go with you to Boston."

Mr. Rouse's face fell considerably.

"Whew!—changed her mind. That's bad. What has she done that for?"

"I cannot tell you. Women can seldom give a reason for their actions. But mademoiselle is quite determined to give up the engagement you offered her."

"But that is folly—madness, in her position. Look here, monsieur," continued the Englishman as he turned in his chair and confronted Valera, "if that girl will only trust herself to me she'll make a fortune. I have travelled half over the world, and seen all sorts of women, but I never saw such a face and figure together in my life before. She'd create a sensation, sir, and that's what the stage wants nowadays. Talent, experience, perseverance, study, everything may go to the winds so long as you'll give the public a new sensation. And I could have done it with your sister. Sir, I would have done it with your sister. Can you say nothing to make her alter her mind again?"

"I am afraid not," said Christobal, pretending to look and feel sorry; "and I am sure both mademoiselle's apologies and mine are due to your—"

"D—n your apologies!" cried the manager, though good naturedly. "What I want is your sister. Here have I been knocking about here, there, and everywhere, on the look-out for something startling, and just when I think I've got it, the girl *changes her mind!* Bother women's minds, they're at all four points of the compass at once. And I'd taken a fancy to mademoiselle, too, outside her appearance, as I was telling her just now. She reminds me forcibly of an old friend I had once in Liverpool. I'm a Liverpool man, monsieur, bred and born in the place, and know every inch of it. But I bet in the whole length and breadth of the town I couldn't find such another face as mademoiselle's. She's glorious—like a colossal statue of the Medici.[*] Well, it's no use crying over spilt milk. I suppose there's nothing more to be said or done about it, sir, and my agreement, and my agreement here is so much waste paper."

"I am quite sure mademoiselle will not alter her mind again, monsieur. I think the suddenness of the proposal, and the distance, and the prospect of our separation, perhaps, have somewhat alarmed her."

"*Is* she your sister?" demanded the manager abruptly.

Valera's heightened colour told the truth for him.

"Very well, then, I won't say anything more against mademoiselle's determination," said Mr. Rouse. "Only tell her from me that if she happens to repent her refusal, or to find an engagement difficult to obtain in New York, she has but to remember my name and address, and if I haven't gone back to Liverpool, I'll do my best to serve her. By George! she is like old Evans," concluded the manager, as he slapped his knee. Valera parted with him with a friendly shake of the hand, and went back to tell Leona that he had settled that business for her, and she was free to go wherever she chose.

Still, the reason of her sudden refusal remained a mystery to him.

* * * * * *

Some two days afterwards, Mr. Benjamin Burrage, manager and proprietor of one of the principal theatres in New York, was sitting in his office surrounded by letters and bills, and in anything but a sweet temper. Every minute was he interrupted in his perusal of

---

[*] Likely to mean Michelangelo's statue of Giuliano de Medici in the Medici Chapel, San Lorenzo, Florence.

applications for employment, for orders, or for personal interviews, by the entrance of the stage-manager or the property-man, with various demands for more hands, more scenery, or more costumes, until Mr. Burrage felt very much inclined to do somebody a damage, and more than inclined to swear. At last, after having to the best of his ability satisfied the requirements of both his subordinates, he turned to the stage-manager and said, "Have you found a captain of the guard yet?"

"I have not, sir."

"How is that? Are there no women left in the city of New York?"

"Plenty; but none that come up to your standard, so far as I can see. I have had dozens of applicants, but none tall enough or handsome enough. You want a perfect giantess."

"*I will have five foot seven!* What would she look beside De Brassey?"

"You'll have to put up with a boy."

"I won't have a boy! Awkward brutes they are at that age! And nothing draws like a fine woman in armour."

"You'll have to send to England for her, then. We don't make the article out here."

"I'll have her if I send to the antipodes."

"Well there are plenty waiting your inspection at the present moment."

"Any tall ones amongst them?"

"Two or three."

"Well, don't you let any one in unless she brings a note of introduction from Westwell. Mind that! It's my strict order."

"Very good, sir. Are you ready to see them now?"

"In half a minute. Let me finish my letters first; and mind what I say to you, Brabant. It's no good sending in any dumpy ones."

The stage-manager retired, and Mr. Burrage reapplied himself to the inspection of his papers. It is no sinecure to be the manager of a theatre. Putting the real business connected with his property out of sight, the worries with which he has no right to be worried, are sufficient to take up all his time. The demands for a free entrance (to which every shoemaker who sells him a pair of boots considers himself entitled)—the distracting appeals for work—the queries on subjects totally unconnected with his office—the requests for autographs, or introductions, or information, would occupy, if attended to, many more days than there are in the week. And even the effort of opening such epistles and casting them on one side is enough of itself to upset the equanimity of any man's temper.

Mr. Benjamin Burrage was good-natured enough as things go. He was a thoroughly honest, upright, and hard-working man, and an experienced actor, who took most of the characters that were in his line upon himself. He was always ready to dip his hand into his pocket to relieve a case of want or suffering, and he was clear-sighted enough to be able to distinguish between merit and self-assertion amongst the men and women he employed, and to reward them accordingly. But he was sharp and brusque in his manner of speaking, calling a spade a spade and never going out of his way to pay a compliment, or to smooth down the rough edges of an unpleasant truth.

Consequently he was pronounced to be excessively disagreeable by those he did not like, and even the few he did like stood rather in awe of their manager finding fault with them.

It was with quite a timid hand that, a few minutes later, the property-man knocked again at Mr. Burrage's door.

"What the devil do you want now?"

"Are you ready to see the ladies yet, sir? They've been waiting a long time."

"Oh, aye! show them in. But one at a time, mind—one at a time."

The first applicant for the post of Captain of the Guard was a tall, thin, antiquated female, of some thirty-four summers, whose long curls, drooping on either side her face scarcely served to hide the crows'-feet about her eyes.

The manager regarded her for a moment with a steady glare, then waving his hand towards a seat, dropped his eyes upon his desk again, and commenced to write and talk at the same time.

"Well, madam, what may your business with me be? My minutes are precious."

"I have ventured to intrude myself upon your presence, sir—"

"Yes, yes, yes! I know all that! *What do you want?*"

The lady, on being thus abruptly appealed to, shook her curls and became nervous.

"Being the eldest of a family of six daughters, now, unfortunately, left fatherless, with a widowed mother to support and look after—"

"Madam!" exclaimed the manager, thumping his desk with an energy that caused the unhappy visitor to jump in her chair, "it's nothing to me if your mother is a wife or a widow. I've no time to listen to such rubbish. I want to know what you've come to ask me for."

"I have a letter of introduction to you from Mr. Westwell."

"Very good. Go on. Come to the point."

"And Mr. Westwell, knowing how much we need money, thought if I could go on the stage—"

"What's your line, ma'am?"

"My what, sir?"

"Your line of business. What can you *do*?"

"I could do anything you wished me, sir."

"*How* could you *do anything I wished you*?" grunted Burrage, contemptuously. "One woman can't fill every part. What are your legs like?"

"*Sir?*"

"Have you got good legs? Not ashamed to show them, eh? What's your age?"

"Well, I'm really not quite sure. Mamma says that—"

"No time to hear what mamma says. Now, look here, my good lady. You're five-and-thirty if you're a day. What the devil do you expect one to do with you at that time of life?"

The tears welled up into the poor woman's eyes from shame and mortification, but she forced them back into their springs again.

"I have often acted in private theatricals, so I thought perhaps—"

"You thought all wrong. Private theatricals have nothing to do with the stage. Now just you listen to me. You wouldn't find a place open in my theatre for you unless you meant to go in for comic old women."

"Comic old women!" almost shrieked the supplicant for histrionic honours.

"Yes, ma'am, and I couldn't take you without training even for that."

"You have insulted me, Mr. Burrage," said the lady indignantly, as she was preparing to leave the office.

"Very good, ma'am, very good, ma'am," replied the manager, not half listening to her words.

"Here, Cheeseman, show the next lady in."

The next lady and the next proved just as unsatisfactory. Fifteen candidates at least passed in review before Mr. Benjamin Burrage that morning, and were dismissed with a grunt of disapproval, with the curt but emphatic sentence "that they wouldn't do."

"I believe all the oldest and most hideous women in New York are in league to come up here and drive me mad," he exclaimed at last. "Why, there hasn't been a good-looking face amongst the lot."

"All the good-looking ones are small," replied Brabant, oracularly. "Never saw a tall, well-made woman in my life yet."

"Then you haven't used your eyes over that foreign critter that's been walking up and down outside the box-office the whole morning, begging you to smuggle her in to the governor," remarked Cheeseman, slyly.

"What's she like?" demanded Burrage.

"Oh, a tarnation fine woman, sir. Such eyes, such a smile, and the size of a grenadier."

"Then why haven't you shown her into me, you fool!"

"You said your particular orders were that no one was to be admitted without an introduction from Mr. Westwell."

"Yes, but how was I to know Juno[*] herself was going to ask for admittance. Bring the girl in at once, Cheeseman, and woe betide you if she falls short of anything you've said of her!"

"I'm not afraid of that," said Cheeseman as he left the stage, and in another minute returned with Leona. She was dressed completely in black—the costume in which she had personated Donna Anita, and wore her mantilla over her shoulder, the only concession she had made to New York fashions being that her beautiful face was shaded by a large black hat, with a curled brim

---

[*] Roman Goddess – Chief goddess and female counterpart of Jupiter. A member of the capitoline triad of deities.

and drooping feather, that suited it admirably.

As she sailed upon the stage with that undulating swimming movement of hers, acquired from the perfect freedom with which her limbs had moved from infancy, and raised her golden brown eyes to the manager's face, Mr. Burrage exchanged looks of congratulation with Mr. Brabant.

"Well, my dear, and what is your name?" he commenced, affably. "Elena d'Acosta, monsieur," she replied, for so she had determined to call herself, in order that Ribeiro might not discover her destination from the playbills.

"What are you—a Spaniard?"

"A Brazilian."

"By Jove, the Brazils are in luck! And how do you come to speak English so well?"

"I learned it from my—from an old man, I mean, who lived in the place where I was born."

"And what do you want to speak to me for?"

"I want to go on the stage, monsieur. I have to support myself, and I don't care for anything but acting."

"But you'd have to stand still on the stage at first, you know, and look on till you learnt your business—eh?"

"I would do anything you thought best."

"That's a good girl. Now just walk up and down the stage three or four times, will you?"

Leona did as she was required, and as the manager's practised eyes followed her graceful movements he chuckled and rubbed his hands.

"That'll do, my dear; that'll do. What do you think of that for my Captain of the Guard, *eh, Brabant?*"

"You couldn't do better, to my mind."

"No big women in New York. No handsome women in New York, *eh, Brabant?* I won't send *you* foraging for beauty again. You haven't half got your eyes about you. Why, where was this southern goddess hid that you never saw her? She's divine, Brabant; she's perfectly divine. I shall constitute Cheeseman my Prime Minister on the spot."

Meanwhile Leona, whose ears the manager's speech was not intended to reach, stood apart, thoughtful and anxious, wondering whether the whispered conversation foreboded good or evil to her.

"What salary do you ask, my dear, now?" inquired Mr. Burrage.

"I never thought of that, monsieur. I am quite a beginner. I do not wish to take any more than you think my services are worth," she answered, with a touch of the old pride.

"Well, now. I'll speak plainly to you, my dear. Your services are worth *nothing*—nothing at all. They may be by-and-by; but at this moment I wouldn't give you a cent a week for them."

"But how then—" she commenced with heaving breast.

"Now, stop a moment; don't be in a hurry. Your services mayn't be worth a cent, but your figure is—at all events to me just now. I want a fine woman to play the Captain of the Guard in the new burlesque of 'Semiramis'* that we're just going to put upon the stage. Will that suit you? I'll give you ten dollars a week down, and a certain engagement for three months. What do you say to my offer?"

"Oh, I'll take it, monsieur," cried Leona, eagerly.

Her heart's desire was gratified at last. She was enrolled as a member of the company of the Memphis Theatre at New York.

But when Valera came to hear of the engagement he grumbled at it. Tobal always grumbled at everything she did—so Leona averred.

"But you've only got about ten lines to speak, *m'amie*. I thought you wanted to become a grand actress. How are you to learn anything by standing on the stage dressed in a suit of armour?"

"But such armour, Tobalito! It will dazzle your eyes only to look at me—all gold and silver scales, with a blue velvet petticoat, and white and scarlet feathers in my casque. It is splendid! I never saw so beautiful a dress before."

"And the public will say they never saw so beautiful a woman," sighed Valera.

"And are you not glad that I am beautiful—if I *am* beautiful?" asked Leona.

"No, *m'amie*, not just at present. It is selfish of me, I know, but I cannnot bear the thought that all the world should be able to go and admire you as I do."

---

* Semiramis was the wife of Nimrod and Queen of Babylon.

"What do you suppose I care for the world?" replied the girl, resenting as usual his air of sentiment. "I want to make money, Tobalito, and if I cannot make it yet by talking, why I will stand upon the stage until I do. The talking will come in good time. Wait till you hear how I deliver my ten lines."

The talking did come, sooner than Leona had anticipated, though not from her own mouth.

Although she had but ten lines to speak for herself, New York talked for her, and before many weeks were over her head, the chief subject of comment in that great city was the marvellous beauty of the Captain of the Guard in "Semiramis."

– CHAPTER 9 –

MR JOHN ROUSE

Just twelve months after the events related in the last chapter, a young woman was standing before a mirror in a pleasant, cheerful-looking room in one of the most respectable—if not one of the most fashionable—streets of New York.

It was Leona Lacoste, or, to designate her as she was generally known, Elena d'Acosta. She had now been a year upon the stage, and though she had not yet made the fortune prophesied for her by Mr. John Rouse, she was earning sufficient money to keep herself in comfort and respectability, and had also managed to lay aside a few dollars against sickness or any other emergency. She was rapidly gaining favour with the manager of the Memphis from her love of her art and steady application to business; and from having stood on the stage to be admired as the Captain of the Guard, had been promoted to fill all the male parts that could be adequately represented by a woman.

As she stood before the mirror thoughtfully trying the effect of a white horsehair wig, it was easy to read from the expression of her face and the lines that had developed about her eyes and mouth, that the qualities of which she had so strongly evinced the possession before coming to New York, had increased rather than lessened with the experience of the year. There was the same strange liquid light in the golden-brown eyes that had driven half the youth of the city crazy to get an introduction to the beautiful Brazilian; the sunny head she had so ruthlessly shorn of its glory when it served her purposes to do so, was again crowned with a rippling veil of chestnut tresses; her complexion—the curves of her mouth, her creamy skin—were as delicate as they had ever been; but there was an older, more matured look about Leona now than the passage of a twelvemonth warranted, and which seemed quite beyond the belief of her eighteen summers. It was *thought* that had done this—thought and anxiety; and even Valera imagined at times the presence of tears; though of what Leona should be afraid altogether passed his comprehension. He had watched over her since their arrival in New York with the solicitude of a father, brother, and lover combined, but had been totally unable to discover any reason for her occasional fits of despondency and restlessness. He attributed them at last to the reaction of her life of excitement, and sighed that it was beyond his power to induce her to resign it.

He had been terribly jealous at first of the sensation she caused and the admiration she excited, and his hot Spanish blood had risen in revolt against the daring aspirants to her favour, who sent her letters, and flowers, and presents as intimations of their wishes. But when he saw how utterly indifferent Leona was to all their advances, how little she valued the offerings or the adulation, and how strenuously she refused the acquaintanceship of her admirers, Valera ceased to thirst for an occasion of taking their blood. It was really not worth while to waste his time fighting for a woman who knew so well how to look after herself, and the most wary and scrupulous lover could not have found fault with the nonchalant manner with which Elena d'Acosta received the advances of the public.

Yet Christobal himself had made no way with her. Affectionate she was to him as she had ever been; he was still her Christal and her brother; and when he was cross and had to be coaxed into good humour again, her Tobal and Tobalito—but there she drew a line. She did not give him all her confidence. Christobal felt, even whilst her kisses were on his brow, that there was a locked chamber in her heart into which he had never penetrated.

Yet could he have rifled it he would not have found much to help to unravel the mystery—only an old letter and a signet-ring, and the memory of hateful, scorching words that burned into her very soul.

She never alluded to it, but it was always there, and her dreams of revenge were fast riveted, if indistinct. She was like the beautiful panther whom she so much resembled. Leona was crouched now, silent and motionless, but her eyes were stealthily set upon the one object of her hate, and she was ready to spring directly the opportunity presented itself.

How absurd to be writing of wild beasts and thoughts of revenge when a beautiful woman is in the case! Leona was more beautiful this year than she had been last, and as Christobal Valera quietly entered her apartments and watched her settling the horsehair wig first to one side and then the other, he thought so too.

"Well, *m'amie*, and how long will it be before you have persuaded that bundle of horsehair to sit to your satisfaction?"

"*Sanctissima!* Tobal, how you startled me! What do you mean by gliding in like a cat o' mountain, and frightening a woman out her seven senses? But how pale you are, *mon frère!* What is the matter?"

"Nothing! A touch of the sun, perhaps. It is powerful enough to-day. And what may that new erection be for, Leona?"

"For the Chevalier de Poigny, in the new melodrama, monsieur. How shall I look in a powdered *queue* and primrose satin knee-breeches embroidered in gold, eh, Tobal?"

"Another male costume," grumbled Valera. "How I hate to see you fill these men's parts, Leona! Cannot Mr. Burrage give you a character more befitting your sex? He is making a perfect trade of you."

"Bah! Stop thy foolish tongue," replied the girl. "The chief gives me the parts I fill best, of course. If you want me to play women, you had better think of some means of exchanging my stature. I am too tall for the boys as it is. I believe I've grown this last year. I shall never find a man to acknowledge I am the right height for a woman," she went on, laughing, "'*just as high as his heart*,' unless I make up to the American giant."

"I know a heart you have never out-stripped," said Valera,

quietly.

"*Mon frère*, you must really be ill! you are beginning to talk sentiment again. I thought I had cured you of that, ages ago. Not only sentiment but nonsense (if they are not one and the same thing), for you know my height has equalled yours some time past."

Which, indeed, was true; for as the friends stood side by side before the looking-glass, there was not a quarter of an inch to choose between them."

"I have news for you, Leona!" said Valera, after a pause.

"Good news, I hope!"

"That is as you take it. I ought to think it good. My employers express themselves so much pleased with the manner in which I have transacted their business during the last year, that they are about to advance me to a post of honour."

"I am so glad! What is it, Tobal?"

"They intend to send me on a mission involving some trust, to one of their corresponding firms in England."

"To England! You are going to England?"

The very name of the country seemed to affect Leona so palpably that she changed colour.

"I believe so. I should have refused the offer on the spot, Leona, entailing as it does, a separation from yourself, but it was intimated to me that to do so would be greatly to militate against my interests in the trade, and perhaps prevent my ever having such a chance of promotion again."

"Of course. You would he mad not to accept it. It is a proof of your employers' trust in you. You cannot tell to what it may lead. When do you start?"

"Next month, I believe."

"It will do you good. Christal, you are really not well to-day. Your eyes look sunk to me."

"It is fancy, m'amie! I am only tired. But with respect to my visit to England. They say I may be absent for a year, and I thought it would be such a good opportunity for you to get an introduction to the English stage, Leona."

"*For me?*" she echoed, sharply. "No, thank you, Tobal. I prefer to remain where I am."

Her Father's Name

"And have you no wish to see England, then?"

The girl's face darkened like a thunder-cloud.

"To see the country my father hated—mix with the people he could not speak of without a shudder. What do you take me for, Christobal? Have I not commanded you never to mention the name of England to me? I will not go! That is enough! Let me hear no more about it! I *remain here*," she concluded, with a stamp of her foot upon the carpet. Valera seemed too weary to argue the matter.

"Very good, *m'amie*. Don't be angry about it," he answered, quietly.

Leona turned round and caught the look of suffering. "Oh! you are ill," she exclaimed, affectionately, as she took a seat on the couch beside him and essayed to draw his head down on her bosom; "rest yourself here, and let me order you some cooling drink. Shall I?" she continued coaxingly, as she pressed her fresh lips upon his feverish forehead.

But the position and the action seemed to torture Valera. He struggled into a sitting posture again. Do what he could, he had not been able to teach his heart to regard Leona as a sister. He could not accept so much from her without wishing for more.

"Any amount of flowers as usual!" he said, with a faint attempt at a laugh, as he regarded the bouquets on the table.

"Yes! some fool sent them into my dressing-room last night. He did not give his name, so I could not return them. General Bastell forwarded me a lovely set of opals yesterday forenoon. I sent them back to him by post this morning, labelled, 'Declined with thanks.' Won't he be in a rage when he opens the parcel?"

"You are a good girl, Leona," said Valera admiringly; "a good, honest girl."

"Holy Virgin! what do you expect me to be? Had I kept the jewels, what would the old General have wished me to take next? Himself, perhaps. *Merci, monsieur!* I don't know about being honest, but I wish you would credit me with a little taste."

"The New Yorkers consider your taste only too exclusive. The complaint is that no one can even get a chance of making himself agreeable to you."

"Let them explain. My exclusiveness must have, at all events, the charm of novelty to them."

"I'm not the one to find fault with it," said Valera, "And when is the new wig to be worn, Leona?"

"To-night. Won't you come and see its *début?*"

"I will if I can. Who plays with you?"

"De Brassey, as usual. What a stick that woman is. By the way, you *must* come, Tobal, for I have to fight a duel for her, and it will remind you of old times to see me handling a pistol."

"Don't speak of those old times, I implore you. I shudder when I recall them."

"What a goose you are. It gave me a fright at the moment, but I have quite got over it now. I often think of poor Guzman, though, and wonder if my shot left any permanent effect on him."

"Your eyes would have wounded him far more deeply had he known who you were. I sometimes fancied he had half a suspicion."

"There you are, off on your hobby-horse again," cried Leona. "A man cannot look at a woman with interest, but you think he must be in love with her! You must be over head and ears in love yourself with somebody or other, or your mind could not be for ever running on the same subject."

"You have heard the rumour, I suppose, about me and the second Miss Halliday?"

"No; what is it?" said the girl, sharply.

"New York is quite certain that since Mr. Halliday has been kind enough to admit me to his Sunday evening gatherings, he is desirous I should become more nearly connected with his family. And the link to unite us is said to be Miss Amy Halliday."

"What! that red-haired little animal!"

"Her hair is not red, Leona. It is a very pretty colour—a few shades lighter than your own."

"Please not to make any comparisons between us. The girl is as freckled as a toad."

"Is she freckled?" demanded Valera, absently.

"Oh! of course, *you* can't see it. That is but natural. Love is blind, as all the world knows."

"My dear Leona, you do not imagine for a moment there is any truth in the report?"

"Well, I should rather hope *not!* I never thought *much* of your taste, Christal, but I should give you up altogether if you stooped to admire Miss Amy Halliday. Not that they wouldn't be glad to get you for her. I have no doubt of that, though you *are* only a corresponding clerk. Mr. Halliday has it in his power to make you almost anything he chooses, and the girl has hung on hand long enough, Heaven knows! She must be six-and-twenty if she's a day."

"She is just my own age," replied Valera.

"Oh! you have taken the trouble to ascertain *that*, have you? Saints defend us! I had no idea matters had gone so far. Well, I wish you joy, Christobal, I wish you joy!" continued Leona, in a heated, fluttered manner. "It will be an excellent match for you, and if a man *must* make a fool of himself he may as well do it by marriage as any other way."

"Leona!—*m'amie!* Have I not told you it is merely a report?"

"It signifies nothing to me if it is a report or no."

"But it is everything to me! How do you suppose for a minute I *could* love Miss Halliday?"

"Oh! men can love anything with what *they* call love."

"But you have always known, I have always told you—"

"Christal, I don't want any explanations! If it will further your interests to marry that woman—or any other woman—marry her! I shall think you're a fool, but that is of no consequence. You will have plenty of companions in folly! Men marry every day, and repent every day into the bargain. Only—only—"

"*I shall lose my brother, that's all,*" replied the girl in a low voice.

Valera sprung to her side, and threw one arm round her waist.

"*Never!* my dearest! you will never lose your brother, come what may. I would rather be your friend, Leona, than the husband of any other woman in the world."

At this assertion, vehemently given, the golden eyes that had just become to look suspiciously soft and humid twinkled with mirth again.

"Ah! you'll never be both at once, Tobal. My friend must be free to be my friend. I will wrong no one by robbing her of her lover."

"I never mean to be the lover of any but yourself, my darling."

Leona turned and took his handsome face between her hands, and looked into his eyes and laughed.

"Chut, chut! little Spanish goose. Don't waste time crying for the moon, for she will never come down to you. But I like my brother Tobalito better than I do any man, and I will be his friend for ever, and for ever, and for ever. So!"

She kissed him on the brow and eyes and mouth, slapped his cheeks each side lightly with her open hand, and humming a tune, applied herself once more to the contemplation of her head-dress.

Such little scenes were constantly taking place between them, and after each Valera felt that he was no farther off and no nearer to Leona than he had been in the wilds of Brazil. Only, whilst she declined a warmer affection from him herself, she evinced a very strong disinclination to his becoming intimate with any other woman.

That evening she looked out eagerly for him as she emerged from her dressing-room at the theatre, but he was nowhere to be seen. She was conscious that the powdered *queue* and the primrose satin knee-breeches embroidered in gold much became her; and although she somewhat dreaded his animadversions on her costume, she knew he could not fail to admire her in it; and somehow—she had so few intimate friends in New York—no applause seemed worth much to Leona unless Valera echoed it. So she stood in her gorgeous attire at the open dressing-room door, watching anxiously all who came behind the scenes, but there was no appearance of her adopted brother. A stranger came by presently, at sight of whom she slightly withdrew, for the purpose of letting him pass. But instead of passing he stopped short, and gazed at the splendid apparition she presented, as though unable to believe his eyes. Leona recognised him then, and, starting back, was about to close her sanctum; but it was too late.

"*Is* it? *can* it be? Yes! surely it is my beautiful little Brazilian!" cried the stranger, as he held out his hand. "And it's you alone I've come this very evening to see. Don't you remember me, my dear? John Rouse, who offered you an engagement in Boston, which you wouldn't take after all, you little baggage, all along of that Spanish fellow with the big black eyes. And now I suppose you've forgotten me?"

"Oh no, monsieur," replied Leona, but with a kind of troubled, uneasy manner, that was very unlike her usual nonchalance. "I have not forgotten you, and I was very grateful for your offer. Only I wanted to come here instead."

"Yes, yes; I understand. It was all that Spanish fellow. And where is he now? You've quarrelled with him long ago, I bet, and got another by this time, or perhaps half-a-dozen, eh? By George! I shouldn't wonder at your breaking the hearts of the whole city in that dress. And so Burrage has got you, has he? Well, I hate Burrage for it, my dear, that's all. I made the first offer, and you ought to have belonged to me. However, I won't bear malice. I wish you every success, and I shall go round to the front and watch your play all through."

"You are very good, monsieur. I am afraid my dress is the best part of me, though."

"Burrage doesn't think so. He's very well pleased with your progress, and says you've got the right stuff in you. Well, don't forget Boston when you want another engagement. I've set my little theatre going nicely there, but I haven't got a woman like you on the boards. However, I shall see you again, my dear, before I go. Ta-ta."

And Mr. John Rouse walked off to ensconce himself in the stage-box, and await the rising of the curtain.

Leona's heart beat fast. She tried to reason herself out of such folly by contemplating the simple fact Valera had tried to impress upon her mind, and no one could carry her off to Boston against her will, or force her into any closer connection with Mr. John Rouse than her inclination pointed to. Yet she felt restless and uneasy by his very presence. A presentiment of evil seemed to come over her, and make her believe she should never be happy till she had heard he had left the city again.

She knew the reason of her alarm, but she knew also that it was perfectly inadequate to the alarm itself. Yet the palpitation her interview with the Boston manager had caused, rendered her so nervous and unlike herself, that she felt she played worse that evening than she had ever done before. The wonderful exactitude with which she mimicked the gait, gestures, and expressions of the other sex, had been the marvel of New York, and the means of her being constantly brought before the public in the character of men and boys. It seemed much more natural to Leona to play a man's part than a woman's; indeed, her own character was almost too strongly marked to enable her to assume the latter winningly and softly enough to be pleasant on the stage. She could portray the passions of jealousy, revenge, or hatred to the life, and as a murderess she was perfection; but the loving, submissive, tender female characters had to be entrusted to girls, with not a tithe of her real deep womanly feeling, because they *looked* so much what they ought to have been. But though Leona, between her uneasiness at missing Valera, and her annoyance at having met Mr. Rouse, fancied she was not doing herself justice as the Chevalier de Poigny, and that that unfortunate lover breathed out slaughter against his traducers in a style not wholly accordant with his undaunted courage, the Boston manager was evidently not of the same opinion. He left the box after the first scene, and came behind, teeming with congratulations and compliments.

"I knew you'd make an actress! I told your Spanish friend so the first time I saw you. Mdlle. d'Acosta, permit me to shake you by the hand. You ought to be proud, mademoiselle; you have made a great success. I never saw a man's part better filled by a woman. You will rival the great Dejazet[*] herself."

"I am on again, almost directly," said Leona, only anxious to get away from her officious admirer.

"The next is the garden scene, where I fight a duel, and I have to be concealed behind the bushes during the opening dialogue. I am afraid I must go. Hadn't you better cross to your box, monsieur? The next set of scenery almost closes the wings."

"Ah, well, I've just caught sight of Burrage, I must speak to him first, and then I'll find my way back as best I can. You'll make your fortune yet, my dear. My prophecy will be justified. See if it isn't."

She shrunk from him slightly, as he patted her on the shoulder, and went at once to take up her place at the wings. As she stood behind the painted bushes where she had (as she told Rouse) to wait during the opening dialouge, she found the scenery blocked her exit at that side.

"There's no exit here," she remarked to one of the scene-shifters. "Can't you move that tree?"

---

[*] Pauline Virginia Dejazet, famous French actress (1798-1875).

"Not very well, miss. The groove's broken. Do you come off this side?"

"No; left."

"We may leave it, then?"

"Oh yes; you may as well, if there's to be any trouble. Move the bush a little forward so as to give me full shelter. That'll do. Thanks."

She was now caged, as it were, with no means of escaping until the scene was over. One piece of scenery leaning against the other blocked all egress. She could do nothing but stand there until she heard the cue for her entrance.

The curtain rose upon the garden scene. The characters concerned in the opening were assembled on the stage. Leona prepared herself for a term of waiting. It was irksome, but she had preferred it to going behind and running the risk of another encounter with the Boston manager. But as she stood there, voices in conversation broke upon her ear. They proceeded from behind the painted canvas that formed the background of the stage, and were distinct to her although inaudible in front. At the first word that reached her she started, for they were the voices of Mr. Barrage and Mr. Rouse that spoke, and the subject of their conversation was herself.

– CHAPTER 10 –

LEONA'S OATH

"She has been a great success here," said Mr. Benjamin Burrage, "and she'll be a greater success still if she goes on as she has begun. She has a genuine love for the art, sir, and I like to see that in my company. I engaged her at first for nothing on earth but her beauty, but I soon saw what she was made of, and her progress during twelve months is wonderful. Her part to-night is a real difficult one, and wants lots of acting. She's the cleverest male impersonator I've ever seen, and makes an uncommon pretty fellow from the front."

"That she does. I've been thirsting for your blood all the

evening, Burrage. I consider she ought to belong to me, for I made her the first offer of an engagement."

"Why didn't she take it?"

"Can't tell you. She was travelling in company with a young Spaniard then, whom she called her brother."

"I know him—Valera. He *is* her brother, or half brother, or something."

"Well, my opinion is, he's 'something.' At all events, after having accepted my terms most readily, the girl suddenly changed her mind, and refused to sign the agreement; and the brother (or whatever he is) said it was the separation from him she objected to."

("I'll be revenged on Tobal for this!" thought Leona, who was listening to every word the men spoke. "What does he mean by making inferences that damage my reputation. *Object to be separated from him*, forsooth! By St. Jago! monsieur thinks enough of himself.")

"Very likely," said Burrage, in reply. "They are always together and I'm very glad the fair d'Acosta wouldn't leave him, my good fellow, however much I may sympathise with your disappointment."

"A manager's sympathy for the losses of his fellow-manager!" replied Rouse, laughing. "I could put all that in my eye and see none the worse for it. But I tell you why I don't believe Valera is any relation to that girl. Because she is not Spanish!"

"She's Brazilian."

"Well, that's not Spanish, though I'm not quite prepared to believe that either. At least she has Brazilian blood in her, but it's mixed with European. You never saw a pure Brazilian with chestnut-coloured hair."

"Don't know that I have, now you come to speak of it," said Burrage, indifferently.

"She is of European build, too, and complexion. The Brazilian blood comes out in her eyes and disposition more than in anything else. She reminds me powerfully of one of my old Liverpool friends. I can hardly disconnect her from him in my thoughts."

"Why, who's that?"

"One of the Evans of the great Liverpool firm, you know."

"Never heard of them."

"Never heard of the firm of Evans and Troubridge at Liverpool? My dear fellow you must be joking. They're largely connected with the West India trade."

"But what have they to do with d'Acosta?"

(At this juncture of the conversation Leona was in danger of missing her cue. Each sense in her body appeared to have frozen except the sense of hearing. She stood bolt-upright against the canvas scenery, straining her ears that she might not lose a single syllable, whilst her heart seemed paralysed with fear of what might be coming).

"Well, nothing, I suppose, except that her expression reminds me of the elder son. Don't you remember the fuss that took place some five-and-twenty years ago about a murder that was committed in Liverpool on a merchant's clerk, and the man that did it could never be traced?"

"I do, now you remind me of it. Wasn't the man that was murdered called Abraham Anson?"

"Exactly so; and a friend of mine, called George, was supposed to be the murderer."

"Nice sort of friends you had in those days."

"No; but listen. There were two brothers, George and Henry, and I had known them from boyhood. The head of the firm was their uncle, old Theophilus Evans, and he had a confidential clerk that had been with him for years, called Anson. At the time the murder took place, George, the elder nephew, was only about two-and-twenty, and the uncle openly gave out that the property was to be divided between the brothers. Well, George was wild, there's no doubt about that. He was a fine, handsome fellow, always getting into a scrape over cards, or women, or some such rubbish, and Anson used to help him out of them. He was awfully fond of George, was old Anson. That's why I never could quite believe George did it."

"What, cut his throat?"

"Not exactly; but the poor man was killed through violence. He used to sleep on the premises, and one morning, it was the month of June—I remember it as if it had happened yesterday—the till was found to have been broken open and robbed, and the clerk murdered. There was an awful stir about it at the time."

"But why did the suspicion fall upon the nephew?"

"Because he bolted! He was never seen afterwards, and witnesses were found to prove he and Anson had had high words the night before over some money George wanted to borrow, and the other wouldn't, or couldn't lend. So I'm afraid there is little doubt who did it."

"*Never seen afterwards!* That's queer!"

"Never! They had the police out in every direction, but it is one of those few cases in which they were completely baffled. How the fellow got off scot-free beats me entirely."

"Perhaps he was murdered too."

"It must be one or the other. Either George murdered Anson, or he shared his fate."

"What do they think in Liverpool?"

"They have no doubt whatever of his guilt. Long ago as it happened, the story is quite fresh in Liverpool still, and anyone will tell it you. It killed the old uncle. He died about six months afterwards, leaving all his fortune to the younger brother, Henry. *He's* rich, if you like."

"Going on with the firm?"

"Oh! I believe you, and got a corresponding house in London, where he lives himself. They do enormous business. I generally see him when I cross the duck-pond."

"Married?"

"Yes; but only got one sickly daughter to inherit all his wealth. By jingo! what that fellow George missed by making that awful mistake. He'd have been one of the wealthiest men in London by this time."

"You believe he committed the murder then?"

"No, sir, I don't," exclaimed Mr. Rouse, emphatically. "I *can't* believe it of him; but he might just as well have done it, as far as this world goes, for you'll never convince it that he didn't. No, no! I believe he's dead, poor fellow! Dead and buried; and I hope he may be with all my heart, for I should be sorry to credit so much ill of him."

"Mr. Burrage, sir," exclaimed the stage-manager, rushing upon them with a frightened look. "We don't know what on earth to do with d'Acosta. She's fainted or something behind the wings, and she ought to be on. Shall we bring the curtain down?"

"Confound it, what's the matter?" cried Mr. Burrage, as he heard the news. "Where's her exit?"

"It's blocked; she ordered it to be left so. We can't get at it, except from the front, and they say she's insensible!"

"Bring down the curtain at once," roared the manager, excitedly. "What the deuce can have happened to cause this? Stay, I must go on in front and make an apology."

And in another moment, breathless and heated, Mr. Burrage might have been heard stammering out to the people in front:

"Ladies and gentlemen, it is with regret I have to inform you that a sudden indisposition on the part of Mddle. Elena d'Acosta compels us to drop the curtain, but if you will accord us your patience for a few minutes, we trust to be able to raise it again, and proceed with the play."

His speech was received with much clapping of hands, but he hardly stayed long enough to acknowledge it with a bow, before he rushed to the assistance of Leona. He found her laid in the centre of the stage, to all appearance lifeless, whilst the other women were loosening her dress and pouring water on her face, and otherwise much interfering with the attempts which nature was making to enable her to regain her consciousness.

At last she opened her eyes, with a sleepy, languid expression, and let them rove slowly round the circle. As they fell upon the figures of Mr. Burrage and Mr. Rouse, the frightened scared look that came into them was apparent to all, and with a violent effort Leona staggered to her feet, as though, then and there, she was about to rush off the stage.

"Stop, my dear! You are not strong enough to walk by yourself, yet," said Mr. Burrage, kindly.

"But where am I? What have I been doing? Why doesn't the play go on?" she inquired, hurriedly, and then perceiving the state of her costume, and of the stage, she continued, "Oh! have I been ill? How stupid of me! What will Mr. Burrage say?"

"Mr. Burrage says nothing, my dear," said that gentleman, answering for himself, "except that the curtain shan't go up again till you feel better. It's the heat and standing so long that's been too much for you."

"But I *am* better, thank you. Do let the curtain go up. Do go on at once! I am all right again now. I am quite able to do my work."

"Drink this," said Mr. Rouse, who had been employed in procuring her a stimulant. "This will fetch you up, my dear, in no time."

She shrunk from the glass he tendered her as if it had been poison, and clung to Burrage's arm.

"You *must* take it," said the latter. "It'll do you good, and then go to your dressing room and arrange yourself, and we'll stop that infernal orchestra and have the curtain up again."

"You aren't fit to go through with it," whispered a sympathising female, who accompanied her to her room.

"I *will* go through with it," was Leona's reply, as she set her teeth together and nerved herself for the coming trial.

Her reappearance on the stage was hailed by the acclamation of the whole house; and every fresh point met with fresh applause which enabled the young actress to keep up until the end. But as the play concluded, all her artificial power faded. She had not even strength enough to appear before the curtain in answer to the many calls upon her name; and Mr. Burrage had again to apologise for her defalcation. All she could do was to murmur, "Do get me a car and let me go home;" and refusing the company of any of her friends, she took her departure to her own rooms alone.

* * * * * *

But it was not to take the rest she so much required after her sudden illness.

Hours and hours after the theatre had closed, and all the members of the household had gone to sleep, Leona sat in her room, pondering over what she had heard Rouse say to Burrage. Her memory, which fainting had somewhat blurred, became distinct and clear again, and she could recall each word that had passed between them with painful accuracy. That great and awful fear, which had never slept since the finding of the letter and the ring, though she had tried with all the strength of her loving faith to her father's memory to stamp it out—oppressed her mind almost to madness. What was it that Rouse had said: *That either George Evans had murdered Abraham Anson, or shared his fate!* She knew—George Evans's daughter knew—that he had not shared the clerk's fate. What then? what then? Was she to believe her father a murderer, against his own dying protestations of innocence, just because Mr. Rouse thought it must be so?

Who was Mr. Rouse that he should constitute himself a judge of her dear father's actions?

Yet if he were innocent why had he left England to make his home in a foreign land under a disguised name? Why had he renounced the expectation of a large fortune to live an impoverished life in Rio Janeiro? Why was he so shy of his fellow-creatures? Why did he call himself Louis Lacoste? Why could he never be persuaded to move out of the stupid little town in which he had fixed his residence, or to visit any larger, more public place, even for a few hours? Why did the threats of that wretch Ribeiro have the power to make the unhappy man cut short the thread of his own existence, sooner than run the risk of their being put into execution?

As these questions presented themselves one after another to the mind of the poor child, she laid her head down on the table and groaned.

They made up a startling array of evidence against her father. There was no doubt of that. A disinterested judge would at once have given it against him. But his daughter was not disinterested. He had been the one great love of her life whilst his lasted; and now she loved his memory with her whole soul. She would not—she could not—believe him guilty, although the facts of his guilt seemed too clear for any filial love to overcome. But whenever Leona tried to put her affection out of sight, and reason impartially upon the matter, the remembrance of the love that had existed between them—of the timid, retired, suffering life he had led—of the silver hair prematurely whitened by secret fear and sorrow, rose up to provoke all her womanly pity for the weak and oppressed—all her womanly resentment against the oppressor; and she argued (as loving women will) in favour of the object of her devotion against all the clearer, higher, and wiser instincts of her nature. It is not because women are ungifted with reasoning powers that they will not reason. In nine cases out of ten they are quite as well aware as the other sex on which side is right.

And in the very fact that they *do* know, lies hid the motive of their ranging their forces on the other. It is a common saying that a woman invariably takes the weaker side, and the weaker is usually the wrong side—for Right is Power.

But they do it from generosity—mistaken, perhaps, but still lovable. Women would cease to be women had they not a few weak points about them. "What! all on one side?" they cry. "The whole world pitted against *one*. What a shame!" And over they go to try what their tender arms can effect in keeping off the enemy.

And this is what troubled Leona so greatly.

In her case, so awful a result hung upon the crumbling of her faith, that it is not to be wondered at if she would have bitten out her tongue sooner than confess she was mistaken. Every time a doubt intruded itself upon her mind, her father's last words—his dying words, as he knew them to be—rose up to battle with the half-conviction, and overthrow it.

"*If, in years to come, they should ever tell you that your father committed great crimes, don't believe them. I have led a thoughtless and dissipated life, but not a criminal one.*"

Each look on his poor worn face—each tone of his suffering, humbled voice, came back to her with the memory of those words. What was to her the opinion of the whole world compared to the half confession which the anticipation of death had wrung from the father she had loved.

"*Don't believe anything they say against me, Leona; your father is true, remember that! Foolish, but true.*"

She *would* believe it. No power on earth should shake her trust again in the complete innocence of the dear parent whose worst crime lay in his weakness. She had been frightened out of that perfect trust. The finding of the letter and the ring after his death had shaken it. But Mr. Rouse's story had thrown a new light upon them. Had he not said that Abraham Anson had always been extremely fond of her father; and what more natural then, that he should have given him the ring as a keepsake. The letter proved the intimacy that must have existed between them.

Leona felt that had she known these facts when she first read that letter it would not have made her so miserable. She drew it from the safe repository where she had always kept it under lock and key, and unfolding its worn and yellow paper, perused its contents anew.

It was dated the 8th of June, five-and-twenty years before, and bore no address:

"DEAR MASTER GEORGE,

"I was sorry to miss you when you called at office yesterday, but the woman says she explained to you that I had been sent for up to the house. The chief mentioned your name. I'm sorry to say he's heard about that business with the Levitt's girl, and wanted me to give him particulars. I pretended to know nothing of the affair, but it appears old Levitt has been up to the house, so I'd get away for a short time, Master George, if I was you. I don't want to have to say anything, so I hope the chief won't put me on my oath; but I think the matter might be settled by money. Levitt's very close-fisted, and I shouldn't wonder if that's all he cares about.

"I am sorry to read the last part of your letter, especially as it seems so urgent. Is there no other way out, Master George? I'd do it for you directly, and welcome, if it was in my power, and that you must know. But if I try and bleed the chief again just now, it will bring the Levitt affair right about your ears. I'm sure you'll excuse me saying you're rather hot at times, Master George, and I'm afraid it would be risky for you and the chief to meet just now. I wish you could go away for a bit.

"I shall be at home this evening if you'd like to step up and talk it over. But don't ask me for the money, for I haven't got it—nor can I get it either. Come as late as you can, for fear of interruption. Master Henry might drop in, he said; and I know he carries tales of us to the chief sometimes. The chief himself was very crusty to-day, and when I asked for a little advance, grumbled at my poor cornelian ring, and said if I was in want of money I had no right to wear jewellery. I have more to tell you when we meet.

"Your obedient servant,

"ABRAHAM ANSON.

"P.S.—I forgot to send you my grateful thanks for your kind remembrance of little Lucy. Never mind about the other loan just now, Master George. I don't like to hear you talk about being desperate."

* * * * * *

The Eighth of June. And the morning on which the murder had been discovered was the ninth. She had heard Rouse say so. This letter had been written on the previous day, asking her father to go late and meet Anson at the office, where, the next morning, he had been found *dead*. And then her father had disappeared, and witnesses had been brought forward to prove that he and the clerk had had high words together the night before—the very night on which Anson had invited him to come—high words about money, which the one wanted to borrow, and the other wouldn't or couldn't lend. How the facts she had heard, and the facts she saw written, fitted into and tallied with each other. How her heart sickened as she watched the pieces of the puzzle accommodate themselves to one another with the greatest ease. How her brain whirled in its endeavour to separate truth from falsehood, and to account by some plausible reason for her father's disappearance, and the clerk's death; or at all events to do away with the various circumstances that so mysteriously bound them together. But everything seemed against her. Even the mention of the cornelian ring appeared written on purpose to divest her mind of the fond idea that it had been given by Abraham Anson to her father! It was hardly likely the clerk had had two cornelian rings, and this one, which on the last day of his life he mentioned as wearing, had his initials, A. A., scratched on the inside of the setting. Who was this "Levitt girl" too, of whom Anson evidently knew so much? Had her father promised her marriage and failed to keep his word, that "Old Levitt" (as the letter termed him), had "gone up to the house" about it? Oh, what was it all about? What was the mystery? How should she ever unravel it, and clear her poor father's name from the disgrace and contumely that had fallen upon it.

At this juncture Leona's long-tried courage failed, and laying her head down upon her outstretched arms, she wept bitterly. It was an awful trial of her fortitude. She believed, and she did not believe. She believed her dying father's word, but the crushing facts that had been unfolded to her opposed themselves to her faith like blocks of granite hurled against a beautiful flower. The blossom has all the life, the perfume, and the freshness, but it cannot live beneath the weight of solid stone. But as the girl wept for her inability to confront and overcome the verdict of the world, a great resolution took possession of her soul. So confident was she that, had her father been guilty of the awful crime imputed to him, he would not have had the courage to say those last words to her, that she felt convinced that it was to her, his child, who had the missing link of his existence, that the Creator had deputed the task of clearing his name from obloquy and shame. The people in England might believe him to have been the murderer, because they knew nothing of his subsequent life—but she, who had heard both sides of the question, was the person of all others best fitted to unravel the mystery to the very end.

And she would pledge her life to the performance of so sacred a duty. As Leona came to this decision she rose from her seat, looking more grand and beautiful in her solitude than she had ever done before a crowd, and raising her eyes and hands to heaven, called on the Almighty to register her oath, and reward her according as she fulfilled it.

She knew she would have to work in the dark. She hardly knew yet how she must work, or when the opportunity to commence would arise. But she felt that her oath was binding. She knew her decision to be irrevocable; and, worn out in mind and body, found further exertion for that night to be impossible to her. So she flung herself upon her bed as carelessly as might be, and strove to forget the turmoil of her mind in sleep.

– CHAPTER 11 –

THE LETTER OF INTRODUCTION

There is many a battle fought in the night that leaves no traces for the rising day to mock at. When Leona Lacoste rose from her bed upon the following morning, she knew she had a self-imposed duty of which she must never again lose sight; yet she applied herself to fulfil the routine of her everyday employments as calmly as if she had registered no oath before high Heaven. Solemn and stately she ever was, for the now civilised life which she had been leading for the last twelve months had had no power to destroy the glorious southern nonchalance which had imbued her being, and those about her could not perceive any difference in the proud bearing and lofty demeanour which made them at all times rather diffident of intruding their confidence upon the beautiful actress. So many a one or, as may be written with greater truth—so, almost *everyone* walks through this world a sealed book to his neighbour, who looks at him and sighs, and envies his placidity, comparing it favourably with the turmoil that rages in his own breast. Mademoiselle d'Acosta went through the rehearsal of some new part that morning in a manner to call forth the honest praise of Mr. Burrage. She even met the Boston manager's inquiries after her health without (apparently) a tremor, and parried the various conjectures that met her as to the cause of her sudden illness with admirable skill. Nor did she feel much more unhappy than usual. The decision at which she had arrived was but the culmination of the doubts and difficulties that had beset her since her father's death. There was no more to conceal and grieve at than she had concealed and grieved at since that time. The only difference in her feelings perhaps was that she experienced less cordiality towards her fellow creatures, and was more ready to suspect and disbelieve them than she had formerly been. Before the day was ended, also, her thoughts received an impetus in another direction. Valera wrote to tell her he was ill. A bilious headache, he affirmed, brought on by over-exertion in the sun, alone affected him, but he must stay at home and nurse it for his employers' sake. Leona had expected to see him that afternoon, and she was disappointed. Somehow, she could seldom interest herself in her ordinary occupations unless Christobal were by her side. It seemed so natural to see him in her rooms—lounging on the sofa and playing with Pepita, or smoking his cigar in the balcony, whilst she was busied in altering her dresses, or copying out her parts. It reminded her of the old childish days when they had always been together, and the absence of Valera put everything out of joint; particularly as that day she required his company, so

Her Father's Name

she told herself, to help to dissipate the unpleasant recollections that still lingered in her mind. And she wrote a jesting but affectionate little note in Spanish, telling him not to be such a baby as to mind a headache, but to come to her as soon as ever he was able, and let her cure it for him. But her answer did not have the effect she imagined. On the next day there was no communication from her adopted brother. Then Leona grew anxious. Impulsive, and accustomed from infancy to accept the dictates of her own heart as the best test of what she should do, she felt no hesitation in calling at Valera's apartments, which were situated a short distance from her own. There she found him in a high fever, and heard that the doctor had been sent for, who, when he arrived, pronounced the young man to be on the brink of an illness, and ordered him at once to bed.

Christobal objected strongly. The prospect which had just opened before him was present to his mind; he felt that he must not be ill, consequently he refused to believe that he could be. The medical man was having a hot time of it when Leona came to the rescue.

"What is this childish nonsense, Tobal?" she said imperiously. "If you are advised to go to bed, to bed you must go."

"But, Leona, consider the consequences of my being ill. It was but yesterday Mr. Upjohn told me my letters of introduction should be ready within the week."

"And if you refuse to obey the doctor's order you will never be able to deliver them. This may be but a passing indisposition, which you would turn by your obstinacy into a dangerous illness. Come, Tobal, if you will not go to bed of your own accord I will put you there."

The young Spaniard laughed at her threat, and dragged himself languidly into the adjoining room. Leona commenced to question the doctor.

"Is he going to be really ill, monsieur?"

"I fear so; but to-morrow will decide. Meanwhile he must be well watched and attended to."

"I shall wait on him myself. Tell me what to do."

"You are a relation of Don Valera's, mademoiselle?"

"I am his sister, monsieur. I should not think of leaving him whilst he is sick."

"I will send a medicine which he must take regularly, and I think ice to his head will relieve the pain. Meanwhile, should he get light-headed, you had better send for me."

Leona bowed her head in answer. She saw trouble advancing on her from the distance like an armed man.

"One word, monsieur. I have engagements that occupy me all the evenings. Will it be difficult to procure a nurse to look after Don Valera in my absence?"

"I can send one at a moment's notice if required. But let us hope he will not require it. He is perfectly sensible and quiet now. The ice may prevent delirium setting in."

As soon as Valera had ensconced himself in bed. Leona commenced to arrange the order of his apartment. He followed her movements with a grateful eye.

"How good you are to me, *m'amie*. Yes, that is right. Place the water-bottle and the sherbet near at hand, that I may reach them readily when you have left me.

"I am not going to leave you, Tobal."

"But that is impossible! How can you stay here?"

"How do other people stay here? There are four walls to enclose them, and furniture for them to use. Where is the difficulty?"

"But, Leona, you do not understand. There are no women lodgers in this house. It is inhabited entirely by young men like myself."

"That is all the more reason that I should remain here then. What do men know about nursing?"

"But your reputation may suffer. People are so apt to talk in this world."

"Bah, Tobal!" she answered, with her ready contempt. "When will you learn how little I care for what the world may say? You are ill, and the doctor declares you require good nursing. That is sufficient. No one nurses you except myself, unless the woman of the house cannot spare time to sit by your bedside whilst I am at the theatre, and then I may have to procure some assistance. But when I am not on the stage I shall be here."

"You are the most generous creature that God ever made," said

Valera, drowsily. He felt unable to argue the point further. The symptoms of the fever he had contracted were already beginning to creep over him. His companion did not comment on his words, but she stood by his side and watched the film that drew over his eyes with sickening fear. She had never been called upon before to measure her affection for Valera by the dread of losing him. But she knew the fatal nature of the fevers of that country, and how rapidly they sometimes run their course. She did not like the sunken look which Valera's eyelids had already assumed, nor the extreme drowsiness which seemed to weigh them down. Had a dozen friends stood in her pathway then and warned her that in resolving to attend on him she would not only risk her character, but lose it, they would have had no effect in making her abandon her post. She was fearless as a lion in a cause of her own adoption, and utterly careless to what others said. So, as soon as she had concluded her performance at the theatre, she settled herself for the night upon the sofa in Valera's sitting-room; greatly, it must be said, to the astonishment and interest of the remaining lodgers in the house, and not a little to the scandal of the landlady. With the morning's sun her worst fears were realised. Christobal was pronounced to be dangerously ill. A professional nurse was engaged to wait on him, whilst Leona was compelled to be absent, and thence followed a week or ten days of anxious suspense, during which the sick man was sometimes worse and sometimes better, but always delirious, and Leona was never quite sure, when she returned from the theatre, whether she might not hear that he was sinking. At the end of that period, however, a decided improvement set in. Valera recovered his consciousness, and, although extremely feeble, began to understand once more what was passing around him, and to take an interest in it. Amongst the first things he asked for were his letters.

"I am not sure if I shall let you have them," replied Leona, playfully.

"Don't keep me waiting," said the invalid. "I am so anxious to know if Upjohn and Halliday have forwarded my letters of introduction, or intend to send another man in my place."

"You need not be afraid of that, Tobal, for Mr. Halliday has sent almost every day to enquire after you, and yesterday the chief clerk called himself to see how soon you were likely to be about again."

"It is very good of them," murmured Valera. "Still, should my convalescence prove a matter of time, they might find it impossible to keep the berth open for me. Give me that large blue envelope, Leona. It has our office seal upon it. Yes, here it is," he continued, eagerly, as his trembling fingers tore the outside cover to pieces.

"*To Messrs Evans and Troubridge, 320, High Holborn,*[*] *London*
"*Favoured by Don Christobal Valera.*"

"*What!*" screamed Leona, forgetting, in her surprise, the necessity of caution.

Her unusual want of self-control brought the hospital nurse bustling into the room to enjoin quiet, and under cover of the little colloquy that followed, she was in some measure enabled to recover herself.

"Why should you be surprised?" demanded Valera, languidly. "Do you know anything about them?"

"No, no, no; how should I? Only—tell me—what have they to do with—Halliday and Upjohn?"

"Why, they are about to enter into business negotiations with them, of course, and I am to settle the preliminaries and get the matter into working order. I shall have three months over there at the least, they tell me. I hope the change will set me up again. I am sure I need it," he added, wearily.

"Of course it will. England is a fine bracing place. But read the contents of the letter, Tobal. Or shall I read them to you?"

She was trembling with eagerness to hear if the letter of introduction would throw any light on the subject that so much interested her.

"*You* read it," said Valera. "When I try to fix my eyes on anything, the room seems to go round."

She unfolded the foolscap sheet of paper and read, in rather a shaking voice, as follows:

"Gentlemen, we beg to present to your notice and kind consideration the bearer of these papers, Don Christobal Valera,

---

[*] Area in central London, forms the southern boundary of the Bloomsbury district.

whom we have deputed to act as our agent in all matters relating to the mercantile negotiations about to be opened between your house and ours. Don Valera is a gentleman whom we have known and employed as our foreign correspondent for the last year, and in whose capacity for business, and strict and honourable dealing we place the utmost confidence. Any attention which you may be enabled to show him during his stay amongst you, will be responded to by a man of birth and breeding, and gratefully acknowledged by ourselves.

"We are, Gentlemen,

"Yours faithfully and obliged,

"UPJOHN & HALLIDAY."

Valera's dull eye gained a momentary lustre as he listened to the words.

"It is complimentary, Leona, is it not? I don't know what I've done to deserve it. And the cashier told me I was certain to be asked to stay at Mr. Evan's house, during my visit to England."

"And why not to the other one's—to Mr. Troubridge's?" asked the girl, with tightly compressed lips.

"Oh, because there is no Troubridge. He's been dead for years. But Mr. Evans—Henry Evans I believe his name is—is a regular millionaire, and keeps open house in London for all strangers connected with the business. Rawlins, the cashier, says I shall find him a very good sort of fellow. He met him once when he was over in New York."

"And shall you stay in his house—his very house?" demanded Leona.

"They tell me so. I believe it is situate in Hyde Park, which is one of the grandest parts of London. *Oh, m'amie*, how I wish you were going with me!"

"What use would there be in my going?" said the girl shortly. But she was thinking all the while how she could possibly invent some plausible excuse for accompanying him. *In the house—the very house!*

The idea made her blood turn with excitement even whilst she shuddered with an awful fear.

"Leona, you look pale. This nursing has been too much for you," remarked Valera, affectionately.

"Not so, *mon frère*. Never did a patient give less trouble than you have done. But you must gain more strength before you set foot on board the English steamer."

"I am much better to-night. I am quite ready to go. The sight of that letter has put fresh life in me, Leona. Fancy being three whole months in England, seeing everything of which we have so often read and wondered at together. And there is even a chance, m'amie, that if the business on which I go is satisfactorily concluded within the time, my employers may give me a few weeks' holiday to visit Spain. Oh Spain, my beloved country!" the young man went on excitedly. "Land of sunshine, and love, and pleasure! How my heart beats at the mere idea of seeing thee again, although I was but an infant in arms when I left thy beautiful shores."

"Tobalito, you must not excite yourself like this. You are not strong enough to think such thoughts. Leave your beautiful Spain to herself for a few days longer."

"How can I leave her to herself, Leona? You are not a Spaniard, or you would not ask such an impossibility. You do not know what we feel for our country, even though we may never have had the happiness of being on her shores; of how our hearts are wrapped up in her future, and bleed at the recital of her woes. Oh that I could shed the last drop of blood in my body to see Spain what she ought to be—gem of all the nations and queen of the sunny south!"

"You will live to see it, never fear! If your country has right on her side, my brother, she will conquer at last. But just at this moment your destiny takes you in another direction. In talking of Spain you have forgotten England!"

"*Pesta!* Why recall me from that heavenly dream of music and sunshine, to contemplate the cold, foggy aspect of the north. How can any one live in England who has once heard of Spain?"

"Yet England may prove your passage to her. Think of that, Tobal."

Already he appeared too weary to think any more. The pitch of excitement to which he had worked himself told terribly on his enfeebled condition, and he lay back on his pillows exhausted—almost sinking. Leona applied all the stimulants he was capable of taking, but without success. His heightened pulse would not subside again, and when the doctor visited his patient that evening, he pronounced the progress of the last two days to have been worse than useless.

"Here we have a relapse, I fear, mademoiselle," he said, as he felt the feverish hand and watched the agitated demeanour of the sick man; "and a relapse in these cases, I need not tell you, is much more dangerous than the original complaint. Can you tell me the cause of it?"

"Don Valera insisted upon having his letters to read, and excited himself greatly over the perusal of some of them."

"Exactly, and has let himself in for another fortnight or three weeks, perhaps, of fever. It is very annoying. I should have had him on his feet in a couple of days otherwise. I forbid letters being mentioned to him again."

There was no need of the doctor making this order, for before the night was over Valera was again totally unconscious of everything that surrounded him. All the weary routine of watching and waiting and sitting up had to be recommenced, but his lion-hearted friend took up the burden without a murmur, and appeared never to think of her own trouble, nor the danger she ran of succumbing beneath the weight of her multifarious duties. The day came, however, only too soon, when the doctor told her with a lengthened face that the symptoms of Valera's disease had assumed an infectious character, and that she must either give up nursing him, or going to and from the theatre.

"And my advice to you, mademoiselle, is to resign the care of your brother to the hospital nurse, who will do all that is necessary for him. There are putrid symptoms about his throat that may at any moment endanger your own life, and since your presence here cannot actually afford him any assistance—"

"You advise me to leave him to die alone," said Leona, sharply. "Thank you, monsieur, but that is not *my* idea of a friend."

"But, mademoiselle, your profession then must suffer."

"Let it suffer!"

"Your means of a livelihood—you will not, I trust, think me impertinent for alluding to such a thing—be cut off."

"Let them be cut off!"

"Of course, if mademoiselle has other resources."

"I have no other resources, monsieur."

"Then there is your health to be considered. Pardon me for saying you are too young, too beautiful, that your welfare is of too much consequence—"

"Monsieur, do you think I am a woman, or do you think I am a brute?"

"I consider mademoiselle to be all that is most attractive, most amiable, most—"

She interrupted him curtly.

"I don't believe it. But if you credit me with all these virtues, add to them, at least, one grain of womanly feeling. You tell me that Don Valera—that my brother—is—is—is—"

She could not go on, but stood before him fiercely biting her under lip, and tapping her foot upon the ground.

The doctor saw her repressed emotion, and tried to, help her.

"That Don Valera is in considerable danger is true, mademoiselle."

"And you want me to leave him, sir?" she went on, rapidly gaining strength from excitement. "To leave, him to die like a dog, a pig, a mule in this strange place alone, whilst I fly from infection like a coward, and for the sake of a few dollars! Monsieur, you do not know the blood of which I am made. What! *Go* when my friend most needs me! Let a hired nurse receive his last looks, last wishes, last sighs? *Leave him!* and when his friends are so far away too? Oh, monsieur! you are not a man. You must be a devil to think of such a thing."

She did not weep as an ordinary woman would have done, but she turned as white as death, and raised her eyes to heaven, and shook so violently that she was forced to steady herself by a chair.

"Forgive me, mademoiselle," was all the doctor could find to say.

"You have mistaken me, monsieur," she answered, proudly.

"I see I have. I did not expect to find so much courage, and generosity, and unselfishness in New York. I will not urge you again to act against the dictates of your nature. Will you let me ask you, though, where Don Valera's friends may be?"

"They live a long way from here, monsieur. In Rio Janeiro, whence we came."

"So far as that? Still they should be told of his danger."

"I will write to his mother at once."

"And summon her, if possible, to New York. It is useless disguising the truth from you, mademoiselle, and you have a courage equal to the occasion. If Don Valera survives this second attack, which I consider doubtful, he will require months of careful nursing to reinstate his health. And for that purpose he will have to leave New York, and go into the country or to the seaside."

She bowed her head in token of her comprehension. She could not trust herself to speak—not even to think, excepting one thing—that this stranger must not be allowed to witness her emotion.

"I will do all that is necessary," she managed to say at last, and then the doctor had the mercy to leave her to fight out the battle with herself in secret.

The next day saw the walls of the city placarded with announcements to the effect that, in consequence of "the sudden and alarming indisposition of Mdlle. Elena d'Acosta"—('sudden and alarming indisposition' may mean a marriage, a quarrel, a freak, anything, in fact, in theatrical parlance)—"the *rôle* of the Chevalier de Poigny, in the highly successful new drama 'English and French' would be sustained by Miss Somebodyelse." The next day also saw a letter on its way down to that insignificant little town outlying Rio de Janeiro, enclosing a sum of money, and entreating Donna Josefa to use it in travelling to the assistance of her son. And the next day, too, saw what was the saddest sight of all—a young man in the onset of existence fighting with a terrible disease that threatened to lay him low, and a devoted and heroic woman risking her life, and relinquishing her only means of support, in order that she might attend upon his necessities, and lighten the only path which she fully believed was leading him to the grave.

What Leona's feelings would have been had Valera died at this juncture, it is impossible to say. She could not have analysed them herself, for she was unaware of their depth or their intensity. She only remembered that Christobal had been her brother and her companion from infancy, and that it would have been as impossible for her to desert him at this crisis as to desert herself. So, cut off from her acquaintances, her occupations, and her ambition, she remained in that darkened room day after day, and did not know from hour to hour whether she should stand alone in the world when the next one struck.

– CHAPTER 12 –

"THREE MONTHS—REMEMBER!"

"It is a long lane that has no turning," and those who have watched by a lingering sickbed, and spent weeks in alternate fluctuations of hope and despair, know that the strain upon the feelings becomes at last so great that any turning is a relief, even though it may lead down to the valley of the shadow of death.*

"Give us certainty," they cry, "any certainty must be preferable to this miserable heart-sickening anxiety and suspense."

And at last the assurance comes—the turning is reached—and, if hope dies with the first view of it, the mourners are ready to retract their former asseverations, and to entreat heaven for the power to accompany the object of their solicitude unto the end of all things.

The time came for Leona Lacoste to see the end of her self-imposed duty, but it came accompanied by its reward. Valera was pronounced out of danger so far as the fever and the terrible putrid throat were concerned, but the exhaustion and complete debility they left behind them made his final recovery still a matter of conjecture, and never had Leona so welcomed the gossiping tongue and garlic-flamed breath of Donna Josefa, as she did when she saw her enter her son's apartments and take up her station by

---

* Psalm 23: The Lord is my shepherd; I shall not want./ He maketh me to lie down in green pastures: he leadeth me beside the still waters. / He restoreth my soul: he leadeth me in the paths of righteousness for his name's sake. / Yea, though I walk through the valley of the shadow of death, I will fear no evil: for thou art with me; thy rod and thy staff they comfort me. / Thou preparest a table before me in the presence of mine enemies: thou anointest my head with oil; my cup runneth over. / Surely goodness and mercy shall follow me all the days of my life: and I will dwell in the house of the Lord for ever.

his bedside. Donna Josefa Valera was like many another mother who has grown-up sons and daughters. She was quarrelsome, argumentative, and generally domineering when Christobal was in good health; induced thereto by a certain jealousy that he had thrown off the submission of childhood, and presumed to think for himself; but when she saw him weakened and prostrate as a child again, with all a child's desire, too, for being coaxed, and caressed, and waited on, her maternal solicitude was in full activity, and Leona had no further trouble in the matter. Give Donna Josefa her accustomed mess of garlic—and in that cosmopolitan city each stranger may find a *cuisine* suited to his own palate—and she was contented and happy to sit by Valera's side for the remainder of the day, and chatter to him on any subject that interested him most. And the man who had been down to the very gates of death, and who was still too weak to dispute, or object, or wrangle, took things much as they came to him in those first days of convalescence, and did not even appear annoyed that the girl who had nursed him so faithfully throughout his illness, should have resigned her place to another. He did not even seem to remember that she had so nursed him.

And for the girl herself?

Proudly and majestically as she had taken her place in his sickroom, ignoring the right of anyone to question her claims to that position, so proudly and majestically she withdrew, without a murmur at being superseded; without a hint even to the invalid, or his mother, of what she felt at quitting the post in time of peace, which she had occupied bravely and unflinchingly whilst the battle raged, and death might have struck her down, at any moment, with one blow.

Without a murmur, but not without a pang. Leona did not know, perhaps, until all the danger was past, how keenly she had felt the peril in which Valera had been placed.

He was so changed that Donna Josefa herself could hardly recognise him. His wavy silken hair had been shorn close to his head; his delicate features were drawn and pinched; his olive complexion cracked and yellow; his soft black eyes fierce, staring, and famine-stricken. His temper, too, naturally so gentle, had now become fractious and irritable; even the sight of his best friend appeared at times to worry him. And when, to these natural drawbacks of recovery, was added an apparently complete indifference as to whether his mother or Leona sat by his side and attended to his multifarious wants, it is scarcely to be marvelled at that the girl who had risked so much more than her life in his behalf, should cease to press her attentions on him, and hint that since his mother had arrived, it was as well she should return to her own apartments.

Donna Josefa was not disposed to combat this proposal. She had never been very friendly with Leona Lacoste, and her surprise at discovering her located in the same house as her son—for the fact of Leona being in New York had been kept a complete secret from her former acquaintances, neither had she disclosed it either when summoning Valera's mother to his assistance—had given rise to more than one unpleasant passage of arms between them.

"I should certainly say it was the most discreet and proper thing that you could do, señora," quoth the old Spanish lady, who was so very particular about the morals of her friends. "It is a pity the necessity for your staying here should ever have arisen, but now that Don Valera's mother has come, there can be no possible excuse for your remaining longer."

"I have no desire or intention of doing so, madame," returned Leona, haughtily; yet she glanced towards Christobal as she spoke, with a hope that he would say something in her defence. But Christobal was lying on his pillows with his eyes wide open, indeed, but his ears fast closed. He was too feeble to disconnect one sound from another in the sentences he heard uttered around him.

"I presume that you *have* apartments of your own," continued Donna Josefa, with her most unpleasant air, as she took a pinch of snuff from an old-fashioned embossed silver box; "it is scarcely desirable for young people of opposite sexes, who are no relation to one another, to lodge under the same roof. Such a thing would not be tolerated in *my* country."

An angry answer was hovering on Leona's tongue, but she glanced at Valera's helpless condition, and checked the impulse to pronounce it.

"Your country is more particular than others in these matters, Donna Josefa," she said, with well-directed sarcasm; "and perhaps your women require closer watching. But the free life of the Brazils has made *me* independent."

"Too independent, I think, by half," rejoined the old lady.

"And yet, had I thought more of myself than of him, your son would have been badly nursed, madame."

"Well, well, well; let us be thankful that the occasion for it is passed. The doctor will be here this evening to say how soon the poor lad may be moved into the country, and then you will return to your occupation, señora, and I trust will never again have such a call made upon your services."

"The Blessed Virgin forbid!" cried the girl, impulsively.

But when the doctor next saw his patient he found they were to be separated sooner than she had anticipated, for he advised Donna Josefa to take her son away from New York as soon as possible, as the only means by which his convalescence could be established.

This proposal was not so difficult to comply with as might be imagined, as Messrs. Upjohn and Halliday had generously decided to continue to pay their clerk's salary until he should be fit to resume his work. But the sudden change brought with it a sudden increase of trouble, with which Donna Josefa, by reason of her age and ignorance of any language but her own, was unfit to cope, and Leona, with her usual nobility of disposition, forgetting everything but that Christobal's comfort demanded her assistance, offered to remain and help his mother to prepare for the journey.

She knew better than Donna Josefa where Tobal's apparel lay, and what he would require during his sojourn in the country; and now, when she realised that the hour of parting with her friend had really arrived, her tears dropped hotly amongst the articles she was folding and packing away, though she took good care that his mother should not be witness to her feelings.

As she was emptying the wardrobe to fill his travelling-chest, she came upon some papers, amongst which she recognised the letter of introduction to the firm of Evans and Troubridge. The sight of it startled her. It seemed to bring back so much to her memory that she had half forgotten in her anxiety for Valera's life. He could not go to England then! That place to which she had at one time almost made up her mind to accompany him! Perhaps he would never go. The post for which he had been intended would be filled by another, before he had regained strength sufficient for the journey, and such an opportunity might never again arise for him—or her. What should she do with the letter? What use was it now to Valera? What possible need could there be for sending it into the country with him? Perhaps it ought to be returned to the principals of the firm. Leona glanced towards the bed. The dusk was drawing on apace, but she could distinguish that Donna Josefa was nodding in her arm-chair, and that Christobal's eyes were closed. She could not ask him his wishes on the subject. She must wait until the morrow. At that moment the landlady's face was thrust cautiously in at the door.

"Hist! mademoiselle."

"Hush! speak low; he is asleep."

"Some one waits to see you outside."

"Say that I am coming."

She placed the letter in her pocket as she spoke, and quietly left the room. On the landing she encountered Rawlins, the cashier.

"I come from Mr. Halliday, mademoiselle. Can I see Don Valera?"

"Not at present! He is asleep, and has a journey before him to-morrow."

"So we heard, and I was sent up here in consequence. Mr. Halliday is afraid Don Valera's recovery may be retarded by his disappointment about this English business, and commissioned me to tell him that he has no intention of sending any one in his place, but shall put off the matter altogether until he is able to take it up."

"It is very considerate of Mr. Halliday. I believe the idea of being prevented going to England has weighed upon Don Valera's mind."

"Well, you must tell him, mademoiselle, that he is to think no more about it. The firm will keep the appointment until he is well enough to fill it, for two or three months, if necessary. I suppose it will take that time to set him up again?"

"I am afraid so. I heard the doctor say to-day that it would require as much as that to regain the strength he has lost in this illness. He is very weak."

"Exactly so. And Mr. Halliday wishes him plainly to understand

Her Father's Name

that there is no hurry about the matter. We have not yet communicated with Messrs Evans and Troubridge, and so there's no harm done. And he's to take his time about it, mademoiselle. Two or three months—it will make no difference to us."

"And you have not yet communicated with the—the firm you mentioned in England, sir—the gentleman to whom the letter of introduction was addressed?"

"Not yet—not with regard to Valera's visit, that is to say. There was no need to do so. The letter we sent him would have been sufficient under any circumstances, for they understand all about the business part of the transaction already; but we should have written privately as well. But now we shall put it off till we see Don Valera in New York again. Remember me to him, mademoiselle, and tell him to make a good recovery and cheat the doctors. We shall write him on these matters in a day or two.

And with a bow and wave of the hand, Mr. Rawlins, the cashier, was gone.

She stood where he had left her, with her hand pressed upon the pocket which contained the letter of introduction. What thoughts were passing through her mind at that moment? What plan was rapidly unfolding in her busy brain? Valera safe for two months in the country with his mother, and she—left alone in New York, with that letter in her pocket. In an instant everything that she had wished and feared and hoped for rushed back upon her mind—her solemn oath came to her memory—she seemed to see a path carved out before her, in which she must walk, whether she would or no. The impulsive nature of the woman began to ferment. Her eyes distended, her nostrils dilated, like those of a war horse scenting the battle; she stood upright and threw out her nobly-proportioned chest and shoulders as though she waited for the saddle to be put upon them. A sudden grand idea had overwhelmed her brain. It took possession of her, and she felt even at that moment that she should carry it out to the end. Every circumstance combined to make it feasible. It was Providence alone that could have directed and arranged it all, and Leona felt the same flow of conscious responsibility driving her onward, that the Maid of Orleans must have experienced when the mysterious voices urged her to the field.

She stood there where the cashier had left her for many minutes, motionless, absorbed. Then hearing herself called by name, with a heightened colour and beating heart, she returned to Valera's apartment, and related to him what she had been told.

It was the one assurance the invalid needed to make his mind easy on the subject of the proposed journey.

"I am very glad," he kept on murmuring, in a weak but contented tone. "I shall soon get well now. I long for the country air and a sight of the fresh green fields. I shall see them before sunset to-morrow, *ma mère*."

"Long before sunset," replied Donna Josefa, as if she were speaking to a weary child, "and then you shall lie on the grass, *Tobalito mio*, and under the shady trees, until you feel quite strong and hearty again."

"How I *long* to be there!" repeated the sick man earnestly. "Oh, how I *long* to be there!"

His whole mind seemed to be set on the idea of getting away from the little heated room where he had suffered so much pain, and been kept a prisoner for so long. It was natural it should be so. Illness is apt to make us very selfish, and forgetful of every one's feelings but our own, and Leona should have been able to make allowances for the condition in which the fever had left her adopted brother. Yet, her proud loving heart swelled with pain as she listened to this little conversation between the mother and the son; though she felt it was another incentive to her not to falter in the path she had chalked out for herself, but to crush every consideration under foot which should attempt to interfere with the fulfilment of the oath she had sworn to keep. Meanwhile, not a word was said about the letter of introduction to the English firm. If the remembrance of it crossed Valera's mind at all, he did not consider it of sufficient consequence to mention. By the time the sun rose next morning, his boxes were packed ready for him to start. By the time it had reached its meridian, Leona stood in his deserted apartments alone. The mother and son were far on their road towards the green fields and shady trees Valera longed for, and even at the last moment he had not appeared to feel the parting with Leona. He who in health became serious if she were but a few hours out of his sight, appeared able to leave her in that great city, friendless, alone, without a fear. The fact is, Valera was too weak to feel anything, except his weakness.

His attenuated hand shook as it lay in hers. The mouth she kissed in farewell was parched, and cracked, and dry. Even the touch of her fresh rosy lips had had no power to excite any response from his.

"Adieu, *m'amie*," he had said, affectionately, but calmly. "Pray that we may meet in happier times. I wish you were coming with us, Leona, but I have kept you from your work too long already. I can never thank you sufficiently for your goodness to me, *m'amie*. Never, never."

And with that Valera had sunk back languidly on the pillows provided for his support, and closed his eyes from the mere exertion of framing those few words.

The carriage drove slowly away, and Leona returned to the vacated rooms to look at them once more, before she took her own departure. The litter attendant upon packing was strewn about them—the bed, from which Christobal had with difficulty been induced to rise, was tossed and tumbled as he had left it. As the girl regarded the place, where, for the last six weeks she had played the *rôle* of a most devoted nurse and companion, and realised that her work was completed, and the end for which she had worked accomplished, she was angry with the tears that, despite her best efforts, would rise to her softened eyes.

"Why am I behaving like a fool?" she said sharply, as she brushed them away. "A short time ago I did not expect Christobal to live. There might have been something to cry for! But he is not only better, but out of all danger, and in another hour or so will be well removed from the influence of the city and its surroundings—will return to it probably stronger than he ever was before. It is often the case that a good fever clears and strengthens the constitution. I heard the doctor say so. Then I am a fool to weep for that which should make me glad."

She passed into the bedchamber as she spoke, and nervously picking up a few pieces of packing paper from the floor, let them drop again.

"Poor Christal!" she thought, as she glanced at the ruffled pillows, "how many restless nights has he spent upon that bed.

How terrible it was to hear him call out in his delirium. Shall I ever forget the time when he leaped from the bed and insisted upon leaving the room? How frightened I was, more so than I have ever been in my life before. I thought that that night he was dying. Oh, my poor brother! What should I have done if he had left me? I have no real friend in the world but him."

Here the rebel tears commenced to fall upon the bedclothes, but Leona did not seem to notice them.

"Poor, poor Tobal! How much he has suffered! How his eyes would follow me about the room, even when he did not seem to recognise me, as though he were imploring me to quench his thirst and mitigate his pain. Once, when I was bathing his head with vinegar, he called me 'Queen of Heaven,' and tried to kneel to me. He always had a grateful heart, my poor Tobal! and he has loved me from the time when we were little children together, and I don't believe, I can't believe—Oh! I wish, I wish," cried the girl, passionately, as she threw herself upon the deserted pillows, "that he had said just a little more at parting than he did."

She sobbed for a few minutes convulsively, then, starting up, as if ashamed of displaying so much weakness even to herself, she dried her eyes rapidly, and, rising, walked up and down the room.

"*Madre di Dios*!" she exclaimed, impatiently, "what am I thinking of? Crying, positively crying, when I ought to be laughing— because my friend is well. *Ought to be laughing!* I *am* laughing—of course I'm laughing!" And here the merriment which she forced from herself sounded sadder than tears. "Or if I'm not, I ought to be whipped. But what fools we women are! Why wasn't I born a man? I might have had more sense in me then. Tobal has double my sense. *He* wouldn't be such a pig as to cry because I had just recovered from a serious illness. I must be going to take the fever myself, I fancy, and that won't do with all I have before me."

She clapped her hand upon her pocket as she spoke, and felt the outline of the letter she had placed there. The touch of it seemed to infuse fresh spirit in her.

"I have ten thousand things to do before to-morrow," she said impulsively, "and I waste my precious time here, whimpering like a school-girl. Leona Lacoste, *I hate you*! You have no more spirit, nor energy, nor courage than the rest of your sex. You have been shut up in these close little rooms with that poor weak boy till you are as bad as himself. Fancy! my *actually crying* because the child was too ill to make me a long speech of thanks and compliments before he started on his travels—when I hate compliments into the bargain! Saint Jago! what shall I require next?"

All this time she had been collecting the few articles that belonged to her, and which she could carry in a basket on her arm. Now she flung her mantilla over her shoulders, and placed a broad-brimmed hat upon her head.

"*Au revoir, mon frère!*" she said, lightly, as she kissed her fingers in the direction of the empty bed. "Please the saints we shall meet again, to laugh together over this little adventure. And I will tease thee, Tobalito, with the account of thine uncomplimentary farewell, and how foolishly vexed I was to think of it afterwards. *Au revoir!* May it be long before I have to watch thee on a sick-bed again, chère!"

She turned to leave the room with the same mocking smile upon her lips—the innocent jest upon her tongue. But before she had crossed the threshold she rushed back, and, with a sudden impulse, fell on her knees and pressed fond passionate kisses upon the pillows which had held the sick man's head.

"The good God have thee in his safe keeping ever, my friend and brother!" she said fervently, as she rose to her feet again and hurried from the apartment, ashamed of the emotion into which she had been betrayed.

* * * * * *

"Here's a nuisance!" exclaimed Mr. Burrage to his stage manager a few mornings afterwards.

"What's up now?"

"That jade, d'Acosta, after having kept me waiting for her for six weeks past, sends word she is obliged to leave New York."

"Why?"

"She doesn't give her reasons, only that she's unfit for work, and must have change. She doesn't even say where she's going to, or when she is coming back. So much for the dependence to be placed on a woman. The fact is, she's been nursing that black-eyed brute she calls her brother through a fever, and I suppose he's been ordered away, and so she must go too."

"That's about the long and short," replied the other. "You know I never believed in that brother of d'Acosta's."

"Well, whoever he is, he's a deuced lucky fellow to have such a nurse. But how am I to replace her? That's the question."

"Ah, I suppose he's been asking the same. I'm sure I can't answer it. You're sure d'Acosta's gone?"

"Sure. I sent word at once to her lodgings; she left yesterday."

"Well, it's no use crying over spilt milk. We must do the best we can without her. Did you write to England by yesterday's mail!"

"By Jove! no. I quite forgot it," cried Mr. Burrage; and in the annoyance caused by the omission, Elena d'Acosta's sudden disappearance was for awhile forgotten.

– CHAPTER 13 –

THE HOUSE IN HYDE PARK GARDENS

When Mr. Henry Evans, head of the well-known firm of Evans and Troubridge, of Liverpool, had, by dint of hard work and steady application to business, doubled and trebled the fortune left him by his uncle some two-and-twenty years before, he thought it time to set up an establishment in London. So he gave up the fine house with its gardens, and hothouses, and pineries, in which he had lived ever since he was married, and which he had furnished with every luxury and convenience procurable by money—he left the friends by whom he had been surrounded since his youth, who had known him through trouble and joy, and been faithful to him under every aspect of life; and came to a new place, to take up his residence amongst strangers, and to find himself encompassed by people and manners and customs to which he was as foreign as though he had belonged to another country. He felt uncomfortable and ill at ease—so did his wife—so, doubtless, did his daughter; but it was the correct thing to do, consequently they did it. People who have been fortunate enough to amass sufficient money to lift all pecuniary care for the future off their shoulders, always seem to imagine that their first duty lies in spending it amongst and upon strangers, instead of the friends and tradesmen who have most claim on them. In consequence of their wealth they find themselves surrounded and courted by a higher class than that with which they originally associated, and they feel that they must needs put themselves on a par with their new acquaintances, by going where they go and seeing what they have seen. And thus it often comes to pass that the fortune it has taken nearly a lifetime to accumulate is frittered away upon a set of aristocratic and fashionable "sharpers," who flatter the *nouveau riche* simply for what he gives them, and laugh at him behind his back for his simplicity and ignorance, and general want of knowledge of society.

Mr. Henry Evans was naturally somewhat above the regulation "*nouveau riche*," both in education and social status. He had held a high place in the society of his native town, and had spent a great deal of his time in London. His birth, manners, and appearance were those of a gentleman, and he was fitted by them to move amongst the noblest in the land. But he had never actually resided in London, and was quite ready to take the advice of anyone as to what he should "eat, drink, and avoid" in that bewildering city. His wife, also, although the kindest-hearted, most retiring, and modest of ladies, had never moved out of the country in her life, and was quite astray amidst the confusion of a London season; and his daughter Lucilla, who had been an invalid for many years past, was unable to do more than follow the lead of her parents. When the three, therefore, found themselves installed in a splendid house in Hyde Park Gardens, and called upon to give large dinners, and dances, and afternoon receptions, in return for civilities shown to them, they felt very much like children led about blindfold, and were thankful—Mrs. Evans especially—to anyone who would kindly take the unusual trouble of entertaining their guests off their hands. And anybody who knows what London is, and what a number of harpies it contains in the shape of needy men and women going about seeking whom they may devour, and ready to bow down and worship the first person they meet who will give them a good dinner, will readily understand how many offers of assistance in dispensing her hospitality good Mrs. Evans received.

There was more reason, perhaps, for Mr. Evans' shifting his quarters from Liverpool to London than for most men in the same predicament. Of late years the firm to which he belonged had greatly increased its connection. The branch establishment in London was crowded with traders and correspondents of all nations, and for these strangers, cast adrift on the inhospitable shores of our metropolis (and no city is less hospitable to a stranger), some sort of entertainment was needed. It was this knowledge that put the first thought of a town residence into Mr. Evans' head. Not but what he might have deputed some one to the office, but he was the head of the firm, and Lucilla had seen nothing of the world; and after all it was the proper thing to do. And so Mrs. Evans, who was one of those good old-fashioned wives who consider that their husbands are intended to rule the house, and who, moreover, may have felt a little elated at the prospect of presiding over an establishment in London, readily acquiesced in his decision. So the house in Hyde Park Gardens was taken for a term of years, and whilst the decorators and upholsterers were having it all their own way, the Evans went abroad, that they might not be behind their neighbours in familiarity with the "grand tour." Having accomplished which feat (with much discomfort and at considerable outlay), they took up their quarters in their new house, where they soon found themselves surrounded by a bevy of accommodating friends, all eager to assist "Dear Mrs. Evans" in her shopping or housekeeping, or to become "dear Lucilla's" nurse and companion, so long as they could repay themselves by driving in Mrs. Evans' carriage, using Mrs. Evans' purse, eating Mrs. Evans' dinners, and even, on particular occasions, coming in for "pickings" from Mrs. Evans' wardrobe, or any other of her possessions. For the sort of friend to which I allude is never "proud." It is amazing, for all their appetites, what amount of humble-pie they will eat from the hands of those who know how to make use of them.

* * * * * *

It was the month of May, and it was evening. From the lower part of the house in Hyde Park Gardens the various sounds of bustle and movement, with occasional bursts of laughter and conversation, showed that a dinner-party was, as usual, going on. In the large drawing-room overhead, furnished with blue satin and gold, Lucilla Evans, the daughter of the house, lay on a couch alone. By her side was a small table, holding strawberries and cream and wine, but she appeared to have pushed it impatiently away. She was too weak to join her father's dinner-parties, so she always waited thus the return of her mother and the other ladies. She had no organic disease, but she had suffered from a weak spine for many years past, and it prevented her taking any active part in life. And the restraint made her fractious. As she listened now to the sounds of feasting from below, her pale face, which might have been pretty, had she enjoyed better health, contracted with pain and envy. She knew she had no right to complain, but it seemed hard that all those people should be eating and drinking at her parent's expense, and making merry over their meal, whilst she, the only child and heiress of the house, should have to lie there unable to partake of it. She turned restlessly upon her sofa as the idea passed through her brain, and she wondered how many of them ever bestowed a thought upon her upstairs whilst they were gratifying their appetites and their vanity. Yet, except for that which it was Heaven's will she should endure, Lucilla Evans had little reason for complaint. She was positively the idol of her parents. Not a wish she ever expressed was left ungratified. She was clothed in purple and fine linen, she fared sumptuously every day. And she would have exchanged it all to enjoy a beggar's health and strength. It is the way of the world. The rich clothes she wore, the luxuries which surrounded her, were as nothing compared to the one thing she lacked. She ever seemed to take pleasure in crumpling and otherwise ill-using the delicate muslin trimmed with the finest of lace in which she could be arrayed, as she tossed from side to side upon her satin couch.

It was infinite relief to her to hear the voices on the staircase which told her that the ladies were ascending to the drawing-room. Lizzie Vereker, a fine handsome girl of two or three and twenty, a perfect specimen of the fast young lady of the nineteenth century, was the first to enter.

"Why, my dear, how dark you are!" she exclaimed. "But

deliciously cool! You should have felt it downstairs. I thought I should have fainted. And that wretch Rivers has been making me laugh so with his nonsense that I had no time to eat my dinner. How are you dear? Better?"

This being a question which was put to Miss Evans by all her lady friends whenever they saw her—which was, moreover, so utterly unanswerable—she took no notice of it whatever.

"You should have the gas lighted, Mrs. Evans," exclaimed an old maid, by name Miss Forrester, who had nobly undertaken the task of setting Mrs. Evans right upon every particular, even to selecting her acquaintances for her. "You should give your man orders always to light the gas before the ladies come up from the dinner-table."

"Oh, of course! I had forgotten it. I am so very stupid," said poor Mrs. Evans, as she trotted across the room to ring the bell.

"Sit down, marquise," continued Miss Forrester, in the most hospitable manner, as she ensconced a pretty fashionably-dressed woman into the largest arm-chair. "I'm sure you're tired. You looked so pale at dinner."

The marquise (it is to be presumed she had some other name, but as her friends always addressed her as if she were the only marquise in the world, it was difficult to arrive at the truth of the matter) took the seat of honour as though she were entitled to it.

"I *do* feel very tired," she said, fanning herself. "These interminable heavy dinners are distressingly fatiguing."

Miss Forrester leant over her and whispered, "They don't know how to do the thing at all, poor creatures; how should they! *Mais on doit souffrir*—you know the rest, my dear."

The marquise, who was considerably powdered and painted, and could not therefore afford to over-exert herself in any way, laughed gently, and lay back in the arm-chair with closed eyes.

"What do you think of the new importation?" asked her friend.

"The boy, my dear? Oh! he's a pretty boy enough. I've asked him to come and see me to-morrow afternoon."

"Your friend, Sir Sydney, may not approve of that, *Fifine*."

"My dear, what nonsense! As if anyone in his right mind could suppose I should ask a child to visit me except out of kindness; his manners are too brusque for society. I mean to polish him up a little."

Meanwhile Mrs. Evans had approached her daughter. She was a charming lady in appearance, not old, not half old enough looking, in fact, to be the mother of the careworn sickly girl upon the sofa—but dressed, by comparison with her guests, so dowdily as to seem twice her age. For although her clothes were rich, and made by good milliners, Mrs. Evans wore them in such a manner as to mar all their fashionable beauties. Her dark-brown moiré* dress hung on her as if she had been a broomstick, whilst her point-lace *fichu*† was twisted like a ribbon round her throat, and her ruffles hung limply from her wrists. Her abundant hair slightly streaked with gray, was tucked away in the staidest manner beneath a matronly cap; for in one particular Mrs. Evans had proved obstinately deaf to the reasoning and advice of her new friends. She would not change the fashion of her cap. She considered the fly-away, fluttering head-dresses which the *modistes* assured her to be the latest fashion, outrageous, and unbecoming (not to say indecent) for a woman of her age; and laugh at her as her friends might, she insisted upon retaining the shape and style which she and her mother before her had always worn. Therefore, though the materials of which her evening cap was composed were irreproachable, it still covered her head, and tied down cosily round her cheerful, pleasant little face, as she came smiling to Lucilla's side.

"Well, my dear, and how do you feel this evening? Not touched your strawberries! Why, how's that? Come, do try some; they are so refreshing."

"I didn't want them," replied the girl, peevishly. "Who's downstairs to-night, mother? What are they doing?"

"Well, there's papa, of course, and Dr. Hastings."

"He's always there. I am sure you might miss him. I'm sick of his name."

"Oh Lucilla, my dear! and when he's so good to you. What we should have done without him on the tour, I'm sure I don't know. What with interpreting for us at the railway stations, and guiding us

---

* Standard style of dress in the mid 1800s, fitted bodice, large full skirts.
† Lightweight triangular scarf often worn to make dresses more modest, ie., to fill in a low neckline.

about, and looking after you, he was quite our salvation."

"We've had enough of him since, anyway. Who else is there?"

"Captain Rivers and Sir Sydney Marchant."

Lucilla drew her mother's ear down to her mouth and whispered "Is he *that woman's* friend?"

"What woman, my dear?" replied Mrs. Evans, in the same tone.

"That marquise, or whatever she is."

"My dear! she is the Marquise de Toutlemonde, a person of very high connections. Miss Forrester assures me—"

"Never mind it now, mother. I hate her, that's all; and wish Miss F. would keep her friends to herself. Who else was at dinner?"

"No one—except the young American."

"What young American?"

"Well, Spaniard, I suppose I should say; only papa says he is connected with his American partners, and has come over on the business of the firm. Such a strange-looking lad, my dear; and so handsome. Doesn't appear to be more than eighteen or nineteen, too; but he must be older, papa tells me."

"What's his name?"

"Don—Don—There, it's quite slipped my memory. But I never can manage these foreign names. Miss Forrester, can you remember what the young gentleman from America is called?"

"Don Christobal Valera," replied Madame La Marquise de Toutlemonde.

"Thank you, marquise. Though I wonder you should think of it so readily."

"Well, *I* should, if anyone, Mrs. Evans, considering he is a countryman of mine."

"Are you Spanish?" demanded Lizzie Vereker, bluntly.

"Certainly. I was born and brought up in Andalusia."

"I shouldn't have thought it, to hear you speak."

"Why not?"

"Your English is so fluent. I suppose it is due to your having lived so long in town; but really, if you hadn't told me to the contrary, I should have said it had quite the cockney ring about it."

The marquise changed the subject by turning and speaking to Miss Forrester in a low tone.

"A very unpleasant sort of girl that—so pert and outspoken in her remarks."

"Particularly so. Wants putting down, I should say. By the way, Miss Vereker, are we to congratulate you?"

"On what?"

"Your engagement to Captain Rivers. You are engaged to him, are you not?"

"Most decidedly not. To become engaged to anyone is the last thing in the world that I think of doing."

"Indeed. I am surprised to hear it. I imagined you were rather partial to the gentleman than otherwise."

"So I am, Miss Forrester; very partial, indeed. I like them all so much, in fact, that I never shall be able to make up my mind to tie myself down to one."

Madame de Toutlemonde closed her eyes, and looked disgusted, as though such a sentiment were altogether too immoral for her to listen to.

"You have shocked Fifine here," quoth Miss Forrester. "She is not accustomed to hear such strong opinions from young unmarried ladies."

It was Miss Vereker's turn then.

"I daresay not. It is the married women nowadays that 'out-Herod Herod.'* By the way, marquise, how is your poor husband?"

"Much the same, thank you."

"How distressing it must be for you to be obliged always to leave him at home, and to be dependent on the kindness of your gentlemen friends for escort. Is it true that Sir Sydney Marchant is your cousin?"

"Who told you so?" demanded the marquise, with a faint access of colour to her cheek.

"No one. But young Taylor mentioned you had given it out at your own dinner-table the other day. So I thought perhaps it might be true."

"He is a sort of cousin of my husband's."

---

* The 'Massacre of the Innocents' is found in the Gospel according to Matthew, chapter 2   There is no non-Biblical source which supports the story that Herod ordered the killing of all boys of the age of two and under in Bethlehem and surrounding area.

"Of the marquis? Really, how strange! Because I know all the Marchants well, and they particularly pride themselves on the unsullied purity of their race."

"Have you any engagement for to-morrow?" suddenly demanded Madame of Miss Forrester.

"No. Why do you ask?"

"I want so much to go to the Crystal Palace Dog Show,[*] and one of my horses has fallen lame."

"Oh, I daresay Mrs. Evans is going, and will be pleased to take you. Mrs. Evans!" raising her voice to reach across the room.

"Yes, Miss Forrester."

"Of course you're going to the Dog Show at the Crystal Palace to-morrow?"

"I didn't know there was to be one."

"Didn't know! Why, my good creature, where are your eyes? It's posted all over the town. You must go. The Palace will be crammed."

"I am so afraid of the heat and crowd for Lucilla. She cannot stand for any time without suffering from it."

"It's not the place for Lucilla, certainly."

"And I don't care to go without her, you see."

"But I'll go with you with pleasure, and so will the marquise, I'm sure. We intended going, and it's all one to us who we go with. When shall you start? About three o'clock I think will be a nice time. We shall be able then to drive comfortably down there and back before dinner-time."

"Well, if you really think I ought to go," said poor Mrs. Evans, dubiously.

"There's no thinking in the matter. I'm sure of it," returned Miss Forrester. "Anyway, Fifine, and I will be here by three to-morrow, and then, if you really don't wish to go—"

"You and Madame will take the carriage and go without me," interposed her hostess. "Ah, that's very good of you. And then you can tell me all about it on your return. For if Lucilla should happen to be too unwell to join us, I really would rather stay by her."

---

[*] Crystal Palace was the site of the Great Exhibition of 1851, also home to the first national motor show, plus cat, dog and flower shows.

"Well, you must do as you choose about that, of course, Mrs. Evans. But at all events the marquise and I will keep our engagement with you. Won't we, Fifine?

"Just as you like, dear. It will make no difference to me," responded the marquise, amiably.

At this juncture, the door opened to admit three of the gentlemen, Sir Sydney Marchant, Captain Rivers, and Dr. Hastings. Sir Sydney was a middle-aged, overblown, sensual-looking man, unpleasant to contemplate, and unpleasant to know—at all events, to most people. From the effusive manner in which he was received by his cousin, Madame de Toutlemonde, however, it may be presumed that she was an exception to the rest of the world.

Captain Rivers was a tall, good-looking soldier, who was evidently on the best of terms with Miss Lizzie Vereker, and lost no time in securing the seat next to her.

Dr. Hastings (or Tom Hastings, as he was called by all his intimate friends) was neither handsome nor tall; but he had a good and strong face, with kind, clever eyes, and a great sense of humour in his composition. He was a Liverpool man, and had known the Evans in their old home, and gladly renewed the acquaintanceship in London. He did not consider Lucilla's case hopeless, and constantly cheered her parents and herself with the prospect that another year or two would see her outgrow the constitutional debility. Mr. Evans thought very highly of the young man's talent, and had installed him as medical adviser to the family. He had even taken him on the "grand tour" with them, that Lucilla's health might not suffer from any imprudence on their part. And his confidence was justified by that of the public. Dr. Hastings was a very clever and rising surgeon, and deserved all his friends thought or said of him. He was, moreover, a man of the world, and not to be easily deceived. During his town practice, he had visited with all sorts of people, and had his eyes wide open. For this reason there were a few ladies and gentlemen (Madame de Toutlemonde and Sir Sydney Marchant, for example) who both hated and feared Dr. Hastings, and lost no occasion of speaking against him. It was strange, however, that Lucilla Evans should have taken a distaste (it was scarcely to be called a dislike) to the man who had really benefitted her health, and was so constantly attentive to her—strange, that is to say, to anyone who did not know the secret of her heart and his. For the cause lay in the fact that Dr. Hastings was too attentive, and that his attentions bore a deeper meaning than mere interest in her as a patient. He was fond of Lucilla Evans, and she felt the influence without acknowledging it; and not being prepared to return his affection, it worried instead of pleasing her. She was a nervous, sensitive girl, who had been brought up in the country, and unused to be flirted with or dangled after, and she could not bear to see that Dr. Hastings' eyes rested on her longer than was necessary, or that he lowered his voice when he addressed her. It would have delighted Lizzie Vereker, who would have drawn on the unfortunate doctor by her smiles and whispers until he was beside himself; but it only made Lucilla Evans fractious and uncomfortable. As he entered the room that evening, and at once made his way up to her side, she bounded into a sitting position with such alacrity as must have been hurtful to her weakened spine.

"Why do you rise? You shouldn't move so quickly—you will injure yourself," he said, gently, as he reached the sofa. "You had better lie down again, or you will not be able to sit up when Mr. Evans comes, and then he will be disappointed."

"I am so *sick* of lying down," said the girl, with a sigh. Yet she did as he told her, notwithstanding.

"I am sure you are. No one feels more for you than I do, who know so well what you suffer. But patience, Lucy" (he had been allowed by reason of their early acquaintance to fall into the habit of addressing her by her christian name), "and it will all come right in the end."

"So *you* say," she answered, somewhat ungraciously. "I shall believe it when I see it."

He took no notice of her mood.

"Have you been out to-day?"

"We drove in the park, as usual. And, as usual, Miss Forrester was stuck beside me all the way, and mamma had to sit on the back seat."

"Miss Forrester appears to be always with you now."

"Not by *my* wish, Dr. Hastings; you may be sure of that. But she is continually popping in at odd moments; and what can mamma do, when the carriage is waiting at the door, but ask her to accompany us? But she is preferable to her friend."

"By the way, I wanted to ask you, Lucy, who is that lady in pink and white?"

"The marquise of something or other."

"How did you come to know her?"

"Miss Forrester brought her here to call on mamma."

"Where does she live?"

"I don't know. Somewhere in Bayswater, but mamma returned the call alone."

"Is she married?"

"Oh, of course. To an old fellow, I believe, who cares for nothing but chemistry and experiments, and is always ill. And so she goes about with Miss Forrester. At least so mamma says. I don't like the woman myself. She's too affected to please me. And I think that man she takes about with her is horrid."

Dr. Hastings looked grave.

"I wish your mamma would be more careful whom she admits to her acquaintance," he said. "There can be very little sympathy between you and this marquise, I should think."

"But she is a great friend of Miss Forrester's," put in Lucilla.

"Yes, yes, exactly so," replied her companion, and then he turned and looked at Madame de Toutlemonde for a little while, as if he had seen her before, and was silent.

"Where's the young American papa brought home to dinner?" demanded Lucilla of him, presently.

"I don't know, I'm sure. Mr. Evans took him into the study, I think, for a little conversation."

"Is he so very handsome, as they say?"

"Handsome! Not a bit of it. He's got a pretty face, but that is not generally considered desirable in a man. He's quite a lad, with the merest down upon his upper lip. The Spanish correspondent, I think your father told me, of some American firm. I don't think you will take much interest in him, Lucilla."

"I don't take much interest in anything," she answered, wearily.

"You shall, some day. Meanwhile, would you like some music? Shall I ask Miss Vereker to sing?"

"I prefer talking. Is this Spaniard very dark?"

"Harping on that Spaniard again! What makes you think of him? No; his hair and eyes are of a reddish colour, I believe, but I really forget. I was not so interested in his appearance as you seem to be."

"I hate dark hair," said Lucilla, brusquely.

Tom Hastings sighed, and passed his hand ruefully through his own dark hair, which, from much thought and study, was plentifully sprinkled with grey.

– CHAPTER 14 –

THE SPANISH CORRESPONDENT

Meanwhile Mr. Evans and the young gentleman who had introduced himself to him as Don Christobal Valera were closeted together as Dr. Hastings had surmised, in the study.

"A few words with you, Don Valera, if you please," the host had said, as the men quitted the dining-room, and he led the way into his sanctum. The stranger followed in silence, As they entered the study and took seats opposite each other, and the lamplight fell upon his face, Mr. Evans could not help remarking how youthful his figure was, and how delicately his features were chiselled.

"Do you smoke?" he inquired, as he pushed a box of cigars towards him. His companion took one, lighted it, and for a few moments they smoked together in silence.

"Messrs. Halliday and Upjohn must have reposed great confidence in you to have chosen you for such an office, Don Valera," commenced Mr. Evans.

"I am young, sir, but I believe myself competent to master all the details of the proposed speculation, and to carry back your ideas and wishes to the New York firm with accuracy."

"I have no doubt of it. The credentials you bring with you are all-sufficient. You have known Messrs. Halliday and Upjohn for more than a year."

"For more than a year, sir."

"And have been their Spanish correspondent for that period?"

"I can write fluently in Spanish, French, or Portuguese, sir. I will give you a specimen of my style, if you will permit me."

"There is no occasion, Don Valera. I have every faith in your assertion. But as the negotiations by which we hope to extend the business of the firm entail correspondence with certain Spanish houses, it was as well to make sure of your ability to conduct it. I may even have to send you to Madrid on the same business."

"I am at your command, sir, and only too ready to do anything you may require. Am I likely to have to start soon?"

"By no means. There's no hurry at all about the matter; in fact, we can hardly get things in train under a month or so. Meanwhile, where are you staying? Have you friends in London?"

"None! I am an entire stranger here. I slept last night at an hotel."

"Then you must accept the hospitality of my house during your visit to England."

"But it will be imposing on your goodness," stammered the stranger. "It is really too much."

"Not another word, my dear sir," said Mr. Evans. "I will not hear of your leaving us again. Your room is ready for you, and I will send to the hotel for your things. Don't think twice about it. We are very seldom without guests in the house, and I make a point of entertaining all the gentlemen who come to London on business connected with the firm. But you are very, *very* young," he added, laying a patronising hand on his visitor's shoulder.

"I am older than I seem," was the youth's reply. He evidently did not like his age being alluded to. Gentlemen who can boast of as much down on their upper lips as the peel of an apple do usually try to change the subject when years are made the topic of conversation.

"That matter being settled," said Mr. Evans cheerfully, "suppose we join the ladies in the drawing-room. I have still to introduce you to my daughter."

As he followed his host up the broad staircase the young stranger could not help looking earnestly at him. He saw before him a man of perhaps forty years of age, in appearance much younger, with a fair complexion, made florid by good living, mirthful blue eyes, reddish hair, which was more than "reddish" in his whiskers, and a tall, well rounded figure. The stranger thought of another head of hair prematurely whitened, of another pair of eyes dimmed with sorrow, of a stooping attenuated form, and a mournful voice, and seeming to gain courage from the recollection, ascended the staircase with a firm step and a resolute expression of countenance. His appearance in the drawing-room caused some little commotion. Lucilla Evans moved tranquilly into an arm-chair, Madame de Toutlemonde roused herself from her state of semi-drowsiness, and Lizzie Vereker neglected to attend to what Captain Rivers was saying to her, as she watched the introduction that was taking place between the young Spaniard and the daughter of their host.

"Don Valera, this is Miss Evans. Lucy, my dear, let me present to you Don Christobal Valera, who has come all the way from New York to visit our firm on business, and who will be our guest, I trust, until it shall be concluded."

Lucilla Evans raised her eyes to the stranger's countenance and withdrew them instantly, blushing deeply. There was something in the face of the new comer that attracted her at once. He, on the contrary, saw nothing before him but a pallid, sickly-looking woman of almost five-and-twenty years of age, of whom his first idea was how little she resembled either her father or her mother, and how much too old she appeared to be their daughter. But as the young lady seemed willing enough after the first minute to talk and laugh with him, he conquered his feeling of indifference, and did his best to make himself agreeable.

"This is your first visit to our country, I presume, Don?" she commenced.

"Quite the first, mademoiselle. I was born and brought up in the Brazils."

"Oh! I thought you were a Spaniard?"

"It is not impossible to be a Spaniard and yet never to have seen one's native country."

"True! I had forgot! But you live in New York now?"

"I do mademoiselle."

"It is a beautiful country, is it not? I have always felt most interested in America, and longed to visit it. But I shall never do that," with a heavy sigh.

"I will tell mademoiselle all she may desire to know," said the stranger, as he ensconced himself in the chair next to her; "that is to say if the relation can afford her any pleasure."

But this monopoly of the Spanish hero on the part of Lucilla Evans did not please Miss Vereker, who immediately quitted Captain Rivers' side to take possession of another seat close to the young couple.

"I want to hear all about New York, too, Don Valera," she interrupted, archly. "I am greatly interested in hearing about new places. Are there many theatres there?"

"Many, mademoiselle, and most beautifully fitted up and decorated."

"Did you often go to them?"

"Very often,"

"How often? Twice a week?"

"More than that; sometimes I went several nights in succession."

"Oh, that must have been charming!" exclaimed Lucilla. "I have so often longed to be able to go to the play, but the fatigue is too much for me. What would I not give to be as strong as you are."

"Each back is fitted to the burden, mademoiselle," said the stranger, gently, "and no one of us can know what the other bears. There are worse calamities in life than the inability to attend theatres."

"Tell me more," said Lucilla. "I like to hear you talk. Have you left many friends behind you?"

"None," replied her companion, bitterly; then, recovering himself, he added, "except a brother. And when I last saw him he was almost too ill to speak."

"That was very sad. I hope he will soon get better, and perhaps be able to join you."

"Do you sing, Don Valera?" interrupted Lizzie Vereker.

"I do, mademoiselle."

"Then do go to the piano and sing us a song; we are really getting as dull as ditch-water. I shall be forced to return to Captain Rivers if this goes on."

"I do not sing to the pianoforte, or I should be happy to oblige you."

"What do you sing to, then?"

"My guitar."

"And have you got it with you?"

"It is amongst my luggage."

In another minute the guitar had been sent for, and unpacked, and laid in its owner's hands. He tuned it, played a short prelude, and then burst into one of those inspiriting Neapolitan tarantellas, the airs of which are so catching.

His voice was rich and mellow, the music a mere bagatelle,[*] the accompaniment light and subdued, and Lucilla Evans, whose nervous organisation could not stand the noise of a shrill voice and a shrieking bravura,[†] was delighted with the singer and the singing, and as soon as the song was concluded begged for another. Don Valera complied by playing a lively Spanish cachuca, which charmed his listener more than the first had done. The picturesque appearance of the musician, together with the novelty of his instrument (for it is a rare thing to hear the guitar well played in England at the present period), made a great impression on the female portion of his audience, and, with the exception of Mr. Evans, proportionately disgusted the men. But that good man, pleased with anything that brought a smile to his daughter's face, applauded the young Spaniard almost as much as the ladies had done, and Don Valera sang ballad after ballad, until some of the company, tired of being kept out in the cold, proposed adjournment to the billiard-room.

"Hang it all," cried Captain Rivers, as he entered that refuge with Sir Sydney Marchant and Tom Hastings. "Enough's as good as a feast. I was getting positively sick of that fellow's squalling. And to see all the women hanging over him in that absurd manner is too tantalising, 'pon my soul it is."

"What they can see in him to hang over I can't imagine," grumbled Tom Hastings. "A fat Spaniard tinkling a guitar. I bet the fellow can neither smoke, ride, nor play a game at billiards."

"None of these d—d foreigners ever can," interposed Sir Sydney. "And this one is a mere boy."

---

[*] Short piece of music, usually for piano.
[†] Piece of music usually played to show of the skill of the performer.

"A mere boy? He looks more like a woman stuck into boy's clothes to me. I should like to try my biceps against his, though I believe he's taller than I am, and broader into the bargain."

"All fat, my dear Hastings, every bit of it fat. You'd knock him into the middle of next week in no time. But that's just the sort of creature the women like to rave about. They'll let him dangle after them and wind their wools, and turn over their music, and sit in their pockets all day long; see if they don't."

"But devil a one of them will marry him," growled Sir Sydney.

"Heaven forbid!" cried Tom. "One might as well talk of their marrying a pussy-cat. He looks about as soft and useless."

"I thought we'd track you," exclaimed the merry voice of Lizzie Vereker, as, followed by the marquise and Don Valera, she appeared on the threshold of the billiard-room.

"You're pretty gentlemen to slope away in the middle of the evening, and leave us poor women to amuse ourselves."

"We thought you were so *very well* employed, Miss Vereker," said Captain Rivers pointedly, "that it seemed a pity to disturb you. Is all the singing over?"

"It is for the nonce, and I have brought the nightingale here that he may enjoy himself with the other birds of night."

"I do not suppose the Don is likely to care for pyramids," said Dr. Hastings, with a sneer. "So thoroughly English a game would have few charms for a foreigner."

"You forget that I am a New Yorker," replied Don Valera, with spirit; "and that New Yorkers have tried everything."

"Indeed. Then perhaps you will take a cue and show us how to play."

"I will show you how *we* play," returned the youth, as he made a stroke that put all that had gone before it to shame.

"Bravo!" cried Miss Vereker, clapping her hands.

"A lucky fluke," observed Rivers.

"Then I'll make another," said the stranger, as he rested his cue on his small white hand (looking so unusually small and white by those of the Englishmen present), and played a still better stroke than the first. The ladies were again loud in their plaudits, and the men began to perceive that the young Spaniard's skill was not entirely due to good luck.

"You have been used to this kind of thing, sir," observed Sir Sydney, grandly.

"I am used to everything, monsieur," was the grander answer.

"Indeed! I should like to hear a list of your accomplishments."

"An intimate acquaintance of the use of the broadsword," replied the Don, regarding hint fixedly; "and a knowledge not only how and when to use it, but *on whom!* Do you wish to hear more?"

"By no means. That is quite enough," said Sir Sydney, uneasily. "We have no time to waste in listening to each other's boasts this evening."

"You begged the question of me, monsieur. Am I to proceed with the game or not?"

"Of course, riding is amongst your acquirements, Don Valera," said Miss Vereker, admiringly.

"It is, mademoiselle, but not in the fashion you practise it in your country. I have been used to ride bare-back, or at most with a pair of stirrups slung across my mustang's saddle-cloth whilst I rode over the pathless prairie with a lasso in my hand."

"How delightful! How exciting! What adventures you must have encountered!" said Lizzie Vereker, with sparkling eyes. "And what did you lasso?"

"Wild cattle, mademoiselle, or horses. But sometimes I went pig-spearing, or shot the wild game, both large and small, which is very plentiful in the Brazils."

"That beats anything *you* have ever done," observed Lizzie to her unfortunate Captain Rivers.

"It is easy to talk," he muttered below his breath, as he moved away to another part of the room. Quite below his breath though. The new comer might be a "fat Spaniard," and "a mere boy," but since they had seen his eyes flash at the mention of the broadsword, they had dropped the idea of thinking it worth while to insult their host's guest.

"It is from the Brazils that the dear little hummingbird comes, isn't it?" asked Madame la Marquise.

"Not only the humming bird, madame, but hundreds of other birds almost as beautiful; and such flowers as, I imagine, you have never dreamt of in England."

"Oh! you must tell me all about them, Don."

"Any day that you wish to hear it, I am entirely at your service," he rejoined, as he applied himself afresh to the game they were playing.

Before they parted that night, the supposed Don Valera had proved to the gentlemen assembled in the Evans' house that he could not only smoke and play a game of billiards, but hold his own with the very best of them there. Lucilla Evans and Lizzie Vereker (who was staying in the house) appeared to be so much taken up with the new comer, that Captain Rivers and Doctor Hastings left them in the very worst of humours, knowing they were to be subjected to the young Spaniard's fascination without the safeguard of their presence. If they had only known the truth, how very easy they might have made themselves.

* * * * * *

As for Valera himself, so soon as he was shown up to the bedroom allotted to his use, he locked the door carefully behind him, threw off his fashionable new habiliments with a sigh of relief, and felt that for a few hours at least he might cast aside the restraint that galled him, and be what he was—Leona Lacoste.

"So far, so good," she thought, as she stretched herself upon her couch. "I have succeeded hitherto better than I could possibly have expected. There has not been a hitch anywhere. My voyage is over. I have met my uncle. I am located under his very roof, with permission to remain here as long as I choose. Now, if the fates are only propitious, and Halliday and Upjohn do not take it into their heads to write some letter concerning Tobal that shall upset my plans, I shall probably gain a clear month to work in.

"Dear Tobal. I wonder how he is progressing, and if the country air has made him strong again. The worst part of this business has been to cut myself off from all communication with him. What will he think of me, *mon pauvre frère*? What will he say? Oh, *Tobalito mio*, I could have done it for naught but one thing— *My Father's Name!* The girl Lucilla fancies me, I can see plainly. How strange it is that I, who, in a woman's garb am generally disliked by women, should excite their sympathies directly I assume clothes to which I have no right. All the girls fell in love with me on the stage when I appeared as a boy. Bah, the fools! How short-sighted they must be. But I must not blame them for it now. Their folly may prove my salvation.

"Lucilla Evans is everything in this house, I can perceive that; therefore, to obtain her favour is to become a general favourite. And I must work upon her liking for me, in order to gain sufficient general information to commence my investigation upon. She looks shrewd, and she is not very young. If I am any judge of age, hers must be five-and-twenty at the least. If that is true, and this sad business happened two-and-twenty years ago, she may even remember to have heard it spoken of.

"But stop! of what am I thinking?

"That man—the Boston manager—said that my poor father was the elder son, and he was only two-and-twenty at the time of the murder.

"My uncle could not have been married so soon. How then can he have a daughter of that age? She must be younger than I imagined!

"Yet I cannot believe it. There are lines in her face which nothing but the passage of time will bring. How totally unlike she is to both her parents. Not a single feature is the same. She looks as if she came of a different race altogether. Anyway my first endeavour must be to make great friends with her, and hear all the family may have to tell me of the details of that terrible time."

* * * * * *

Acting upon this determination, Leona exerted herself to the utmost to foster the fancy that Lucilla appeared to have taken for her. She hovered about her couch all day, delicately attentive to her many little wants, and always ready to converse or to hold her tongue as the invalid seemed best inclined. Dr. Hastings, who had been accustomed in his rough way to fetch and carry for Lucilla, but whose intentions had ever been better than his mode of carrying them out, sunk terribly in her estimation as nurse by comparison with the new comer. Don Valera's voice was so low and musical, it never went through her head as poor Tom's did; and his hands were so firm and gentle, he never let the cushions slip, or clashed the teacups, or made any other jar to startle and alarm her. And he would sit for hours by her sofa reading to her, or talking of those far-off beautiful countries which she could never hope to see for herself, singing quaint foreign songs to the soft accompaniment of his guitar. In a few days it seemed as though Lucilla could go nowhere and enjoy nothing, unless this Spanish youth were by her side. She drove out with him in the carriage, he walked beside her invalid-chair in the Park, he carried her meals up to the drawing-room; in fact he waited on her like a servant, and became more necessary to her happiness every day. Mr. and Mrs. Evans saw their daughter smiling and contented, and were delighted with the improvement, never minding whence it came; Leona perceived the influence she was gaining over Lucilla's mind, and praised heaven for the good fortune that had given her such an ally. Since they conversed, when together, on every topic under the sun, it was not difficult to her woman's tact, to bring round the conversation to the subject she preferred to speak on; and thus it came to pass that, as they were driving together one morning, about a week after her arrival, in the quiet shady roads round Wimbledon and Roehampton,* she made her first attempt to gain some information respecting the Liverpool murder.

"How lovely the trees are!" observed Lucilla. "Who would think we were but a few miles out of London? I should think your Brazilian forests could hardly boast of finer specimens than those chestnuts, Don Valera?"

"Ah, mademoiselle! you can have no idea of the vegetation of the Brazils until you see it. It is almost too beautiful for earth. And yet amidst such wealth of loveliness as nature shows us there, people can still rob and ill-treat, and murder one another! Crime is not so prevalent, I think, in this climate. You are colder, more patient, and more forgiving than the children of the south."

"I don't think we are! We have dreadful murders committed in England, sometimes; but mamma does not like me to read such accounts, because I dream of them at night. It must be terrible to be murdered; to have your throat cut, or to be shot, or poisoned. The mere thought of it makes me shudder."

---

* Areas in south west London.

"Yet you must have heard a good deal of that sort of thing in Liverpool, mademoiselle. The people about there are a very rough lot, are they not?"

"I don't think so—not worse than others, I mean. Papa had a sad case happen once in his warehouse, though—"

"Yes, yes," said Leona, eagerly. She fully believed she was going to hear the story now.

"A very dreadful case. A poor woman killed her baby, and hid the body under some empty casks that were packed away there. But that is all I know. They will not let me hear of such things, as I said before."

"I have heard, mademoiselle—that is, I read in an old newspaper—oh, years and years ago—of another that took place also, if I remember rightly, on your father's premises."

"Did you?" said Lucilla, with wide-open eyes. "How was that?"

"It was the murder of a man, I believe, and the murderer was never traced."

"How strange! I never heard of it. It may have been some other firm, not papa's."

"No. I am sure it was the house of Messrs. Evans and Troubridge."

"Oh, Mr. Troubridge died in a fit. Perhaps you are thinking of that, Don Valera?"

"No. This was the murder of a clerk of the name of Anson, which happened about two-and-twenty years ago. Has no one ever mentioned it to you?"

"Never. I fancy you must be mistaken. Only I was not much more than a baby at that time. I am just five-and-twenty. It is strange you should imagine it happened in that year, though."

"Why?"

"Because it is just two-and-twenty years since papa and mamma sent me away from Liverpool, to be brought up down in the country."

"Why did they send you away, mademoiselle?"

"I was a sickly little thing, I believe, and country air was recommended to me. I was brought up in Sussex, by a Mrs. Gibson. I never knew I had a father or a mother till I was nearly eight years old; and then they came down to Sussex one day and took me home to Liverpool. I remember I was so astonished. They seemed quite like strangers to me. But they were so kind. I was soon as happy as I could be. But it *was* funny—wasn't it?"

"*You never saw Mr. and Mrs. Evans till you were eight years old?*" said Leona, musingly.

– CHAPTER 15 –

ON THE SCENT

"Never saw your parents till you were eight years old?" repeated Leona, in a tone of surprise.

"Oh! I had seen them before, I suppose, Don Valera, but that was the first occasion I can remember doing so."

"And you are their only child, too!"

"And a good thing for them, if the others would have been half the trouble that I have been. But mamma did have another child— a little boy, who died soon after he was born. She has often told me of him. I am sorry I was not a boy too, for papa's sake."

"I am sure he would rather have you as you are, mademoiselle."

"Do you think so? Anyway it is of no use wishing things to be different from what they are. You went to see the marquise yesterday, Don, did you not?"

"I had that honour, by madame's special invitation."

"And who did you meet there?"

"Sir Sydney Marchant, Miss Forrester, and three gentlemen whose names I do not remember."

"No other ladies?"

"None except Miss Forrester, and—I mean except Miss Forrester."

"You are keeping something from me, Don Valera. Why should I not know of all the company, then?"

"I assure you I have told you all!"

"No beautiful young lady, with melting eyes and golden hair, to take you captive?"

"Had there been such, she could have had no influence on me, mademoiselle."

"Why? Is your heart already gone?"

Leona gave a sudden sigh.

"I think it is. At all events I have not left it at Madame de Toutlemonde's."

"Ah, Don! I am afraid you are no better than the rest of your sex. But it is strange (is it not?) that there should be no ladies present at the luncheon but the hostess and Miss Forrester?"

"I did not think it strange. I have seen a great deal of the world, mademoiselle, and I should not care—I mean if I were a woman—I should not care to make a friend of the Marquise de Toutlemonde."

"You don't like her," said Lucilla, with an air of content.

"I do not, indeed! But I say it to you in strict confidence. I have no right to abuse the lady's hospitality."

"I am very glad you don't like her," observed Lucilla, "because I don't either."

"Had not your father an elder brother once?" asked Leona, harking back to the old subject.

"Oh yes," said her companion readily, "his brother George—but he died long ago. There is a miniature of him in the study, but papa always keeps it locked up in one of the drawers in his writing table. I saw it once and asked who it was. Then he told me."

"He was very fond of him, perhaps?"

"I think he must have been. I know mamma said I mustn't mention his name again to papa, because it upset him. But it all happened long before I was born. Raymond had sometimes spoken of him to me. Have you observed that old woman who always accompanies me to the carriage with my shawls and wraps? She is Raymond. She was papa's nurse, and has lived in the family more than forty years. I found her crying one day, poor old thing! and when I asked her the reason, she said it was her bonnie Master George's birthday, and it made her sad to think of him. I thought it very nice and affectionate of her. Don't you?"

"Very nice," repeated Leona, mechanically. She had already made up her mind, if possible, to get on the right side of Nurse Raymond.

They arrived at home to find the luncheon-room and table filled by a set of visitors, not one of whom had received an invitation to attend the meal. But, thanks to Miss Forrester and a few such enterprising spirits that had now become the rule in the Evans' household, people dropped in and out just as they chose, at all hours of the day; and the poor dear hostess thought it very convenient that they should do so, without giving her the trouble to ask them, and remained perfectly innocent of the fact that she was being "fleeced" without mercy, and that her splendid mansion had been turned into a mere house of call for the lunchless and the tired.

Foremost amongst the self-invited guests that day were two old maiden sisters of the name of Lillietrip, who lived chiefly upon such chance visits to their friends, and knew the exact breakfast, luncheon, and dinner hour of all their acquaintances. They were gushing, enthusiastic, youthful creatures, of about sixty years of age, withered and skinny to a degree, but still young! oh so young! in their thoughts, manners, and mode of expression, and used to take huge fancies to strangers at first sight, which they discarded as soon as they found the new-made friends attracted more attention than they did themselves. They lived together in a suite of rooms where they allured visitors, especially young men, on the pretence of attending fancy-dress balls, private theatricals, and musical parties, but which visitors, finding by experience that the chief part of such entertainments consisted in seeing and hearing the Misses Lillietrip act, dance, and sing, were accustomed to fight shy of lending their countenance to the proceedings; or if they went, were bold enough to cause not a little amusement for themselves whilst there. This last alternative, however, was always highly resented by the Misses Lillietrip, especially if the offender happened to be a female, younger and better-looking than themselves, and fortunate enough to have induced some of the gentlemen present to be amused at the same time. They would speak sharply of her as "bold" and a "forward" and "designing," and even hint (but strictly behind her back) that her reputation was not wholly above reproach. They had been much troubled with one or two such recreants lately, and been obliged to give out in consequence (but also strictly behind their backs), that they had been forced to "weed" their little society, and were determined in future to receive none such as cared for them for themselves alone. Miss Forrester and Madame de Toutlemonde had been heard to observe that in that case the Misses Lillietrip would have very few flowers left in the garden of their acquaintance, but of this the sisters were of course blissfully ignorant. The two ladies above mentioned were not amongst the "weeded," chiefly, it was supposed, because Miss Forrester had a very sharp tongue, and an utter contempt for the feelings of her friends, and that it was her royal will and pleasure, for reasons best known to himself, that the Marquise de Toutlemonde should accompany her wherever she went. I say *for reasons best known to herself*, but that does not preclude the public from guessing at them.

And Madame de Toutlemonde gave nice little dinners in her cosy house in Bayswater, and generally had a brougham at her command, and orders for the opera and other places of amusement. Moreover, she paid well to secure the fidelity of her few female adherents. And Miss Forrester was needy and dependent—too poor to go into society—often in want of a dinner, and a thorough time-server. She could not brave the world's opinion, but she ignored what passed beneath her eyes—in consideration of her scanty purse. She was also at the Evans' luncheon table that day, with, of course, the marquise.

The Misses Lillietrip flew at Lucilla as she entered the room, as if they had been her oldest and dearest friends. They cajoled, they condoled, they flattered, and fawned, and caressed, like two aged and attenuated pussy-cats, giving vent to their delight or their sorrow, by little juvenile screams and infantile groans. They kept their eyes meantime, though, upon the young Spaniard, of whom they had already heard. They liked his appearance. He looked young and soft and impressionable, and as if he would be easily taken in. And it was generally very young men whom these ancient sirens managed to allure to their home in Portman Square. Their fishing, if successful, usually resulted in the capture of some infinitesimal minnow or undeveloped tadpole. And to secure a real Spanish don for one of their receptions would be delightful. They had talked of it coming along. They had even improvised a party for his special benefit. And they lost no time in bringing the subject forward.

"My dear Lucilla," they exclaimed (the Misses Lillietrip always talked together, and interrupted each other, so that it was difficult to know which was the speaker), "we have come here on purpose to-day to ask your dear mamma if you would all come to a little gathering at our house on Saturday; just a few charades, you know, and a little dancing and so forth; your mamma and papa, and yourself and any friends, of course, you may have staying with you—this gentleman for instance (glancing towards Leona)—if he will honour us. You've not introduced me, my dear."

"I beg your pardon. Don Christobal Valera, Miss Lillietrip—Miss Charlotte Lillietrip."

"Delighted, I'm sure, Don Valera. Well, as I was saying, it will give us the greatest pleasure to see you all on Saturday, but your dear mamma won't say yes till she hears what you think about it."

"So good of Mrs. Evans, so like her, so kind," answered Miss Charlotte.

"Mamma is afraid of my back. I cannot stand any fatigue," said Lucilla, wearily.

"And you are tired now. You must sit down," said Leona, fetching her a chair.

She smiled her thanks for the attention before she proceeded with her conversation.

"But if mamma and papa are going, and—and—all of us, I think I should like to accompany them, though, of course, I can't dance, you know."

"My dearest girl, you shall do just as you like. We hope to have some charades, and they will amuse you."

"Shall *you* go?" asked Lucilla, timidly, of Leona.

"That is as you wish, mademoiselle," she replied, with a pretty foreign accent, over which the Misses Lillietrip went into dumb raptures.

"*I'm* going," exclaimed Lizzie Vereker, "and I shall act too. What charades do you propose to have, Miss Lillietrip?" The sisters were not overpleased at this generous announcement, Miss Vereker being one of the ladies they would fain have "weeded" from their society, had she not been so intimate with the Evans. She was too handsome and attractive and outspoken to permit them to be comfortable in her presence.

"We have not decided yet, Miss Vereker, and we must get our

gentlemen first. Will your friend act?" continued Miss Lillietrip, turning to Lucilla, and indicating Leona.

"I don't know if he can. Have you ever acted charades, Don Valera?"

"Sometimes, mademoiselle."

"Will you do so, to oblige these ladies?"

"If *you* are to be there to see me, I will."

A thought had flashed into Leona's ready brain at the idea. It might prove feasible or not, but at any rate it would be as well to secure the opportunity. It was this that made her agree so readily to Lucilla's proposition.

"If you act, I shall make a point of going," rejoined Miss Evans.

The Misses Lillietrip were delighted. They invited all present for Saturday evening, and they secured Don Valera to visit them the day before, and make the necessary arrangements for the successful production of the charades. They were gushingly enthusiastic over him, until Leona had the utmost difficulty to be civil to them. As soon as ever she could slip away from them she did. Lucilla went to lie down after luncheon, and Leona escaped to her own room, to think over the puzzling intelligence she had heard that morning, and to try if she could make it bear in any way on the mystery she was bent upon unravelling.

She took out a private memorandum-book, in which she kept a record, in Spanish, of any evidence she considered worth preserving, and wrote down:

"*Lucilla Evans was sent away from Liverpool into the country, to the care of a Mrs. Gibson, two-and-twenty years ago, when she was three years old, and does not remember to have seen her parents till she was eight.*"

"That is a very remarkable circumstance," thought Leona, as she closed her book. "In the first place, I have heard nothing of Henry Evans being married at the time the murder was committed, whereas this child appears to have been three years old, when the father could not have been much more than one-and-twenty. That seems improbable. And why should he and his wife have parted with her for five years afterwards, and never visited her—nor had her home—during all that period? Did they quit England after my poor father quitted it? I must find that out. I must find out, too, what part of Sussex Mrs. Gibson lived in, and see if it is not possible to have an interview with her. I wonder how much or how little she knows. I might go to her as the child's old nurse—as Raymond, for instance if she has never met Raymond. *Caramba!* That reminds me of how useful the nurse herself might be. How am I to get over her? She is very much attached to Lucilla. I will begin by praising that young lady."

It was not long before the opportunity she wished for occurred. The voice of Mrs. Raymond, who occupied the position of half-housekeeper, half-lady's-maid, in the establishment, was heard in the corridor, bringing an idle servant to book, for leaning out of the window instead of attending to her work.

"How often am I to tell you the same thing, you impudent hussy? you think of nothing, morning, noon, or night, but smirking at the men."

"I wasn't smirking at no men," returned the girl. "Well, if you wasn't, it's only because there was no men to smirk at. Come, you be off, do, and carry all them things downstairs. This is no time of day to have the passages littered up with mops and pails of water."

"Mrs. Raymond," said Leona, as the housekeeper's dress rustled past the open door.

"Did you speak, sir?" was the woman's answer, given in the most dulcet of tones, as she appeared upon the threshold.

For all the females in the house, from high to low, were taken with the appearance of the young foreigner. They thought him so very handsome and nice spoken.

And, indeed, Leona, in the fashionably-cut clothes which she had been careful to procure, did make a very beautiful boy.

"Forgive me for troubling you, Mrs. Raymond, but if you would take pity on the ignorance of a poor stranger, I should be so much obliged to you. What am I to do with the linen, the shirts, the collars, you understand me, that I wish to have washed?"

"Dear me, sir, don't think twice about it. I will look after all that for you. If you will only be so good as to throw them on one side, I will see they are properly got up and replaced in your wardrobe."

"But it will trouble you too much, I fear."

"No, indeed, sir. And I am quite sure you've not been used to look after such things yourself."

"*Madre de Dios!* madame, no! Nor yet to have such women as

yourself to do it for me. In the country from which I come we have only blacks to wait upon us."

"Lawk a mercy, sir, and how ladies and gentlemen could ever abide them black creatures, I can't think. The mere thought of them makes me creep. I should never fancy anything they touched again."

"We are obliged to bear them, Mrs. Raymond, we have no other attendants. And I do not think, if we had, that we could allow women like yourself to be our servants."

At this speech Mrs. Raymond bridled. She was a fine upright old woman of perhaps five-and-sixty, and still bore the traces of having been a handsome girl.

"Well, I'm sure, sir, and what else are we good for. I wonder?"

"Mademoiselle Lucilla, I fancy, thinks you are good enough for anything. She was talking to me of you this morning."

"Ah, bless her sweet heart!" said the housekeeper; "she's too much a lady to speak ill of anyone. She's a real angel is Miss Lucilla."

"So *I* think, Mrs. Raymond. But she has reason to love you. You were her father's nurse, were you not?"

"Aye, that I was, sir. I was taken into the Lime House nursery before ever Master Henry was born, and I stayed there till after he had lost both his pa and his ma, and was breeched and sent to school, and then I went as housemaid to his uncle, Mr. Theophilus Evans, with whom the young gentlemen lived, and when Mr. Henry married, he brought me home to his house, and so you may say I've been with them through sorrow and joy for five-and-forty years. And that's a long time for one family's service, sir."

"It is indeed! No wonder they speak of you as a friend more than a servant. But you spoke of the young *gentlemen*. Has Mr. Evans a brother?"

"He *had,* sir," she replied, with sudden gravity.

"Is he dead?"

"We believe so, sir. He went to foreign parts, and hasn't been heard of since."

"How very strange! Was he a sailor?"

"No, sir."

"A soldier?"

"No, sir. He was nothing but a gentleman. But *such* a gentleman! I've heard Master Henry called good-looking, but he's nothing to what Master George was."

"Oh, his, name was George, was it?"

"Yes, sir, it was; but it quite slipped out of my mouth, and I hope you won't mention it again, for the master doesn't like his brother alluded to. It was a sad business for the family, and least said is soonest mended."

"Was Master George very wild then?"

"He was wild, sir, God bless his heart, though there wasn't a soul but loved him through it all. And, for my part, I shall never forget him—never! I don't know what set me off talking of him so, I'm sure," she continued drying her eyes, "unless it is that you remind me of him, sir."

"I remind you of him!" cried Leona, startled.

"You do indeed, sir; though it seems strange to say so, and I can't tell you in what. But several times when I've carried Miss Lucy's shawl down to the carriage, and you've been sitting by her side, I've stood and looked at your face—(you'll forgive the liberty, I hope, sir)—and wondered how it was you brought poor Master George so powerfully to my mind. 'Tisn't your eyes, for his was the beautifulest brown; nor yet your nose, I fancy it must be something in your smile, and the colour of your hair. Master George had just your coloured hair, sir; and I think Master Henry sees it too, for I often catch him looking at you when your head's turned another way."

"A strange fancy," laughed the young foreigner, rather uneasily. "How comes it that Mademoiselle Lucilla is so unlike both her parents, Mrs. Raymond?" he said suddenly a moment afterwards.

The housekeeper's face betrayed her disquietude at the unexpected question.

"Don't you consider her like them, sir?" she said rather evasively.

"Certainly not. No one could. I should never have taken her for their daughter if I had not been told so."

"She is a dear, good young lady as ever breathed," rejoined Mrs. Raymond. "But I must be going—I have business below. I won't forget about your things, sir; and if there is anything else that I can do I hope you won't scruple to ask me."

"Don't go so soon. I want to talk about Mademoiselle Lucilla. Has she been long ill?"

"Ever since she was fifteen. And that's ten years ago, sir."

"How very young Mr. Evans must have married."

"Many gentlemen marry young; though I don't hold by it," replied the housekeeper, getting flurried.

"Was he married when his brother died, or went away, Mrs. Raymond?"

"Lor'! sir, I don't know why you should put these questions to me at all. They can't concern you to know. There's Miss Lucy, as handsome a young lady as you'd wish to see, and there's her pa and ma. If you want to know more than I can tell you, you'd better go straight to them."

"I'm sorry I offended you, madame. It was quite unintentional. But Mademoiselle Lucilla has been good enough to honour me with her friendship. Is it not natural I should be interested to learn all I can concerning her?"

"I beg your pardon, sir. Perhaps I spoke too hasty. But the thought of those times always cuts me up. I was very partial to Master George, sir."

"I am not surprised to hear it, madame, if he was all you say. But perhaps you will meet him again some day. He may not be dead. He may be still living in those foreign lands."

"Oh, no, sir, there's no hope of that; for it's so long ago, we should have heard news of him before now if he had been alive, poor dear. But there, it's no use talking. If he were alive he'd never come home again. I know that for one."

"Did he quarrel with his friends then?"

"Yes, sir, he did; and now I hope you'll ask me nothing more, for I can't tell you."

"I have had a purpose in asking, Mrs. Raymond. I have been a great traveller, and am likely to travel still more. Were I to meet the gentleman we have been speaking of, I might recognise him from your description."

"He wouldn't thank you to recognise him, I fancy, sir. He knows where he has got friends if he wants them."

"I have met all sorts of people in my wanderings, and have

heard all sorts of secrets. You say I put you in mind of Mr. Evans' brother. I'll tell you of whom your young lady puts me in mind, Mrs. Raymond."

"I never think Miss Lucy's like anyone but herself."

"Oh, I don't mean to say they're quite alike, only there's a strong resemblance. Did you ever come across a family of the name of *Anson*?"

"*Anson*, sir?" the housekeeper repeated in a gasping voice; then, feeling she had partly betrayed herself, she added very slowly, "I've heard the name, sir, it's a common one in this country."

"I knew some people of that name once," said Leona, deliberately, and keeping her eyes fixed upon Mrs. Raymond. "And your Mademoiselle Lucilla so resembles them in feature and general style, that before I heard she was Mrs. Evans' daughter I was just going to ask if her name was not *Anson*."

"Oh no, sir! indeed it isn't her name," exclaimed the housekeeper, with most unnecessary vehemence. "Her name's Miss Lucy Evans, sir. You mustn't go talking about of her looking as if she had another name, sir, because the master will be very much annoyed if you do and if it were to come back to me, sir, and to your having talked with me about it, I don't know what mightn't happen. I don't indeed."

"Be quieted, my good woman; be calm," said Leona. "Not a word shall pass my lips of what you have said to me to-day."

"I oughtn't to have said as much as I have, I daresay," whimpered Mrs. Raymond; "but you drew it out of me somehow before I knew where I was; and you remind me so strong-like of poor master George that I hardly seem to remember a word that's gone from me."

"And no more do I. And if I did 'tis as safe as the grave," said Leona, as she watched the housekeeper leave the room.

* * * * * *

"At the same time, my good madame," she said to herself, "your chattering has told me all I want for the present to know. I suspected it this morning. I am sure of it now. '*Lucilla is not my uncle's daughter!*' That is the first fact! Whose is she then? Abraham

Anson thanks my dear father in the postscript to his letter for his kindness to '*Little Lucy!*' If—as I almost believe—this girl is the offspring of the murdered clerk, there arises a second question to be answered:

"*Why did my uncle adopt her, and pass her off as his own child?*"

"I cannot see my way clear before me yet, but I am on the scent."

– CHAPTER 16 –

THE MISSES LILLIETRIP

Her conversation with the housekeeper cost Leona several sleepless nights and speculative days. She had arrived at that scene in the life-drama she had sworn to play out by herself when half the actors were upon the stage, and the plot was commencing to unfold itself; and yet the chattering and commotion about her were so great she could neither hear nor understand the meaning of what passed before her. Her thoughts were in inextricable confusion, and from day to day she could not decide what steps to take next. One fact was very apparent—that Mr. Evans' interest was awakened in her. Not only did he show it in the way Mrs. Raymond had pointed out—by gazing earnestly at the young Spaniard whenever he imagined he was unobserved—as though he was trying to discover what it was in Leona that attracted him, or to connect his fancy with some link of the past—but he attempted to prove it by more substantial methods. He appeared almost jealous of the partiality which Leona evinced for Lucilla, and seized every opportunity of securing her company for himself. He used to ask her to join him in his morning walks, when he would draw out from her, as much as possible, the history of her past life—where she had been reared, how educated, and of whom her family consisted. These questions Leona would parry to the best of her ability; and such as she was compelled to answer, she did as though she were indeed the person she represented herself to be. Then her host would take her with him into the City, and introduce her to the various members of the firm, by whom she was at first received (as she had been by Mrs. Evans' guests) with shrugs of the shoulders and looks of incredulity. But, being presented to the gentlemen who conducted the Spanish correspondence of the great house, and proving herself a proficient in reading, writing, and speaking that language in all its ramifications and branches, she rose immensely in the estimation of her companions and ceased to be mentioned with expressions of contempt. Did no pang of remorse assail Leona Lacoste at this period, for the deception she had practised on those who had received her with such unmitigated kindness and perfect trust?

Not the slightest!

She had but one object in view. She looked upon her mission as sacred, and considered nothing underhand or dishonourable that was necessary to forward the project she had pledged herself before high heaven to carry out—the clearance of her dead father's reputation from obloquy and reproach. She never stopped to consider if she had any right to accept the benefits showered on her in another name. Her eyes were steadfastly fixed upon one point, and she would have gone through fire and water to attain it. She had taken a cordial distaste to Mr. Evans, which no kindness on his part could mitigate. She disliked his company, she revolted at the interest he evinced for her, she shrank inwardly from the touch of his hand, or the sound of his voice. She regarded the luxury with which he and his family were surrounded as the price of her father's blood. She saw them revelling in everything they could desire, without a thought, apparently, of him who had forfeited his share of the good things of this life, to go forth and die an exile in the wilderness, branded with the infamy of a crime of which he was completely innocent, and which yet must have been committed by—whom? For the sake of the task before her she was obliged to submit to her uncle's peculiarities, and pertinent inquiries, and fellowship; for in intimacy with him and him alone lay her chances of discovering the truth, but the submission galled her spirit. And when it came to his offering her pecuniary benefits, her pride drew the line and became actively rebellious. And yet Mr. Evans proffered this assistance in the most delicate and generous manner. He took occasion, one afternoon, whilst Leona sat with him in his study translating an English letter into Spanish, to intimate that it might be another fortnight or three weeks before the firm would require his services professionally. "Meanwhile," continued Mr. Evans, "I trust that you are enjoying your stay in London, and making the best use of your time."

"I am enjoying it more than I could have hoped for, monsieur, thanks to the hospitality of yourself and madame."

"Our metropolis cannot compare in point of gaiety and sunshine with one of your beautiful southern cities; but still there is very much of interest in it, especially to a foreigner; and I should not like you to quit London again without having seen all that there is to be seen here."

"You are very good," replied Leona, "and I think madame concurs with your wishes, for she takes me almost every day to some new place."

"That is not quite what I mean. There are many things and places to be seen in town that ladies cannot go to, but sight-seeing costs money, as I have often been made to feel. And money runs away faster than we can ever make it. I do not know what arrangements Messrs. Halliday and Upjohn have made with you, Valera, but I am detaining you longer in England than they probably anticipated, and for my own pleasure or convenience. Under these circumstances I feel bound (and I hope you will see it in the same light) to charge myself with your extra expenses. I think you will find sufficient ammunition there," he continued, passing a sealed envelope across the table, "to carry on the war a little longer, and the only favour I ask of you is that when it is expended you will be sure to let me know."

But the Spanish correspondent pushed back the sealed packet, with an expression of wounded pride and sensibility which Mr. Evans had never seen on the face of any salaried clerk before.

"I thank you, monsieur," said Leona in a voice that slightly trembled, "for your intentions on my behalf, but I never accept money that I have not earned."

"Let us consider that you have earned it then, my dear fellow, by your attentions to my wife and my daughter. I do not know when Lucilla has found a companion before in whom she expressed so much interest."

"I am indebted to madame and mademoiselle for their good

opinion of me, which I feel to be entirely undeserved, but that cannot alter this matter between us. I have sufficient money for myself, monsieur."

"Very good," said Mr. Evans, as he threw the rejected gift into the drawer, but he seemed vexed and disappointed as he did so. "We will let the subject drop. You must believe, however, I had no intention of offending you, Don Valera."

"Oh no, monsieur, indeed, and I feel your goodness very much—but—but—it is impossible to me, that is all."

"I am, at all events, glad to know that you have no occasion to lay yourself under such an obligation to any one. It is not every young man in your position that can say the same."

"I am fortunate," said Leona, simply, as with burning cheeks she reapplied herself to her task of translation.

Presently a servant entered with a summons on business that Mr. Evans felt must be immediately attended to. He rose with a gesture of annoyance.

"It appears as though I could never get half an hour to myself. If you wish to proceed with that translation, Valera, you will find the rest of the document in that drawer; but there is no hurry, there are my keys. Lock the writing-table before you leave the room, there's a good fellow, and keep the keys till we meet again. I shall be back to dinner."

And in another minute he had gone, and Leona was left alone. Here was her opportunity. Ever since Lucilla had spoken to her of that miniature of her uncle George which her father kept under lock and key in one of his study drawers, Leona had longed to rifle the writing-table and see the portrait for herself. For supposing (and the thought had occasionally flashed across her mind) it should be all a mistake; and that George Evans, with whom she had been led to associate her father's identity, should prove *not* to be the George Evans of the firm to which she had under false pretences, attached herself! It had been all hearsay hitherto. She had received no conclusive evidence. But a sight of the miniature, should she find it to have been taken from the face she knew and remembered so well, would settle her doubts at once. She waited breathlessly with the keys in her hand till she heard the hall-door close after Mr. Evans; then hurriedly securing herself against intrusion, she commenced her search. Drawer after drawer was ransacked of its contents before she came to what she looked for. Private letters, professional papers, receipts of consequence and bills of value, passed in revision before her, but she never stopped even to glance at them. With all her anxiety to clear her father's name, and her determination to let no obstacle stand in the way of her filial duty, Leona Lacoste would have scorned to have read a private letter without permission, as she scorned to accept money from the man whom she believed she was working in the dark to ruin. There *are* women who consider it no dishonour to be dishonourable—unfortunately there are many—but the instinct of all noble natures is the same; and the nature, educated or otherwise, who will stoop to listen at a door or read a letter not intended for its perusal, never mind to attain what end, will never rise under any circumstances to be noble. It may be restrained through fear, or propriety, or shame, but if it be not instinctively too grand to grovel, its uprightness will be at the best but a sham.

Leona Lacoste had been born noble. Her fiery untamed nature was full of faults; and to attain a purpose which appeared of more consequence to her than the rest of the world put together, she could act a part which she believed would injure no one but the guilty. But her host's private papers were safe with her. She passed them over with no more notice than was necessary to let her see the portrait she looked for was not amongst them. But at last she came upon it. At last, in the lowest drawer, hidden beneath a store of unused writing-paper, she spied a small oval red morocco case, much worn and discoloured, which, on being opened, disclosed the features of her father. She could not mistake them. Young, *debonnair*, and handsome, as George Evans had appeared at one-and-twenty, with his laughing eyes and winning smile, his daughter could yet trace the expression that had become overshadowed by trouble and fear before she knew it, and recognise the thick curls of chestnut hair that had whitened from the same cause. She had hardly thought the sight of him as he had been would so much affect her; but the tears gathered thickly in her eyes as she gazed at the miniature, and compared it with the wreck that he had died. As she looked at him through the blinding mist her emotion had evoked, it seemed as though he called out to her from the past to see what the injustice of public opinion had done for him, and to be steadfast to avenge his wrongs. She examined the portrait minutely, and taking in every detail of form and colouring, was struck with its startling likeness to herself at the present time, rendered all the more striking by her assumed attire. She no longer wondered that Mr. Evans should regard her with attention, or that the housekeeper should say she reminded her of "poor Master George." She was only surprised they could live in the same house with her and not discover who she was. But she forgot that the lapse of years since George Evans disappeared, and their total ignorance, even of the country to which he had escaped, rendered it unlikely that her appearance would have the power to do more than raise his memory.

She recalled the vivid past to Mr. Evans; the past that he had been vainly trying all these long years to forget—that he would fain have thrust from him as the enemy of an evil dream, and that was all. And yet for the very sake of what that past had caused him to suffer, he would have been kind to the young stranger if she would have permitted him. But he made her suffer too. Had she followed her inclination she would have run away and never looked upon his face again—that face so like, and yet so unlike her dear injured father's handsome features.

But she had her part to play, and having well once put her shoulder to the plough, was not the woman to turn back until the harrowing was completed, never mind whose back suffered in the fulfilment of her duty.

She replaced the miniature where she had found it, and locked the drawers. She could not proceed with the task of translation; when the brain is fermenting with a new project, or excited over a strange discovery, our natural powers go from us. So Leona closed her study door behind her and sought the presence of Lucilla Evans, whose dull eyes lighted up with pleasure as she perceived her friend cross the threshold of the drawing-room.

* * * * * *

The Misses Lillietrip had secured the attendance of Don Christobal Valera the day before they were to give their charade-party, in order to hold a consultation as to the scenes they intended to represent. He was punctual to his appointment, and found Miss Vereker already installed in office, with some five or six other ladies and gentlemen who had promised to take part in the performance. The Misses Lillietrip were in great form. They always were on the eve of private theatricals or charades, and they invariably insisted on playing the young and lovely heroines themselves, and thus came in for the largest share of the spurious spooning that necessarily went on. And to those ladies who have never had any experience of the genuine article, the theatrical substitute seems to afford somewhat of satisfaction. There is no accounting for taste. When Leona was first made to understand that whatever was acted the Misses Lillietrip intended to adopt the *rôles* of heroines, she was at a loss to comprehend how they could ever suppose they would look the parts. But then, she was not aware that they possessed two beautiful flaxen wigs in their boxes upstairs, and that, according to female reasoning, flaxen curls and a liberal amount of rouge will cover a multitude of crow's feet and wrinkles. As a matter of fact, the fairer the hair the older appears the skin: and a complexion that might pass muster under a dark brown wig, looks coarse and ruddled beneath locks of gold—but let that pass. To quote an old saw, "Where ignorance is bliss 'tis folly to be wise;"[*] and certainly the Misses Lillietrip had no intention of being wise on this occasion, nor any fear apparently of placing their withered arms and cheeks in close proximity with Don Valera's blooming complexion and smooth, plump hands. A few of the preliminaries having been arranged, Miss Charlotte Lillietrip (who considered herself quite an infant by the side of her elder sister) took it into her virginal head that the young Spaniard must require some instruction in the mode of English love-making, and proceeded therefore to show him a few of her favourite *poses*, and initiate him into the manner in which she desired he should receive her arch smiles and languishing glances; whilst Lizzie Vereker, who would have had no objection herself to play ladylove to the pretty boy whom she had bantered so unmercifully and

---

[*] Quotation from the English poet Thomas Gray (1716-1771) from the poem 'Ode on a Distant Prospect of Eton College'.

unsuccessfully during the last few days, as to make her almost inclined to give him up as a fool, sat enthroned in an arm-chair, and laughed until the tears ran down her cheeks; and Miss Charlotte, anything but pleased at the ridicule thrown on her acting, remarked snappishly, that if Miss Vereker could do it better she would prefer, perhaps, to take the principal part herself, and leave her hostesses to play waiting-maids and old women.

"*Of course* I should prefer it, infinitely," replied the audacious Lizzie, no way daunted by Miss Charlotte's sneer; "and I think I should *look* the part quite as well as you will, into the bargain. But you are not going to keep Don Valera the *whole* evening to yourself, are you? You'll let me come in for a share of the kissing, I hope. Consider my feelings."

Leona laughed at this speech heartily—knowing what she knew, and the Misses Lillietrip looked proportionately disgusted.

"You make me feel quite nervous, positively," said the guileless Charlotte, with a look of modest alarm. "I shall never be able to act if you speak in that way. It is only by regarding such things entirely from a business like point of view that one is able to go through with them. Don Valera must understand what I mean; I am sure he is too much of a gentleman to misinterpret."

But at this juncture Lizzie's shrieks might be heard all over the house, and Leona was scarcely less amused.

"Indeed! you must believe me, mademoiselle," she commenced, "that I never had a thought—a notion—"

"A wish, a desire, a craving," cried Lizzie Vereker, "for unhallowed pleasures. Of course he hadn't. Why, Miss Lillietrip, Don Valera is the most moral of men—I can assure you of that on my own authority, for I've been trying to make love to him ever since he came to Hyde Park Gardens, and he won't have anything to say to me."

"This is absurd. This is turning the whole thing into a farce," exclaimed Miss Lillietrip, with as much offence as if they had met for the most solemn of purposes. "If this is to go on we had better break up the meeting at once, and not have any party or charades at all."

But this was carrying the joke too far.

"No, no! mademoiselle," cried Leona, who had a purpose in

wishing to act with them. "I, for one, cannot consent to such a terrible disappointment. And after you have promised, too, to let me play your lover. Let me at least have that pleasure," she continued in a low voice, "*if it be for one evening only.*" And the request and the whisper combined proved too fascinating. The Misses Lillietrip consented to be appeased, and the party gathered amicably round the table, to discuss what words they would select for acting. Several were suggested, and rejected or accepted, as they were considered suitable or not. At last some one proposed "Outcast," and was negatived by general agreement.

"The word is too commonplace—too short," remarked Miss Vereker; "besides, how could we act it?"

"Look for another," said Miss Lillietrip to the gentleman who held the dictionary.

"Outcast—Outcast," mused Leona, and then, after a moment, "might I suggest that we reconsider that last word?" she asked.

Anything that Don Valera proposed was agreeable to the Misses Lillietrip, who immediately discovered that "Outcast" would make a first-rate charade.

"I think we might have a worse," said Leona. "I see a little romance to be woven from that word."

"Oh, that is charming!—so original!" said Miss Charlotte, as she pushed her chair close to Leona's. "Do tell it to us, Don."

"Let us imagine then for the first syllable, 'out,' that there are two brothers, one of whom is unjustly accused of a crime of which the other is really guilty, and that the innocent man permits himself to be turned out of doors by his father sooner than lay the blame where it is due. We might work up this scene into something very telling, I think. There would be the parting from the girl he loves," added Leona, turning to Miss Charlotte, "who never really believes that he is guilty."

"*Of course not!* What woman who really loved would?" exclaimed the romantic young thing, with upturned eyes.

Do go on—this is interesting," said Lizzie. "*Marvellously* clever," chimed in Miss Lillietrip. "Then for 'cast,' One might portray the injured man, cast away—either at sea or in a foreign land—and enduring great hardship from the knowledge of how they had misjudged him at home, and that he might never have an opportunity of retrieving his character in their eyes. Here I think," went on Leona, turning to the elder Miss Lillietrip, "he might encounter a temptation to be faithless to his betrothed from the love of another beautiful woman, whose lot shall be cast in with his own. And that part would do for you."

"Charming! charming! A lovely idea," cried both the sisters at once.

"The scene for 'Outcast' must be at his home again, where they are mourning him as dead, and where, believing him to be so, his guilty brother makes full confession of his crime; in the midst of which the 'Outcast' must return, brought back by the woman who loves him hopelessly, and who joins his hand with that of his betrothed. This is a very simple outline of my conception," continued Leona, "and we must talk it over, of course, and fill it in. It is an idea, that is all."

"It is excellent!—very good indeed!" was the general verdict.

"Oh! it is more than that, a great deal," said the enthusiastic sisters; "it is sensational, romantic, poetic, to a degree. You are a genius, Don Valera, a thorough genius; we can never thank you sufficiently." And, elated with the thought of having equal opportunities of embracing the handsome young Spaniard, the Misses Lillietrip bore him off with them to the next room for secret counsel and the doubtful refreshment of stale sponge-cakes and bad sherry.

Lizzie Vereker sat in her arm-chair, kicking her heels against the floor. She didn't approve of the proposed charade. There was no part for her in it, and she set Don Valera down as a brute or a fool.

As they drove back together in the Evans' carriage—having arranged to return on the following morning for rehearsal, Leona perceived for the first time the perverse young lady's mood.

"What's the matter?" she said kindly. "Have you a headache, Miss Vereker?"

"No."

"Why are you so silent, then?"

"Why should you care to know?"

"Because I like to hear you talk, as everybody else does."

"Indeed! I shouldn't have thought it."

"Now, I'm sure something is the matter, from your tone of

voice. Have I offended you?"

"Why should you think you had?"

"Because I was afraid of it," replied Leona, as she glanced in her companion's face. She had acted a boy's part so long that she sometimes almost came to think she was one.

"Are you *really* afraid? Would you be sorry if I did not like you?" demanded Lizzie, eagerly.

"Of course I should."

"Then I *do* like you. There!"

"That's right! I am very glad to hear it," replied Leona, as she laid her hand on Miss Vereker's. She also liked the high-spirited, imprudent girl sincerely; for there was something in her independent way of thinking that accorded with her own. But she was surprised at the vehemence with which Lizzie seized her hand and squeezed it.

"You kept no part for me in the charade," she said, with a half sob, "and so I thought you didn't want me to act with you."

"Oh my dear! what a mistake!" exclaimed Leona, falling unconsciously into her natural character. "How could you suppose for a moment I would rather act with those two ugly old women than with you? But I had a design, well (remembering herself)—I can hardly tell you *why* I did it, but it was not, at all events, because I preferred anybody to yourself."

"Then I don't care *why* it was!" replied Lizzie, as she lifted up a very bright face so close to Leona's that it only seemed natural to my heroine to kiss it. The minute she had done it though, she saw by the blush that dyed her companion's cheek, how imprudent she had been, but it was impossible to explain the action away again. She must let Miss Vereker think what she chose.

"Forgive me! I didn't mean to do that, mademoiselle," she said apologetically.

But Lizzie Vereker only laughed at her dismay.

"You shouldn't have done it," she said. "You are a very naughty boy, and I ought not to forgive you—at least all at once!—but there!"—placing her hand in Leona's, "I suppose I must; only, don't you do it again—*till next time!*" she added, with a look that said, "next time may be at once, if you choose to make it so, Don Valera!"

But it was Leona's turn to blush now, as the truth burst on her mind—and she did it right royally!—thereby making Miss Vereker decide in her heart that "the boy was a fool after all!"

But what was this Leona was bringing on herself? She feared she would have to snub Lizzie Vereker for the future.

– CHAPTER 17 –

THE ACTED CHARADES

As will be surmised, it was Leona's strong dramatic instincts that had led her to think of furthering her solution of the mystery that enveloped her father's life and death by the acting of a charade. The play scene in Hamlet, with various other *dénouements*, formed after the same pattern, had been floating through her brain when she pressed the word "Outcast" on the consideration of the Misses Lillietrip. But the more she thought of the design the more she liked it. When in company with Lizzie Vereker—who had commenced to call the attention of the public to the secret understanding which she conceived to exist between them, in a manner which was most embarrassing to poor Leona—she returned next day to the house of the maiden sisters, she had brought her first idea of the charade to such a state of perfection as to elicit the shrillest screams of approbation from those ladies. She laid the scene of the first syllable in Germany, and the second in Spain, thus bringing in the aid of pretty costumes to heighten the effect of the little drama. And to crown all, she appeared ready armed with the sketch of a second charade, in which Lizzie Vereker was to take the principal part, and have full opportunity of showing off her ankles and her acting.

So everybody was pleased, and Leona became feverishly anxious to watch the effect of her plan, and fearful lest, at the last moment, something might occur to prevent the attendance of those whom she most wished to be witness of her efforts. But nothing went wrong. All the inmates of Mr. Evans' house assembled at the dinner-table on the eventful day, smiling and ready for the evening's amusement.

Lucilla looked almost pretty, in the palest of pink dresses, whilst excitement in the anticipation of an unusual pleasure had tinged her cheeks with the same colour as her robe, and Tom Hastings, who sat opposite, appeared unable to take his eyes off her for admiration of the change. Mr. Evans came in late—he usually came in late—but rubbing his hands with a satisfied expression on his face.

"Just got all my business over in time, Valera," he said, as he took his seat at table, "and very glad of it too. I should have been sorry to miss this evening. I met Miss Charlotte Lillietrip in the Park just now, and she is in ecstasies over your performance. Acting is not much in my line, private or public, but I suppose you've been used to it. Have a great deal of that sort of thing in New York, eh?"

"Occasionally, sir. It is a fashionable amusement there, as here."

"Ah! brings young people together, of course. That's a fashion that will never go out I fancy. Well, and who else takes part in these famous charades. You, Tom?" he continued, addressing Dr. Hastings.

Tom looked unutterable scorn at the idea.

"*I*, sir? I have something better to think of, I hope, than dressing myself up in frippery, and strutting about a drawing-room for the edification of my friends. I leave that to less busy a people."

Lucilla resented the innuendo sharply.

"It must be more amusing than making pills, anyway," she retorted.

"I said nothing against the *amusement* of it, Lucilla. I expect to be uncommonly amused myself, this evening."

"This is mightily condescending of you, I am sure," exclaimed Lizzie Vereker. "Perhaps you will find something to laugh at in me, since I am to be one of the dramatic corps."

"Oh you are going to act, Miss Vereker, are you?" interposed Mr. Evans. "Then I conclude a gallant captain has been at drill, too, during the last few days."

"If you're alluding to Captain Rivers, you are all wrong, Mr. Evans, for he certainly is not going to act with me to-night. He couldn't do it if he tried."

"Well, I think you might give me the benefit of the doubt, Miss

Vereker," said the gentleman in question, in an aggrieved tone, "considering this is the first time the subject has been mooted."

"Oh, I see you can't act, by your face. It has always the same expression on it."

If that were the case, Captain Rivers' habitual expression must have been a very unpleasant one, judging from that which Miss Vereker's words called forth. But he kept his temper admirably.

"That is because you always see it when looking at yourself," he answered.

"Well, don't say it's the reflection from mine, for I shouldn't take that as a compliment, Captain Rivers."

"Your nature's not so transparent as you give yourself the credit for," he said, gloomily.

Leona perceived plainly that the men of the party were as much set against her as the women were on her side. The knowledge only made her smile. She knew that she had but to change her clothes to turn the tide in a contrary direction; and the jealousy hurt her no more than the flattery pleased.

She was walking through the world with her eyes fixed upon one point only.

The dinner-hour had been advanced that day in order to accommodate the Misses Lillietrip's charade party, and as soon as the meal was despatched they started for their destination. Here the usual preliminary fuss, bustle, delay, and inconvenience attendant on an amateur theatrical dressing-room went on upstairs; whilst the patient audience in the drawing-room sipped weak tea and nibbled cold tea-cakes, in order to beguile their impatience. All the pleasure, as is inevitable with such entertainments, was for the performers—all the boredom and *ennui* for the spectators. In the Misses Lillietrip's dressing-rooms the utmost excitement prevailed. One had, of course, been put aside for the gentlemen to change their clothes in; the other devoted to the use of the ladies. But from the furtive exclamations of horror, and shrieks of laughter that occasionally reached the ears of the party in the drawing-room, it was evident that some sort of collision was taking place upstairs—that Miss Lillietrip had been surprised in her blue dressing-gown by Don Valera on the landing, or that the fair Charlotte had been startled out of all her propriety by a knock at her door, and a hoarse voice demanding assistance in the shape of pins, or needles and thread, whilst she was in the very act of putting up her own scanty and undeniably dyed hair under the celebrated flaxen wig. Then some of the gentlemen's things didn't fit, and some of them wanted tapes tied and hooks fastened. And, to crown all, the handsome young Spaniard insisted upon "making up" Miss Charlotte's face himself; and after having smeared her with glycerine, dusted her with powder, blacked her under her eyes, and rouged her on the eyelids, cheekbones, and lips, found he had so vastly improved her personal appearance that he actually gave her a resounding kiss, in reward for her patience and amiability. This was the climax. Miss Charlotte liked the salute amazingly— nothing better—but could not have done anything so staid as to enjoy it quietly. She must needs give a girlish scream of mingled terror and delight, which brought all the other ladies round her to inquire the cause, and made Lizzie Vereker give Leona a look of displeasure that almost startled her.

The next minute they had assembled on the stage formed by the back drawing-room, and the curtain had risen on the first scene of the charade "Outcast."

Under Leona's practical direction, the little drama had really been most creditably got up. The interior of an apartment, half kitchen, half sitting-room, in a German farm-house, was faithfully depicted. The costumes, too, with which she was well acquainted, had been followed quite closely enough for representation. There was to be seen the old German farmer, in his quaint habiliments, smoking his pipe, with his *frau* knitting stockings by his side, and the *mädchen* moving about the room, laying the table for supper. Presently there entered to them one of their sons, pale, travel-stained, disordered. They noticed his appearance, and inquired the cause. He answered them shortly and gloomily. Whilst engaged on their supper they were surprised by the officers of justice, with an order for the arrest of their son, on the charge of murdering a certain merchant who had been found dead, and robbed of his possessions. The parents were horror-stricken. They called on their son to refute the dreadful accusation. At first he was unable to speak—then he denied it. The officers produced the articles found near the murdered man—a glove, a knife, a handkerchief—and the accused man recognised them as belonging to his brother. At this juncture it was Miss Charlotte Lillietrip's turn to act, and she made the most of her part. Leona had wished to keep her as much as possible in the background, but the flaxen wig and short German petticoats were not to be outdone. Down in the front of the foot-lights they dropped, as with uplifted hands and streaming eyes the ancient *mädchen* attested the innocence of her betrothed. Whilst she was hard at it, Leona, dressed as a German student, entered on the scene. Her dramatic talent, added to her processional knowledge, at once impressed her spectators. They became interested—absorbed. The rest had been child's play—*this* was earnest. When she started back on being accused of the murder, her audience could almost see her countenance blanch. When she turned her eyes in deliberate silence upon her brother, they knew that he was the guilty party. When she took the weeping *mädchen* in her arms, and bade her farewell, some of the women began to cry. And when she finally submitted to being led away by the officers, and turned at the door to gaze once more on her accuser, they all saw and understood that the brothers had changed places, and that the younger was sacrificing himself for the elder.

At the conclusion of the scene the applause was long and loud, but it was all intended for Leona.

The second word was more difficult to represent. It is not easy to transform a modern back drawing-room into the shore of a desert isle. However, it was sufficiently successful to convey the idea of what it was meant to be. And here the wrongfully accused brother, who, although justice had not been able to convict him of a crime he never committed, had been unable to remain in his native country under the suspicion of guilt, was to be seen cast away in company with part of the crew of a Spanish vessel, in which he had been journeying to the New World. In this picture Leona had all the acting to herself, and she acted splendidly. The woman seemed inspired. She threw herself into the part as though it had been created for her. She thought of her dead father's secret lamentations, and what he would have said had he given them vent, and her words came pouring from her mouth as though she had learned them off by heart. The student she represented spoke of his home, of all he had hoped to do, to be, and to make for himself; then of his brother's ingratitude, of his own wasted life, of the dark mystery—the knowledge of the cloud hanging over his name, of the suspicions entertained of his innocence by his family, gave him. And when he went on as solemnly to implore heaven to send some means by which the truth of his tarnished honour might be restored, and his name redeemed from a shameful and undeserved ignominy, the people sitting in the front drawing-room forgot they were only looking at a charade, of which they were expected to guess the meaning, and held their breath and trembled, or wept in concert with the actor, as their sympathies best inclined them. Even Dr. Hastings and Captain Rivers were obliged to confess that "the fellow knew what he was about." They forgot even to laugh at the absurd figure cut by Miss Lillietrip as the beautiful Spanish girl who drew out his sad history from the homeless wanderer. Leona's acting was so real, it shed a halo of truth upon all its surroundings, and made the spectators overlook everything but itself.

But as the curtain dropped upon the second syllable, and she gained the upper landing again, she found her fellow-actors in earnest colloquy.

"You don't mean to say he is gone? Why, did you not see him get up in the middle and leave the room? It created quite a commotion."

"But why?"

"Because Don Valera's acting affected him so much, I suppose. I know no other reason."

"Well, I'm sure it was enough to do it. I was nearly crying myself the whole time."

"What is it all about?" inquired Leona, as she came upon the chattering group.

"Only that you've driven Mr. Evans away. He was completely upset by the charade."

"Nonsense! How could that be?"

"I was watching him from the side all the time," said Miss Charlotte, "and I saw him fidgeting on his seat and changing colour; and then Mrs. Evans spoke to him, and he was quiet a little bit, but at last he could evidently stand it no longer, for he made a sudden jump up and rushed from the room."

"But he will return surely," said Leona.

"Indeed he will not return," cried the Marquise de Toutlemonde, who had found her way upstairs, "for we have just heard from the servants that he took his hat and left the house. A fine sensation you have created, Don! But I don't wonder at it, for my heart has been in my mouth all the time you have been acting!"

"It was *perfection!*" exclaimed Miss Charlotte, with clasped hands.

"It is time to begin the finale," said Leona, anxious to disperse her clustering admirers; and in a few moments she found herself standing on the stairs alone.

He had actually gone then. Her uncle had fled before the memory of the past. Her ruse had succeeded—but how? Was it brotherly affection—the sting of an unforgotten grief, that had driven him away? or was it *the consciousness of guilt?* She had not time to fight out this question with herself at that moment; she must judge by his future conduct. Beside her was Madame de Toutlemonde (who had already been rather offended by the seeming indifference of the young Spaniard to her charms, trying to get up a flirtation with her.

"A penny for your thoughts, Don!" she exclaimed sweetly, with her head on one side.

Now Leona had taken a great dislike to this woman, simply because she saw that she was not what she assumed to be. She could laugh at and with the old maiden sisters; she could amuse herself with teasing Lizzie Vereker; or bear with much patience the pressing attentions of Lucilla Evans; but she had a repulsion towards Madame la Marquise. She hated her soft voice and wheedling ways; she despised her painted face and modish dresses. These might be fitting traps wherewith to lure that feeble creature man, who will run after a petticoat fluttering from a broomstick; but they were too paltry to excite anything but the contempt of an open-eyed and honest woman. Leona recognised in Madame la Marquise one of those improper ladies, or lady-like improprieties—which shall we call them?—who infest society in the present age, and gain footing in many a house where the master and mistress are lavish of their hospitality, and unsuspecting of evil. The men of a family have too often their own reasons for not exposing the true character of such hybrid ladies; and the women have no opportunity of hearing the truth, until one day some man more bold or less interested than the rest, expresses his surprise at meeting them in respectable society, or gives a private caution to the mother of the establishment; and inquiries are set on foot and discoveries made, and the place wherein they were received as honoured guests knows them no more.

Leona, with her knowledge of the world and general society, had read Madame de Toutlemonde's character at a glance. Had she been what she professed to be she would doubtless have enjoyed the fun of being made love to by a really pretty woman as much as anyone, but being female and honest, the instinctive shrinking of her sex from all that is polluted and impure came upon her as often as she was brought in contact with the marquise; and when she found that they were standing on the same stair she intuitively moved a step higher.

"Now, that is unkind," said Madame la Marquise. "Do you mean to pretend there is not room enough for us both on one step, Don?"

"I pretend nothing; but I am anxious not to crowd you."

"Suppose I like to be crowded—by *you*," she answered.

"Then I should say you have very bad taste, madame. Your dress is too pretty to be crushed."

"Bah! what signifies my dress? That is but an excuse for evading my question. Tell me, Don, why is it you do not like me?"

"Who has told you that I do not?"

"Yourself. I read it in your eyes."

"I advise you not to look there, madame; they are not such easy books to interpret as you imagine."

"Let me learn how to read them, then," urged the lady, coming nearer. "Teach me, Don."

"I have not the knowledge myself, madame, neither would my eyes say anything to you."

"You are cruel—both cold and cruel. I cannot understand you. What are you made of—ice or marble? I thought your countrymen had souls of fire."

"Perhaps so—in a good cause."

"And am *I* not a good cause, you saucy boy?"

"You are a beautiful one, madame."

"Come, that's not so bad. We are getting on. I will give you a kiss for that," said the Marquise, as she lifted her face to Leona. But the girl could not embrace her. She had kissed both Lizzie Vereker and Miss Charlotte Lillietrip in play, but she shrank from madame's painted lips as though they had been poisoned.

"Hush! I hear my cue," she said, pushing past her down the staircase. "It is time I joined Miss Lillietrip," and before the other could stop her she was gone.

Madame de Toutlemonde stood on the stairs, angry and confounded. Was it possible this wretched boy had actually refused to kiss her? She grew so heated over the idea, she was compelled to go back into the dressing-room and powder her face again. Madame de Toutlemonde was not wholly unused to rebuffs, but they seldom came from the sex she believed Leona to be, and she was indignant at the supposed insult. As she puffed her face and arranged the curls over her forehead, she determined that she would have her revenge of him. The young upstart should learn that he could not refuse her favours with impunity. And when she had sufficiently cooled herself, she resumed her seat amongst the rest of the audience, and talked aloud and yawned audibly during the remainder of the evening's performance. For it is a peculiarity of ladies of the type of Madame la Marquise de Toutlemonde, that as soon as they are offended, they can be just as rude, ill-mannered, and spiteful as they were before smooth-spoken and amiable. A cat with its claws sheathed, and a cat with its claws out. That is all the difference between their good tempers and their bad.

Notwithstanding madame's temper, however, the charade "Outcast" went on to its close. It was observed that Don Valera did not act with so much spirit in the last scene as he had done in the two first. The fact is Leona's mind was occupied with thoughts concerning the reason of her uncle's absence, and speculations as to his return.

These made her absent and inattentive to the work in hand, so that Miss Charlotte's gushing tenderness at the restoration of her lover did not meet with all the return she had anticipated, and the curtain fell rather flatly.

Leona was angry with herself afterwards for this distraction. What right had she to spoil the entertainment of her friends, to gratify her own morbid fancies? Had she not plenty of time for thought at home? Taking herself to task after this fashion, she resolved to do her best in the succeeding charade, where most of her play was to be with Miss Lizzie Vereker, and when she came on the stage, she found that that young lady was quite determined to keep her up to her work. The action was confined to modern life, but there was a great deal of love-making in it; and Lizzie, who had been debarred, greatly against her will, from taking any part in the first charade, had made up her mind that the people in front should see what *she* called "spooning" in this. She had rehearsed the character, after a fashion, the day before, but Leona had no idea she intended going so far as she did that night. Even for two women personating lovers, the action was very strong, but under the supposed circumstances of sex, it almost passed the limits of decorum. Yet, do what Leona would, she could not make the headstrong and imprudent girl lessen her familiarities or her caresses. Miss Vereker (like some other amateurs) appeared to imagine that the mere fact of "acting" dispensed with the reticence of daily life, and that she might indulge her wayward fancy without control. And the immediate presence of Captain Rivers, in a large arm-chair, close to the foot-lights, only seemed to urge her on to wilder flights of imagination. She was at the very height of her love-making, and Leona, who, if she was not to repulse her in public, was compelled in some measure to respond to her advances, had just folded her rather warmly in her arms, when a loud scream from some one in the audience was quickly succeeded by a burst of hysterics, and amidst a general rising of the guests, the curtain was obliged to be let down, and the charade brought to an untimely conclusion.

"*Who* is it? *What* is it? cried Lizzie Vereker, impatiently. "How annoying to be interrupted in this manner! I believe it's that booby, Lucilla Evans."

"Never mind I'm sure they have had enough of it, and it is quite time to give over," replied Leona; who, now that the excitement of the evening was past for her, was beginning to feel weary and depressed.

"Oh dear! Oh dear! isn't it distressing?" exclaimed Miss Lillietrip, hurrying in to them. "We mustn't have any more acting to-night, for poor dear Lucilla is taken so ill—over-tired, I suppose, or over-excited. She's not used to these things, you know—and they've carried her up to my bedroom, and Dr. Hastings has gone with her. But you mustn't let it break up the evening—and I hope you'll come and have some refreshment, Don, for you must need it I am sure; and how we can ever thank you enough for all you've done and gone through to-night, I don't know." And thus talking, lamenting, and extolling, Miss Lilletrip ushered her guests into the supper room.

Meanwhile Lucilla Evans, who had been thus unexpectedly upset by the fatigue or the heat—*or the acting*—was conveyed upstairs by her mother and Tom Hastings, and placed upon Miss Lillietrip's bed.

She had begun by a loud shriek, then she had gone off in a sort of faint; on being revived from which she had commenced to laugh hysterically; and having been scolded into another mood, was now lying on the pillows weeping silently.

"What can I get for her?" exclaimed Mrs. Evans, in distress. "What do you recommend, Tom! Brandy and water, or sherry, or coffee? Is there anything that will do her any good?"

"Quiet, my dear Mrs. Evans, a few minutes' rest and quiet, and then take her home and put her to bed. Lucilla is not accustomed to such fatigue as she has gone through to-night. She ought never to have come here."

"I wish I never had! " said Lucilla, weeping.

"But, my dear girl—" commenced her mother.

"My dear madam," interposed Dr. Hastings, "will you go and fetch a glass of wine, and leave Lucilla alone with me. I must forbid her talking or being talked to for a few minutes."

Good Mrs. Evans trotted off obediently to do the doctor's bidding, and as soon as the door was closed after her he turned to his patient.

"Now, Lucilla," he said, sternly, "I cannot have any more of this nonsense, or I shall speak to your father about it."

"Oh, Dr Hastings! you would not—you *could* not! You do not know—"

"I know far more than you have any idea of. But I have been watching you closely for some time past, and the absurd fancies you have got into your head are no secret to me."

"*What* absurd fancies?" inquired Lucilla, with dogged boldness.

"Don't provoke me to mention them, for they're nothing to be proud of; and I am quite sure of what steps Mr. Evans would take were the matter confided to him."

"I shall *hate* you if you speak to papa about it," said the girl.

Tom Hastings changed countenance, but he did not give in.

"Then don't let me see any more hysterics, he answered immediately.

"Is she better?" asked Mrs. Evans, re-appearing with the glass of wine.

"She is *going to be*, I trust, my dear madam," replied the doctor. "Drink this, Lucilla—that's right. And now, the best thing mamma can do is to take you home."

"Not till they *all* come," said Lucilla imploringly.

"They *will* all come, love," replied Mrs. Evans. "It must be high time to go, and the carriage is at the door. Will you accompany us, Tom?"

"No, thank you!" rejoined the doctor, shortly, as he turned on his heel and left the room.

– CHAPTER 18 –

LUCILLA'S ILLNESS

There was a general look of dissatisfaction on the faces of the guests left behind at the Misses Lillietrip's, as the carriage which contained Mrs. Evans, her daughter, Lizzie Vereker, and Don Christobal Valera, rolled away from the hall door.

Captain Rivers and Dr. Hastings, who were gnashing their teeth with indignation, the one at Miss Vereker's too evident admiration of the handsome Spaniard, the other at Lucilla Evans' fit of hysterics, retired to the farther end of the supper-room and indulged in a hearty and wholesome abuse of the absent foreigner. Madame de Toutlemonde, whose instincts drew her their way, had soon joined the conclave, with her friend Miss Forrester, and all four united in denouncing the folly of the women and the impudence of the man.

"How Lizzie Vereker's father can permit his daughter to pull about a man like that in public, beats my comprehension," remarked Miss Forrester, spitefully. "I suppose the girl *has* a father, hasn't she, or some one to look after her? It was perfectly shocking to see her! What on earth would a woman be thought of who went on in that way *off* the stage?"

"Don't mention it," cried the virtuous marquise, with a shrug of indignation, "it was outrageous, indecent. I shall never speak to Miss Vereker again!"

"Well, I think you are going a little too far in saying that. I do indeed, by Jove," said Captain Rivers. "Miss Vereker never behaved in that way before she met this confounded Spaniard."

"It was every bit his fault," agreed Tom Hastings; "and if these old women" (indicating the Misses Lillietrip by a jerk of his elbow) "weren't a couple of fools, they would never have asked him to act. Who wanted to see him lumbering through every scene? But I suppose the old girls are in love with him, or some such folly."

"Everybody seems to be in love with him," said Miss Forrester.

"I'm not, my dear, for one," replied her friend.

"Well, no, Fifine. I hardly meant to include you. But Miss Lucilla's hysterics look very like it. I perceived they came on at the height of the embracing between Don Valera and that forward minx, Lizzie Vereker."

"Oh, as to that I think you're mistaken," interposed Dr. Hastings, quickly. "Miss Evans is very used to attacks of the kind. She is not strong enough to come out in the evening, and I have often warned her mother against hot rooms and late hours. I should be very sorry to attribute her illness to anything but the most ordinary cause. Besides, this Spanish Don, as he calls himself, is almost a stranger to her."

"So he is to Miss Vereker," remarked the marquise.

"But Miss Vereker's love-making was all in the course of the charade. You don't suppose she meant anything by it?" said Captain Rivers, uneasily.

"I really don't know what to suppose, Captain Rivers. Young ladies are so exceedingly strange in their behaviour nowadays. But I cannot see, for my own part, what there is to admire in Don Valera."

"He appears nothing but a lubberly boy to me," remarked Miss Forrester, to whom Leona had always been distantly polite.

"A perfect cub," said the marquise.

"An undersized, flabby foreigner, with a complexion and hands like a woman. I believe the animal uses rouge," added Captain Rivers, contemptuously.

"With a squeaky voice, and a face as smooth as a billiard-ball. What can a girl see in such a hybrid! Why doesn't she take to hugging one of her own sex instead. But no, forsooth! He's a don, or he says so, and a Spaniard, and there's some romance attached to the idea, and so the silly creatures flutter round him as if he were that martyred hero of modern history, the Emperor Maximilian himself. I have no patience with it all," grumbled Dr. Hastings.

"What made Mr. Evans leave the company so suddenly?" inquired Miss Forrester. "I don't think he can have conceived such a partiality for this Valera as his daughter has."

"I don't know what called him away. Business perhaps, or he was sick of the performance, as he well might have been," said Rivers. "By the way, Hastings, how would the old gentleman fancy a snatch between his heiress and this unknown adventurer, eh?"

"Like it! I should imagine he would cut her throat first."

"Well, I think he ought to be warned, if there was any friend sufficiently intimate with the family to take so delicate a matter on himself. It would be perfect cruelty not to open his eyes. And I should think the old lady was not much good as a chaperone."

"*Much good!*" echoed Miss Forrester. "How should she be? Why, they've lived in the provinces all their lives! She has no more idea of London manners, or the usages of society here, than my cat. And she'd let that girl bolt with anyone under her very eyes, and never know anything of it till it was over."

"You wrong Miss Evans, in supposing she would ever so far demean herself as to consent to an elopement with anyone, Miss Forrester," said Hastings, warmly. "She may be countrified, but she is a girl of the highest principles."

"Oh! I don't doubt it. But these silent streams run very deep, sometimes; and your mealy-mouthed misses are generally the ones who contrive to help themselves on the sly. I daresay butter will not melt in Miss Lucilla's mouth when you are present, doctor, but then you must remember young ladies are hardly likely to show off their tricks before their medical man."

"I fancy she forgot you were present when we had that little *exposé* this evening," said Madame. "But now, really, Dr. Hastings, if you are a friend of the family, her illness might form an excellent loophole for your ordering the poor girl away. It would really be a pity to see a nice woman like that sacrificed to a needy adventurer."

"And Miss Lucilla's removal would necessitate Miss Vereker's return home," put in Captain Rivers; "so that you would be killing two birds with one stone, Hastings."

"And conferring a real obligation on your friends," said Miss Forrester. "Mr. Evans and his new *protégé* left together, could not do much harm to one another."

It was wonderful how eager they all suddenly became to further the interests of the Evans family. Captain Rivers had an urgent reason to see Lizzie Vereker removed from Don Valera's influence—Dr. Hastings naturally desired Lucilla's absence, from the same cause—Madame de Toutlemonde wished to have her revenge on the heartless Spaniard—and even Miss Forrester foresaw a large increase of benefits likely to accrue from the unused luxuries of the house in Hyde Park Gardens. And so, one and all, they suddenly discovered that the Evans had been so good to them, and were so estimable in themselves, that it behoved them as Christians to see they were not imposed upon, and made miserable by the impostor they were nurturing in their household.

"I begin to think I should only be doing my duty in speaking to Mr. Evans on the subject," said Tom Hastings, thoughtfully.

The quartette had now been conferring together for too long a time not to excite observation.

"What are all you naughty people talking about in this corner?" cried kittenish Miss Charlotte, as she shook a skinny finger at them. "You really must make your conversation more general, or we shall insist upon knowing the subject of it."

"We were saying what a delightful evening we have had, and how clever your charades were, Miss Lillietrip," replied the marquise, unhesitatingly.

"Ah, you mustn't call them *our* charades, Marquise, for that charming Don Valera got them all up from beginning to end. Doesn't he act beautifully? What a name he would make for himself upon the stage. As I said to him to-night: 'Don! why don't you turn professional?—you'd make your fortune;' and he coloured up—positively he coloured—as he replied, 'You flatter me, madame.' He is very charming in his manner, don't you think so? So thoroughly foreign. My sister and I are quite in love with him, I assure you—positively and truly—we fight about him. How did you like our dresses, Marquise? Pretty, were they not? The Don chose the colours. I think his own dress was superb. I wonder where he got it from. And the fair wig altered his appearance so entirely in the second charade, I hardly knew him. But we like him in his own hair best. So uncommon. What a pity dear Lucilla was taken ill. I wish you could have given her something to revive her, doctor. We were disappointed at their all leaving so soon. Still, we hope soon to have the pleasure of their company again. These charades have been so successful, my sister and I think of getting up some more, and they have all promised to act for us; and perhaps next time, if we have something *very quiet indeed*, Miss Lucilla might be persuaded to take a part in them."

"*Not if I can prevent it!*" thought Dr. Hastings, as the loquacious Charlotte began to chatter to somebody else, and the quartette dispersed about the room. "Why, the very devil seems in this Spanish brute. Even these dried-up old women flutter their wings at sight of him. *More charades?* No! I think we've had enough of them. Madame is right, change of air will be the best thing in the world for Lucy. The weather is very hot for the season of the year, and London is the worst place on earth for an invalid. I'll get her mother to take her down to Bournemouth or St. Leonards, until this foreigner is on his way back to New York. Confound the brute! How I wish we had never had a sight of his ugly face!" Which only proves how much imagination has to do with our convictions, and how differently the same objects may appear to different eyes.

Whilst the real Christobal Valera, fighting against the inroads fever had made in his constitution, and struggling with the dreadful doubts engendered by Leona's mysterious disappearance, was dreaming of her lost face as the loveliest vision that had ever blest his sight, Dr. Hastings, viewing it from another and more distorted point of view, pronounced it *ugly*, and believed it to be what he said.

Whilst Lucilla Evans, who in her weakness and timidity shrunk from the generality of the sterner sex, as something too rough and loud-spoken to give her any pleasure, considered Leona Lacoste, in her male attire, to be the very perfection of all she had ever dreamed of as amiable, and gentle, and winning in a man, Captain Rivers spoke contemptuously of the disguised woman as *"an undersized flabby foreigner."*

Whilst Lizzie Vereker thought the supposed Valera the most charmingly handsome and fascinating boy in creation (and Leona could be very fascinating when she chose), Madame la Marquise dubbed him "bearish, ill-mannered, and a fool;" and Miss Forrester marvelled that any of these people should take the trouble either to like, or dislike, or be afraid of, so utterly contemptible and insignificant a personage as Mr. Evans' Spanish correspondent.

But Dr. Hastings was afraid of him; and after a night's cogitation, resolved at all hazards to tell Mr. Evans that town air was likely to injure his daughter's health. He broached the subject very cautiously, but the merchant took alarm at once. It has been observed before that the object of Mr. Evans' life appeared to be to give pleasure, or heap benefits upon this girl. No pleasure was worth anything if Lucilla could not take part in it. No luxury was worth the procuring unless it were to add to her comfort or enjoyment. For her sake he had come to London and furnished his splendid house, and for her sake he was ready to give it all up to-morrow, and take a trip to the Andes, or the Himalayas, or any other outlandish and inaccessible quarter of the globe.

"But you are getting on too fast," said Dr. Hastings, as his friend proposed one plan after another. "There is no need whatever that you should break up your establishment, or even leave town yourself. Lucilla is not ill, but this warm weather makes London atmosphere very enervating, and I should strongly advise her mother taking her down quietly to the seaside until the season is passed, and you are able to join them there."

"And you really think that is all that is necessary? Because, you know, my dear Tom, money is no consideration, and if you advise the climate of Italy or Spain—"

"My dear Mr. Evans, you quite mistake the case. Your daughter's constitution wants bracing, not relaxing. Sea-bathing would do her all the good in the world. It is evident town does not agree with her. She had a very weakening attack of hysteria whilst at the Misses Lillietrip's last night."

"So her mother told me. She quite alarmed me with her account of Lucy's illness. What do you suppose can have caused it, my dear Tom?"

"Nothing but fatigue and heat, joined to a little excitement. But the fact that so small an excitement can produce such unusual results with her, is proof positive she should not indulge in it."

"It would certainly be inconvenient for me to leave town at present," said Mr. Evans, thoughtfully. "I expect to he very busy for the next week or two; besides I have that fellow Valera on my hands."

"If you can get Lucy out of London, there is not the least necessity for any one but Mrs. Evans accompanying her."

"I am afraid they will find it very dull at the seaside all by themselves. Lucilla appeared to be so delighted at the prospect of her little party at the Lillietrips."

"Exactly so, and see the harm it did her. She has no strength for dissipation."

"I hope she won't object to go, Tom; but you see we have never thwarted the dear child in anything."

"I should think she would hardly be so unreasonable as to risk her health by refusing to take my advice. But if you think she will feel the change, sir, why not send down Miss Vereker with her? They appear to be excellent friends."

"So I will; and for the matter of that, Valera might go too, till I want him. We can't begin his business for another fortnight at the earliest."

"I don't think I should send Don Valera with them, Mr. Evans," quickly interposed Tom Hastings. "I would not even broach the subject if I were you. What Lucilla wants is perfect rest and quiet, and you will excuse me for saying that a man who is incessantly talking, or singing, or acting, is not calculated to ward off excitement from an emotional woman. If you send any one but

Miss Vereker and her mother with her, you may just as well keep your daughter at home, for the sea air will do her no good at all."

"You really think so? Well, I'm surprised to hear it, for I have always thought Lucy took so much pleasure in Valera's society. He's not like us great rough Englishmen, you know, Tom. There's something so nice and quiet and soft-spoken about the boy, that appears to suit the timid nerves of my poor delicate little girl. However, if you say she had better go alone, there's an end of it."

"I am quite sure that the fewer companions you send with her the better, and they must certainly be of her own sex. You will forgive my having mentioned the subject, Mr. Evans. I thought it but right you should know."

"I should never have forgiven you if you had not mentioned it, my dear boy," replied the merchant, as he held out his hand. "I know the friendly feeling you entertain for my family, and can never sufficiently thank you for the interest you take in us. My wife shall broach the subject to Lucy before the day is over, and you shall know the result to-morrow."

But the result was very different from what they had anticipated.

On the proposal being made to her, Lucilla Evans at once plumply refused to leave London. She didn't care what Dr. Hastings' opinion was. He was a nasty, spiteful creature, to have spoken to papa about her at all; and she was not going to take his advice. *So there!* She was very happy in London—perfectly happy and perfectly well—and she liked going out to parties; and she meant to go to the next she was asked to, whatever Dr. Hastings might think or say. Meek little Mrs. Evans was at her wits' end what argument to use next. She had been so much accustomed for years past to be completely ruled by her invalid daughter, that she no more dreamed of interposing her authority in the matter than of carrying Lucilla bodily out of London.

"But, my dear," she said, persuasively, "if it is for the sake of your precious health, you know—"

"It's not for my health, mamma; it's because the wretch has got a spite against me, and wants me to go, because he sees I'm happy here. But I won't go till the season's over. It's my first season in London, and I mean to enjoy it, as far as I can. Fancy turning out of this house just as we've furnished it from top to toe, and all! It's ridiculous—absurd. Nobody but a stupid old doctor would have thought of proposing such a thing."

"But Dr. Hastings has always been so careful of you, my dear. And he considers London too relaxing at this time of the year, and that Bournemouth or Brighton would do you so much more good—"

"Bother Bournemouth and Brighton! I won't go then, mamma—once for all. And, pray, what would papa do, cooped up in this house alone? *He* can't leave the business to look after itself. it's too absurd. Pray don't say anything more about it."

"Oh my dear! your father would do well enough without us. Tom would be backwards and forwards, naturally enough, to see him; and his gentlemen friends would come and dine with him. And then there's young Valera staying in the house, you know."

But at the mention of that magic name, Lucilla burst into tears, and the murder was out.

"Oh mamma! don't take me away—pray don't take me away! I don't want to go—I can't go," she sobbed. "I should be so wretched if I couldn't—if I couldn't—"

"If you couldn't *what?*" demanded her mother, with perfect innocence.

"If I couldn't see *him*," exclaimed Lucilla, with a fresh burst of grief.

For a few moments Mrs. Evans was all bewilderment. "Is it your papa you mean, my dear?" she asked in a mystified manner; "because of course he would run down to see you at the least every week or so."

"No! no! no! I don't mean papa."

"Dr. Hastings, then?"

At this juncture had Lucilla Evans been a gentleman she would certainly have used a naughty word. It is very hard that there should be no naughty words that a woman may use with impunity in the time of need. Why should one sex be legally permitted the privilege of safety valves, whilst the other must explode without caution?

But in this, as in all things, the men have the best of it.

"Bother Dr. Hastings," cried the young lady, energetically. And here I must remark that had she spelt "bother" with four letters instead of six it would have meant no more than it did. "Haven't I told you, mamma, that I hate his very name. I wish I had never seen him—nasty, selfish, interfering creature."

"But stay, my dear, *who* is it that you are so unwilling to leave? Confide in me, dear Lucilla. You know that your papa and I have but one wish, and that is to make you happy."

"Oh, can't you *guess*?" asked the girl emphatically.

"You don't mean this young Spanish friend of your papa's, do you?" said Mrs. Evans, as if she were suggesting the most unlikely thing possible, and fully expected her daughter to refute it.

"*Of course* I do! Who else is there worth caring about in all the world? Oh, mamma! he is so nice—so clever—so amiable—I have never met any one like him in my life before. When he is with me, playing chess, or singing, or talking, the time passes away so quickly; and when he is gone—oh! it is all so dull and blank. And now you want me to go down to the seaside, and leave him up here in town with papa, and I can't. I can't, mamma. It would kill me to go away. Oh I do say that I may stop in town till the end of the season."

"But, Lucilla," said Mrs. Evans, whose breath had almost been taken away by this unexpected announcement, "am I to understand then—am I to tell your papa—"

"Oh! you're not to tell papa anything," exclaimed Lucilla. "You are not to say a word about it, mamma. Promise me you won't. Only persuade him that I am quite well and happy here, and that there is no need for me to go to the seaside, and don't let me see that wretch, Dr. Hastings, for the next few days, or I shall kill him."

"And you have actually conceived an attachment for that boy, Valera," said Mrs. Evans, musingly.

"Oh! don't put it in so many words. It sounds dreadful. I only like him, you know; and everybody does that. Only, why should I go away? Promise me you won't breathe a word to papa about—about *that*—will you? Oh! why was I ever such a fool as to say anything? But it slipped out before I knew what I was doing. Only *promise*—won't you?—that you'll never say anything to anybody."

Mrs. Evans promised, as a matter of course, and likewise, as a matter of course, she made her way straight down from Lucilla's side to her husband's study, where she told him the whole story.

"My dear Henry, I've got a terrible piece of news for you. Lucy's in love with that Spanish friend of yours—she has just told me all about it; but I promised the utmost secrecy, so you must consider this communication as strictly confidential."

"Lucilla in love with Valera! Why, she's old enough to be his mother."

"Well, not quite that, my dear, but she must be several years his senior. However, whether or no, the mischief is done, and she utterly refuses to go to the seaside away from him."

"Has Valera been speaking of love to her?"

"I should imagine not. Lucy said nothing about that. Only it's very evident what is making her ill. It's the worry and fretting, and suspense. She begged I would say nothing to you on the subject, but I felt it to be my duty. She was in a terrible state of distress just now."

"*In love with Valera*," said Henry Evans, musingly. "Now, what are we to do about it, my dear?"

"What can you do about it but let matters take their course, Henry. It's most unfortunate in every way, but it's not to be thought of, is it? We know nothing about the young man, even if he were fond of Lucy."

"True; but I fancy I know as much as is necessary. And as for money, my dear, you know she will have plenty for both. The first question is, how will disappointment affect the girl's health? She is very delicate and sensitive, and fretting may do her a great deal of harm. You mustn't let her get depressed or anxious. Keep up her spirits, and if after awhile she seems really in earnest, why—"

"You wouldn't let her marry him?" cried Mrs. Evans, in astonishment.

"Why not, my dear? why not? What object have I ever had with regard to Lucy's bringing up except her happiness? At any risks or personal loss to myself, it must be secured. And I don't know that young Valera would be such a bad match for her. He is a gentleman, there is no doubt of that, and we have tried to make Lucilla a lady. They might both do worse."

"Well, I'm glad to find you take it in that spirit," said his wife, "and it's as well I told you. I suppose the seaside trip is to be put off then?"

"Most decidedly! Go at once and set Lucy's mind at rest on that score. I will have nothing done, or even proposed, that is in any way distasteful to her. My wish is that she has her way in all things. And with respect to the other business, don't let her know you have told me; but watch, my dear—watch, and I will watch with you."

– CHAPTER 19 –

AN EXCEPTIONAL PROPOSAL

Leona had not seen so much of Mr. Evans since the evening of the charade party, or perhaps it would be more correct to say that she had avoided him more. She had every desire to watch his actions, and gain further proof of what she suspected from his conversation, but intuitively she shrank from the close contact she had hitherto maintained with him. His strange behaviour at the representation of the charade had excited her worst suspicions. Nothing but guilt, she argued, and the fear of detection, could render a man so weak and sensitive. Unpleasant memories might have been raised in his breast by her acting, but had he been innocent, he would have been able to stamp them down, and curb himself to sit out the little drama. Such ideas necessarily raised a great barrier between their familiar intercourse. Leona had never liked her uncle. Now, she positively hated him. Her distorted imagination made her picture in him the murderer, whose crime had driven his brother and her father to drag out the remainder of his life in exile; whose meanness could permit another to carry the burden of his guilt upon his shoulders; and whose conscience could permit himself to be enriched and wax fat upon the wealth his treachery had earned for him. She thought, if this were true, that nothing in the whole world could be more wicked, base, and contemptible than this same uncle of hers; and she held as much aloof from him as possible, brooding on her supposed wrongs, and turning over in her mind by what means she should bring the criminal to detection.

Mr. Evans saw the change, but he naturally attributed it to the intelligence he had heard from his wife, and concluded that Valera was either questioning his own heart, and the probabilities of his success with Lucilla; or having observed the girl's predilection, was meditating on the best course of action to be pursued with regard to her.

"In either case," thought Mr. Evans astutely, "the lad would naturally be shy of me. If he aspires to Lucy's hand he probably imagines it is a presumption I shall never forgive. Whilst, if he does not care for her, he would be equally afraid of offending me in consequence. And I must not forget that his hopes of advancement lie, in some measure now, through myself. But I won't have the young fellow's mind biassed. He's a good lad, and a gentlemanly lad; but it would be a great thing for a clerk to marry Lucilla, and I must know a little more about him before I let matters come to a crisis. Meanwhile the young people shall have complete licence to associate with one another, and find out their own minds. And then, if I see it all go on favourably, I'll have a quiet talk with Valera, and discover what he wishes."

In consequence of this decision on the part of Mr. Evans, which was duly repeated to his wife, Leona found herself thrown even more than before into the society of Lucilla; and unmindful of the trap laid for her and the eyes watching her actions, she fell readily into the snare. The truth was, she rather liked the companionship of this quiet sickly girl who was so ready to devote long hours to the familiar conversation by which Leona hoped to find out much of what she desired to know. She saw day by day that Lucy welcomed her more and more warmly, and attempted to detain her longer; and she was pleased at the interest evinced in her, and did all she could to show she felt it. She had never kissed Miss Evans as she had done Lizzie Vereker.

Not only had that little episode taught her to be more careful, but she scarcely ever remembered, whilst by Lucilla's side, that she wore the garb of a man. For the girl did nothing to remind her of it. She was too passive, too depressed, too much absorbed in her own weakness, to display any violent emotion. The affection she had conceived for Leona was perhaps the highest flight of love-making to which her sickly imagination had ever soared; yet it was, after all, but a very diluted imitation of the grand passion, so much so that the person towards whom it was directed never recognised it as such. She saw that Lucilla's eyes brightened at her approach—that she appeared content and happy whilst she sat by her sofa playing chess or singing Spanish serenades to the accompaniment of the guitar; perhaps even she may have felt the hand she held morning and evening, tremble a little in her grasp, but, after all, what do such symptoms amount to? One woman may evince them for another, and Leona was glad to be able to please the invalid by any attentions in her power. So she continued to sing to Mr. Evans' daughter, and to play chess and talk with her, until their pleasant intercourse was brought to an unexpected close after this manner.

It was morning, and the breakfast at the great house was just concluded.

Lucilla had been absent from the meal, and mamma Evans had reported privately and mysteriously to papa that her absence was caused by a violent headache, brought on after a prolonged fit of crying the night before, induced by her having seen Lizzie Vereker slip a three-cornered note into Don Valera's hand as they were all going up to bed.

"And really," concluded Mrs. Evans, "I think it is time you spoke, Henry; for Lucy seems to be always crying about something or other now, and her appetite is nothing to what it used to be."

The effect of which advice was that, as the breakfast-party were leaving the table, Mr. Evans asked Valera to accompany him to his study. Leona followed her uncle briskly. She hoped he was about to open the subject of business between them; for not only was she getting sick of the idle life she was leading, but she knew that before long, answers to the letters announcing her arrival in England must be received from the New York firm, and necessitate her flight. She wanted to be more generally engaged before that crisis arrived, so that her disappearance from the present scene of action might be the easier accomplished; and she longed to have the opportunity to embark upon a larger field of discovery, and bring her long-desired object to a close.

She had lingered on in the house in Hyde Park Gardens, picking up from day to day such crumbs of information as she thought might prove useful to her in the future; but she had felt of late that she had come to the end of her tether, and there was nothing more to be gained by remaining there. And she had had the seed of the next step to be taken germinating in her brain for weeks past, and only needing a word, as it were, to bring it into being. And that word she was just about to hear.

"Sit down, Valera. Make yourself comfortable. I want your attention for a moment or two before I go out this morning."

"About the business, I presume, monsieur," said Leona, seating herself.

"Well, no; not about the business exactly. I want to speak to you about Lucilla. You are very good friends with my daughter, are you not, Valera?"

Mr. Evans looked Leona steadily in the face as he said this, but Leona did not blush.

"Miss Evans has been kind enough to permit me to enjoy a good deal of her society, monsieur, and I think I may say, without presumption, that she regards me as a friend. I *hope* she does."

"Exactly so. And friendship between two such young people as yourselves is but another name for affection, eh?"

"Yes. I think Miss Evans likes me," returned Leona.

Mr. Evans thought the young man had rather a cool and unembarrassed way of expressing his feelings; but perhaps he wished to find out the father's opinion on the subject before he confessed his own.

"I think she does, too; and as this may lead to a still greater intimacy between us, I should like to know all you can tell me about yourself, Valera—your birth, parentage, and connections; bringing up, expectations, and so on. Treat me as a friend, my dear boy, and tell me everything."

Now, when Leona had resolved to take Don Christobal Valera's name, she had resolved also to borrow his antecedents. She knew that, at the best, it could be but a very short time before the fraud she had perpetrated would be discovered, and that when that came to pass she must vanish, and Christobal have his own again. She argued that whilst she bore his name (so long as she did nothing to disgrace it) she could not harm him by adopting his relations, and therefore she had never hesitated to speak of them, as she now did, boldly and without reserve.

"I fear I have very little to tell you, monsieur, that you have not already heard. My grandfather was an Hidalgo, of Spain, who was banished from his country for political intrigue, and settled in the Brazils. There my father was born and married; there he begot me, and died before I was ten years old. My mother, Donna Josefa, with the help of the padre, brought me up somehow; and, with the assistance of my godfather, who was a merchant at Rio, I procured the appointment of Spanish correspondent in the firm of Messrs. Halliday and Upjohn, which has given me the advantage of your acquaintance. My faith, as you know, is the faith of my country and forefathers. As for my prospects, they are *nil*. Had I any, monsieur, I should not now be a clerk in a counting-house. You will forgive my warmth, I trust, but the remembrance nettles me."

"All right, Valera. Don't say a word about it. The letter I received from your employers told me you were a gentleman. Your own appearance and manners more than confirm the statement. As for your prospects, I was foolish to mention them. I might have known they were bounded by the trade in which you have embarked. Though, with interest and friends to back you, the circle may be a wide one. Look at me."

"You have certainly been *most fortunate*, monsieur," said Leona, significantly; "but, if report speaks truth, you have been happy enough to inherit also the wealth of others."

"*Happy* enough!" repeated Mr. Evans. "Ah, Valera, people who speak of me like that do not know the truth."

"Perhaps not, monsieur."

"But I did not come here this morning to speak of myself, but of you. Of course I knew you had no fortune, but in mentioning your prospects, I should rather have asked, do you intend to adhere steadily to the trade you have chosen?"

"Unless something better turns up," replied Leona, cautiously. "I have a great and glorious object in view, Mr. Evans, a noble ambition before me, and I mean to pursue it to the end, or perish."

For the moment she had forgotten herself, and feared she had said too much. But Mr. Evans attributed her enthusiasm entirely to her desire to gain Lucilla.

"Just so. I guessed as much. Now, my dear Valera, you have been candid with me, and I shall be the same with you. Mrs. Evans and I have observed your affection for Lucilla, we could not fail to do so, and hers for you; and we are quite willing, sooner than destroy the dear girl's happiness, which is very precious to us, to smooth over all little difficulties, and let it end in the usual way."

"*In the usual way*?" repeated Leona, with open mouth.

"Yes, in your marriage. We should not, perhaps, have been so hasty in bringing matters to a conclusion had not Lucy's health been so delicate, but as it is—"

"*Lucilla wishes to marry me!*" said Leona, with the same look of blank astonishment.

"Well, I have not yet sounded her on the subject. I wished to speak to you first; but naturally I conclude she does, and that your own hopes aspire to that end also. Now, I know that the idea must be rather a startling one to you, and perhaps you have hardly even dared to hope to yourself that it might be; but since Mrs. Evans and I have seen that Lucilla's happiness is concerned in it, I resolved to tell you that, as far as money is concerned, the way will be smooth enough before you, as I have more than I require for my own need, and have always determined that the want of it should be no obstacle to Lucilla's having the man of her choice."

Leona took out her handkerchief and wiped the perspiration off her brow.

She was a brave woman and a bold woman, but she was not quite prepared for this. At first she thought of utterly disclaiming having taken any interest beyond that of friendship in Miss Lucilla Evans, and repudiating the idea of marriage between them as something sacrilegious. But the next moment's thought made her see how imprudent under the circumstances such a course would be. It would naturally rouse the indignation of her host, who would consider his daughter's affections had been trifled with, and banish her from his house without the shadow of a chance of regaining an entrance there. And Leona had learned to be very wary how she trod upon the social eggs amongst which she moved. She leaned back in her chair with her handkerchief still pressed to her brow, and thought.

"Take your time," said Mr. Evans mildly; "I see I have surprised you. Don't hurry yourself."

An idea flashed through her clever brain. She perceived how by temporising she might turn this matter to her own advantage.

"You *did* take me by surprise, monsieur," she said, after a moment's pause; "the prospect you hold out to me is too flattering—so brilliant—so far beyond my poor deserts—it has taken my breath away."

"I thought so, Valera, but take courage. My daughter loves you. She has confessed as much to her mother, and we are both disposed to favour your suit."

"Madame and you are too good—too condescending," murmured Leona, "and I can but trust you will never regret your kindness. If to be the—the—*husband* of Miss Evans is not too exalted a lot for me—a position to which I can never do credit—then, monsieur, what remains for me to do but to accept your generous offer, and bless the day you made it? Yet, if you will not think me too bold—"

"Say what you think, Valera. I wish you to be perfectly frank with me."

"Rumours have reached me—they may be idle tales, and in that case you will pardon my mentioning them—but I *have* heard that Miss Lucilla is not your own daughter, monsieur! Is that the truth?"

Mr. Evans knitted his brow at this question, but he answered it promptly.

"Don Valera! I will be open with you. Under the circumstances I should have been so in any case, although I cannot conceive who has had sufficient interest in my private affairs to discuss them with a stranger—"

"Pardon me, monsieur, but I have spoken of Mademoiselle Lucilla to all the world—"

"Ah, very true; but I, myself, have never spoken of the subject, nor intended to do so, except to the man Lucilla might marry. *She is not my daughter, Valera.* I tell you so frankly—but she is as dear to me as if she were, and her dowry will be the same as though she had been."

"And may I ask, then, whose daughter she is?"

"I suppose you have a right to do so, though it can make no difference to you, as all her relations are dead. Her father was an old and trusted friend of my uncle's, Mr. Theophilus Evans. His name was Anson—a good name in our country, Valera—but he died suddenly, leaving this one orphan child behind him. No one appearing disposed to take charge of her, my uncle, with his usual generosity, immediately placed the infant under the care of a widow lady in the country, and when I married I brought her home to my wife, who, having no little ones of her own, has been a real mother to Lucy ever since. And that is the whole history, Valera."

"It does honour to your goodness and purity of intention, monsieur," remarked his hearer, dryly.

"Oh, as to that," rejoined the merchant, wiping his heated face, "least said soonest mended. There is the girl, as much a lady as any you'll find in the land, and she has chosen you for her husband. She might have looked higher, but I'm an advocate for people listening to what their own hearts say in such matters, and, as I've observed before, her fortune goes with her."

"Lucy told me that she had once lived in the country with a Mr. and Mrs.———" said Leona, pretending to puzzle over the name, which, for her own purposes, she was most anxious to ascertain rightly.

"A Mrs. Gibson," replied Mr. Evans promptly. "Yes, to be sure, Mrs. Gibson, of Willowside, in Sussex; though I should hardly think Lucy could remember that time."

"She seemed to remember it very well, monsieur, and the fact of your fetching her away to Liverpool."

"Strange! I should have thought the child must have forgotten it all long ago, though I hear the old lady is living yet. Still, it little matters now."

"No, indeed," said Leona.

There was a pause between them, neither knowing what to say next. Mr. Evans broke it by observing:

"Well, Valera, I suppose then we may consider this matter settled?"

"In what way could I answer you but one, monsieur, when you know that my fortunes hang upon the issue of the question? That I am utterly unworthy of the honour you design for me, I feel more and more with every word you say. But it is not in my power to refuse so much happiness. It has overwhelmed—blinded me. May I ask one great favour of you? I received this morning an invitation from some friends I made at the Misses Lillietrip's, to spend a few days with them at Streatham, and at the end of that time—Monday or Tuesday at farthest—I shall have had leisure to think over this great and unexpected proposal, and to thank you for it as I should. At the present moment I am stunned."

"I think your idea a very sensible and reasonable one, Valera. Lucilla knows nothing of what has passed between us, so that her mind will not be disturbed by suspense or agitation. You will say nothing, of course, to her on the subject; but go to your friends, and from there you can write to me, if you prefer it, and tell me all your mind."

"Monsieur is too good," said Leona, in a voice that slightly trembled. For liar and murderer as she believed the man before her to be, she could not help feeling that in this instance, at least, he was treating her with greater kindness than she deserved. Yet the weakness was momentary; for with the next breath she drew she remembered that he was but trying to forward the happiness of the *murdered man's child*, as a propitiatory offering to the manes of his remorseful conscience.

"I will just put my things together, bid adieu to madame and mademoiselle, and start for Streatham at once then," she said, rising to her feet.

"Just so, Valera, and the carriage will be at your disposal when you choose to order it," replied Mr. Evans.

"And you will say nothing to Lucilla until I return?" she added, looking wistfully into his face.

She did not wish the feelings of the poor sickly girl, who had been so very weak as to fall in love with her, to be more roughly handled than was necessary.

"*Certainly not!*" was Mr. Evans' decisive answer. "Not a word shall be broached on the subject until you give us leave;" and thereupon Leona, sorely against her will, was forced to take an apparently friendly farewell of the man she hated, and had sworn to hunt down, if needful, to his death.

There was some little surprise exhibited in the drawing-room at the announcement of her departure. Mrs. Evans peered at her inquiringly above her spectacles, but was reassured by Leona's blushing cheek and quiet smile. Lizzie Vereker openly gave vent to her expressions of disgust, and professed to be so offended that she would not shake hands with the young Spaniard at parting. But poor Lucy laid her hand so confidingly in hers that Leona's heart smote her for the mischief she might have caused; although the ludicrous side of it was so omnipresent with her, that she was longing to get away to some place by herself, if only to be able to indulge in a genuine shout of laughter at the absurd mistake into which the poor invalid had fallen. She managed to shake free of all three ladies at last, and (Mr. Evans having already quitted the house) to pack her possessions (they were not numerous) without the fact becoming noticeable. She declined the use of the carriage, and drove in a cab to the Victoria Station,[*] where she deposited her luggage. Then she looked out for a small hotel in the vicinity, where she ordered dinner, and allowed herself time to think over her plans. With a brain of fire, and an energy of iron, she was not long either in bringing them to perfection or putting them into force.

As soon as her meal was concluded, she sauntered into the Buckingham Road,[†] and with ready money at her command, found no difficulty in procuring all that she required from one or other of the numerous emporiums of female millinery that pervade that district.

At a latish hour a young man strolled upon the platform of the Brighton Railway.[‡] He had a light portmanteau, which he was anxious should be put into the carriage with him. He was also very anxious to secure the compartment to himself.

"Want to go alone—expect a friend to join me a few stations farther on. Don't you twig, old fellow?" he said jocosely, as he dug the guard in the ribs with his little cane.

The guard did "twig," but he didn't see the force of the argument just yet.

"Very difficult, sir. Express train, you see. Going against orders," he answered firmly, until a glittering yellow sixpence found its way miraculously into his palm, and he altered his tune, and said he would "try his best to oblige the gentleman."

---

[*] Opened in 1858.
[†] In south west London.
[‡] By the 1830s Brighton was the most popular seaside resort in Britain. The London to Brighton line was finished in 1841.

Which best was so very good, that the gentleman presently found the door of his compartment locked, and a large placard with "Engaged" stuck across the window, whilst he and the light box he had desired should travel with him were flying through the night air at the rate of forty miles per hour, and no stoppage to speak of all the way.

When, at last, the panting engine drew up in the Brighton terminus, and the active porters, throwing the carriage-doors open, came to that one marked "Engaged," they discovered its solitary occupant to be a very beautiful woman, dressed in the height of the fashion, with a spotted veil drawn tightly over her face.

"Want a cab, miss?" exclaimed three of them at once.

"If you please. And will you tell me which is the best hotel to go to here?" she answered, in the prettiest of foreign accents.

"Oh, the Grand* is the best, miss," was the porter's reply. "A fine big'un, close to the sea." And thereupon the beautiful woman was put with her luggage into a cab and driven off to the Grand Hotel.

"And now," she thought, as she found herself once more safely landed on a new field of action, "now for one night's rest, and then to find out what I can from Mrs. Gibson of Willowside."

– CHAPTER 20 –

THE RECLUSE OF WILLOWSIDE

Brighton, which is always gay and pleasant, was looking its very best when Leona first saw it, and to the Brazilian-bred girl, who had never had an opportunity of visiting a large watering-place in her life before, offered every inducement to remain a few days amongst its novel attractions. But she was too seriously bent upon accomplishing the object of her life to have leisure even to think of such frivolities as bands, aquariums, piers, esplanades, and cockle-boats.

Her whole desire was to find out the geography of the country,

---

* Brighton's Grand Hotel is an iconic Victorian hotel, opened in 1864.

and how far Willowside might happen to be from Brighton. A friendly waiter at the "Grand," taking compassion on her foreign extraction, and not entirely untouched by her lofty style of beauty ("like one of them big female statties at the aquarium[*]," as he remarked confidentially to his fellow-waiters), took upon himself to procure the desired information for her; and she ascertained that a few hours' travelling by cross-country trains would bring her to the village where Mrs. Gibson was said to reside.

"But it's a rare poor place, miss, I hear," said the friendly waiter, "and no hotel anyway near it. I don't know how you'll manage, unless you're going to friends."

"I am going to friends," replied Leona, shortly; for she was unwilling to let anybody know more of her movements than was absolutely necessary; and glad to find that Willowside was at some distance from Brighton, and a place unlikely to attract attention.

But as she travelled down to it, she was unable to tell herself what issue she expected from an interview (even if she obtained it) with the quondam guardian of Lucilla Anson. All the information she had gained through the Evans was that, on her father being murdered, the child had been placed with this lady till she was eight years old, and then taken back to Liverpool to live with Henry Evans and his wife. Whether the girl's true parentage had ever been confided to Mrs. Gibson was doubtful; and even if it had been, she was unlikely—living in that remote Sussex village—to have heard more than—or even so much of the murder and its surroundings—as Leona herself. All these facts were indisputable, and yet she would have left a stone unturned by not going to see Mrs. Gibson. She could not even say what she *hoped* might come of it, she only knew that it was part of her task to go.

Leona looked very handsome as she travelled down to Willowside. It was the first time she had ever adopted complete English female costume, and the passengers by the same train turned to gaze at her again and again as she passed. She had robed herself completely in black—the only colour that her unusual

---

[*] Brighton Aquarium was designed by Eugenius Birch, the architect responsible for the West Pier. Work on the Aquarium began in 1869, the building was opened in 1872.

height would bear—but she looked like a queen as she moved majestically across the platform, and might have been drawn for a reclining Cleopatra as she cast herself grandly upon the cushioned seat of the carriage. In order to avoid singularity she had been compelled to adopt the inevitable false chignon behind, but her own thick short curls still adorned her brow and the sides of her head, and were very suitable to her style of countenance. As the name her father had adopted in his exile bore no significance in England, she had determined to use it when assuming her own part, and was travelling as Miss Lacoste. What she intended to say to Mrs. Gibson, or how account for her unexpected visit, she decided with herself as she went along. Willowside was an out-of-the-way village at the farther end of Sussex, and Leona had several changes to make, and intervals of waiting to try her patience, before she reached it. At the close of the summer's afternoon, however, she found herself at the nearest market-town, and engaged what accommodation she could procure there for the night, before she walked on to Willowside.

"Do you know an old lady of the name of Gibson, living at Willowside?" she inquired of the fresh-looking country girl who brought her some refreshment previous to starting.

"Do you mean the bed-ridden lady in Acacia Cottage?" demanded the girl.

"I suppose so. Are there two of that name in the village?"

"Not that I know of, miss. But this one's a regular invalid. I don't think anyone's seen her not for years—except it's the woman that looks after her. She's been very bad, so I hear, this ever so long time, and can't remember anybody or anything. I come from Willowside myself, miss."

"Indeed. I'm sorry to hear Mrs. Gibson is so ill," said Leona, wondering if she had made that long journey for nothing.

"Have you come to see her, miss? for I don't think they let no one in. The old lady never goes out of one room, except into the other. But perhaps you're a relation, and it may be different."

"I shall, at all events, try," replied Leona; and after sundry directions concerning turning to the right and turning to the left, which sounded almost like Greek in her unpractised ears, she set off walking across the fields to Willowside.

The information of the girl at the inn had so depressed her that she anticipated no results at all from her excursion. It was hardly likely she would be admitted to the presence of the invalid; and if she were, she could not expect to gain much useful knowledge from a memory weakened by old age and paralysis. Yet she still determined to try.

An hour's walk across the fields brought her to Willowside, and Acacia Cottage looked very pretty and rural, embowered in honeysuckle and climbing roses. Leona had to ring two or three times before any one attended to her summons, and then the door was opened by a hard-featured, middle-aged woman.

"What are you pleased to want?" she inquired, in a tone which indicated that the stranger could only have stopped to ask some question, perfectly irrelevant, of the inhabitants of the cottage.

"Does Mrs. Gibson live here? I want to see her," replied Leona confidently.

"*You want to see the mistress!*" said the woman, in a tone of surprise, as she came outside the door on to the steps. "But you don't know her?"

"I know some old friends of hers, and I want to ask her if she can give me any information about them at the present time," said Leona confidently.

"Oh!—ah! But you don't know *her*? I thought so. I know everybody that she's known for the last thirty years."

At this assertion Leona pricked up her ears. If the mistress's memory proved valueless, the servant's might serve her purpose equally well. She immediately put on her most fascinating manner.

"Ah, then, you must be that very good friend of Mrs. Gibson's I hear of, who tends her so carefully, and never spares any trouble on her account. Is it not so? Pray let me shake hands with you."

The woman looked gratified, and hastily rubbed her bony hand upon her canvass apron.

"Well I'm sure, miss, you're very good. Yes, I do look after the old lady, and a precious trouble she is to me, as you may guess. But I don't remember your face, miss, and—you'll pardon me I hope—but you're not Sussex bred, are you?"

"Oh no. I am not English. But I love England, madame, and all its people, and I have an English friend whom Mrs. Gibson once knew, of whom I have lost sight, and I came over to Willowside expressly to see if I could gain any information about her present address."

"And what might the lady's name be, miss?" demanded the woman, inquisitively.

But Leona was afraid that if she gratified her curiosity too readily she would refuse to let her have a sight of Mrs. Gibson.

"I hope you will let me see your mistress," she went on, persuasively. "I will not stay long, or talk much, to fatigue her. But I am very anxious to hear from her own mouth whether she remembers, or knows anything of my friend."

"Lor! miss, you wouldn't get nothing out of the mistress. She's been but a poor creature these many years past, and don't remember anything from day to day. She's lost the use of her limbs too, and has to be carried about like a child, and nice work it is for me, as you may imagine. There's no rest for me, day nor night, and what with her fads, and one thing and another, it's enough to wear a woman out."

"I am sure all her friends ought to be very grateful to you for your kindness to her, madame," said Leona, as she slipped a sovereign she had reserved for the purpose into the woman's hand. The Sussex charwoman (for she was nothing more) looked at the magic coin with amazement. She had seen from the first that this foreign lady was very different from those that usually passed through the village. Leona's commanding presence and handsome dress, her pretty modulated speech, each word of which dropped slowly and distinctly from her lips, her gracious manner and expression, had already had an effect upon Mrs. Gibson's servant. But when the climax came in the shape of a sovereign, and the title of "madame," the significance of which was patent even to Sussex ears, the charwoman was completely conquered. She closed her hard-working hand firmly over the unexpected present, and unmistakably smiled.

"Of course, miss," she went on, "if you really want to see the poor old woman, why there she is! I'm not ashamed, nor afraid, that no one should see her at any time of the day, for I keep her as neat as a new pin, as our clergyman has often said, when he comes to give her spiritual comfort. But I fear you'll be disappointed about her memory, for it's gone as clean as this tooth from the side of my head, and Mary Jones is just the same to her as Betty Brown, or Sally Anyone else."

But, as she spoke, she pushed the hall door open, and Leona had gained the object she had worked for—an entrance to the presence of Mrs. Gibson.

Through the open parlour she could descry the figure of the frail old woman, propped up by pillows in an armchair, with wistful eyes turned meekly, but unmeaningly, towards the direction whence the voices reached her.

Leona did not stand on further ceremony, but, with a hasty word of thanks to the servant, passed at once into the sitting-room, and approached the invalid.

"You do not know me, madame, I am aware," she commenced, "but I have come to see you to ask after a dear friend of mine."

The old lady looked at her without speaking, then turned to her attendant.

"What does she say, Wallis?"

"She says she's come to get news of a lady as you knew, mum," bawled Wallis into her ear, with the apparent idea that the louder one speaks the better a weak-minded person can understand.

"I don't know her," replied Mrs. Gibson, shaking her head.

She was a delicate, lady-like looking old person of perhaps seventy, but she did not strike her visitor as being so childish as her servant had made out.

"My name is Lacoste," replied Leona, going to the point at once, "and I want to find out the present address of Lucy Evans, who used to live with you when she was a child."

"She don't know no Lucy Evans," affirmed Wallis, decisively.

"No, I don't know Lucy Evans," repeated the old lady, feebly.

"Nor never did," added the servant.

Leona started. She trusted to Wallis's memory more than to that of her mistress. Was it possible she could have mistaken the name, the address, the identity altogether of this paralytic?

"But if you have been with Mrs. Gibson thirty years you must remember," she said, turning to her first acquaintance; "Lucy Evans was here about two-and-twenty years ago. She came from Liverpool, and she went back there when she was eight. A fair child, with blue eyes and pale-coloured hair.

"Are you speaking of *Lucilla Anson?*" demanded Wallis, curiously.

"Yes, yes. I didn't know she was here under that name. She was adopted by a Mr. Evans, you know. You remember her, don't you?"

"Oh yes, miss, I remember *her*," said the servant, dryly.

"Well, it is of that young lady I want news. We knew each other afterwards, long afterwards; but I have heard her speak of Mrs. Gibson, and Willowside. Where is she now? What is she doing? Is she married or single? Tell me all about her."

"I know nothing to tell," replied Wallis, with compressed lips. "The child was placed here for a spell by Mr. Evans, and a nice trouble she was from first to last. I was precious glad to see the back of her for one. The old lady here had several other children to take care of at the same time, but I don't suppose she remembers one more than the other."

"What is she talking about?" demanded the invalid, querulously.

"Do you remember Lucilla Anson?" bawled Wallis at her again.

The old woman paused a moment, as though waiting for recollection to come back to her. Then a look of terror passed suddenly over her features, and she began to wail:

"Oh, blood—blood! They murdered him, Wallis. Don't you remember they murdered him? See, they are doing it now! Don't let them come near me! They will murder us both. Let me hide!" and with childish alarm she seized the servant's apron and folded it over her own head.

"Don't you talk such rubbish, or I shall send you to bed," said Wallis, authoritatively. "You see what she is, miss. Quite gone, as you may say, and no rhyme nor reason in anything she says. It's no more use talking to her than to the table."

"It's a curious fancy of hers though, associating Miss Anson's name with blood, because you know, perhaps, her father *was* murdered," said Leona, with the idea of making a bold stroke for her information.

"Oh, you've heard that, have you, miss?" returned Wallis, with a look of relief. "Well, it's no use denying it, then, though me and the mistress were bound over to secrecy at the time, on account of the child not coming to the knowledge of it. It was a dreadful thing, warn't it? I've most forgot the circumstances now; but I know the murderer never was found, which was a great pity, for if ever a fellow deserved to swing, he did."

"I quite agree with you," replied Leona; "and Mr. Evans was as anxious to bring him to justice as any one. Mr. Evans is a very nice gentleman, isn't he?"

"I never see him, miss—"

"You never saw him? Then I suppose *Mrs.* Evans fetched the child away from Willowside?"

"No one fetched the child away, miss. I took her up to London myself, by Mr. Evans' desire, and then a young gentleman from the office met her, and I suppose he took charge of her to Liverpool. I never saw Mr. nor Mrs. Evans in my life. They was too fine, I fancy, to trouble Willowside."

"That is strange," mused Leona. She remembered that Lucilla had mentioned her putative parents taking her home from Sussex to Liverpool, and naturally fancied they must have visited Willowside. Why had her uncle avoided the personal acquaintance of Mrs. Gibson? But the fact made an idea which she had conceived for the future all the easier of execution.

"I wonder why Mrs. Gibson did not take Miss Lucilla home to Liverpool?" she said to Wallis.

"Lor, miss, the mistress had plenty to do at that time, without running all over the country with her pupils. She kept a school, you understand; quite private it was, and very respectable. But we never held much account of Lucilla Anson. Indeed, I recollect when the mistress first heard who the child was, she was in two minds about taking her at all. It would have been very unpleasant for us if the story about her father had got wind in the village. They are very particular in Willowside, miss."

"No doubt, madame. And so Mrs. Gibson never went to Liverpool?"

"Not she. What would she have to do with a nasty dirty town like that, all docks and shipping? She never had a call to go."

"Nor seen Mr. or Mrs. Evans?"

"No, nor seen them neither. Nor Miss Lucilla since she left us. Nor didn't want to. We'd enough bother with her while she was here."

"Well! I see you cannot help me to her present address, madame, so I need not trouble you any further. I am infinitely obliged to you for the trouble you have taken, and I hope I have not wasted too much of your time."

"Oh lor, no, miss, and I wish I could have obliged you, I'm sure. But you see how it is. The poor old lady's good for nothing, and hasn't been for the last five years; but if she weren't she couldn't have given you any satisfaction, *I* know. We've never had word of Miss Anson since I left her in London that day, and I don't know whether she's dead or alive. And shouldn't know her from Adam if we met. Which we're not likely to do, unless she travels down here as you have done; for my mistress and me, we're both Sussex bred and born, and haven't moved out of the county for the last twenty years, nor shan't do it till we go to the churchyard. So I wish I could have obliged you, miss, but it's out of my power, and I wish you a very good evening, and—yes, that's the way back, miss, across those fields."

Leona having passed out of the presence of Mrs. Gibson without any more useless words, was just about to retrace her steps to the place she had come from, when a sudden thought struck her. "One moment, madame," she exclaimed, recalling Wallis to the garden gate; "if neither Mr. nor Mrs. Henry Evans have ever been to Willowside, would you tell me who brought Miss Lucilla Anson down here when she was first placed under Mrs. Gibson's care?"—for she fancied that her uncle might have travelled with the child without discovering his identity to the school-mistress.

"A sort of a servant, miss; at least she wasn't quite that neither. I don't know *how* I should call her."

"It was a woman, then?"

"Oh yes, miss, it was a woman."

"You're sure it was not Mrs. Evans herself?"

"Well, if it *was* Mrs. Evans, he must be a queer sort of gentleman to have married her. She was a big strapping woman, with a stride like a grenadier, but she seemed monstrous fond of the little girl, and cried when she parted with her."

"Did you hear her name?" demanded Leona, satisfied that at no period could little Mrs. Evans have been transformed into a "*big strapping woman."*

"Now you come to speak of it, I *did* hear the child mention her name. Let me see, *Levitt!* Yes, that was how she called her—*Rebecca Levitt.*"

"*Levitt!*" repeated Leona, with a sudden remembrance of the murdered clerk's letter to her father, and the consciousness of another link being forged in the chain that was to lead to her discovery.

"Yes, miss. Do you happen to have heard it too?"

"Oh yes; I knew it very well. I suppose you are sure that *was* the name, madame?"

"Quite sure, miss," reiterated the woman; and then Leona commenced her walk back to the inn in earnest.

As she went, her brain was throbbing with the information she had obtained, and the uses to which she intended to put it. To an ordinary listener, perhaps, she might not have appeared to have heard anything more from Mrs. Wallis's lips than she had done from those of Lucilla—only that the child had been placed there and taken away again, and there was an end of it. No clue to the mystery of her adoption—not even a confirmation of the fact that Henry Evans was the chief instigator of the arrangements made for her benefit, nor a recognition of him as the person who had interested himself in her welfare whilst there.

But in these very circumstances lay the most valuable intelligence Leona could have received. Mr. and Mrs. Evans were equally unknown to Mrs. Gibson. The parties had never met. *They* had never visited Willowside. *She* had not gone to Liverpool. For reasons of his own (probably, as Leona surmised, to avoid future recognition), Henry Evans had strictly avoided making the acquaintance of the lady in whose charge he had placed his adopted child. He, therefore, could have no knowledge of her personal appearance.

Nor, in her present condition, was Mrs. Gibson ever likely to quit Willowside. Wallis said they had neither of them been out of the county for the past twenty years. Here was another circumstance that promised greatly to aid the new project Leona had in her head.

Added to this, there was the fact of Rebecca Levitt having

accompanied Lucilla to Sussex on the first occasion of her going there to be looked into. Who was Rebecca Levitt?

The name had conjured up a host of surmises in Leona's heart. She remembered the words of Anson in the letter to her father: *"I'm sorry to say he's heard about that business with the Levitt's girl."*

What business? What girl? Could she be identical with Rebecca Levitt, and if so, why did she cry over the parting with Abraham Anson's orphan? All this was fresh matter for speculation and inquiry, and Leona felt the energy, which had been rendered somewhat dormant by her prolonged stay with the Evans, stirring anew in her at the thought. She had always intended to make Liverpool her next stage of action. She wanted to be on the very spot where the murder was committed—amongst the very people who remembered its commission. But she had been puzzled to think under what character to go amongst them—on what plea to institute the inquiries which she trusted to follow up to her desired end.

Now her doubts were solved—her visit to Willowside had made all things easy to her.

She must enter Liverpool in a disguise which ran no chance of detection. *She would go there as Mrs. Gibson.* She must have a plausible excuse for making acquaintances and asking questions.

Her ostensible object should be to find out Rebecca Levitt for news of Lucilia Anson.

– CHAPTER 21 –

MISS GIBSON

Leona Lacoste did not part readily with a determination once arrived at, but when she came to sit down quietly in the Brighton Hotel, and think over the difficulties of successfully impersonating an old woman like Mrs. Gibson, she was fain to cast about her mind for some more suitable idea. For there is no disguise less easy to maintain by daylight than that of a wrinkled old crone by a plump, smooth-skinned young woman. The imitation may pass muster beneath the gaslight, but it would certainly be detected under the searching glare of day. Not only has the fair, firm flesh to appear shrivelled, discoloured, and empty, but the eyes must lose their brightness, the throat become drawn, the hands bony, pinched, and misshapen. Grey hair, false eyebrows, and paint judiciously applied, may do a great deal towards gaining the desired effect, might even accomplish it for one or two interviews. But Leona foresaw that in the disguise she adopted for Liverpool she would probably have to return to London, and be again subjected to the scrutiny of the Evans, and therefore she abandoned the idea of personating Mrs. Gibson, and determined to appear instead as a niece of that old lady, who had been asked by her aunt to institute inquiries respecting Miss Anson on her way up to the North. The preparations for this disguise gave her very little trouble. Cosmetics she already possessed, and having procured a grey front and a few plain articles of attire, such as a female of the middle-class might wear, she put a thick veil over her face, settled her bill at the "Grand," and drove away with her boxes to a smaller hotel. Here she went straight up to her bedroom, whence, in the course of an hour, she emerged—a middle-aged woman. Her chestnut curls all tucked away beneath smooth bands of grey hair completely altered the expression of her face; whilst her dark arched eyebrows, dashed with white, and a few crow's-feet artistically penciled at the corners of her eyes, drew off the attention from the liquid amber-coloured orbs, that could gleam so wrathfully or lovingly beneath them. She descended to the sitting-room, where her meal was prepared for her, such a staid, matronly-looking body, with her old-fashioned cap tied under her chin, and a small three-cornered shawl pinned discreetly over her bosom, that the maids who had watched her arrival, nudged each other to look at her now, and whispered, "Did they ever think she was such an old 'un, to judge by her voice."

Not but what Leona had great command also over her voice, and could alter it to suit her own fancy. But she had hardly had time to think about what voice she should assume when this little incident occurred. By the time she reached Liverpool she had accustomed herself to a tone which no one would have recognised as that in which Don Christobal Valera had ensnared the heart of poor Lucilla Evans.

The acting and managing partner of the firm of Evans and Troubridge in Liverpool at that particular moment was a Mr. Lionel, a bachelor of some forty-five or fifty years of age, who was noted for his gallantry to the fair sex.

It was a standing remark that whenever a woman had occasion to enter the office or the warehouse (which was very seldom), "Old Lionel," as the clerks irreverently termed him, could pay no attention to business, however pressing, until she had passed out of sight again. So incurable was this amiable weakness on the part of the manager of the firm, that his subordinates had been known, on more than one occasion, to play the double trick of sending some pretty woman on a false errand to his office, in order that they might watch his delight at her reception, and ridicule him for all that passed during the interview afterwards. But, naturally, only when his back was turned.

It was, therefore, with a wink of intelligence to his brother clerks that the sauciest of the lot demurely announced to Mr. Lionel one morning that "a lady" wished to speak to him.

"A lady! Watson," exclaimed the manager, pricking up his ears. "Who is she? What is she like?"

"Her name is Miss Gibson, sir; and—she's very nice-looking, sir."

"Oh, show her in, Watson, show her in," said Mr. Lionel; and thus, thanks perhaps entirely to the love of mischief on the part of Mr. Watson, Miss Gibson gained admittance to the presence of the head of the firm.

But though the grey-haired woman who presently appeared to Mr. Lionel was not "all his fancy painted her," she was quite sufficiently "nice-looking" to engage his attention. "Nice-looking," indeed, was just the term to apply to his visitor; for though the hair, and the eyebrows, and the crow's-feet belonged to the supposed Miss Gibson, the clear eyes, the dimpled chin, the beautifully-formed mouth, and all that Leona Lacoste could not paint out of herself remained to make the woman look as though age had overtaken her through trouble or sickness, rather than crept upon her unawares.

"Miss Gibson, I believe. Pray be seated, madam," said the manager, courteously.

"I presume that I am speaking to Mr. Evans?" commenced the stranger, as she accepted the offer.

"Oh, no! I am Mr. Lionel. Mr. Evans is not in Liverpool at present, but if your business with him is not of a strictly private nature, I have no doubt I shall be able to act for him."

"You are very kind, sir. Perhaps you will allow me to trouble you with a few questions. I have called here at the request of my aunt, Mrs. Gibson of Willowside. She had charge, many years ago, of a Miss Lucilla Anson, a ward, I believe, of Mr. Evans?"

"Yes, yes!—well?" said Mr. Lionel, becoming grave directly.

"And as I was passing through Liverpool, on my way north, my aunt was anxious that I should see Miss Anson, and send her word how she is, and if she is married, and so on, or get her address that she may communicate with her by letter."

"Miss Anson—who, by the way, is always termed Miss Evans now, by the desire of her adopted father—is not in Liverpool, nor likely to return here. She is alive and well, and still unmarried. You can tell your aunt so far, but I think I must consult Mr. Evans before giving you his private address. There is always a certain amount of etiquette observable in these matters, you know."

"Mrs. Gibson thought that having had the charge of the young lady for so many years, and being fully acquainted with the history of her birth and her father's death—"

"Indeed!" said Mr. Lionel, bringing his chair closer and lowering his voice, "was Mrs. Gibson told the secret of Miss Anson's adoption by Mrs. Evans then?"

"It was pretty well known over the country, sir, though it may be forgotten by this time. And the hand that Mr. Evans' brother had in the business too."

"Hush! my good lady; pray speak lower. The unhappy circumstances you allude to are not such public property as you imagine."

"But everybody knows that Mr. George Evans disappeared at the time of the murder, sir, and that there was no suspicion cast on anyone else. I thought that fact was plain enough, though it's no concern of mine."

"True, as you say, it's no concern of ours. But you must not be offended if I ask if your aunt has any idea of using this knowledge of hers in order to—"

While Mr. Lionel was looking about for a word, Miss Gibson supplied it.

"In order to extort money from Mr. Evans or Miss Anson? No, sir. We have no need of that. We are not well off, but we've not yet come to robbery."

"My dear lady, you must not misinterpret my meaning."

"I do not, sir. But I will tell you candidly, that Mrs. Gibson's desire to know Mr. Evans' address arose from the hope he might be able—and willing—to put me in the way of filling the situation of a housekeeper, or any place of trust. My aunt is now a very old woman, unable to do anything more for her own living, and she did her duty by the child Mrs. Evans placed under her care, and has guarded the secret of how she came to lose her father; and thinks she has—or rather I may have through her—some little claim in consequence on the gentleman's consideration. For we hear he is very rich."

Mr. Lionel felt this was not a case to be dismissed hastily. He knew that women's tongues are long and loud, and that should he irritate Miss Gibson to proclaim her wrongs, all Liverpool might soon be ringing again with the story that his partner had been trying so many years to put to sleep. He saw that he must be cautious to keep Miss Gibson in good humour—more than that, he must keep her under his own eye until he had communicated with Mr. Evans on the subject.

"You are perfectly right, madam," he said, after some little consideration, "and were my partner here, he would be the first to tell you so. Are you making any stay in Liverpool?"

Now, Leona, with her usual quickness, saw at once by this cautious answer how the land lay. She had made no plans when she entered the office, having determined to be guided entirely by the force of such circumstances as might meet her there. The event had proved better than all her anticipations. She had the power to make them fear her, and her reply to Mr. Lionel's question was given in accordance with her new discovery.

"That just as it suits my own pleasure, sir. I can stay or go as I see fit, but I think I shall remain till I've heard something one way or another from Mr. Evans, that is, if you'll be so good as to give me his address."

"Well, I've already told you that I think I must ask his permission for that first, and meanwhile I will write anything you wish to say to him. Have you got lodgings yet, Miss Gibson?"

"No, sir, I only arrived in Liverpool this morning, and I don't even know where to look for them."

"I am sure Mr. Evans would not like to think you were put to any inconvenience while waiting for his answer. He will be the first, I feel assured, to acknowledge the strong claim your aunt has upon his gratitude (for he is much attached to his adopted daughter), and to find fault with me if I have in any way neglected it. I am a miserable bachelor, Miss Gibson," he went on airily, "but I have tolerable accommodation for visitors in my house, and a highly respectable old housekeeper to look after my lady guests! so if you will accept the offer of rooms there during your stay in Liverpool, I can promise you shall be as quiet and undisturbed as though you were under your own roof, and I shall feel it an honour to be of any use to a friend of Mr. Evans."

Leona did not know at first what to say to this proposal—how to decide—whether it would hamper or accelerate her search after the truth. But she saw no way of backing out of it, and she had a strong—almost a superstitious belief in the Fate which was bound to carry her on to the end of her sacred mission. So she accepted the offer of Mr. Lionel's rooms.

"I'm sure I'm much obliged to you, sir, for taking such care of a stranger, and I think I should be very foolish to say No. And I suppose it cannot be for long that I shall have need to trouble you."

"The longer the better, as far as I am concerned," returned Mr. Lionel gallantly; "but I shall communicate with Mr. Evans on the subject to-day, and I do not think you will have to wait for his answer. I shall have the pleasure of seeing you again, I hope, to-morrow, when we will talk further on this matter. Meantime, I am sure I can trust you to mention it to no one."

"Certainly, sir," Miss Gibson replied.

Mr. Lionel drew pen and paper towards him, and hastily wrote a few lines.

"These are for my housekeeper, Mrs. Hodgett, desiring her to see you have everything you may require," he remarked, as he folded the note, "and I will send one of my clerks round to my house with you."

"My luggage is waiting at the door, sir, on a cab."

"Very good. Then there need be no delay."

He opened the door of his sanctum, and called into the outer office.

"*Levitt!* Is Levitt there, Johnson? Send him here to me at once." And thereupon a cry of "*Levitt! Levitt! wanted immediately,*" sounded through the establishment.

Leona started. Here was that name again—the name mentioned in Anson's letter, that was borne by the woman who wept at parting with Anson's child. What mysterious chain of circumstances bound that name of Levitt with the destinies of the Evans family? She had hardly had time to ask herself the question when the present owner of the title appeared.

He was a good-looking lad of fifteen or thereabouts, with dark eyes and hair, and a bright complexion, who looked as though he could be wicked enough if he chose, but was all meekness and sobriety before Mr. Lionel.

"Here, Levitt, you are to go round with this lady to my house, and give this note to Mrs. Hodgett, and tell her she is to make Miss Gibson as comfortable as possible, and that I have to go over to Manchester this afternoon, and shall not be home till late—ten, or half past. Do you understand?"

"Yes, sir."

"And after you have seen Miss Gibson safely there, you are to come straight back to the office. Do you hear?"

"Yes, sir," replied the meek Master Levitt, who seemed to carry some remembrance in his face of a former occasion, when he had not come "straight back."

"I am sure I am much obliged to you, sir," said Miss Gibson, with a sweeping curtsey.

"Pray don't mention it," returned Mr. Lionel, as he bowed her out of the office. "Mr. Evans would, I am sure, be greatly annoyed if he found it otherwise. I am only acting as his representative."

Notwithstanding the stranger's gray hair and modest attire, there was an amount of tittering in the office when it was discovered to what point Master Levitt had been desired to navigate her, and, for all her boasted strength of mind, Leona was not sorry when the young gentleman had finished giving directions to the cabman, and, taking his seat by her side, was driven away with her. She looked at his laughing face and wicked eye more than once before she ventured to ask him if he knew Mrs. Hodgett.

"Know old Mother Hodgett! Rather think I did. So will you by to-morrow."

"Why, is she such a formidable old lady then, Master Levitt?"

"You wait till you see her. My eye! I'd sooner 'twas you going to stay with her than me."

"Perhaps she doesn't like young gentlemen so well as I do."

She was careful not to call him a "boy," and check the growth of his budding confidence.

"Do you like 'em? Well, I think you look rather jolly, you know. But as for Hodgett, I never put my foot over her threshold if I can help it."

"If she makes herself as unpleasant to me," said Miss Gibson, "I shall look out for some lodgings."

"Why didn't you get lodgings at first? I would if I'd been you. I wouldn't stay with old Lionel if he'd give me a guinea a day."

"Are there many lodgings to let in Liverpool?"

"Heaps and heaps. My mother lets 'em right down on the docks."

"Does she? I wonder, if I have to stay here long, whether your mother would let me have a room with her?"

"I am sure she would if I asked her: and we've got the whole house empty now. There's only mother and me and uncle Bill lives there, and he's nobody."

"You shouldn't speak of your uncle in that way, young man, it isn't respectful."

"Oh, but he is nobody. He's silly, you know—soft—what do you call it? I knock him about just as if he were a baby."

"Poor fellow! I knew a lady of the name of Levitt years ago. I wonder if it was your mother? Do you mind telling me her name?"

"Mother's name is Mary Anne."

"Oh! This Miss Levitt's name was Rebecca."

"*Aunt Becky!* Oh! I've never seen her, she lives in Paris or

London or somewhere. Bill talks of her sometimes, but mother won't let him, because it makes him cry."

"I should very much like to call upon your mother, and talk to her about the lodgings. Do you think she would let me come?"

"Of course she would. Our address is No. 3, Dock Buildings. We often have sailors lodging with us. I wanted mother to let me go to sea, but she wouldn't."

"Are you her only child?"

"That's all, ma'am, and quite enough, as some people say. But here's Old Lionel's house. And when are you coming to see mother? Don't come in the day or I shan't be at home."

"I'll come this evening if it's fine. I have nothing to do in this place."

"All right then. I'll tell her, and then if you like the rooms you can take them, for you'll soon be sick of Mother Hodgett, I can tell you. Vinegar's nothing to her. Here, hie! Cabby, stop! First door on the right. That's it. Now, ma'am, here you are."

Master Levitt's graphic description of Mr. Lionel's housekeeper proved but too true. Vinegar was nothing to her. She answered the door in person. A prim, stiff, starched old woman, with a sour mouth and a fallen-in jaw, who appeared to regard all of her own sex who had not quite reached her standard of womanhood as natural enemies. Miss Gibson looked fully five-and-forty, but there is a long stretch between that and seventy, and Mrs. Hodgett, having snatched her master's note from Master Levitt's contaminating fingers, and perused it with a pursed-up mouth, turned looks of suspicion even on her middle-aged visitor.

"Well, of all the unreasonable things," she commenced, "to expect a body to turn out her rooms at a moment's notice, and for a person as she never set eyes on before! And what are *you* staying here for?" she continued, turning round upon the lad, who was gazing at her with his mouth wide open with delight; "you've done what you were told to, I suppose? Be off to your work, you lazy varlet, and don't stand gaping at me as if you'd never seen a respectable woman before."

"Never have! That's why I gape," replied Master Levitt, audaciously. "Haven't done what I was told to either! I've a message for you, old lady, from your master, and you'd better attend to it, or it'll be the worse for you."

"You hold your imperent tongue, and tell me what it is!"

"Why, that you're to make this lady as comfortable as you can, and she that she has everything she wants. Roast turkey, ice cream, green peas, asparagus, &c. &c. &c. Whether in season or out of season. Do you understand that?"

"He never said anything of the sort," grumbled the old housekeeper.

"Didn't he though? You'd better believe it, or he'll let you know the reason why. And the governor's going over to Manchester this afternoon, and won't be back till three in the morning, and you're to sit up for him and keep his supper hot."

"I sit up! I sit up till three in the morning! An old creature like me, with every bone aching with the rheumatics! I don't believe the master sent any such message. But how's one to know what to believe or disbelieve when he keeps a set of devil's imps like you to carry his orders backwards and forwards? Oh dear! oh dear!"

"Well, you can believe it or not as you choose," shouted the boy as he went down the street; "but don't say afterwards that I didn't tell you."

And with that Master Levitt disappeared. Mrs. Hodgett shut the hall-door with a groan and ushered her unwelcome guest into a sitting-room.

"You seem a quiet sort of a body," she said, as she scrutinised her appearance. "I suppose I needn't turn the house upside down for you?"

Leona's object was to conciliate the old housekeeper, so she immediately disclaimed the idea of such a thing.

"I should be very sorry if you took any trouble at all on my account, Mrs. Hodgett. I have a little business connected with the firm, and as I am only in Liverpool for a few days Mr. Lionel insisted upon my coming here. The plainest food in the world will do for me. And as I have a great many things to do in the town, I shall be out of doors most of my time."

"Oh! very well! you can please yourself about that, so long as you don't want me to go with you. For I've enough worry downstairs, with only one girl to do the cooking and housework, without running after visitors. If the master meant this to be a lodging-house he should have told me. And then to send up his orders by a worriting young varmint like that Levitt. It's enough to put any woman out. Do you want breakfast to be got for you now? It's past twelve o'clock."

"I should very much like a cup of tea," replied Leona, who had tasted nothing that morning.

"Just what I thought it would be," grumbled Hodgett, as she prepared to crawl downstairs; "worry, and trouble, and cooking, going on from morning till night. It's begun already, and it'll never leave off. Well! I don't call *this* waiting on a single gentleman, and so I shall tell him, and if he can't live without—"

The rest of her soliloquy was lost in the depths of the kitchen stairs. If Leona's mission had not been such a solemn one, she could have laughed heartily at the old woman's exhibition of temper. But the boy Levitt's information had startled her, and she was rather glad than otherwise to find that Mrs. Hodgett's dislike would remove all bar to her movements whilst she was Mr. Lionel's guest. For her food, she was blissfully indifferent as to what they might place before her. English cooking was distasteful to her palate after the highly-seasoned dishes of the Brazils. And if she could not eat what Mrs. Hodgett supplied, she had but to go out and get her meals elsewhere. What were meals to a woman who felt herself trembling on the brink of a discovery that should clear her father's name from shame!

Leona never anticipated that the search she was prosecuting might end in convincing the world of her father's guilt. Her faith was as strong as her love! She had no knowledge, but she had feeling! She *felt* that he was innocent, and it was this beautiful unswerving filial faith that led her on, without the least doubt of ultimate success, through circumstances of difficulty that would have caused a less brave spirit to turn back and throw up the game long before.

But Leona Lacoste was a woman who would *never* give in—until she died.

– CHAPTER 22 –

"UNCLE BILL"

It was about six o'clock on a fine summer's evening when Leona took her way towards No. 3, Dock Buildings, Liverpool. She had been feverishly anxious to commence her pilgrimage earlier, but two reasons had deterred her. One was the lad's request that she would wait until he was at home. She felt it would be better if he related the circumstances of his meeting with her, and the need that might arise for her requiring apartments, to his mother first. He seemed to have taken a fancy to her, and he was an only child, and probably exerted considerable influence at home. Then, too, she wanted time before she met these Levitts to think over the sentences in Abraham Anson's letter that alluded to their name, in case anything occurred by which she could gain fresh information concerning it. She had drawn forth the letter from its hiding-place—her bosom—and well pondered over those portions that mentioned the family that seemed in some mysterious way to have been mixed up with her dead father's fortunes.

"I'm sorry to say he's heard about that business with the Levitt's girl, and wanted me to give him particulars. I pretended to know nothing of the affair; but it appears old Levitt has been up to the house, so I'd get away for a short time, Master George, if I was you. I don't want to have to say anything, so I hope the chief won't put me on my oath, but I think the matter might be settled by money. Levitt's very close-fisted, and I shouldn't wonder if that's all he cares about. But if I try and bleed the chief again, it will bring the Levitt affair right about your ears."

This was all that related to the Levitt family, but Leona saw that the letter had been chiefly written with the view of cautioning her father on this particular subject. Of course she guessed that the "Levitt affair" was a love affair; but how far had it gone? and why should the clerk have been so alarmed lest it should reach the "chief's" ears? "Old Levitt," the father of the girl, to whom allusion was twice made, had probably been employed in the firm, which rendered any trifling with his daughter more likely to annoy the head of it, particularly when the trifler was his own nephew. Leona considered that even an ordinary flirtation, which was destined to end in nothing, might, under the circumstances, be spoken of in as serious a manner. But she could not understand how such a piece of *badinage* could be thought worthy of compensation by money. It must have been an injury that went deeper than a flirtation. And it was to procure this money to patch up his own folly that her father was supposed to have robbed his uncle's till, and murdered the man who was so anxious to befriend him!

Leona's lip curled even whilst her frame shuddered at the pitiful idea! Her mind was full of these thoughts as she asked her way to Dock Buildings, which were at some distance from Mr. Lionel's house and situated in a less fashionable quarter of the town. When she came to them she found a plain but cheerful row of small dwellings, close to the quay, where all manner of lading and unlading was going on. Dock Buildings were evidently frequented by the seafaring tribe. There was quite a marine appearance about the pink-lipped conch shells, and lumps of rough coral, that adorned the solitary plot of grass or flowers that stood before each doorway; and a card with the inscription—"Apartments for a single gentleman," was displayed in almost every window. No. 3 was amongst the brightest and most cheerful-looking of the lot. There was an evidence of care about the little place that betokened the industry of the inhabitants. The tiny front garden was filled with blossoming annuals, the steps were as white as snow, and the palings looked as if they had been painted yesterday.

Leona's knock was immediately answered by the lad Levitt himself. He had certainly taken an unusual fancy to his middle-aged acquaintance.

"Here's the lady, mother," he shouted, to some one in the back part of the house. "Do come in, Miss Gibson, and sit down. I say, how have you got on with Mrs. Hodgett? What did she give you for dinner? Old boots and garden snails? She's close enough to do it."

"Not quite so bad as that, Master Levitt," replied Leona, as she followed him into a tiny, neatly-furnished parlour. "Did you tell your mother I was coming to look at the rooms this evening?"

"Of course I did, and here is the old woman to corroborate the statement."

The "old woman," who was a comfortable, matronly person of about forty, now entered, with a broad smile on her face, and shook hands with Miss Gibson, whom she evidently considered on an equality with herself. Leona was glad to perceive this, and immediately proceeded to keep up the illusion, knowing that the more familiar she could become with her new acquaintances, the more she was likely to get out of them.

"I hope you expected me," she said, as they exchanged greetings. "Your son here was good enough to invite me to come over and have a look at your apartments this evening, as I may be in want of some myself before long."

"Oh yes. Harry told me all about it, ma'am," replied Mrs. Levitt, "and as soon as ever I heard that Mr. Lionel had sent you to stay with Mrs. Hodgett I said, 'Well, if she doesn't change her quarters as soon as ever she can, she'll be the first person that ever liked 'em.' So sit down; Miss Gibson, and make yourself comfortable. And now you'll have a cup of tea with us, fer I'm sure Mrs. Hodgett hasn't given you anything fit to drink since you've been in Liverpool, has she?"

"Well, it wasn't very strong, certainly," said Leona, laughing; and Mrs. Levitt remarked, as she bustled about to set the tea-service, that she expected it tasted more of the water than anything else.

They sat down to tea together; she, the mother, and the office lad, but Leona looked for the advent of "Uncle Bill" in vain.

"Well, your face is free enough from wrinkles," said Mrs. Levitt, after she had been examining her visitor closely. "I shouldn't say you had seen much of trouble in your day, ma'am."

"Indeed, you are mistaken, Mrs. Levitt, I may not show it, but I've had many a care. It's care alone that's brought me up to Liverpool."

"Indeed now, I never should have thought it! I hope you haven't got any money in the business. Not but what the house is as safe, as safe can be, but I hate speculations of all sorts. It was that brought my poor husband down to an untimely grave."

"You are a widow, then?"

"Bless you, yes! and been so ever since this lad here was four years old. Mr. Levitt was employed under Evans and Troubridge. That's why they took on Harry as soon as he was big enough."

"And I'm sure I wish they never had," interposed Harry, with his mouth full.

"Hold your tongue, you foolish boy," replied his mother. "It was the most natural thing for them to do. The Levitts have worked under them—and worked well, too—for four generations past."

"So I have always understood," said Miss Gibson. "I knew the family twenty years ago. My aunt brought up Miss Lucilla Anson, the daughter of the head-clerk—who was—you remember!"

"The daughter of *who*, ma'am?"

"Of Mr. Anson, who was murdered, you know. You recollect the murder that took place here about that time, surely?"

Here the mother glanced at her son, who rose from the table, and closed the parlour door carefully.

"I didn't know as Anson had a daughter," remarked Mrs. Levitt.

"It was before your time perhaps."

"It happened before my marriage with Mr. Levitt, though, of course, I've often heard him speak of it. It was a sad thing altogether."

"Very sad, and particularly as Mr. George Evans had a hand in it."

"How, ma'am, did you know Mr. George?"

"Yes, well."

"And you believe he murdered poor Anson? Don't they believe so in Liverpool?"

"Such as remember it I suppose do, but he never came back to tell the truth for himself, and the story's mostly forgotten now. Though they do say that's the only reason Mr. Henry Evans—Mr. George's younger brother, you know, ma'am—has left Liverpool to live in London. The whole family is up there now."

"And is Miss Anson living with them? My aunt is very anxious to find out her present address."

"You quite surprise me, ma'am, with your mention of Miss Anson, for I never heard tell of her before. Mr. Evans has one daughter, I believe, but as for the other, it's quite news to me."

"Well, I can assure you it's true, Mrs. Levitt, and I daresay there are several other things that I could tell you about the Evans that would surprise you to hear. Those great people have so many means of keeping their secrets close."

"Ah, you may well say that, ma'am! but my James, he never was a man for telling about others. Often and often he aggravated me to that degree with his secrecy I could hardly abide him; and his father, old Mr. Levitt, was for all the world as bad. Not a word could you ever get out of either of them."

"Is old Mr. Levitt still alive?"

"Dear me, no! He died twenty years ago. He never was himself after the murder. He quite shut himself up from society and wasted away. But then he had his own reasons for fretting, poor old gentleman."

"Ah! you mean about his daughter?" said Leona, making a shot at the truth.

"Lor! ma'am, you seem to know everything about everybody."

"But I know Rebecca Levitt personally. She came down to my aunt's house with Miss Anson."

"With Miss Anson! Well, I never! Now, did she?" exclaimed Mrs. Levitt, in three volleys of surprise.

"So, of course, I heard all about that little affair with Mr. George."

"Did you know they were married then?" exclaimed Mrs. Levitt. At this question Leona's presence of mind forsook her. She felt her colour fade, her face change, her limbs tremble.

"Married! No. Good heavens! they were never *married*," she cried.

"Well, as I used to tell my James, it seemed unlikely, for the girl had no lines to show. But you see, before Mr. George disappeared, there had been a great noise about him and Rebecca, and old Mr. Levitt was quite mad about it, and determined to make him do her justice; but, when the murder took place and he was gone, of course there was an end to it, and he wouldn't have seen them man and wife if he could. But it was then—so I hear, ma'am, for I wasn't in Liverpool at the time—that Rebecca stood out for it that she had been married to Mr. George, and that he had the lines with him. And I believe she sticks up for the truth of it to this day."

Her Father's Name

"But where is Rebecca now?" stammered Leona. She hated herself for her want of self-control, but if this were true—*what was she!*

"Ah! that's more than I can tell you. She left Liverpool before I came to it. My husband did hear once as she was married to a jeweller of the name of——. Now, what was that jeweller's name, Harry? I know it was not English, but I can't for the life of me lay my tongue to it."

"Perhaps your uncle might be able to remember it. Didn't you tell me you had an uncle living with you?" said Leona, appealing to the boy.

"Uncle Bill! Not he. He cannot remember his own name, can he, mother?"

"Oh no. He's been quite a poor natural ever since he came back from America," replied Mrs. Levitt.

"America! Has he been to America?" demanded Leona, hastily.

"Yes, ma'am. He ran away to sea, poor foolish fellow, the very night that Mr. George Evans took himself off. There was quite a commotion about the two disappearing together. Some thought as Mr. George had arranged it on purpose so as to throw the suspicion on poor Bill, but everyone knew as he was more than half a fool, poor fellow, and his father was here to stick up for him, so it passed over. But years after, when old Mr. Levitt was dead and gone, this poor silly was brought back to my husband with scarcely a rag to his back by a stranger who had taken pity on his condition, and we've never been able rightly to make out what happened to him meanwhile. He's lived with us ever since, for I couldn't turn him out when James died, and I suppose he'll bide on now till the end. There's only one subject that excites him, and that's the mention of his sister Becky, and so I never let him hear her name. And that's why I wouldn't bring him into the parlour this evening, because Harry told me you wanted news of her."

"I hope you will let me see him before I go, though," said Leona, "for I take a deep interest in all the family."

"*Antoine* was the name of Aunt Becky's jeweller, mother," interrupted the boy, as the remembrance flashed on him.

"To be sure it was. And I suppose she's Mrs. *Antoine*. A curious name to go by in a Christian country."

"But if she was married to Mr. George Evans, how can she be married to *M. Antoine?*" said Leona.

"Well, ma'am, the less said about that, I suppose, the better. She couldn't be married to both of them, could she now? For Mr. George may be alive and well at this moment, for aught we know. But all families, great and small, have their secrets, and I daresay poor Becky, married or not married, ain't worse than half the ladies in the land."

"I should very much like to see Rebecca again," mused Leona. "I suppose you never heard what part of London she settled in?"

"No, ma'am, no; and I don't even remember if it was London or Paris. My James never seemed to covet any communication with her after the business of the murder; indeed, he didn't like the mention of her name. But 'tis a long time ago now, and my motto is, 'Let bygones be bygones.'"

"With regard to the murder of Mr. Anson—was no suspicion ever cast on any one else?"

"I believe not, ma'am. I never heard of it, I think everyone was quite convinced it was Mr. George, and his running away looked like it, didn't it now? If he had only stayed to answer questions. But he was clean gone the very next morning—as clean gone as that poor fool Bill, who did turn up again as you may see. And the till being robbed, too. It was a shameful business, I don't think anybody ever had a doubt in the matter, even to poor Rebecca, for she never held up her head after it came to light, and the only time my husband saw her afterwards, he said he shouldn't have known her in the street, she was so changed."

"I wander what made Mr. Henry Evans adopt Anson's child. It was hardly necessary," said Leona, thoughtfully.

"Ah, there you puzzle me, ma'am, for, as I've told you, your mention of it is the first I ever heard of Anson having a child. I know he was a widower, but from first to last I never heard speak of a family. And Becky took her down to your aunt's, too?"

"That she certainly did, and cried very much when she parted with her."

"Well, that beats everything; but it's a mystery to me. Will you come and look at the bedroom now, ma'am, if you've finished your tea? It's always ready to be seen, I'm proud to say."

Her Father's Name

Leona rose, and followed Mrs. Levitt up the narrow staircase to a nice clean little bedroom, looking over the busy quay.

"You wouldn't mind the noise and the bustle here after a bit," remarked her would-be landlady, "and the masts of the shipping seem quite like company to me. Have you ever been on the sea, ma'am?"

"Yes."

"Ah! Well, I haven't, and I don't wish to, either; but I like to live near the traffic. We have all the big steamers from America unloading here. There was one came in only this morning. Such a lot of passengers as they bring. The hotels won't hold them sometimes."

Leona admired the room, and appreciated its proximity to the quay to Mrs. Levitt's entire satisfaction, but was unable to say when she would take possession of it, or whether she would require it at all.

"For I am waiting for an answer to a letter that Mr. Lionel has sent to Mr. Evans on my account, and when it arrives I may have to go on at once to London."

"It's all the same to me, ma'am. My rooms are never empty long, and I'm very glad to have had the opportunity of making your acquaintance, particularly as you've been so nearly connected with the family. Here's poor Bill, if you'd like to have a peep at him," added Mrs. Levitt, as she opened the door of a side-room.

It looked out upon a strip of garden at the back, and the sprays of a climbing clematis were intruding through the open window. Seated with his back towards them, and unoccupied, save by twisting the scented blossoms in his fingers, sat a man of not more, perhaps, than fifty years of age, although his hair and beard were grey. He was such a fine, broad-chested fellow, and looked so strong and hearty, that Leona could hardly believe she saw the poor natural she had been told of, until her companion went up to him and laid her hand upon his shoulder.

"Now, Bill," she said, as though she were speaking to a little child, "where are your manners? Here's a lady come to see you. Can't you make her a nice bow, and say 'Good evening?'"

But Uncle Bill, taking no notice of the appeal, kept his eyes steadily fixed upon the spray of clematis he was destroying.

There now, see what mischief you are up to, breaking off the flowers in that lavish way. Leave them alone, do," said Mrs. Levitt, slapping his hands, "and stand up like a man and make your duty to the lady."

At this renewed adjuration, Uncle Bill consented to turn his head and look at the stranger, but the minute his eyes fell upon her face, he gave a sharp cry, and trembling hid his face in his hands.

"Lor! now! what's took the fellow?" exclaimed his sister-in-law, as she attempted to shake him into reason. "He's just like this, ma'am, night and day. You never know where to have him, nor what he'll do next. Here, Bill, hold up, I say, or I'll send you straight off to bed this very minute! there!"

"I didn't do it," said the man, in a strangely-terrified tone of voice. "They said I did it; but some one held my hand, and it was all in the dark—in the dark—in the dark! *Why was it in the dark?*" he interrupted himself suddenly to demand of Mrs. Levitt.

"Bless you! how should I know? Because it wasn't in the light, I suppose. There, hold your tongue, do, and don't talk any more rubbish."

"*He* didn't do it," said Bill, pointing at Leona with his finger.

"He takes you for a man now," cried Mrs. Levitt. "Was there ever such a natural?"

"If you slept, you couldn't feel," continued Bill, as he turned his mournful eyes upon Leona.

"No, Bill, I couldn't," she replied, anxious to draw him into conversation.

"But three days is too long to sleep; and yet you did not die. And you believed it, you believed it!"

"Yes, I believed it," said Leona.

"Why have you come back here? Do you mean to tell of father?"

"Why, if he isn't off on his father now, and I don't know that I ever heard him mention him before! He's as good as a play, poor Bill is; you never know what tricks he won't be up to next."

"Mother, you're wanted!" shouted Harry from belowstairs.

"Who is it, my dear?"

"It's Captain Gray; and he can't wait."

"Lor! Miss Gibson, do you mind my running down for a

minute? You can stay in the next room if you prefer it to this."

"I would rather stay here," replied Leona. She was longing to be left alone with Bill.

"*Where is your father?*" she asked him, as soon as Mrs. Levitt had disappeared.

The fool looked round mysteriously before he answered.

"I mustn't tell, or he will beat me. I mustn't tell anything—how it happened, or why I went away. Hush! they are coming."

"But you went away with Mr. George, didn't you?"

"Why, *you* are Mr. George," replied the idiot, with a look of cunning delight at his supposed discovery. "Why do you try to hide yourself under this?" pulling at her skirts.

Leona started. The poor fool had seen a likeness to her father, even under her disguise. But he mustn't be allowed to bruit about his knowledge. She must turn the current of his ideas.

"Nonsense!" she said sharply. "I am a woman. I used to know your sister Rebecca."

At that name Bill burst out crying. "Oh, poor Becky!" he moaned, rocking himself backwards and forwards; "poor, poor Becky! Hush-a-by, baby; hush-baby. He'll never own it, Becky. It's no use. He daren't do it. *Father shall make him do it?* Ah, yes! if father can—if father can! Poor Becky, poor Becky!"

And then, suddenly changing his tone to one of entreaty, he continued:

"It wasn't me, Becky. Don't look at me with them eyes, or you'll kill me. What if it had been *him?* What then? What then? Oh, poor Becky! Poor, poor Becky!"

"Now, if he hasn't set off on Becky!" exclaimed Mrs. Levitt, in a tone of vexation, as she bustled into the room again. "You'd better come downstairs, ma'am, for he'll never leave off till we've shut him up for the night." And thereupon she insisted upon conducting Leona back to the little parlour where they had had their tea.

But during the remainder of the time that she stayed there she could still distinguish the tones of the poor fool upstairs moaning over the same burden

"*What if it had been him? What then? What then? Oh, poor Becky! Poor, poor Becky!*"

– CHAPTER 23 –

A VOICE FROM THE PAST

It is marvellous to what an extent human nature can control itself when under the fear of discovery, or the necessity for caution. To all outward appearance Leona was interested in the garrulous gossip of Mrs. Levitt until the last farewell had been exchanged between them; but as she left the little house, and refusing all Master Harry's offers of escort, commenced to wend her way back to Mr. Lionel's, she fairly staggered beneath the remembrance of the dreadful doubt that had been communicated to her.

Her father married to Rebecca Levitt! It was impossible. He could not have so disgraced himself. He could not have done her so irreparable a wrong! Yet, even whilst she pondered, there flew into Leona's mind so many instances in which men had, just as weakly and inconsiderately, done their children an irreparable wrong, that she shuddered and ceased railing. Suppose her dead father *had* committed the youthful folly of which he was suspected! What was the upshot? Rightfully or wrongfully, he found himself banished to a foreign country, separated from all his friends, alone, without love, or sympathy, or comfort! What more natural, if under such circumstances, he had found himself unable to resist the temptation to accept the affection of a young and attractive woman, and make her the sharer of his sorrows and joys? Her father had seldom mentioned the name of her mother to her. The packet of letters she possessed told her nothing. They might have been written from a wife to her husband, or a mistress to her lover. They breathed but expressions of the most tender and confiding affection. Her father's love for herself had been very devoted. Had he made it so, to try, in some measure, to repair the awful wrong he had done her? As poor Leona thought on these things, and tried to throw her mind back into the past, and disinter some word, or look, or action, that should throw light upon the mystery that puzzled it, she felt her brain reel with the momentousness of the question. *She*—who had so prided herself upon her European blood and ancestry; she—who had believed her father to be one of the most honourable and upright gentlemen the world had ever produced; she—to be compelled to know herself to be nothing, worse than nothing—a nameless, parentless, base-born outcast!—the child of a murderer! For here Leona began, for the first time, to falter in her perfect faith in her father's innocence! If he were capable of the one crime he might have been capable of the other! And the idea of a disreputable marriage, to be denied or concealed, seemed to imply a more tangible reason for the terrible events that followed it, than the mere fears of discovery of a few youthful follies or extravagances. Blinded by the tears that overflowed her eyes as Fancy conjured up one fearful image after another to her mind, and too much absorbed in her own miserable imaginings to take much heed of the way she was going, Leona roused herself after a while to the knowledge that she had lost her road. Liverpool is a large and bewildering place to a stranger, and though she had certainly started in the direction of Mr. Lionel's house, she had as certainly permitted her feet to miss some turning or other that should have conducted her towards it. She was first made aware of the fact by a porter running up against her with a large bale upon his shoulder, and as she stepped out of his way she fell against a truck that was being wheeled in the opposite direction. It was now nine o'clock at night, and as dark as it ever becomes at that time of the year. Leona started from her absorbing reverie to find that she had left the narrow way of the streets and gained the docks. Before her rose the tall masts of the shipping, dimly defined against the darkening sky, whilst all around lay bales of cotton, and silk, and fibre, and casks of sugar, and rice, and molasses, and piles of iron, and wood, and all the other species of merchandise that make England the golden land that it is—waiting their removal on board ship, or their consignment to their relative owners on shore. The hour was too late for much traffic to be going on. The numerous public-houses that surrounded the wharves had claimed most of the workers of the day, as the shouting, and swearing, and singing that proceeded from them proclaimed. But here and there some one might be seen working after hours. Some few porters were still conveying goods or luggage to their destination, and one or two groups of better-dressed people, passengers apparently by some of the numerous steamers lying in dock, were standing about the quay, either inquiring for their luggage or giving directions concerning it.

As Leona came upon this scene, she felt quite dazed and giddy. Her heart and her head were beating tumultuously, and at first she hardly realised where she was. But when she did so, she stopped for a moment to recover herself. The moon had risen above the tall black masts in the river, and was shining down upon her with a calm and tranquilising light. The night air blew refreshingly across the water, and seemed to clear her feverish and giddy brain. She felt grateful for the support which nature's elements afforded her, and drawing into the shadow, sat down upon an unused truck to rest herself. Whilst she was in this position some gentlemen passed her, followed by a porter. They were talking together, and in a moment she recognised the accents of her beloved Spanish tongue, and became all interest and attention.

"You will scarcely get your luggage at this time of night," said the first speaker. "You had better make up your mind at once to do without it till to-morrow morning."

"But I cannot do without it," replied the second. "It is a small portmanteau, but it contains the actual necessaries of the toilet. They promised to forward it to-day. It is most provoking."

"Which steamer, sir?" demanded the porter.

But Leona did not wait to hear which steamer. At the sound of that second voice she had nearly started to her feet, and only by a strong effort of will controlled herself from calling out his name aloud.

For it was the voice of Christobal Valera.

They had passed so quickly that she had not had an opportunity of distinguishing his features, but she could not be mistaken in his voice.

It was Christobal. Her brother, her friend—her one beloved companion—in England, close to her, almost within her arms. As the truth struck her, she had nearly run after and claimed him. But then she remembered her disguise, and her reasons for assuming it and all the consequences that must ensue from discovering her identity, and shrunk back again, feeling the necessity for concealment press harder on her than it had ever done before. But still she might see him, he would not recognise her. She might look on his face and judge of his well-doing by his looks—her poor

Tobal! whom she had left so ill and languid—from whom she had existed so long without a line to say if he had lived or died!

As Leona decided thus, she started after the gentlemen, and came up with them just as they had reached the edge of the quay, and were looking somewhat despondently after their messenger, making his way towards the plank bridge that connected the wharf with the New York steamer, which displayed but a single light to show that anyone was awake on board of her.

"I very much fear they will refuse to let you take away any of your possessions so late as this," repeated the speaker who had spoken first before.

"What a croaker you are, Guzman," replied Valera. "The baggage was to be all had up from the hold this morning. I must have it. There's no question about the matter. I leave for London the first thing tomorrow."

She crept nearer to them as they spoke, and tried to look as though she too were waiting for news from the steamer. She could see him plainly now. His large, dark eyes, his delicate features, and silky moustache. She could even distinguish on the little finger of his left hand the gold ring she had given him when they were children, and which she had often laughed at him since for continuing to wear.

The moonlight glanced on the trinket, and made it glitter; and something in Leona's eyes made the glittering circle dance. She was too much occupied with the one thought that Christobal was standing before her even to feel surprised at recognising in his companion, the identical Don Guzman with whom she had fought the duel on her journey from Rio to New York. All her thoughts were absorbed in the knowledge that the greatest friend she possessed was close to her.

Presently, as Christobal gazed over the water, she heard him sigh.

"*Presto!* What ails you now?" exclaimed Don Guzman. "Dreaming of the blue eyes of the fair Lilias, eh, Valera?"

At these words Leona's hearing quickened.

"Perhaps," said Valera, vaguely, as he sighed again.

"What, another!" cried Guzman. "I didn't think you were quite so far gone as that. But, in truth, Don, you have not been in good spirits lately."

"I do not know that my spirits were boisterously happy at any time, Guzman. I have many troubles of which I say nothing, and the fact of finding myself in a strange country, away from all my old associations, brings them more vividly to my mind."

"New scenes will help to disperse them, Valera."

"I trust so. But I came to England with a secret hope which seems to have faded with the first view of her shores."

"Well, the view from these docks is not soul-inspiring. A good night's rest will make you see things in a better light. Here comes the porter with your valise. He has got it, after all. I congratulate you. And now let us retrace our steps to the hotel. You go to London the first thing to-morrow morning, do you not?"

"The first thing to-morrow morning," repeated Christobal, indifferently, as they turned away.

Leona watched their retreating figures until they were lost in the surrounding darkness; then, groping her way towards a pile of goods, she sat down upon the nearest bale, and burst into a flood of tears.

It was late before she reached Mr. Lionel's house, and Mrs. Hodgett professed to be quite scandalised. "*She* had never heard of such a thing before, not she; as ladies tramping out on the street half the night, which she'd always been told it wasn't considered respectable for folk to do; and she hoped that Mr. Lionel might take notice of it, that she did."

Leona pushed past the grumbling old creature, with scarcely a "Good-night," and found her way up to her own bedroom. She was in no condition either to argue the point or to excuse herself. All she wished was to be left alone, to think over what was to be done next. A few hours back, had her plans been demanded of her, she would have expressed her determination to remain in Liverpool until she had found out all that was to be discovered with respect to her father's secret connection with the Levitts. But now—since she had encountered Christobal upon the wharf, and heard his destination, she was all eagerness to follow him to London. She felt as though she must breathe the same air as he did. The sight of him had acted on her like the taste of blood upon the tiger. She thirsted to see him again.

So she began to hope that Mr. Lionel's appeal on her behalf to Mr. Evans might be responded to by some desire to speak to her in person, and to think that if it were not so she must go to town on her own speculation. But she was not disappointed. At an early hour the next morning the surly old housekeeper, informed her that her master wished to see her before he went to the office, and on her entering the dining-room she found him ready charged with directions concerning her.

"Good morning, Miss Gibson. Pray be seated. I trust Mrs. Hodgett has made you as comfortable as the poor resources of a bachelor's establishment will permit. Mr. Evans has lost no time in replying to my communication respecting you, Miss Gibson. I received his answer this morning."

"Oh, ho!" thought Leona to herself, "so you considered my claim of sufficient importance, then, to demand a telegram, for by no other means could Mr. Evans have heard of it in time to write by the afternoon post."

But all she said aloud and demurely was, "Indeed, sir!"

"Yes. I told you he would be the last person to deny such a plea as you bring forward in support of your claim to his patronage. My partner is a kind-hearted man, as well as a good and generous one. He perfectly remembers and acknowledges the care which your good aunt bestowed upon Miss Lucy Evans (you will please to note in speaking of that young lady, Miss Gibson, that Mr. Evans much objects to hear her mentioned by any name but his own), and would wish to requite it, if possible, by being of use to you. You told me, I believe, that your object was to obtain some place as housekeeper or nurse?"

"Any place of trust, sir. I have not been used to menial offices."

"Of course, of course; naturally. Mr. Evans hopes he may be able to help you to some such situation, but he would wish to see and speak to you first. He desires me in this letter," continued Mr. Lionel, carelessly twisting about the sheet of notepaper he held in his hand, "to ask if you will go to London and see him on the subject."

"It is a long way to go for an uncertainty," remarked Leona, thinking it wiser to make a few preliminary objections.

"It is a long way," acquiesced Mr. Lionel. "My partner is quite aware of that fact, and that you may not be prepared to run about the country on a mere speculation. But—will you excuse me for a moment, Miss Gibson," he continued, interrupting himself suddenly, and preparing to leave the room.

"Certainly," replied Leona, remarking with secret satisfaction that he had already in an abstracted manner laid his partner's letter on the mantle-shelf.

As the door closed behind him, she sprung from her seat and seized the paper. It contained but a few words:

"DEAR LIONEL,—

"You have acted perfectly right. Send the woman on to London at any cost. Pay all her expenses, bribe her if necessary, or bring her yourself; but make her come straight from your house to our office. I think I have a plan for keeping her under my own eye.

"—Yours in haste, HENRY EVANS."

She had scarcely replaced the letter in its former position when Mr. Lionel re-entered the room with some bank-notes in his hand.

"My partner being unwilling you should be hampered by any unforeseen expense in travelling, Miss Gibson, has begged me to give you these from him, and to request you will use them to defray the cost of your journey to London."

As he spoke he tried to place two five-pound notes in her hand. But she drew backward.

"I am much obliged to Mr. Evans for his offer, sir, but I am in no immediate want of money."

"But come, Miss Gibson, you will not refuse to take them, I am sure. Money is always acceptable, whether we have our pockets full or not."

"I must refuse, Mr. Lionel. I told you yesterday I had no design to beg from Mr. Evans."

"Well! I suppose you must have your own way, but my partner will be annoyed to hear of it. When do you intend to go to London? There is no hurry, you know. My poor rooms are at your service for as long as you choose to use them."

"You are very good, sir, but I think the sooner I see Mr. Evans the better. Should my application to him prove unsuccessful, I must go on to my friends in Scotland. You have not yet given me the address in London where I am to call."

"Ah! to be sure; well, here it is—Messrs. Evans and Troubridge, 320, High Holborn. You will not forget it."

"I will write it down," she answered, "and I shall start to-day."

"So soon?" said Mr. Lionel.

"Yes, sir. I have no time to spare."

"Why, I have just seen a young gentleman who had come over from America on business with the firm off by the train. You might have travelled together, if I had known it, and Don Valera could have taken care of you on the journey."

"What name did you say, sir?"

"Don Christobal Valera. By the way, a most curious thing happened the other day to our London firm. But I will not detain you, Miss Gibson. The story might possibly possess no interest for you, and, if it does, you will hear all about it when you get up to town, for they can talk of nothing else in the house at present. If you are quite determined to leave us to-day, there is an excellent train at eleven and another at twelve. You will not, in any case, be in time to see Mr. Evans, but he will, doubtless, give you an interview the first thing tomorrow morning."

"I thank you, sir. I shall present myself at the office in Holborn as soon after ten o'clock to-morrow morning as possible. I am extremely obliged to you for all the civility and kindness you have shown me, Mr. Lionel. It may prove the turning-point in my career."

"I trust it may lead to a comfortable berth, somewhere," replied Mr. Lionel, as he bowed her to the door. "A snug housekeeper's place to some rich old bachelor; eh, Miss Gibson? How would that suit now? or head nurse in a duchess's family?"

"I would rather have the first, sir," replied the supposed Miss Gibson, gaily; and Mr. Lionel chuckled, and said she was a sly puss, and he wouldn't trust her to remain Miss Gibson long if she once got some unfortunate bachelor under the domination of her eyes.

Two hours after she was travelling back to London, and Mr. Evans had received a telegram to that effect.

* * * * * *

The following morning he sat in his office, expecting her promised visit with anything but pleasurable anticipations. For so many years past the subject of his unfortunate brother's crime and self-banishment had been so completely tabooed that he had almost come to believe that the world had forgotten it, and he would never hear it mentioned again. And to have it crop up through a stranger, and one who visited Liverpool, and for aught he knew might be induced to take up her residence there, was very annoying. His whole aim had been to hush the matter up, so that the interests of the firm might not be damaged by the memory of so ugly a story; and now to be told that this woman, who had been intimately acquainted with members of his family at the very time of the occurrence, had appeared with the whole story fresh in her memory, and ready to be retailed on the slightest occasion, provoked him beyond measure. From the moment of receiving Mr. Lionel's telegram he had resolved on one thing. Miss Gibson must either be bought *up*, or bought *out*. She must either be bound down by gratitude to hold her tongue, or she might be bribed to adopt an exile, where it might wag without detriment to his family or himself. But before he decided on which course of action to pursue, he must see what sort of woman he had to deal with. He had never met the aunt, but he had heard excellent accounts of her. If the niece were like her, she might be a person of delicacy, with feelings to be appealed to, and a sense of honour which would make her shrink with horror from the idea of betraying the trust of the family who befriended her. With such ideas coursing through his brain, Mr. Evans waited the advent of Miss Jane Gibson with feverish anxiety. As she entered his private office he almost trembled. But there was nothing in her appearance to alarm him. On the contrary, when he looked up and encountered the smooth, placid face, and bands of grey hair, surrounded by the plain net cap and quaker-like bonnet, that this middle-aged person presented to him, he felt reassured. Leona had taken the extra precaution during this interview of shielding her glorious eyes with a pair of spectacles, and though Mr. Evans slightly started as she first met his view, her further appearance aroused no remembrance in him of the gay *débonnair* boy who had so mysteriously disappeared from his family circle.

"Miss Gibson, I believe," he commenced, nervously. "Pray be

seated, madam. My partner, Mr. Lionel, informs me that you consider, in consequence of certain services rendered in past times to my daughter, that—"

Now, Leona had fully weighed the worth of the stress Mr. Evans, in his letter to Mr. Lionel, had laid on the necessity of her being sent up to London "at any cost," and determined to find out of how much consequence her knowledge was to him. So she interrupted him here without ceremony.

"I beg your pardon, sir. You are alluding, I suppose, to *Mr. Anson's* daughter?"

Mr. Evans frowned.

"Whatever name that young lady maybe entitled to by rights, she has been known now for many years to the world *only* as my adopted daughter, Miss Gibson—"

"Very good, sir. So I have heard; but I thought that between you and me—"

"*Between you and me*, Miss Gibson! What do you wish me to understand by using that expression—*between you and me*?"

"That there is not the same necessity for caution, Mr. Evans, as there would be were you speaking to a stranger. *I know all!*"

"All—all? What do you mean by all?" he repeated, with a sickly smile, although the hand with which he played with his ivory paper-cutter shook as he awaited her reply.

Leona drew her chair closer to his.

"All about the murder of Abraham Anson, sir," she said in a low voice, "and the part that was taken in it and *by whom—and the reason why you wish Miss Lucilla Anson to be known by the name of Evans.*"

– CHAPTER 24 –

"DIAMOND CUT DIAMOND"

As Leona uttered these words, Mr. Evans rose hurriedly from his chair, and turning the handle of the door, glanced into the passage beyond, to satisfy himself there were no listeners to their conversation. And as he reseated himself she saw that even in that short time his face had grown whiter and more troubled, and felt she was on the right track.

"You speak very strangely, Miss Gibson," he said, as he passed his handkerchief across his brow, "and too openly to be agreeable. If, as you affirm, you know, or have heard, all the details of that unfortunate business, your good sense and natural delicacy of feeling must surely point out to you the propriety of not making the subject a common one."

"Certainly, sir; and hitherto my lips have been closed to all. But considering the time at which, and the circumstances under which Miss Lucilla Anson—"

"I must beg of you, madam, to call that young lady by her accustomed name," interrupted Mr. Evans, almost fiercely.

"I beg your pardon—Miss Lucilla Evans. Considering the time and the circumstances, as I was saying before, sir, it is scarcely likely that I should not be acquainted with the whole story of her birth, particularly as I know Rebecca Levitt."

At that name Mr. Evans started up as if he had been shot.

"*Rebecca Levitt!*" he exclaimed. "Why, she's dead years and years ago!"

"Not at all, sir," replied Leona, coolly. "On the contrary, she is living and married, or supposed to be so."

"Whom did she marry? Where does she live?"

"I am not quite sure if I should be justified in telling you that, without her consent, sir. Rebecca has kept out of your way for a long time, and doubtless had her own reasons for doing so."

"Miss Gibson, tell me the truth," said Mr. Evans, solemnly, as he wheeled round and confronted her. "Is this a plot on the part of Rebecca Levitt and yourself to obtain possession of any property of hers that she may imagine to be in my hands?"

This most unexpected question opened up such a new field of conjecture that Leona was for a moment bewildered, and hardly knew what to answer. But one thing was certain. This idea of Rebecca Levitt being close at hand, and producible at any moment, was an alarming one to Mr. Evans. And she must not let him know that his fear was unfounded.

"*A plot*, sir," she replied. "I am surprised that you should think fit to use such a term to me. How or for what reasons should I be concerned in a plot against you? My aunt, Mrs. Gibson, had the charge of Miss Lucilla for several years, and did her duty by her. She is now too old and feeble to work any more; in fact she has become childish, and is under the charge of an attendant. Under these circumstances I feel myself obliged to earn my own living and support her. What is more natural than that I should apply to you for assistance—to you, who are the most wealthy of all her former employers? But that you should consider me capable of—"

And at this juncture Miss Gibson's feelings getting the better of her fortitude, her voice broke down, and her handkerchief went up to her eyes.

"Indeed, my dear madam, you are quite mistaken. I had no intention of wounding you in this manner, but I must confess that the name and remembrance of Rebecca Levitt are alike distasteful to me. I am quite ready to acknowledge how much I am indebted to your good aunt for the care she took of my adopted daughter during her childhood, and to return her kindness in any way in which I am capable, to yourself. Will you tell me openly what are your circumstances, and how I can afford you assistance?"

"My circumstances, sir, are such that I am on the look-out for any situation in which I can earn my own living."

"I suppose you want some very superior situation, though, such as superintendent of a gentleman's family, or companion to a lady? You would not undertake any lower office, eh?"

"I would undertake anything, sir, by which I can get my livelihood," said Leona, thinking only of the best answer by which to keep up the character she had assumed.

"If that is the case, I may be able to help you. Were you attached to the person of Miss Lucilla Evans when a child?"

"I was always fond of children," she replied, evasively.

"Should you know her again, do you think, were you to see her?"

"Yes, sir, I am sure of that."

"Then, would you like to undertake the charge of her, that is of her apartments, wardrobe, &c.? My daughter is an invalid, Miss Gibson; and lately, I am sorry to say, she has been more delicate than usual. Our old nurse and housekeeper, Mrs. Raymond, has been her attendant hitherto, but she has been laid up with gout for some days past, and will never, perhaps, be able to resume her duties about Miss Lucy. At any rate the companionship of a superior person like yourself would always be a comfort to her, and relieve Mrs. Evans of a large share of trouble. Now, do you fancy that is the sort of position you would like to fill?"

As Mr. Evans' intention broke on her mind, Leona's heart throbbed with joy. She had never dreamt of such good luck as this: to be taken back into the very house she had been obliged to fly from, and in a position where there would be less probability, perhaps, than in any other, of the discovery of her identity. To be able to prosecute her search in the quarter where she would be most likely to obtain information—the kitchen floor—and at the same time to be intimate with the upper storeys, and close to him whom she had no doubt was already installed in the place she had left vacant in the household. She could hardly believe in her good fortune. Her eyes, sparkled with the delight of success, and her pleasure was apparent.

"Indeed, sir," commenced she, "there is *nothing* I should like better."

"I am glad to hear you say so, Miss Gibson. Mrs. Evans and I have been talking for some time past of the necessity of getting some one for the purpose I have named, and I see no reason why you should not fulfil our requirements. Your name is sufficient guarantee for your character. With respect to your duties, my wife can better inform you than myself; but your salary will be liberal—eighty pounds a year."

Again Leona was pleasantly taken by surprise. Why this unusual salary for a head servant, unless some sinister motive lay beneath the generosity?

"You are, indeed, very good, sir," she replied, "and if I can do all that Miss Evans will require of me, I shall be but too happy to accept the situation."

"Very well, then; consequent on Mrs. Evans' approval (of which I have no doubt), we will consider that matter settled. But I have a little bargain to make with you concerning it, Miss Gibson."

"What is that, sir?"

"That the subject on which you have spoken to me to-day—the story of—of—Mr. Anson's unfortunate death, shall never be mentioned in my house. It is needless to tell you that Miss Lucy *knows nothing of her parents*. She believes herself to be my child, and not a hint must be breathed in her presence to upset that conviction. If, as you say, *you know all*, you must be aware of the urgent necessity there is for *concealing the name of her father from her*."

"Of course I am aware of it, sir."

"It would be putting her to useless shame, to torture, to misery, to let her know it!" continued Mr. Evans, covering his face with his hands.

"I quite agree with you," replied Leona.

He looked up, half frightened of this woman, who professed to know everything, and took it all so calmly. Intuitively he felt that she was not deceiving him in saying so—that his family secrets *were* in her possession, and that it behoved him to conciliate her as much as possible.

"I am glad of that. I felt, as soon as I saw you, Miss Gibson, that you would not only perceive the necessity for caution, but preserve it out of the goodness of your heart. We will make this bargain with each other, then; that my house shall be your home under the circumstances we have already alluded to, and that in return you will preserve an inviolable secrecy with regard to the past. It is all done and finished with, Miss Gibson, and can never be undone. It is far better to bury it in silence."

"You are doubtless right, sir," she said evasively.

"My next condition is, Miss Gibson, that the person we mentioned—if, as you say, still living—does not come to my house without my knowledge."

"That I can safely promise you, so far as it is in my power to prevent it."

"Perhaps it is wrong of me to say I am sorry to hear that Rebecca Levitt is still alive, Miss Gibson; but I heard, and I hoped, that she had died many years ago. For all our sakes—and especially for Lucilia's—you must see it would be better we should never meet again. She has been silent, and apparently willing to forego all her claims upon us so long, that I concluded death had ended her troubles. But since it is not the case, it would be extremely impolitic of her to rake up old matters anew."

"Her claim is a very strong one, sir," remarked Leona, putting out thereby what is termed "a feeler."

"Well; yes—yes. I acknowledge that. But still the question is: What good can she do herself by bringing it forward? And especially if she is married. Would it not be wiser for every reason to let the matter rest?"

"*I* should think so, sir. And with poor Mr. George away, too, or dead—no one knows which—"

"Dead, Miss Gibson, dead. There is no doubt, after all these years, of my poor brother being dead. If I thought otherwise—if I *could* think otherwise—" continued Mr. Evans, with unmistakeable agitation in his voice.

"And yet there's many a one returns, sir, who has been given up for dead by his friends and relations."

"Don't speak of it, Miss Gibson; pray don't speak of it," he continued, in the same tone, "or you will utterly unfit me for business. That old grief can never be forgotten, but we have not mentioned it for years. Your coming has unfortunately revived its memory, but I trust this is the last time you will allude to it. I will be frank with you. My firm is, as you know, one of the most prosperous in England. My position in society is by no means despicable, and I have considerable wealth at my command with which to keep it up. Under these circumstances you must be aware how detrimental the propagation of such a scandal as we have been talking of would prove to my name, both in business and in fashionable circles, let alone the sorrow which the remembrance causes me. You will therefore oblige me if from this hour you entirely drop the subject. I never wish to hear it mentioned, nor even alluded to in the remotest manner. And, in consideration of which, it shall be my care to see that you want for nothing, whether in my house or out of it. Are we perfectly agreed on this matter, Miss Gibson?"

Leona was anything but perfectly agreed to a bond that must render all the trouble she had taken futile, but she could not affect even to appear to differ from her supposed patron. So she got over the difficulty in some clever, shifting, feminine way, and took her leave, bound to appear before Mr. and Mrs. Evans the same evening, and make the final arrangements for taking up her abode with them. As she left the presence of her uncle, and found herself in the glaring streets again, Leona could hardly believe in her good luck. As the door closed upon her retreating figure, Mr. Evans rubbed his hands, and congratulated himself on his diplomacy. It was a complete case of "diamond cut diamond." It had been agreed between them, in the course of their conversation, that she would call in and see Mrs. Evans that same evening. So, a little after eight o'clock, Leona presented herself at the familiar door, and heard through the open windows the sounds of laughter and talking from the dinner-table at which she had so lately sat a welcome guest. She was shown into a small study on the ground floor, where in a few minutes Mrs. Evans found her. The little lady, generally so brisk and lively, looked less so than usual, Leona imagined, as she walked demurely into the room, and begged her to be reseated in the chair from which she had risen.

"My husband tells me he has already, in some measure, explained to you the kind of person we require to attend upon Miss Evans. She has a maid to keep her wardrobe in order, and dress and undress her. But she is, unfortunately, in very delicate health, and often lies awake at night. We want some one, therefore, to be more of a companion than a servant, to read to her when she is restless, to see she takes her medicine regularly, to accompany her occasionally in her drives, and to be near her when she lies upon the sofa."

"To wait upon her, in fact, madam, as a mother or a sister might wait upon her were she dangerously ill."

"Just so, Miss Gibson. I see you perfectly understand what we require. I do a great deal of it myself, but I have my house and my friends to look after, and cannot be always by Miss Lucy's side. Sometimes, I fear, you may find her rather fractious—her illness, which arises from a weakness of the spine, is apt to make her so. And added to that, I much regret to say that the dear girl has experienced a great disappointment lately. But that has nothing to do with our engagement, nor would the story possess any interest for you."

"Anything which affects Miss Evans' health will possess, I hope, for the future, an interest for me, madam; but where there is no necessity for my hearing her private affairs, or those of any of the family, it is best they should remain untold."

Mrs. Evans was enchanted with this reply. She thought she had never met with any person who impressed her so much at first sight with her judgment and propriety as Miss Gibson did.

"There is one thing I am rather puzzled about," were the next words she said, "and that is, how I am to manage about your meals, Miss Gibson? My husband tells me you know his family well," she went on frankly, "and so you must know that I am country bred and born, and have not much knowledge of town customs. I should wish to make you as comfortable as possible, and to do everything that is right, if you will just tell me what are your ideas upon the subject. Of course I couldn't think of asking you to take your meals in the servants'-hall, but I am afraid you will be lonely eating them by yourself; and it is only on her worst days that Miss Lucilla takes hers in her bedroom. Now, what will be the best arrangement to make about it?"

The question was put so ingenuously that it did not seem unnatural that Leona should slightly deliberate before answering it, and during those few minutes of delay she reviewed her forces as a general reviews his troops, and decided on the servants'-hall.

"I will not deny, madam," she replied, "that I am unused to the society of my inferiors. My appearance and manner will have told you as much already. But since I have consented, and with the utmost gratitude to you for the offer—to enter your family in the capacity of a sick nurse to Miss Evans, I would prefer to take up my proper position in the household. Were I to take my meals alone I should only excite the envy and distrust of the servants, neither am I fond of eating myself. With your permission, then, I will dine in the hall with the others."

"I think you have come to a very sensible conclusion, Miss Gibson, though I should not have ventured to propose it. You will find all my servants respectable and superior people. Mrs. Raymond, the housekeeper, is especially so."

"And now may I venture to ask, madam, how soon you wish me to enter upon my duties?"

"Whenever you please, Miss Gibson, to-night or tomorrow. It is all the same to me. We are rather in confusion just now, our housekeeper being laid up, and two guests having arrived unexpectedly yesterday."

"Can I be of any use in filling her place?"

"I daresay you might. It is very good of you to propose it. But I should never dream of asking you to do anything more than I have already mentioned."

"I shall be glad to make myself useful in any way in return for your kindness," replied Leona. And then it was agreed between them that she should enter upon her service the following day, and consider that her salary commenced from the same date.

As Mrs. Evans, in her familiar countrified manner, was showing her out of the hall door, Leona heard that of the dining-room open, and caught a glimpse of a file of men in evening dress taking their way upstairs. There was Mr. Evans, who did not at that moment seem to wish to recognise her; there were the everlasting Captain Rivers and Tom Hastings; and lastly came Don Guzman and a slight figure, the sight of whose back alone made Leona's heart throb with mingled pain and pleasure.

"Are you suffering? Your face is so suffused," said kind Mrs. Evans, as she noticed Miss Gibson's complexion change.

"It is only the heat, madam. Even at this hour of the day there seems to be scarcely a breath of wind."

"You may well say so. It is stifling. We were thinking of sending Miss Lucy to the seaside next week, and now that you are coming to look after her, I imagine we are certain to do so. Good evening. Any time to-morrow that is most convenient to yourself will do for us. Good night. Good-bye."

And so she was kindly dismissed.

When she reached the next turning she stood against some railings for a few minutes, just to recover herself.

Oh, it was hard—bitterly hard—to see him and not to speak to him! Leona's heart was bursting to know everything that concerned himself and her. How he had passed his convalescence—if he had discovered the trick she had played upon him—what Dona Josefa had said upon the subject—above all, what he had thought or believed.

Now that she had seen him again, that she knew he was within a few yards of her, it seemed incredible that she could have been satisfied to remain without news of him three long months. He—her brother—her Tobal! The boy who had played with her from childhood—the man who had been her nearest friend and counsellor and companion!

But she was going to live in the same house with him. That thought was a balm to all her present ill. To-morrow she should sleep under the same roof as Tobal—should hear his name, perhaps his voice, and see his face every hour!

Leona went home to the hotel where she had stayed the night before, and slept long and well under the sense of that conviction.

* * * * * *

Meanwhile, Don Christobal Valera, who had come to England immediately on the receipt of the news by the New York firm of the fraud that had been perpetrated in their name upon their London correspondents, was receiving from Mr. Evans a full, true, and particular account of every circumstance connected with the mysterious appearance and disappearance of the young man who had assumed his name and presented his letters of introduction.

"Such a nice boy as we all thought him," said Mrs. Evans. "The only thing that ever struck me about him as strange was his extreme youth. He professed to be two-and-twenty, but he did not look more than eighteen—if so much."

"You will pardon my great curiosity, I hope, upon the subject," replied Don Christobal, "but you must be aware it possesses an overpowering interest for me. Would you mind describing to me over again, as minutely as you can, every detail of the appearance of this impostor?"

"I can tell you to a T, Valera," interposed Captain Rivers, who had taken as great a fancy to the real Simon Pure as he had taken a dislike to the false one. "He was an undersized, flabby, little beast, with fat white hands, pink cheeks, a rosebud mouth, and every other description of horror. He used to loll about with the women all day, and boast tremendously of achievements which he never saw, and—"

"Stop, Rivers!" said Mr. Evans; "you are unjust in your description. You never liked the lad, and you are prejudiced against him. But Valera desires an accurate knowledge of his appearance, remember, for other purposes than the gratification of personal spite. Our firm and his have been deceived and cheated by this pretended Spanish correspondent, and we want to discover the offender, and bring him to justice."

"The sooner the better, I should say," grumbled the Captain, *sotto voce*.

"Had he not been so effeminate-looking, the young man would really have been handsome," continued Mr. Evans, turning to Valera, "for he had beautiful features."

"What coloured hair and eyes?"

"A deep red or chestnut colour, and very thick and curly. I am speaking of his hair. As for his eyes, it is not so easy to describe them. I am not much in the habit of looking at people's eyes, but I could not help noticing Valera's—I beg your pardon, Don—it's difficult to drop calling the impostor by his assumed name. They were the most peculiar eyes I have ever seen, large and long, of precisely the same colour as his hair, only with black eyebrows and lashes, and the most extraordinary yellow light about them."

"A yellow light!" cried Valera, suddenly. "How very peculiar. I never heard of such a thing before," he added a moment after, in a sedater tone.

"Nor I. I used to look at the boy with astonishment. His eyes seemed to change like a panther's. Sometimes they looked as black as night, at others, clear as amber. Where are you going, Don?" he continued, as the young man left his side and walked in a bewildered manner towards the open window.

"Only for a breath of fresh air. Your cramped atmosphere chokes me, monsieur," said Christobal, as he leant his feverish brow against the sill, and gazed up into the dark blue star-spangled sky.

The stars seemed to look back upon him with their yellow light, and confirm the suspicion that had arisen in his mind.

"Black as night, clear as amber," he repeated to himself. "As sure as those stars never change their lustre, those eyes must have belonged to *her*. Yet Leona *here*—in the country she vowed she never would visit, as an impostor in name, and sex, and position, as a defrauder of *my* rights, the rights of *me* whom I thought she so much loved. *Madre di Dios*! I would sacrifice every prospect I have in the world sooner than believe it true."

– CHAPTER 25 –

A NOVEL POSITION

"Caramba," cried Don Guzman, "the description answers pretty accurately to the appearance of that little friend of yours, Valera, who nearly gave me my quietus on our road to New York. *Sapristi!* I shall never forget the coolness with which that lad put a bullet into me. And all because I had doubted the purity of your Spanish blood. Can it be Leon d'Acosta that has been personating you? You told me you had lost sight of him lately."

"The same idea has passed through my brain," said Christobal. "And yet I cannot think it possible."

"Why not? The boy had an affectionate heart and plenty of courage; but our own welfare is always the first consideration with us."

"Not with—with *him*," replied Valera.

"It is strange," remarked Mr. Evans, "that I never had any doubt about this young fellow from the beginning. I am generally considered 'cute' enough in business matters, but he completely took me in. He had such a refined courtier-like air about him, and made himself so general a favourite. As for the women," continued Mr. Evans in a lower voice, "he made complete fools of them—what with his acting and his singing."

"Did he act well, this boy, as if he had been used to it?" demanded Valera.

"Splendidly. He took us all by surprise one night at a friend's house. I don't care much for such things myself, but I confess he astonished me. And he had a very fine voice too, and sang to his guitar in several languages. He spoke English as well, if not better than you do yourself, Don."

"Did he appear familiar with the Brazils?"

"Perfectly so, and from what you tell me, with every particular concerning your family and antecedents. I think he must, at some time or other, have been intimate with yourself or your friends."

"Tell us how it was you lost your letters of introduction, Valera," said Guzman. "How did they go? When did you first miss them?"

"Well, that I can hardly tell you. Just as I had received them from the firm I fell dangerously ill of typhoid fever, and know nothing that happened for weeks afterwards."

"*Après?*"

"As soon as I was well enough I was taken away to the country for change of air and thought no more of letters until I was told they had been already presented in England by some one assuming my name."

"And have you no idea *who* had an opportunity of getting at your private papers?" said Mr. Evans.

"There was no *man* associated with me at the time," replied Christobal, evasively.

"May I ask who nursed you during your illness?"

"My mother and a female friend of hers. As far as I know, no one else touched anything that belonged to me."

"It is all very mysterious," said Mr. Evans; "and even if we catch the lad, I don't see what we can do to punish him. He has defrauded no one as yet. He had not the time to do it. I suppose he must have received some intimation of your arrival before he left here, for he and I had had some private conversation that morning—"

"I wish you wouldn't talk so loud, Henry," said Mrs. Evans, coming up to them. "Your voice reaches the other end of the room, and poor Lucy is listening to every word you say. If you *must* talk about that horrible, deceitful, wicked young man, take Don Valera into the conservatory."

"All right," replied Mr. Evans, obediently, as he moved away with his guest. "You will understand, Valera, that under ordinary circumstances I should not repose in you, or anyone, the confidence I am about to do now; but I consider it is necessary you should know all. On the very morning this impostor left us, I had been talking to him on the subject of my daughter and himself."

"Had he presumed to—to—*address* Miss Evans, then?"

"He had, as she believed it. Any way, there was a sort of understanding between them; and my daughter, being a very spoilt child, made herself ill by fretting after him, so I thought it time to put in my oar. We had a long conversation on the subject."

"And what *did* he say?" asked Valera, curiously. He would have burst out laughing in his host's face, believing as he had commenced to believe, had his mind not been too mournfully exercised on his own account. As it was, he had difficulty in appearing as serious as he should have done.

"He seemed startled at first, as though he had hardly expected such a communication on my part. When I had made him fully understand my meaning, he appeared—as I have no difficulty in believing now that he felt—extremely flattered. He acknowledged the preference he experienced for Miss Evans; and in consequence, believing it was all right, I reposed a confidence in him which I much regret to have parted with. Notwithstanding that, I promised it should be all straight sailing for him. I remember now that I was rather surprised at the diffidence with which he met my offer. I suppose the young rascal had received some intimation of your arrival, and knew that under any circumstances he would not be able to keep up the ball much longer."

"Did he agree to marry your daughter, then?" demanded Valera.

"Well, not exactly. He shilly-shallied with the subject, and I ascribed his hesitation to his modesty. He said he was engaged to spend a few days with some friends at Streatham, and asked leave to postpone further discussion of the subject till his return. Of course I assented. I had no wish to force my daughter on him. All I wanted was to secure her peace of mind. *The scoundrel!*" added Mr. Evans, angrily.

"I hope Miss Evans has not felt his defection much?"

"She could not but feel it, Don. She is very sickly, and spends most of her time on her back, and this fellow had made himself almost necessary to her. She has plenty of friends, but his gentle ways and winning manners suited her nervous temperament better, I suppose, than the roughness of most men. She fretted more than enough at his going to Streatham. When we discovered he had never been there I thought she would have had a serious illness from suspense, and your arrival has been the crowning blow. I insist upon her mixing in society, because I know solitude is the worst thing for her, but I do not know what mischief may not be silently working in her system the while. The fellow deserves to have his neck wrung."

"Might not change of scene prove beneficial to Miss Evans?" said Christobal, unwilling to discuss the advisability of wringing the neck of the unknown impostor.

"My wife and I have talked of it more than once, but the girl is unwilling to go. However, we have lately secured the services of a very nice and respectable attendant for her, with whom we think she may be induced to visit the seaside. A family is a great responsibility, Don Valera. You are fortunate in not having, as yet, encumbered yourself with one."

"I do not know what would become of my very slender and uncertain prospects if I had," replied Christobal, with a laugh that broke off in something very like a sigh.

* * * * * *

When Leona returned to the Evans' house on the following day, she felt herself to be a person of some little importance. She knew that Mr. Evans would have repeated to his wife all that he knew concerning her, with a caution respecting the treatment he wished her to receive, and that in her turn Mrs. Evans would have communicated his sentiments, more or less, to the servants of the household. She was not surprised therefore on presenting herself to find that the footman ushered her into a private room, where she was presently joined by her new mistress, and welcomed with every appearance of cordiality.

"Mr. Evans and I have been laying our heads together, Miss Gibson, and come to the conclusion that, if it is agreeable to yourself, you and Mrs. Raymond had better take your meals together in her little sitting-room upstairs. I am sure you will like Mrs. Raymond, she has been in our family forty years, and is a most good-tempered, chatty old lady. Will you come up and see her at once (she is confined to her room, as I told you, with the gout), or will you be introduced to Miss Lucy?"

"I will do whichever is most agreeable to yourself, madam."

"Then I think it will be pleasanter for you to take off your bonnet and make yourself comfortable first, Miss Gibson, and when you have had a cup of tea you can come to my room. This way." And, going before her, Mrs. Evans trotted up the staircase until they reached and entered the housekeeper's apartment. Although Leona knew but little of the domestic life of servants, and the style of their treatment in England, she had kept her eyes sufficiently open to be aware that, for the station she had assumed, her reception was a very unusual one. Her statements then to her uncle had had the desired effect. He was afraid of what she might have to disclose. He dreaded the old story being raked up again. What might he not have to dread when she had found out and sounded Rebecca Levitt, or Antoine? For to discover this woman's whereabouts, and to hear all the evidence she might be able to bring to bear upon the subject of Abraham Anson's murder, was Leona's next design.

Mrs. Raymond received her more cordially than might have been anticipated of one head servant welcoming another. The truth is, the old housekeeper had seen her day, and was thankful for the prospect of any help in her duties. She had been too long with the Evans to feel jealous of an interloper. She knew (and for the same reason that made the security of the new comer) that whatever happened she would never be deposed from the place she held in their household. They could not afford to offend so old a servant. So, after a careful scrutiny, that resulted in a grunt of satisfaction, Mrs. Raymond made Miss Gibson welcome to her sanctum, and gave her such a cup of afternoon tea as only housekeepers and such as have the run of the storeroom know how to brew for themselves.

The first conversation between the two women ran naturally upon Miss Lucilla, and the shameful manner in which she had been treated by the "furrin young gentleman." Mrs. Raymond did not restrain her tongue during the discussion. She had evidently been made cognisant of the position Miss Gibson had formerly held towards the family, and assumed that she must be perfectly *au fait* with everything that concerned its members. She animadverted freely enough on the conduct of the supposed Valera, and the scandalous manner in which he had eventually "cut and run"— "just for all the world, my dear, like a life-guardsman on leave that I was engaged to be married to when I was a girl—the handsomest creature as ever you saw, with blue eyes and fair hair, and standing six foot two in his stockings, if he stood an inch—and who borrowed ten pounds of my poor father on account of the expenses of the wedding trip, and then ran away and rejoined his regiment, and we never could get no satisfaction out of him afterwards—never!"

"But this young gentleman hasn't robbed anyone, has he?" demanded Leona, trembling for her own honour. If Mrs. Raymond had answered "Yes," she would scarcely have been able to avoid betraying herself by a denial.

"Bless you, no, my dear; and he had one of the nicest faces as you ever set eyes on, with beautiful brown eyes. What coloured eyes are yours?" demanded Mrs. Raymond, suddenly interrupting herself as she turned about and confronted her new acquaintance.

"They're of a brownish colour, too, but very weak," replied Miss Gibson, as she resumed the spectacles she had laid aside for a moment. "I can't bear the light upon them at all."

"Bad for needlework, I should say," suggested the housekeeper. "Very bad," replied Leona, who, possessing little or no skill with her needle, was delighted at having found an excuse that should absolve her from exhibiting her deficiency in that respect.

"Well, it's a pity, but it doesn't much signify here," said Mrs. Raymond, "because Miss Lucy's maid looks after her wardrobe, and I expect you're to be more of a companion than a servant to her."

"I believe so, from what Mrs. Evans told me."

"She said the same to me, and that you knew pretty near as much of the family as I do. That's why I was going to mention the poor young gentleman's eyes to you. I can't keep from calling him poor, because he did remind me so of Master George. His eyes were the very moral of his."

"That's strange, isn't it, when they were no relation to each other?"

"Well, I don't know. Your eyes remind me of Mr. Valera's, too, though you never heard of him before today. It is the colour, I suppose, that makes the resemblance. Although, I must say, I used to be foolish enough to wonder to myself if that poor boy could be any kith or kin to our Mr. George."

"Why Mrs. Raymond, how could he have been?" cried Leona, looking and feeling really startled by the housekeeper's suspicion.

"Well, my dear, I daresay it was only an old woman's fancy, but the likeness at times was powerful. And you see, Mr. George went to foreign parts, and this lad, he came from foreign parts; and though we've heard nothing of our poor dear since he left England, and don't know if he's dead or alive, still, anyway, he might have left a family behind him—but there, I'm foolish, and don't you get repeating a word of what I've said to Mrs. Evans or Miss Lucy, or I shall never hear the end of it."

"Don't be afraid. I shall repeat nothing. Only you know the rumour there was about Mr. George before he left England, and I should think he would scarcely have married in the face of it."

"Lor, my dear! I said nothing about marriage. And who do you think would marry a poor creature with a curse upon him like that? It was only my nonsense, no doubt; but I must say, the first time I caught a good sight of Mr. Valera, he took my heart away."

"Can you give me Rebecca Levitt's address?" said Leona, trying to speak naturally, and as though the answer were of no moment to her.

"No, I can't," replied Mrs. Raymond, sharply; "and if I could I wouldn't. She's been dead and buried, so I hear, these ten years past; and dead or alive we don't want her about this house again. She's brought misfortune enough into it for one lifetime, I should think, and I wonder at any calling themselves friends of the master's taking the trouble even to mention her name."

"I am sure I beg your pardon," said Leona, humbly. "I have no more reason to like Rebecca Levitt than you have; but I've cause to believe she's not dead, because I was speaking with some of her relations only the other day in Liverpool."

"Well, 'tis a pity she ain't dead then," rejoined the housekeeper, "for a more deceitful hussy never breathed. I wish the whole family had been drowned in the Red Sea before we had set eyes on them. They're at the bottom of all the misery we've ever had."

"Yet Mr. Evans employs some of the Levitts still in his house at Liverpool."

"He has his own reasons for that, my dear, as you may well believe. But I don't think he could stand even the name of that Becky being mentioned before him again. That's the bell to Miss Lucy's room. Mrs. Evans said she would ring it when she wanted you. If you've quite done your tea, perhaps you'd better go."

Miss Lucy's room was a pretty little boudoir, opening from her sleeping apartment, and where she usually spent her mornings. Leona had often passed an hour there with her guitar, and her heart smote her sensibly as she entered it now, and saw poor Lucilla stretched upon the couch, looking so feeble, and languid, and worn out. Mrs. Evans was seated by her daughter's side.

"This is Miss Gibson, my love," she said, as Leona made her appearance. "Will you let her sit with you whilst I run down to your papa? You can tell her just what you want."

"Yes," replied Lucilla, wearily.

"Take a chair by the side of the sofa, if you please, Miss Gibson, and keep the flies off Miss Evans with this fan. Her handkerchief and eau-de-cologne bottle are on that table, and there is lemonade in the ice-cooler in the corner. You will be sure and tell Miss Gibson all you may want, love, won't you?"

"Yes," repeated the girl, in the same tone.

"Some friends may come up to see her by-and-by, Miss Gibson. You must admit them or not, according to her orders. I shall not be gone more than an hour. Good-bye, dear Lucilla." And with a kiss to the invalid, Mrs. Evans trotted out of the room.

"Can I do anything for you, miss?" said Leona, as she approached the sofa.

"Nothing, thank you," replied Lucilla, with closed eyes.

Leona took Mrs. Evans' vacated seat, and commenced to fan the languid invalid. As she was thus employed she examined her with interest, and was shocked to see how great an alteration her disappointment had made in her. Lucy's face had always been pale—now it was drawn and sallow, and the dark, leaden-tinted circles round her eyes showed how many tears the poor child had shed over the defalcation of her supposed lover.

Leona had never professed to feel more than friendship for Lucilla; but her conscience smote her as she remembered that but for the deception she had practised, her sentiments could never have been misinterpreted. With all her courage, and determination, and apparent insensibility to the feelings of others, our heroine had a kind heart, and she felt terribly sorry for the ludicrous error into which Lucilla had fallen; and her sorrow gave birth to a desire to relieve it.

If she could manage to engage the girl's attention (so Leona argued to herself), and gain some influence over the girl's mind, she might, with the many opportunities of converse open to her, continue to undo some of the mischief she had caused. The fancy Lucilla had taken for her in her masquerading costume being but one-sided, was not likely to prove lasting; and there was Dr. Hastings, as Leona well knew from former observation, ready to step into the breach, and offer his patient all the consolation in his power. As she sat and silently examined the havoc fretting had made in the girl's appearance, Leona resolved to do all she could to favour Dr. Hasting's suit. But to attain that end she must first win Lucy's liking and confidence.

She was roused from her reverie by finding that her charge's eyes had opened, and were fixed upon her face.

"I don't want any more fanning, thank you. It chills me. Why does mamma say I knew you when I was a little girl? I never saw your face before."

"Oh yes, miss, you did! Down at Mrs. Gibson's, in Sussex, years ago. Don't you remember Jane Gibson?"

"No, I do not," replied Lucilla, shaking her head. "You must be mistaken. I never forget a face that I have once seen. And there was only Mrs. Gibson there and a woman—I forget the name we used to call her—Watson, or Walters, or something like that."

"Wallis, you mean," interposed her companion; "an old servant, Wallis. She is still living at Willowside with my aunt."

"Yes, that was her name, I remember now. So you must have been at Willowside at some time, but not with me."

"Oh yes I was! but it was so long ago you have forgotten me, Miss Lucilla."

"I never forget faces," repeated Lucilla emphatically; "and you were not at Willowside at the same time that I was."

Leona became somewhat alarmed at this obstinacy, which might lead to unpleasant inquiries. She was so unused to children, and their ways, that she had miscalculated the strength of a child's memory, and she did not quite see her way out of this fresh difficulty. But her mother-wit came to her assistance. She knew if she removed the spectacles she wore that Lucilla would see something familiar in her eyes, for which, from her dress and gray hair, she would be unable to give a tangible reason. And from the confused memory that would follow Leona thought she saw the means of convincing her of the truth of her own assertion.

"I am sorry I should have passed so completely out of your mind, Miss Lucilla," she answered, "but I know the reason why. I had brown hair in those days and strong eyes, now my hair is nearly white, and I am compelled to wear glasses. I think if I remove them you will have less difficulty in recognising me."

She suited the action to the word, and Lucilla gazed on the eyes she had so lately decided to be the most beautiful in the world. But crow's-feet had been delicately pencilled at the corner of each eyelid, and the black brows above were nearly white, so that her first glance elicited a little cry of pained surprise, the second mystified her. She felt that she had, and yet she had not, seen them, and the face to which they belonged, before. And the consequent confusion that ensued in her mind, brought about the very result that Leona had anticipated. Lucilla could not decide for herself, so she was fain to accept the decision of another.

"You know me now, you see," remarked Miss Gibson.

"I suppose I do," replied Lucilla, in a wondering kind of way. "Your face looks familiar to me, and yet I cannot associate it with Willowside, nor have I any idea where I have seen it before."

"You were such a mere child at that time, remember."

"I suppose that must be it, yet it seems strange I should forget. Perhaps you were not always in the house, Miss Gibson."

"I was in and out, and about. I remember you perfectly, Miss Lucilla, and so does Wallis. My poor old aunt is too foolish now to remember anybody."

"Hark!" interposed Lucilla, "was not that a knock at the door? It must be the doctor. Let him in, Miss Gibson, please."

And Leona, rising hastily and letting the spectacles, to which she was so unaccustomed, fall from her lap, went forward to do her new mistress's bidding, and found herself face to face with *Christobal Valera!*

– CHAPTER 26 –

LEONA IS DISCOVERED

As the door opened their four eyes met, and in that moment he recognised her. He had no time to take in the details of her costume: the eminently respectable black silk dress; the primitive collar and cuffs, and the old-fashioned cap with lilac ribbons that adorned her head. He had no time to mark the gray wig—the white eyebrows—the painted wrinkles—he saw only Leona's eyes, those eyes that were so unlike any other eyes on earth; those rich, fathomless brown orbs, with the restless light playing across them, like sunshine glistening through a thick tracery of leaves. Lucilla had not been able to recognise them, because even had she stayed to consider whose eyes they resembled she would only have sighed at the memory they recalled, and been quite unable to associate the appearance of this middle-aged woman with the fascinating youth whose loss she deplored. But Christobal had seen and studied Leona's countenance under every sort of disguise. She would not have been able to deceive him by her male attire, nor directly her eyes met his could the supposed Miss Gibson keep up her *incognito*. And as recognition flew to his face and made it glow with sudden pleasure and surprise, Leona saw as plainly as he did that she was recognised; and yet the space of time occupied by a flash of lightening might have covered what it has taken so many words to put down on paper.

"*M'amie!*" he exclaimed, without the slightest disguise, and as she heard the word Leona believed that all was over with her. But the next moment Cristobal had recovered himself, and though our heroine was trembling from head to food her courage did not desert her.

"This is Miss Evans' room, sir. Do you wish to see her?"

"*Pardon*! Yes!" he answered. "I was commissioned by Madame Evans to bring these flowers"—intimating a large bouquet he carried in his hands—"to mademoiselle, and to ask if it is her pleasure to drive in the Park this evening."

"It is Don Valera, Miss Lucy," said Leona, turning to the couch. "Do you wish to see him?"

"Oh, yes! Let him come in," said Lucy, indifferently. She had heard the exclamation he had given vent to on first meeting Miss Gibson, but it had conveyed no meaning to her ears. She knew neither French nor Spanish sufficiently well even to understand to which language the expression belonged; and she was so accustomed to hear the numerous foreigners that frequented her father's house using their native idioms, that if she noticed it at all, it was only to wonder whether Don Valera was taking an oath, or uttering a prayer to his favourite saint. So that the visitor was permitted to enter, and whilst he was paying the usual amount of compliments a man considers due to the daughter of the house he is staying at, Leona's agitation had leisure to subside, and she could think of the best means to prevent Christobal further betraying her identity. Not but what she believed that, once assured of her wish, he would respect it; but she had everything to explain to him, and she feared that his impatience might make him forgetful of the harm he might do her by his indiscretion. She knew that, having once detected her in a false position, Christobal would never rest until he had learned the truth, and that the sooner she could give him an interview the better. So, with her back turned toward the couch where they were conversing together, she tore a leaf from her pocket-book and hastily scribbled on it, in Spanish:

"Be silent—be patient—for the love of God, and I will tell you all. This evening, when they go out in the carriage, I shall remain in this room."

She crushed the paper in the palm of her hand, and held it so waiting.

In a few minutes Don Valera rose to go. He was evidently making a great effort to speak lightly; but Leona could detect the nervous tremor in his voice.

"Then, mademoiselle, I am to convey to madame your consent to dine with her this evening?"

"Oh, yes! if mamma wishes I will go. It is all the same to me," replied Lucilla.

"Pardon, mademoiselle, but I venture to surmise you will not find it all the same when you get out of this warm room into the cool fresh air. It is very charming in the Park to-day."

"Perhaps you will accompany us, Don?"

"With pleasure, mademoiselle, if I gain the consent of madame. I will go and tell her that you will be ready—how soon?"

"In half an hour."

"In half an hour. *Au revoir,*" said Valera, as he bowed and prepared to quit the room. Leona walked swiftly to the door and held it open for him. As he passed through it he gave her a glance that cut her to the soul. She responded to it by thrusting the piece of paper in his hand.

Then he turned and looked back upon her from the landing, and had she obeyed the impulse of her heart, she could have run forward and clasped her arms about his neck, and cried for joy at seeing him again. But the exigencies of her position were strong upon her, and she shrunk backwards instead, and closed the door upon him.

"If you'll open the second long drawer of that wardrobe, Miss Gibson, you'll find a pale-blue walking costume and bonnet. I'll wear them to-day. Will you do my hair before I leave the sofa? Thank you. How nice and firm and plump your hands are. They're just like a girl's. And you brush hair beautifully. You seem to brush all the pain out of my head. I should have it done frequently, only my maid pulls at my hair and tangles it so, that it is pain instead of pleasure. But your touch is wonderfully soothing."

"I am so glad you find it so, Miss Lucilla. I know what a good effect brushing the hair has upon nervous pain. I will try the effect of it when your are restless. It might often send you to sleep at night."

"I think it might, but I should not like to give you so much trouble. What do you think of the gentleman who was here just now, Miss Gibson? He is considered to be very handsome."

"I think he *is* handsome, Miss Lucilla, for a foreigner. But you don't think there are many men like Englishmen, I'm sure."

"Indeed I do! There was a young gentleman staying with us the other day"—here poor Lucy stopped and sighed—"he was a Spaniard too, like Don Valera, and he was the handsomest man I've ever seen in my life."

"Indeed, miss. What was he like?"

"Oh! he had such beautiful hair," cried Lucy, delighted to find a new listener for the topic that absorbed her. "A kind of a deep chestnut colour, and a straight nose, and such glorious eyes, and teeth as white as pearls, and such pretty little hands and feet."

"Dear me, miss! that seems more like the description of a young lady than a gentleman to me. A man should be broad and lusty, and tanned by the weather; and have good strong limbs to protect himself and others with. I am afraid the young gentleman you speak of couldn't have been of much good out of a drawing-room."

"Oh! but he sang divinely, Miss Gibson, and played the guitar, and acted so well; in fact I think he could do everything."

"Well, Miss Lucilla, I should like to see your paragon, though I don't fancy I should hold him of much account beside a gentleman like Dr. Hastings, for instance."

"Dr. Hastings! Why, when did you know him?"

"I don't know him, miss, and I've only seen him once since I've been in the house. But I noticed what a fine, strong, manly gentleman he is, and Mrs. Raymond told me his name. Now he's what *I* call handsome, if you like."

"Tom handsome!" mused Lucilla. "I never even thought of him in that light. But he is very strong. He can carry me as easily as if I were a baby."

"Ah, and as good as he is strong, miss, I am sure. Anyone could see that at a glance. Will the other gentleman be here again soon?"

"What, Don Valera?"

"No; the handsome young gentleman you were speaking of."

"He was Don Valera."

"But is not that the name of the one that visited you just now?" Lucy saw the error she had made, coloured and hesitated.

"Yes—but—"

"They are brothers, perhaps."

"Oh no. They're no relation to each other, but they have the same name. I don't think he's coming back again—not just yet, that's to say," continued poor Lucy, rapidly and incoherently—"and—will you please to get me out my parasol, Miss Gibson—and a pair of gloves—and—I think mamma must be ready by this time, if you'll just go and see, and tell her that I'm dressed, and will wait here till the carriage comes round."

Leona saw through the earnest desire to get rid of her, born of poor Lucy's personal fear that she had said more about the defalcant Valera than was either necessary or prudent. She was willing enough to let the subject drop for the present, foreseeing plainly that the foolish little heart would before long unbosom itself again. And she was right. For what she did not know was that Mr. and Mrs. Evans, from a mistaken idea that they were acting for the best, had strictly tabooed the mention of the false Valera's name, and refused to let Lucy discuss the subject of her feelings respecting him with anybody. Consequently the poor girl's heart, left to brood over her disappointment, was positively bursting to relieve itself by placing confidence in some sympathetic mind.

It is the greatest error possible to suppose that a trouble is increased by discussion. On the contrary, air it freely, and it will probably die a natural death in half the time. It is the pent-up grief that will not expire, but feeds upon the heart until it has drained it of all life and energy. Some people cannot talk of their trouble. So much the worse for them. It proves how deep it lies, how sorely it has wounded. It is like a terribly diseased limb, to uncover which even is agony. But when they can talk, and wish to talk, do not prevent them. Be patient and merciful. Listen to the oft-repeated tale again and again, without a look that shall warn them they have wearied you. Hear how handsome *he* was—how beautiful *she* looked—how divinely each one of them sung or danced, or wrote, or played—not once, or twice, or a dozen times (that is if you love the narrator), but as often as your tormentor chooses to inflict it upon you without a sign of impatience, or contempt, or fatigue, and great shall be your reward. For of all the acts of mercy registered in heaven, surely to bear our fellow-creatures' burdens after this fashion must be amongst the highest. The relief of such vent for a broken spirit is incalculable—the want of it renders the burden almost too heavy to bear.

Yet the best of mortals on occasions refuse it to their fellow-sufferers, on the score that it will increase their disappointment to dwell upon it. They betray the merciful exemption they have had from such suffering by the mere idea.

* * * * *

The carriage had rolled away from the door, and, as Leona, peeping behind the blind of a front window had observed, without Valera. The House in Hyde Park Gardens was now nearly empty. The afternoon visitors had departed; the ladies gone out; the gentlemen not yet returned from their various avocations; and the servants, congregated in the basement, were enjoying the first interval of leisure they had had that day. Leona lingered about Lucilla's room, confident that Valera would join her as soon as ever he considered it prudent to do so.

And he came even sooner than she had anticipated, not creeping silently up the staircase, but with a dash and a bang, as if the whole house belonged to him, that frightened her to hear. Into the room he rushed rapidly, energetically, as if no power on earth should keep him another moment from her side, and, slamming the door behind him, ran forward and clasped her to his heart. Leona had intended to act a little, more for the sake of any who might overhear their interview than in the cause of prudery; but when she felt Christobal's arms tightly wound about her, and his face laid against her own, every consideration vanished before the knowledge that her dearest friend was with her again, and she cried with joy and excitement.

"*Tobal! Tobalito! mon frère, mon cheri!*" she kept on repeating, in broken tones, as she allowed the young man to embrace her according to his will.

"And so I have found you again, *m'amie!*" he exclaimed, as soon as there was a pause, "after all these weary months of suspense and waiting, and horrible doubt, I have found my sister again. Do you know what you have subjected me to by your silence and mystery, Leona? Do you know how I have suffered, scarcely risen from a sick bed, and unable to gain any tidings of you, except that you had left New York? *Madre di Dios!* my worst enemy could not have devised a more cruel fate for me than has been inflicted by your hands. Tell me the reason of it! Why did you throw up your engagement at the theatre without letting me know? What influence has drawn you to visit a country to which you have always expressed the greatest antipathy? And why do I find you in my employer's house in a disguise, unbefitting your birth, your beauty, or your profession? There is some terrible mystery in all this, Leona."

"Tobalito! forgive me for all I have made you suffer! I did not forget you. If it had been possible, I would have made you my confidant. But there was no alternative."

"You speak in riddles, *m'amie*."

"It is so long a story, you must give me time for explanation. I will have no more secrets from you, Tobalito. I will tell you everything, but it must be on one condition."

"Name it, Leona!"

"That you do not in any way attempt to stop me in the path of duty I have chalked out for myself."

"Have I ever attempted to turn you from your duty, *m'amie*?"

"You promise then?"

"Tell me first, why do I find you under this disguise?"

"Because it is necessary to my design. It is not the first I have adopted since coming here. Cannot you guess, Tobal? I am the person who stole your letters, and introduced myself here under your name. I could not accomplish the design I have in hand under that character, so I adopted another in order to enter the, house again."

Valera dropped her hand, and sunk into the nearest chair.

"Oh, Leona, Leona!" he murmured, "I suspected this; but I would rather have heard any other confession from your lips."

The girl flung herself at his feet, her grey hair and prim attire contrasting strangely with her ardent eyes and impetuous manner.

"Tobal, speak to me! Where was the great harm of it? I would have died sooner than injure you. But you could not travel at that period; and I knew that as soon as you were fit to do so, the firm would provide you with fresh letters of introduction. The only risk I ran was to myself."

"But why—why, my darling? What object could you have had in undertaking this mad freak? What are you doing in this house? Why have you sunk yourself to the level of a servant?"

"My answer is almost contained in your questions, Tobal. You have known my nature from a little child. Why should I do that which is naturally abhorrent to me unless I had some great and important end in view?"

"What end can you have?"

"The most powerful of all—the clearance of my dead father's name from the charge of *murder!*"

At that word Valera started from his chair.

"Leona, you must be dreaming. This is a delusion, an hallucination on your part. Who ever dared to couple M. Lacoste's name with so foul a charge? Why did you not tell me of this before? Whoever he had been, even to a king upon his throne, he should have retracted the calumny, or felt the power of a Spaniard's revenge."

"Thanks, *mon frère*," said the girl, quietly, though her eye kindled at the sight of his enthusiasm in her father's cause, "I love you for your championship; but I am the only one who can search out this matter to the end, and I have sworn before heaven not to rest until I have done so. Do you remember what I told you on board the steamer, Tobal, as we were journeying from Rio to New York, and the reason I gave you for wishing to quit the place where we were born?"

"I do remember, Leona, but I regarded your communications simply as the effect of a heated and youthful imagination."

"There was more in my resolutions than you gave me credit for. And when I got to New York and heard the subject renewed, found that the infamous charges brought against my dear father were well known and far spread; and that his real name and the names of his accusers were common property, the fire of my indignation burned higher than before. Then your letters fell into my hands, and the temptation to use them was too strong. Forgive me, *mon frère*, it is all that I can say. I have made you the only excuses in my power."

"But I am still mystified, *m'amie*. Granted that your suspicions are correct, and that your poor father was falsely accused of so base a crime, of what earthly avail to you could be the use of letters addressed to the firm of Evans and Troubridge? Why could you not have come to England under your own name and character?"

"Because my father's name was Evans, Christobal; because he was the brother of the man in whose house we now stand; because my uncle has unjustly inherited the property that should have been his; because, as I firmly believe, Henry Evans himself committed the murder for which my poor father suffered a life-long banishment."

"Leona, you must be mad! You cannot think of what you are saying," cried Valera. "For heaven's sake cease these awful accusations, for should you be over heard you may ruin yourself for life."

"My father was ruined for life," replied Leona, "and his death is at the door of his accusers. Do you think *I*—his daughter—shrink from sharing his fate? I tell you, Christobal, I have sworn the most solemn oath to avenge his memory, and if it led me to the gallows as a reward, I would not falter in my duty."

"I know as well as most men, all the courage of which you are capable, Leona," said Valera, as he wiped the beads of perspiration from his forehead, "but I must have further proofs of the authority on which you are acting before I can approve of your present conduct. You are rash and inexperienced, and may lead yourself into some terrible labyrinth of difficulty, by bringing a false accusation against so eminently respectable a man as Mr. Evans. It is difficult for me to believe on your bare word—though I know *you* believe it—that your father *was* the brother of my employer; still more to think that the latter could be capable of the criminality you impute to him. And allowing it all to be true, how can a woman like yourself expect to find the means of bringing it home to him? And if you can, will it be advisable to let the world know that your uncle is a murderer?"

"The world thinks my dear father was one!" cried Leona, excitedly. "Am I to let his memory rest under such a blight, in order to spare my uncle? I have made several discoveries since I have been in England, Christobal, and I see my way already to the end. I will tell you everything, from first to last, if you will swear to keep my secret inviolate."

"Should I be justified in doing so?" asked Valera, who, between love, and duty, and honour, was becoming sorely perplexed. "I have been sent over here in a position of trust, and received—notwithstanding the obstacles you placed in my way—with the greatest hospitality and frankness. Can I remain in this man's house, and receive his confidence, knowing all the time so dark a plot is hatching under his very roof to destroy his respectability?"

Leona's lip curled with indignation.

"*His respectability*! The respectability of an undiscovered assassin! Go on, then, Valera. Act as you think most honourable and best. Betray my identity, my designs, if you will; but you will effect but one object by your intervention."

"And that is—?"

"*Our total separation.* Not for a few months, or a few years—but *forever, and ever, and ever*! I swear it, Tobal—so help me heaven! You have come to the knowledge of my presence here through a mistake, an inadvertence. If you make use of your knowledge to circumvent the fulfilment of my solemn oath, I will never see you nor speak to you in this life again. Now for your decision."

"Never see me, nor speak to me again in this life! Me, *me*, Leona, who have loved you from your very cradle? Oh, *m'amie!*" exclaimed the young man passionately, as he fell on his knees and clasped her round the waist. "You might threaten me with the gallows sooner. If I lose the whole world for it, I cannot, *cannot* give, you up."

– CHAPTER 27 –

LEONA'S STRATAGEM

"I knew it," cried Leona triumphantly. "I knew that you cared for me too much, Tobalito, to become my worst enemy now."

"Your enemy! As if that word could ever be applicable to me, when every thought of my life has been yours, Leona, and will be until life ends."

The girl stooped down, and kissed the young man in her old frank way upon the forehead.

"You were always my good brother and friend," she murmured, "and I love you, Tobalito. It is agreed then. When you leave this apartment, you go back to the family circle as utterly unconscious that the person they call 'Miss Gibson' is Leona Lacoste as though you had never seen her before."

"If you say it *must* be so, I shall obey you, Leona. But is there no other course open to us to pursue, *m'amie?*"

"What course should there be?"

"Is it of no use," continued Valera wistfully, "my pleading with you for myself. Of no use my urging the long weeks I have endured of doubt, and suspense, and misery, whilst I have thought you dead or faithless, as a reason for your having a little pity now on me—if not upon yourself?"

"What do you mean, Tobal?" she questioned sharply. "It is you who are speaking in riddles now, and I have no clue to guessing them."

"I mean, dear Leona, that if you are determined to pursue this quest, I want to share the risk with you. I want to be your right protector as well as your friend, *m'amie*. I want, in fact, *to marry you*!"

She had been holding his two hands in hers till now, but at these words she threw them away, and a look of distaste, mingled with contempt for her companion's weakness, mounted to her speaking face.

"*You want to marry me!*" she repeated incredulously. "When I have just told you that all my thoughts and hopes are set upon the accomplishment of my oath. Are you raving? How *could* you marry me, even were I to consent, under the circumstances?"

"Had I your consent, Leona, the rest would be easy enough. We are not under parents or guardians. We have but to walk into the nearest church and get married."

"*Après?*" said the girl mockingly.

Valera was silent.

"Go on, monsieur," she continued. "Suppose we accomplish this admirable design, what then?"

"It is impossible to talk to you whilst you are in this humour," repeated Valera. "You turn the most serious subject into a jest."

"Pardon me; I was but demanding information. You ask me to become your wife—I, to whom, as I have just informed you, each moment is precious in the pursuit of an inquiry that affects a name far dearer to me than my own. I wish to know in what manner your proposal is intended to alter my designs? How will a marriage with you further it? Shall I bring my father's accusers to justice any the sooner in consequence? Or will my disguise be rendered less difficult or more effective by the change in my name and position?"

"Of course, if you only look upon my offer in that light," said

Valera, gloomily, "I have nothing further to urge in its behalf. I find you here in England, alone, unprotected, and in an equivocal position. I wish to relieve you of all this."

"By what means, monsieur? By obtaining the legal power to force me to give up my design, and appear in my true character. *Merci!*" and with a mock curtesy she turned away from him.

"*M'amie*, you do me wrong. I love you, love you passionately, and you know it; and I ask you to be my wife. Is there any such insult in that, that you turn round upon me like a tiger?"

"You have hinted at such a contingency more than once before, Tobalito, and I have given you my answer. Don't worry me about it again."

He sighed, and she turned and came back to him.

"Come now, my brother, cannot you be satisfied with my affection as it is? I love you, Christal, more than anyone in the world. What can I say better?"

"But you do not love me in the way I want you to love me, *m'amie*."

The crimson blood flooded Leona's face and brow, and made the light in her eyes glow; but she would not acknowledge she was in the wrong.

"Then you must learn to be satisfied with *my* way, Tobal. Confess, now. Were I in your power, would you be content to let me remain as I am, dressed up to personate an old woman, and perform all sorts of menial offices for Miss Lucilla Evans?"

"*Caramba!* No."

"I have caught you, then, you see, my brother. It is well I am more on my guard than you are. Were I to yield to your wishes, you would upset all my plans, and spoil the hopes of a lifetime. No, Christal, I have chalked out my path, and I shall walk in it without deviating to the right hand or the left. I will *do* nothing, and think of nothing, until I have accomplished the work before me."

"And when it *is* accomplished, *m'amie*?"

"Wait till it is accomplished, Christal."

"Tell me," he said, catching her hand, "will you marry me then?"

Leona paused, and regarded him thoughtfully. "I think not, Tobal. I think that I shall then go back to New York and the profession I love, and be content to keep you as my brother and my very good friend until my life's end."

"You have no heart!" cried Valera, as he flung himself upon the sofa.

"I should have no reason were I to comply with your request, Tobal. Listen to me. There are circumstances—more than I can tell you of now—doubts, surmises, that will prevent my marrying *any one* until they are cleared up—but I heard a carriage stop at the door. I must leave you. It may be the family returned. One word, my brother. You remember your promise and mine. If you attempt to betray me we part for ever."

"I will never betray you, Leona." She threw herself beside him, kissed his hands and his face, and flew out of the apartment.

Christobal rose slowly from his position and followed her example. What was he to think of the wonderful revelations Leona had made to him—of the promise that had been forced from himself? He felt half guilty as he dressed for dinner, and remembered that he could never again meet his host with the same open friendly greeting he had hitherto done. He even questioned whether he ought to remain in the house and accept Mr. Evans' hospitality, while he was cognisant of the dark plot hatching against his respectability. Yet, on the other hand, he had great faith in Leona's perspicuity and judgment, and believed he could trust her not to move in the matter until she was on the right scent. It was all terribly perplexing and confusing though, and Don Valera's absence of mind was noticed by all the party assembled that evening. It was not until an animated discussion commenced concerning the Marquise de Toutlemonde (whom her friends had at last discovered not to be entirely *sans reproche*), and in which the name of the person who occupied his thoughts was introduced, that Valera could bring himself to take any interest in the matter in hand. The Misses Lillietrip—according to their usual custom—had appeared about dinner-time, and been asked to take their places at the table; and they were full of the terrible discovery they had made concerning Madame de Toutlemonde, and which had been patent to all the world except the good simple creatures who gaped, open-mouthed, at the recital.

"My dear Mrs. Evans, I assure you if we had known what we

now know, she never should have entered our house. So shocked as we were when dear Lady Polecat told us—I thought poor Charlotte would have fainted. But it has taught us a lesson. One cannot be too particular in London."

"My dear Miss Lillietrip, you quite surprise me! Whatever is the matter with Madame la Marquise! Such an elegant creature too! Her dresses were quite a picture! I cannot believe anything was wrong. Do speak plainer."

"Well, my dear! I can hardly do so at the dinner-table, you know—and before the gentlemen. But still I have no doubt you can understand. Lord Toffey is a *very intimate* friend of hers, they say, and both her carriages belong to the Baron de Raby."

"Dear me! I think it is very kind of him to have lent them to her," remarked simple-minded Mrs. Evans.

"I wish, if he's got a third to spare, he'd lend it to me," cried Lizzie Vereker, boldly; at which Miss Charlotte opened her eye, and Captain Rivers frowned.

"You can't think of what you are saying," said Miss Lillietrip. "Charlotte and I have been quite hysterical ever since we heard the news. It is so dreadful to think we should have been seen about with such a woman. What will people say? They may take us for the same sort of characters."

"Oh no they won't, depend upon it!" interposed Captain Rivers, quietly. "I wouldn't be afraid, Miss Lillietrip, if I were you. I wouldn't indeed. I am quite sure no sensible person would ever take you and your sister for anything but what you are."

"I'm sure it's very good of you to say so," whispered Miss Lillietrip, much complimented by the captain's faith in her morality. "Old ewes dressed lamb fashion," whispered Lizzie Vereker into Captain Rivers' ear.

"Hold your tongue! You're very naughty. I'm angry with you," he said, in a way that proved they had much advanced in intimacy since we met them last.

"I don't care," pouted Lizzie.

"I'll make you care next time we are alone," he answered confidently.

And Miss Vereker only laughed and looked pleased at the prospect.

"But respecting poor Madame de Toutlemonde," recommenced Mrs. Evans; "I really don't understand what there is wrong about her."

"I think you had better leave the discussion for another occasion," said her husband.

"I'll tell you everything when we are upstairs," said Miss Lillietrip, consolingly.

"But are you sure you're correct? For it seems so hard if there should be a mistake—"

"Begging your pardon for interrupting you, Mrs. Evans," said Captain Rivers, "Miss Lillietrip is not mistaken. The lady she alludes to should never have entered your house. I was astonished when I saw her here. But it was not my part to interfere."

"Well, I am surprised to hear you say so. It was Miss Forrester who introduced her to us, and I thought she was always so particular."

"Miss Forrester is a regular time-server," cried Lizie Vereker, "and particular about nothing so long as her acquaintances give good dinners, and have carriages of which she can make use. Papa always calls her the 'toad-eater.' See how she turned round upon that nice young fellow Valera!"

It was at this juncture that Christobal began to take an interest in the proceedings.

"Hush!" said Captain Rivers to Lizzie, although Lucy Evans was not of the dinner-party.

"I shall not hush, Willy; and you'll be good enough not to order me about, as if I were a baby. He *was* a nice young fellow, wasn't he, Mr. Evans? I thought him most jolly; and his turning out not to be Don Valera; and cutting off just at the very time he was most wanted, has nothing whatever to do with his personal characteristics, has it? I liked him immensely."

"You needn't tell us that. You showed your preference openly enough," remarked Rivers.

"Oh! not half what I did when we were alone. You should have seen us together in the close carriage, Willie."

"My dear Lizzie, I am sure you don't mean what you say," interposed Mrs. Evans.

"Don't I?" said the girl, audaciously. "You never saw your

double, Don Valera, did you?"

"It has yet to be discussed who he is," replied Christobal, evasively.

"He was *so* handsome, Don, and so fascinating. And didn't Madame de Toutlemonde think so—that's all!"

Valera was so much amused at this idea, and evinced his enjoyment of it so freely, that Mrs. Evans became fearful to what extent Lizzie's excitement might not lead her, and proposed an adjournment to the drawing-room.

"I am exceedingly annoyed with you," whispered Captain Rivers to Lizzie as she passed him.

"And I hate you," she rejoined in the same tone. They were engaged to be married by this time, and were, to all appearance, the most quarrelsome couple that had ever proposed to link themselves together for life. They fought and made it up again twenty times a-day in public. But they never fought when they were alone. And for all their contradictions they loved each other the more heartily, perhaps, that there was no false sentimentality mingled with their undoubted affection.

* * * * * *

When Lucilla Evans returned from her drive, languid, dispirited, and fatigued, she found her new attendant in the most orderly of dresses, ready to relieve her of her walking attire, and to wait upon her during the meal, which she now almost invariably took in her own room.

"Mamma told me to tell you, Miss Gibson," she said, as she sent away the third or fourth dish untouched, "that you are to consult your own convenience about taking the air, and that if you have been used to walk at any particular hour, she begs you will continue to do so."

"Your mamma is very good, Miss Lucy; but I should not think of leaving the house so long as I can be of any use to you. What do you propose to do this evening?"

"I'm sure I don't know. Lie here, I suppose, and wish that I was dead!"

"You don't mean that, miss. I was in hopes you would let me

put on you one of your pretty white muslin dresses, and go downstairs to the drawing-room."

"I'd rather stay where I am. They've got a lot of people down there to-night, and Lizzie Vereker and Captain Rivers, and they're always chaffing me, and I hate being chaffed."

"Perhaps you would like Miss Vereker to visit you here instead?"

"No! I'd rather be alone, thank you," but as she said the words, Leona saw a tear steal out of the corner of Lucilla's eye and roll slowly down her cheek. She perceived that the girl was just in that condition when her heart would be most open to the consolation of a sympathetic friend, and determined at once who that friend should be. She did not again mention the subject that appeared so distasteful to Lucilla, but commenced to speak to her on general matters instead; telling her one or two tales of American life, which she affirmed she had heard from a brother-in-law, and which diverted her companion's thoughts to that degree that she had eaten half her dinner before she remembered that she was not hungry. And then Leona opened both doors and windows, and let the evening breeze circulate freely through the rooms, telling her patient (still, of course, second-hand, through the fictitious brother-in-law) that that was the secret of keeping one's health in tropical climates.

"I think we are too much afraid of draughts in England, Miss Lucilla. We live so shut up during the winter, that we cannot persuade ourselves but that a current of air must be dangerous all the year round. Yet, in hot climates, where the doors and windows are thrown open on every side, colds are unknown. It is too little air that gives us cold, not too much."

"It is very refreshing after such a warm day," said Lucilla.

"And you would feel much cooler if you did not lie down, miss. Come, now! try sitting in this arm-chair close by the window, and let me take down your hair, and run the brush through it."

Lucilla had never been so well cared for yet, for Mrs. Evans, with all her solicitude, was too fussy to make a good nurse. But Miss Gibson's hands were so firm and tender, and her voice was so richly modulated, and her conversation so cheerful and animated, that the poor sickly girl could not help feeling the influence of her genial companion. But Leona had another remedy in store for her—to prove more potent she hoped than any of the others. When she guessed that the time had come for the ladies to quit the drawing-room, she proposed to fetch Lucilla a cup of coffee. As she tapped at the drawing-room door and made her request, Mrs. Evans naturally came up to her.

"How is Lucy, Miss Gibson? Is she coming down to-night?"

"May I speak to you for a moment alone, madam?"

"Oh, certainly," replied Mrs. Evans, as she drew Leona aside.

"Miss Lucilla is very well, madam, but she is slightly depressed. She does not feel inclined to join the party in the drawing-room, nor to have any of the ladies upstairs. Yet I think a little company would do her good."

"I think so too, Miss Gibson, but if she won't see anyone, what are we to do?"

"If I might make so bold as to suggest it, madam, perhaps a visit from the doctor might cheer her up a little. I think she might be the better for a soothing draught when she goes to bed too; and if he sat with the young lady for an hour or so he would be able to decide what is best to give her, without mentioning the subject of medicine, to which she seems very averse."

"The doctor! What, Dr. Hastings? There is no objection whatever to his seeing Miss Lucy if she will see him. He has known her from a little child. I will tell him when he comes up from the dining-room."

"If you will allow me, madam, I will save you the trouble as he passes through the hall."

"Oh, by all means, Miss Gibson, if you will be so good, and then you can let him know just what you think she wants. The ladies had better not go upstairs then?"

"I should say not, madam. Miss Lucilla is quiet now, and reading a book, but she has been very hysterical since coming in from her drive."

"Well, I leave her with perfect confidence in your hands, Miss Gibson, for she appears to have taken a great fancy to you. Only, should she want me at any time, just let me know."

And then Mrs. Evans returned to her discussion with Miss Lillietrip on Madame de Toutlemonde's poor battered character, and Leona found her way downstairs.

"Dr. Hastings is just the sort of bluff, manly fellow," she thought to herself, "to knock all the nonsense out of poor Lucy's head that I so unwittingly put into it. She cannot really have liked me. It must have been a delusion. And Dr. Hastings really likes her. So that if by any means in my power I can further this matter, so as to efface the remembrance of the other, I shall not feel quite so guilty about it as I do now."

As the gentlemen issued in a file from the dining-room they found this highly-respectable middle-aged female, in cap and spectacles, waiting for them in the hall. Valera started and coloured as he caught sight of her, and then rushed rapidly upstairs. Mr. Evans stopped and wished her good evening, asking if there was anything he could do for her.

"No, thank you, sir, it is the doctor I want to speak to."

"Nothing wrong with Miss Lucy, I hope."

"Nothing of the least consequence, sir," and then Mr. Evans and the other men felt they were in the way, and left her alone with Dr. Hastings.

"Now, what is it, nurse?" he inquired, as they stood together under the gaslight.

"I have been placed in charge of Miss Evans, sir, and feel responsible for her well-doing. Little as I've seen of her, I can plainly perceive her illness is more of the mind than the body."

"You are quite right there, nurse."

"She is perfectly able, sir, to walk about and come downstairs like the others, but she's moping herself to death instead. She fancies she can't eat, or talk, or exert herself in any way, but it's all fancy. I wished her to have company up in her room this evening, but she refused. But I think it would do her good to see *you*, sir."

"*Will* she see me?" he asked, with a kindling eye.

"I'm sure she will, sir; or at least that I can manage it, if you will give up an hour to her."

"Oh, I'll give as many as you like."

"If you will sit and talk with her whilst I go out for a little while, she'll be forced, as it were, to exert herself, till I come in again. And force is necessary in some cases, sir. And Mrs. Evans sends her compliments to you, and she'll be much obliged if you will do as I say."

"I shall be delighted to oblige Mrs. Evans in anything."

"I told her, sir, that Miss Lucy required a little medicine, just for an excuse, but she wants nothing in reality but a little diversion. She is very sad just now, and her heart will open to any kindness. And I'm sure a little of your lively talk will do her all the good in the world."

"You're a very sensible woman, nurse, and see things in a wonderfully clear light. If we had more nurses like you, there wouldn't be so much sickness in the world."

"And if we had more doctors like you, sir, there wouldn't be so many young lady patients," said Leona, significantly.

Tom Hastings stopped short, and stared at her.

"Bless my soul! Miss Gibson—you don't mean to say—"

"I mean to say, sir, that Miss Lucy doesn't know what she's fretting for, and that it's your business to go and find out."

"And I *will* find out, by Jove!" said Dr. Hastings, as he followed her upstairs.

She took him straight into the room without any ceremony.

"Here, Miss Lucilla, is the doctor come to see you," she said briskly; "and as I'm going out for half an hour to get a little air, he says he will kindly sit with you till I return."

"I can sit by myself, perfectly well," said Lucy, quickly.

"Oh! you'll let me stay, won't you?" asked Tom, as he took her hand; "I will be very quiet, Lucy, and not say a word if you do not wish it, or I will fan you, or read to you. It is better you should not be left alone while your nurse is away."

"Of course it is. She *mustn't* be left alone. It would prevent my ever going out if she were," interposed Leona.

And stealing past the closed door some moments afterwards, she bent her ear to the keyhole, and heard the low-toned conversation that was going on inside, broken occasionally by a soft laugh from Lucilla, with a smile at the success of her stratagem. Only as she passed the drawing-room door on her way downstairs the smile faded from her features, and gave place to a wild look of longing that was much more like pain.

– CHAPTER 28 –

MADAME ANTOINE

Naturally the first means by which Leona tried to find out the address of Rebecca Levitt was through the Post Office Directory. Here she was confronted by the names of nine "Antoines;" naturalised Frenchmen, pursuing their avocations in London. Of these, four were jewellers, two pawnbrokers, one a bird-stuffer, one a perfumer, and one a dentist. She noted the addresses of all of them, but in case the vague account she received from Mrs. Levitt, of Liverpool, should have any truth in it, she determined to try the jewellers first. And since the Evans were talking freely of the chances of leaving town for change of air, she felt she had no time to lose. But after a few days spent in her new situation, Leona experienced no difficulty in getting out to pursue her inquiries. The ladies were only too kind in pressing her to lighten her duties as much as possible. Indeed, so attentive was Mrs. Evans to her slightest wish, that she felt surer each day that, instigated by her husband's commands, her mistress's great object was to keep her content to remain where she was. But with all four of the jewellers Leona failed in her object to discover Rebecca Levitt. To each one she demanded an introduction, in the name and character of Miss Gibson, urging as an excuse that she was the bearer of messages from Madame Antoine's relations, and having unfortunately mislaid the address given her, was compelled to make inquiries on her own behalf. But at each house she received a polite answer in the negative. Two of the jewellers had never been married, none of them had even heard of the name of Rebecca Levitt. Leona began to fear her Liverpool informants had led her altogether astray, or that Madame Antoine had settled in Paris instead of London. Yet if she were above ground she resolved to find her, were she hidden in Paris or Vienna, or any other continental city. She would not call her life her own until she had dragged all that was to be dragged of this secret to the light.

She was returning home one evening after a fruitless interview with the fourth and last jeweller, weary and dispirited. She intended to try the pawnbrokers, bird-stuffer, perfumer, and dentist, but she had little hope of them. And as she neared the house, walking slowly and with a downcast air, Christobal, smoking near the open dining-room window, caught sight of her, and before she could ring the servants' bell, he had opened the hall door. Her first glance at his face brought a flash of pleasure, the next a look of fear. She had grown afraid, from several little encounters they had had on the stair-case lately, lest, in his desire to enjoy her newly-recovered company, he might become careless of the embargo she had laid upon him.

"You should not have done it," she said, in a low tone of warning, as she walked past him into the hall.

"*M'amie*, you will not leave me like this; you will give me a few minutes to myself this evening? Fancy what I must suffer, shut up day after day in the same house with you, and yet unable to exchange a word!"

"It is not safe we should do so," she replied.

"Come into the dining-room for one moment now. It is empty."

"I cannot. I might be discovered there."

"And what then?"

"It would raise suspicion, to say the least of it."

"And you think that I can go on like this, without a word—a kiss?"

"It is absolutely necessary."

"Leona, you are heartless, unfeeling—you care for no one but yourself."

"Perhaps so, Tobal."

"Do not call me by that name! It is a mockery—a falsehood! It means that you love me, whereas you do not care one straw whether I suffer or rejoice."

Her lip trembled, but she answered quietly, "You must think what you please, *mon frère*. I have already given you my reasons for behaving as I do. If, after that, you choose to misunderstand me, I cannot help it."

"You *can* help it, and I will make you," he answered fiercely.

"I think not. You are a Spaniard, and will never break your word; and there is no other way by which you can circumvent my plans."

"Is there not? We will see."

"I am not afraid," said Leona, with apparent indifference, as she left him and went upstairs. But she was not indifferent—far from it. Alone she shed some bitter, burning tears over Christobal's unkindness; but she knew his impetuous nature, which a tender word, or a look, or a kiss from her would set burning like lighted flax, and she dared not indulge herself or him until the time for hardness and endurance was past, and the task she had set herself completed.

It was more difficult to obtain interviews with the pawnbrokers than it had been with the jewellers. The latter were men of substance and position, who were not afraid of what a visitor might require of them; but the hands of the former were not entirely free from dirty work, and they were not sure what business even strangers who came in the garb of respectable men or women, might not have with them. From the first shop Leona was dismissed with a curt and surly negative, which betrayed as much suspicion as it excited; and to the presence of the second M. Antoine, pawnbroker, she could not even gain admittance. He appeared to be the owner of a large establishment—half of which was devoted to the sale of second-hand plate, watches, and jewellery, and half to the mysterious business which is conducted beneath the shadow of three gold balls; but to all her inquiries for the master, she received rough answers to the effect that M. Antoine did not live there, and they had no instructions to give his address to anyone. Yet some instinct made Leona linger about this shop more than she had done about the others. She reiterated her request in the jeweller's department several days consecutively, but without success. She attempted to enter the pawnbroker's part of the establishment, but found the counter so crowded by customers that no one else had any attention paid to them. Then she thought of bringing some article of her own to pawn; and selecting a solid gold chain, which had been handed down to her amongst her mother's things, she presented herself once more at M. Antoine's establishment, and patiently waited her turn to be served. There were two men standing behind the counter. One was a fair-haired young Englishman, the other an undoubted French Jew; and with her first glance at him Leona felt convinced that (notwithstanding the assertions of the shop men that he did not live on the premises) she saw the master of the establishment.

He it was who priced every article that was placed upon the counter; he it was who endorsed the pawn-tickets, and grudgingly paid the money lent; and he it was, in consequence, to whom Leona determined to address herself.

"What can I do for you, miss?" demanded the apprentice, presently, but she put him to one side. "I wish to speak to the master," she said firmly, and something in her dress and manner made him yield to her. He whispered to the old Jew, who immediately turned his keen eyes and gold spectacles upon her face.

"What is your business?" he demanded, abruptly.

"I wish you to value this chain for me, M. Antoine."

The man did not disown the title she gave him, but turned the massive gold links over and over in his hand.

"Three pounds ten," he said presently.

"It is worth five times that money," she answered.

"Well, let us say five pounds then. Will you take it in gold or notes? What name and address?"

"My name is Miss Gibson. I am a friend of your wife, M. Antoine, Rebecca Levitt, that was. You might take that fact into consideration, I think." As she mentioned and rather accentuated the words "Rebecca Levitt," M. Antoine looked up at her, sharply and fiercely—then dropped his eyes again upon the chain he was holding.

"I say I know Madame Antoine," repeated Leona.

"You are mistaken. There is no Madame Antoine," replied the Jew, with closed lips.

As he said the words the fair-haired apprentice flashed one look of surprise from his side the counter. It did not occupy an instant, but it was enough for Leona. She was about to reply, when the heavy swinging doors were pushed slowly open, and the face of a girl, stained, pinched, and dirty in appearance, yet unmistakably of Jewish origin, was thrust timidly into sight.

"Mother's so bad to-night," she said. "She does nothing but cry, and we've had no dinner since the day before yesterday."

"Go to the d—l with you!" screamed the old Jew, in a voice of rage, as he stamped his foot behind the counter. The starved face disappeared as quickly as it had come, but the child still lingered about the outside of the door.

"Charles," said M. Antoine, "go and send that girl away at once. I won't have a lot of beggars hanging about the place."

As Charles crossed the shop to do his master's bidding, and caught Leona's eye, was it fancy, or did he actually wink at her? Whether or not, the expression of his face set all her blood boiling, and made her as anxious to get out of the shop as she had been to get into it.

"Shall we say five pounds for the chain, mees?" continued the pawnbroker.

"Yes, if you cannot let me have more on it. But I wish you would give me Madame Antoine's address."

The old Jew's rage at this second allusion to his supposed wife was comically undisguised.

"I tell you, mees, there is no Madame Antoine. God dam. Am I not to be belief in my own house? There is plenty more of my name. Why should I have a wife because you think I have? Is it not enough that I say no? I cannot bear these questions that have nothing to do with my business. You must take your money, or you must take your chain and go. There is no Madame Antoine in this place that you can see. God dam. It is most provoking to be questioned in this way."

"I will take the money, I think, monsieur" (she foresaw she might need another excuse for worrying the testy little pawnbroker), "and I hope I haven't annoyed you. But you must remember I want news of a friend."

"Well, then, I know nothing of your friend, mees. And here is the money and the ticket; and I wish you a very good day. Charles, see to the business whilst I make a note of this transaction."

And apparently anxious to elude further inquiry, the Jew bolted into an inner apartment, upon which Leona gathered up her money and prepared to depart. The shop was again crowded with applicants for relief, but the fair-haired apprentice managed to waylay her on her road to the door.

"The child will give you the address," he whispered, as she passed him.

Her Father's Name

The child! yes! she had thought of that, but hardly imagined there could be any connection between her and the well-to-do pawnbroker. Now, fearful of losing sight of her, she darted out of the shop like lightning. But there was the poor little attenuated form and starved face still leaning hopelessly against the window-frame.

"What are you waiting here for?" said Leona, kindly.

She was a girl of about thirteen or fourteen years of age. Her face was grained with dirt, and her rough hair was twisted up in an untidy knot at the back of her head; still, as she lifted her black lustrous eyes to meet Leona's glance, it was evident she would have been handsome had she been well cared for.

"I'm waiting to see if father will give me any money for mother. We've had nothing but bread to eat for the last two days, and mother's so ill she can't stir. And he *must* give it, he *must*," she added passionately, while the tears overflowed her eyes and mingled with the dirt upon her cheek.

"But what if he won't?"

"I'll sit here till the policeman comes and orders me on, and then I'll make a row and everybody will hear it, and he'll be obliged to give me something to keep me quiet. The wretch! I hate him!" said the girl vehemently, with a clenched hand in the direction of the door.

"Then M. Antoine is your father?"

"Yes, he is. I wish he wasn't."

"And your mother is Madame Antoine?"

"Of course she is. But father and she haven't lived in the same house for years. She's so bad," continued the child pathetically.

"She's been in bed for weeks."

"May I go and see her with you?"

"What good will that do?"

"I may be able to help her a little. I knew a person of her name many years ago. I think she must be the same. Perhaps she might like to see an old friend if she is in distress."

"Can you get her something to eat?" said the girl, thinking of the main chance.

"That I will, and you too. Let us go and buy it now, and take it home together."

"But you won't like to walk with me."

"Give me your hand and you shall see."

She took the child's dirty hand in hers as she spoke, and led her on, till they should reach the shops they needed. "What is your name? What am I to call you?" said Leona, presently.

"Rebecca. It's mother's name as well as mine."

Leona's heart gave a great bound. She had succeeded in her search at last. Her excitement became so great that she laid in a stock of meat, bread, and groceries, that made the eyes of her strange companion sparkle with astonishment; and then, calling a cab, she told Rebecca to direct the driver where to take them.

The girl gave some address that, in her ignorance of London thoroughfares, conveyed no idea of locality to Leona's brain, and they rattled away together through the hot dusty streets until the cab stopped at the entrance of a dirty purlieu in the back slums of Tottenham Court Road.

"I don't think we can get up here, miss," said the driver as he came round to the door.

"Oh no!" cried the little girl, "but I'll carry the things;" and loading herself with parcels, she tumbled out of the cab, which Leona dismissed, and led the way up a filthy court to the door of a still more filthy-looking house.

"We used to live in a better place than this," she said, apologetically; to her visitor; "but since mother's been so bad she can't work, and there's nothing to pay the rent except what Tommy and I get."

So anxious was Leona to ascertain if she had really hit on the right person at last, that she did not even ask how "Tommy" and her informant earned the money for the rent, but, stumbling after the girl into the dark close passage, asked if she had not better inform her mother first that a lady wished to speak to her.

"All right," said Rebecca; "and you stay here till I come back, miss."

Leona placed her back up against the dirty wall, in order to let the stream of lodgers that seemed constantly passing backwards and forwards go by, and waited the child's return with as much patience as she could. Presently Rebecca came back with the uncouth message: "Mother's very much obliged for the things, but she says, *who are you?*"

"Tell your mother my name is Gibson, and she knew my aunt many years ago at Willowside."

But the effect of this communication was not so satisfactory as it was intended to be. In a few minutes Rebecca returned to say that mother was very sorry, but she was too ill to see anybody that day. Leona felt that she had made a mistake somewhere, and determined to retrieve it. She could not turn her feet away now that she had gained the very threshold, without a sight of Rebecca Levitt.

"Go back," she said to the girl, "and tell your mother that I am very sorry she is ill, but I have something to say that she ought to hear. I have news for her of *George Evans*."

Leona heard the child's shrill voice delivering this second message a couple of storeys above where she stood, and the cry of surprise that followed it. And then Rebecca's unshod feet came flying down the rickety stairs again with double speed, and she called out breathlessly to her new acquaintance:

"Please come upstairs, miss, as quick as ever you can, for mother's took very bad, and she wants to see you directly—this very minute."

And, making her way up the dark steps as best she could, Leona followed her little companion to the bed room of her mother.

– CHAPTER 29 –

THE MYSTERY OF LUCILLA

A group of children was hanging about the doorway to stare at the unusual apparition of a visitor to their mother's dirty room, but Leona, only eager to ascertain if she had really found the person of whom she was in search at last, pushed past them without comment, and followed Rebecca into the apartment. It was meagrely furnished, and the want of fresh air and cleanliness made itself painfully apparent to more nerves than one, but Leona had no eyes except for the bed that stood at the farther end, and the wretchedly-attenuated figure that lay upon it. From the ideal she had built up on the descriptions afforded by Wallis and Mrs. Levitt of Liverpool, and making allowance for the time that had elapsed since they had seen her, Leona had come to picture Madame Antoine as a full-blown, highly-coloured, and coarsely-constituted woman of middle age. And so, under happier circumstances, the poor creature might have become. But sorrow and sickness are great refiners if they are not beautifiers, and they had combined to temper down Rebecca Levitt's country homeliness until she was but a shadow of her former self. Leona could not at first believe that the emaciated woman who leaned upon her elbow staring anxiously into her face, and breathing laboriously with expectation the while, could be the person she desired to see.

"Are you Rebecca Levitt?" she demanded, in a voice of astonishment, too much taken aback to observe her usual caution.

"I *was!*" replied the woman, slowly. "And what business can you have with me, that concerns the dead and gone?"

"You speak of George Evans? How do you know that he is dead and gone?"

A change seemed to come over the invalid's countenance. Her eyes looked wild and troubled.

"They told me so," she answered vaguely, "or else—or else—*how should I be here?*"

At this juncture she glanced at the cluster of children, six or seven in number, hanging, open-mouthed, about the bed, and shuddered.

Leona, with a woman's rapid intuition, guessed her feeling, and, misinterpreting the reason of it, shuddered with her. She thought it indicated that the rumours she had heard in Liverpool were true, and that her father had indeed been married to Rebecca Levitt. She felt she must ascertain the truth if she died for it. And the most powerful means of arriving at it, she knew, would be by the pretence that he still lived, to urge whatever claims he might have upon her.

"He died years and years ago," continued the woman, half inquiringly. "He *must* be dead—they all said so!"

"I fancy I know more about him than you do," said Leona, quietly; "and I have been searching for you for some time to tell you so. Can you send the children away?"

"Go away, all of you, and do not come again until you are told!" exclaimed the mother, sharply; and then, as the door closed upon the dirty, dishevelled, and much disappointed little group, she turned to her visitor, and clutched her hand with feverish anxiety.

"Tell me all! tell me everything!" she exclaimed. "Is George Evans still alive?"

"Had you not better feed the children first, and have something to eat yourself?" said Leona, glancing at the packages she had purchased on the way. "You are weak and ill, and not fit to go through an exciting conversation without taking some nourishment."

"No, no! tell me of him first. I cannot eat or rest till I have heard what you have come to say. *Children!* what are the children compared to *him*—to him? I had a child once; but no matter, no matter! Go on; tell me, is he in England?"

"How could he be in England whilst he is under a charge of murder, Madame Antoine? What did he leave England for except to escape it?"

"But you don't believe he murdered Anson?" demanded Madame Antoine, anxiously.

"*I do not.*"

"No, no; no more do I. But if I had known he was alive; if I were only strong and well, that I might rise and go to him, and tell him all. But I am good for nothing!" she added, with a deep sigh, as she fell back in her bed.

"Madame Antoine—"

"Ah! don't call me by that hateful name."

"I must call you so; you have no other now! You do more than disbelieve that George Evans committed that foul murder; you *know* he did not!"

"Who are you that can read my thoughts!" cried the woman, starting up again with knitted brows. "You told the child your name was Gibson, and you came from Willowside, but I never saw you there."

"Perhaps not! You were only there once yourself, remember, when you took little Lucilla down to Sussex, and placed her under the care of my aunt."

At the mention of Lucilla's name, to Leona's surprise, Madame Antoine began to sob. It was painful to see her rocking herself backwards and forwards whilst the tears oozed through her thin fingers. "Oh, don't speak of it; don't speak of it!" she cried.

"I know it is an unhappy subject, but it is to speak of it I am here this morning. I have been trying to trace you for a long time, Rebecca Levitt, and now that I have found you, you must hear me speak."

"But why? What interest have you in the matter?"

"Every interest possible. I am employed in the Evans family. I know George Evans' daughter."

"What, my darling?" exclaimed Madame Antoine, in a shrill voice, as she grasped Leona's arm, "Have you seen my child?—my lover's child? Oh, tell me how she is—how she looks!"

"I think you have mistaken my words," replied Leona, now scarcely less agitated than her companion. "I did not know you had ever had a child—besides the ones I saw here this moment."

"Why should I be ashamed to tell of it, now when I am dying so rapidly that I do not know from day today whether the next will not prove my last? Yes, I *had* a child, of which George Evans was the father, and I was proud of it—proud of it and of him—proud to know that I belonged to them both. Now think of me what you will." And as she concluded Madame Antoine cast herself down upon the bed, and buried her face in her hands.

Leona placed her hand upon the prostrate woman's head. Why should she not? She was pure and upright, and honourable herself, and the creature she pitied might have that to disclose to her that would ruin her life's happiness; but she was a woman, sick and suffering; and her father, whose memory, whatever wrong he might have done her, Leona could never cease to love and cherish, had honoured her with his preference—perhaps with his name—therefore was she sacred in the eyes of his faithful daughter.

"Do not touch me," murmured Madame Antoine, as she writhed beneath the pressure of her visitor's hand.

"Why should I not? Believe me that I wish to be your friend—that I came here for no other purpose."

"I am not worthy!"

"No one is worthy of any good that heaven sends him if we

look at it in that light. But come now, Madame Antoine, let me tell you the reason for which I have found you out. Your suspicions with regard to George, Evans are correct. *He is dead!*"

The woman made no exclamation of surprise or suffering at the news. She only writhed again, with her face still hidden, and uttered a low moan.

"But he has left a child behind him—not yours, but another," said Leona, observing the start occasioned by the reference. "And it is on behalf of that child, who is in sore need of your assistance, that I traced you to your home."

"What child?—what child?" muttered Madame Antoine. "He had no child but mine."

"Not when you knew him, perhaps, but afterwards. He left this country, as you know, under a false and cruel charge of murder, and settled in a foreign land, where after a while he married. It is this daughter who has now come to England to claim justice for her father's name, and asks you to help her in clearing it. Will you not listen to her for the sake of the love you bore him?"

But the effect of this announcement was very different from what Leona had anticipated. Dying and deserted as she was, all the woman was yet strong within Madame Antoine's breast, and her first burst of grief was not for the certainty of her lover's death, but the news that he had forgotten her for another.

"*Married!*" she exclaimed in so strong a voice that Leona could scarcely believe it was the same as that in which she had spoken hitherto. "George married! Oh my God! why did I ever let him leave me? Why did I ever let them make me believe that he was guilty? I was strong and young then—I was free to go where I chose—and I loved him as never woman loved a man before! My handsome, noble, good-hearted, George! The father of my child! Why didn't I leave everything and follow him? I wanted to do so. I was nearly mad because they wouldn't let me; but they held me back and threatened me, and told me he was a murderer, and I believed them until it was too late—too late. And it has ended in this; and he forgot me, forgot me, and married another woman! Oh! every minute will be an age now until death comes to release me from this pain!"

"I don't think he forgot you, madame," said Leona, gently.

"George Evans never forgot anyone who loved him, but he was in a strange land, alone and unhappy, and he was bound by no legal ties to you."

"We were bound by our love and our child to one another."

At this admission Leona's heart gave a great bound of thankfulness, but she continued calmly: "We must not judge of men's feelings by our own, madame. George Evans doubtless loved you very dearly, but he believed that you, in common with the rest of the world, had condemned him as a criminal, and that he should never see you more. And he needed the solace of affection and sympathy, and when it came to him in the shape of a woman's love, it is hardly to be expected he should have resisted it."

"And then he died," murmured Madame Antoine.

"And then he died—very unhappily, very miserably—and his last injunction to his daughter was that she should strive by every means in her power to clear his name from a wicked calumny that had embittered all his life. And it was with that view she came to England, and it is with that view asks for your assistance now, to help her by telling all that lies in your power concerning that unhappy business."

In her anxiety to make an impression on her companion's mind, Leona had somewhat dropped the artificial tone she naturally adopted, and it rang out so full, clear, and youthful as to rouse all Madame Antoine's suspicions as to her identity.

"You have deceived me!" she said quickly. "Your name is not Gibson, who are you?"

"*I am George Evans' daughter!*" cried Leona with a sudden impulse, as she pulled off her glasses, bonnet, and wig, and threw herself on her knees beside the bed, "and I have come here to-day to say to you: 'Rebecca Antoine, you loved my dead father better than you did yourself! Help me to clear his name from this foul charge that he may look down and bless us both from heaven!'"

The woman gazed at her for a few moments almost in alarm, then seizing her face between her two hands, she gazed at her features as though she could never look at them sufficiently.

"*His* eyes," she exclaimed, with an hysterical gasp, "*his* mouth, *his* brow! Oh my George, my George, my George! How much I loved him! And he is dead, and you are his child; *his* child, as much as mine is. Oh, kiss me, kiss me for his sake! and if I die for it you shall know *all!*"

She opened her arms as she spoke; and as Leona felt herself folded within them, she believed her battle was won.

"Can you help me?" she cried.

"I will tell you *everything*. What does it signify now? He is dead; my oath is no longer binding. And I would never have taken it, had I not thought my George was gone for ever. Oh, you are so like him! What is your name?"

"Leona; it is a foreign name. My mother was a Brazilian."

"Don't talk to me of your mother. Tell me of your father—of yourself. When did he die, and where?—my brave, handsome George! And did he speak of me and of the child—the dear child they took from me?"

"I will tell you everything you wish to know if you will eat something first," said Leona, glad to be able to waive an awkward question; for never, so far as she knew, had a thought of poor Rebecca Levitt crossed her father's mind. "You are exhausted with this exciting conversation, and will be unable to continue it without sustenance. These poor children, too. They looked so hungry. Let me feed them and yourself first, and then I will tell you all I know of my poor father's life and death."

"You will not leave me?" said Madame Antoine, anxiously.

"I will not, indeed. I will remain with you until you have no further need of me," replied Leona, who felt she had entered on a mission she must fulfil until the end, whatever that end might be.

"Then do as you think best," said the dying woman, as she fell back exhausted on her pillows. Leona, having first resumed her disguise, went to the door, and called back the poor starving little children, who were only too eager to respond to her invitation. Her heart was beating rapidly with expectation the while, but the true womanly instinct that was ever uppermost in it prevented her from wanting anything at that particular moment so much as to see those hungry little ones fed. It was good to watch the avidity with which they seized upon the food which her forethought had provided for them, and the delight with which, after having satisfied the first keen pangs of appetite, they carried the remainder away to have a feast upon the stairs; on which Leona left all further care of them to the eldest sister, and directed her attention more particularly to their mother, who appeared to be in the last stage of consumption. On seeing her considerably revived by the administration of some warm arrowroot, which she mixed herself and made warm for her over a neighbour's fire, Leona ventured to ask Madame Antoine how she came to find the wife and children of a man so well off as the pawnbroker in so pitiable a condition of poverty.

"Your friends at Liverpool, from whom I obtained the first traces of your address, seemed to imagine you were in the most flourishing circumstances."

"Let them continue to think so," gasped Madame Antoine. "It is for that reason that I have held no communication with them for years!"

"But has there been any quarrel between your husband and yourself, that he thus neglects you and the children?"

"No open quarrel, but a suspicion which he will never forgive. I slaved for him for fifteen years, and he turned me and the children out of the house, and has barely allowed us sufficient money to keep life in us since."

"And what was this suspicion, madame, if I may ask the question?"

"You shall hear it in due course. Am I to tell you my story first, or will you tell me yours?"

"If you do not mind, let me hear what you have to say first. I have already been several hours away from home, but I do not feel as if I could leave you until you have told me all you know concerning the murder of Abraham Anson."

"I will do all for you in my power, for to-morrow maybe too late. Come nearer, that I may not have to raise my voice more than is necessary."

– CHAPTER 30 –

LEVITT'S CONFESSION

Leona drew her chair closer to the bedside and Madame Antoine laid her hands on hers.

"You are so like him—so very, very like him! It seems almost as if the days of my girlhood had come back again, and he was sitting by my side and talking to me. Ah well! perhaps I shall see him before long. Who knows?"

She was silent for a minute, and then went on.

"What I have to tell you involves more names than one! but if it injured all the rest of the world I would disclose it for the sake of benefiting my George's child. You are his child—you are not deceiving me?"

"Why should I deceive you? Do not my features speak for themselves?"

"Oh yes, they do! I might doubt your tongue—I cannot doubt your eyes! My dear, the blame of Anson's murder was thrown on your dear father's shoulders to screen the real culprit."

"And he was—?"

"Wait, and let me tell you in its proper turn. When George and Henry Evans were lads of seventeen and eighteen, I was a rosy-cheeked girl of the same age, and my father, Richard Levitt, was employed in their uncle's firm as clerk, Mr. Anson being the cashier. I need not make this part of my story long, my dear. Your father was handsome, and thoughtless, and fascinating, and I was a motherless girl with a hard father, and took every opportunity of escaping from home to meet my lover, and the result of it was that shortly after my seventeenth birthday I found I was likely to become a mother. Ah! I shall never forget the terror of that time. I believed that if my father were to find it out he would kill me, and I was half dead with fear and misery. Well, George stood up for me, young as he was, with the courage of a lion. He sent me straight away to some good people in the country, who nursed me through my confinement, and then he went to my father, and told him the whole story from beginning to end, and begged him, for my sake, to keep it quiet for a little while."

"'And what do you mean to do for the girl now you've ruined her?' says my father."

"'I mean to marry her,' says George boldly. Ah! how often I've heard the story repeated. It seems as if I had listened to every word. 'How can you marry at your age without your uncle's consent?' says my father."

"'I don't mean directly, but as soon as I'm a man, and able to choose for myself,' replies George. 'Don't be afraid that I shall forget Rebecca, Mr. Levitt, for I love her, and I mean to do the right thing by her.'"

"'And what's to become of the child meantime?' roared my father. (Oh, he was a violent, passionate man to deal with!) 'You don't suppose my daughter can come back to Liverpool with a brat at her back, and keep her character, do you?'"

"'I have provided for that,' said George. 'I will take the child if you will receive Becky back, and let her live with you until I can marry her.'"

"Well, so it was settled. I suppose my father thought the chance of my marrying a gentleman too good to be missed; and so long as the child was not allowed to burthen him, he cared little about my feelings at parting with it. My poor baby was left at the farmhouse, in charge of the people who had nursed me, and I came back to Liverpool, and no one, except George and my father, were the wiser for the reason I had stayed away. Things went on then much as usual. I wasn't happy, for I fretted after my baby; and my father took to bullying poor George in a way that was very hard to submit to, considering the difference in their stations. So then he became wild, and my father was always bringing me home tales of his extravagance and his riotings, and the bad company he kept, and upbraiding me for my past conduct with him, until I was regularly miserable, and used to tell George that I'd rather go away at once, and work for my child's living and my own, than be subjected to such treatment. I think the dear lad was afraid I might leave him if I hadn't some tie there, and so, unknown to all but me, he sent for my baby from the country (she was a great girl of eighteen months old by that time), and made arrangements for her being kept in Liverpool, where I might see her now and then, and comfort myself with thinking of the time when we should all live together.

"Now, Mr. Anson was a great friend of George's, and had stood up for him to old Mr. Evans, the uncle, times out of mind. He was a widower, a quiet, kind sort of man, who had rooms over the offices of the firm, and kept the keys of the till, and had everything of value there under his charge; for the partners trusted him as if he had been one of themselves. He had often sent poor George money out of his own purse, and had still oftener persuaded Mr. Evans to advance his nephew some; for the thought of me and my father's wrong had weighed on the poor boy's mind, as I told you before, and had driven him to be very reckless and extravagant, and he seemed always in debt. Well, one day, I remember it as well as if it were yesterday, George came up to me and said:

"'Who do you think has promised to look after the child for me, Becky? Why, Anson! Isn't it jolly of him? He's told the governor that it belongs to his late wife, and he wants to have it to live with him, and the governor's given him leave to do so. And there it can be, as snug as possible, till you and I can marry and claim it, and he's going to call it Lucy Anson, so that—'"

"*What!*" cried Leona, darting from her chair, and interrupting Madame Antoine's narrative, "is Lucy Anson my father's daughter and yours?"

"Lucilla was her name. I called her Lucilla after my poor mother. To be sure she is. Heaven bless her! But where have you heard of her before?"

"Did I not tell you that I am living with Henry Evans?—that I am acting the part of hired attendant on your daughter, that I am, in fact, nursing, dressing, and waiting on *my own sister!*"

At this piece of intelligence Madame Antoine became much excited.

"I asked you the question before," she said, "and thought that you denied it. Oh! tell me how she is—what she is like! I have not seen nor spoken to her for years—for *her* sake, that she might know of no shame connected with me, but I have never forgotten nor ceased to dream of her. She was so fair and white, with golden hair and blue eyes. The sight of these children's eyes makes me shudder when I remember hers—my George's child!"

Leona may have thought in her own mind that the dark piercing orbs that M. Antoine had transmitted to his little family, were more to be admired than Lucilla's sickly washed-out blue eyes; but she kept her opinion to herself. It was evident that for poor Madame Antoine, as for many another of her sex, life had ended when she lost her first lover.

"Lucilla has not strong health," said Leona kindly, "but she has every luxury and convenience, and Mr. and Mrs. Henry Evans love her as if she were their own daughter. Are they aware that you are her mother?"

"Oh yes! Henry Evans knew it from the beginning. His brother had no secrets from him; and after the child went to live with Mr. Anson, they used to speak of it openly amongst themselves. Indeed, I am afraid we were too open; for after a while my father found out whose baby it was, and threatened both Anson and George with exposure if the latter didn't fulfil his promises and marry me off-hand. Anson tried to keep peace between them. He thought it would be a very bad thing for George to marry without old Mr. Evans' consent, and I've thought since that he hoped by delay to prevent his marrying me altogether, for of course he ought to have looked much higher than the daughter of his uncle's clerk. But to the last, George always held to it that, sooner or later, he would do me justice. But the end came only too soon. I think my little Lucy was about three years old, and my father had been more than usually violent and overbearing in his talk, when one morning we heard the dreadful news that poor Anson had been found murdered in his office, and that George had disappeared from Liverpool. Of course it made a great commotion. There was an inquest and a coroner's jury, and they brought in a verdict of 'Wilful murder' against my poor George, and the police were out after him in every direction, but he never turned up. I was half mad, as you may well suppose, my dear, with fear for him and misery for myself, but no one heeded me in the general disturbance. My father was the chief witness on the inquest, and he deposed to there having been high words between Anson and George the night before the murder, and threats having passed between them. But it was one of those cases that seem as if they must remain a mystery for ever; only, as George had runaway, all the suspicion was directed against him. As soon as I ascertained the dreadful rumour I had heard was true, my first thought was for my baby; but when I went to fetch her from Mr. Anson's house, regardless of what anyone might say, I found that she had been already removed by old Mr. Evans. I went up to the great house, frantic with anxiety, and told him all my story, which he had already heard from Mr. Henry. The old gentleman was very good. He was more cut-up than he liked to-show at George's disappearance, and he didn't say one word of reproach to me—only he wished to keep the child and bring it up for his nephew's sake. I cried, and said I couldn't part with it; but they talked me over between them, and persuaded me it would be for my little daughter's good; so I let her go to Willowside to Mrs. Gibson's care, and I took her down there myself, and after that I think I went well-nigh crazy with grief. I hoped against hope that my lover would return, or that his name might be cleared from blame, but neither happened. Then—after some five years or so—my brother William, who had runaway to sea the same night that poor George left home, turned up again very queer in his mind (he had always been strange from a lad), and my father took to his bed and died, leaving me a sealed letter, with strict injunctions not to open it till ten years had elapsed from the day of his death, unless George Evans returned to England before that time. Old Mr. Evans was dead too, then, and Mr. Henry had married, and adopted my little Lucy as his own child, and George had never been heard of, as you know. So, being sick of my life in Liverpool, I left it and came to London, where I fell in with Antoine and married him, thinking that a comfortable home might help to make me forget the past. But it didn't. My husband proved to be a miser, and each child was a source of misery to him because it was a source of expense. He was trying to get rid of me and them from the beginning, and he seized the first opportunity to turn us out of doors. When ten years had elapsed from my father's death, I opened the letter he left me. I had not been very curious on the subject before, but I little thought what it contained. Child! *The murderer of Abraham Anson was my own father, Richard Levitt.*"

"*Madre di Dios!*" cried Leona, lapsing into herself in her surprise. "And he could let *my* poor father bear the onus of his own crime for so many years! He was a double murderer, madame. He killed

George Evans as well as Abraham Anson."

"Do you think *I* have not felt this as deeply as yourself? Do you think I have not cursed the author of my being for his perfidy and sin? When I read that letter, I raved openly about it. My husband heard (for the first time) of my former conduct, and swore he would never have anything to say to me again. He drove my children and myself from his doors, and has supported us on the barest pittance the law can force him to allow us since. And even now, when he knows that I am dying, he has no pity."

"But the letter? Have you got it still? Did you never make any effort to clear your lover's name by means of it?"

"I would have, had I imagined he was alive, or had left anyone to share his supposed disgrace. But fifteen years had passed since he left England so mysteriously, and not a word had been heard of him, except through my brother Bill, whose intellect had quite given way. So I thought it best, for the sake of all concerned, to say no more about it. The past was past and almost forgotten. To revive it might have afforded satisfaction to the Evans family, but it would have injured my child, and shed irretrievable ignominy on my dead father. So, for their sakes I was silent; and I should have gone down into my grave had you not come, with your father's face and your father's smile, to remind me that I owe him a duty before I go to meet him again."

"You will give me the letter?" said Leona, earnestly.

"You shall take it for yourself. It is at the bottom of that writing-desk, and here is the key. A piece of parchment tied with a green ribbon. It is properly signed and attested. No question can be raised as to its validity."

Leona seized the paper, which she found as indicated, and tore it open. It was a full confession of the crime, written and witnessed in a regular clerk-like form. After the usual opening formula, it went on to describe the manner in which the murder had been committed:

"I had been very uneasy in my mind for some time past"—so ran the confession—"about my daughter Rebecca. Mr. George Evans had promised me over and over again to marry her, and I believe that he would have done so except for Mr. Anson, who was always preaching patience to me, and dissuading the young man from doing anything in a hurry, for fear of offending his uncle. And Mr. George was getting very wild too, and was always betting and playing at cards, and losing money in various ways, which didn't look to me like settling down into the married state. On the day of the accident"—it was remarkable that throughout this statement the word "*murder*" was never once used with regard to Anson's death—"I had had an interview with George Evans, and we had parted bad friends. I had reproached him with want of faith to my girl, and to me, and had threatened to go straight up to his uncle and tell him the whole story, as I had threatened Mr. Anson only the day before.

"George swore that want of money was the only thing that prevented his marrying Rebecca, and that he should call on Anson again that evening, and see what could be done about it. I didn't half believe his statement, seeing he had so often trifled with me before, and when the night fell, I took my lad Bill, who was a strong, lusty fellow, though never over bright in his intellect, and walked up to Anson's rooms.

"I had a good thick stick with me, and so had Bill; for I was getting tired out with excuses and puttings off, and I just meant, if George Evans wouldn't come to terms, to give him a jolly good thrashing, and nothing more.

"When we got, up then, we found the gentlemen together, but George had had more than enough liquor, and was in a very excited condition. I stated my case, and explained my terms, but Anson had been talking to George beforehand, and persuading him to leave Liverpool and let me do my worst, and he seemed quite to have veered round and taken up his friend's opinion. They talked big at me, both of them, and dared me to bring forward my daughter's claims, and Anson called her by a name that set all the blood in my body on fire. So I fell upon him. I hardly know how it happened, but I suppose I must have cracked him on the skull, for he went down like a shot and never spoke again.

"George was too drunk, apparently, to know what had happened, but I did: and when he came dancing towards me and making a noise, I felt his blustering must be stopped for the moment, and I gave him just such another crack and silenced him.

"Then Bill—poor fool!—sat down and blubbered, and I had

time to think what was best to do. It was early in the morning, about two or three o'clock (for we had sat up arguing for hours before this happened), and I knew that whatever I did I must do quickly, before the daylight appeared. I turned over Anson's body—it was already beginning to grow stiff.

"'Bill,' I said, 'have you a mind to be hanged?' The poor fool stopped blubbering at this, and looked up, trembling with fright.

"'What do you mean?' he asked.

"'Why, I mean just this—that the crack of your stick has killed Anson, and if you don't want the police after you in another hour or so, you must help me to carry Evans quietly away.'

"Poor Bill hadn't enough sense to remember if he had hit the clerk or no, so he became all anxiety for his own safety.

"'What am I to do, father?' he said, shaking from head to foot like a leaf.

"'Help me drag Evans out into the passage first. There, that will do. Now you keep by him and wait for me.'

"I crept back again into the office, where we had been quarrelling together. The till was open, and some coin was scattered on the table. Anson had evidently been in a mind to help George when he came in. I gathered up all I could; not that I wanted it, but that there might seem to have been a motive for the accident; gave Anson's body two or three more cracks to make them believe there had been a struggle, and left it, face downward, on the floor. Then I joined Bill in the passage, and between us we managed to set Evans on his feet and drag him out into the street; though what with the blow and the liquor, he was so stunned that he understood nothing of what was going on. It was some distance from the offices to my house, which was near the docks, but we only met one policeman on the way.

"'Is he ill?' he asked, alluding to George.

"'Ill,' I replied. 'He's so jolly drunk he can't stand.'

"'Where are you taking him to?'

"'Home, to be sure. He's my son.'

"'Very good. Look after him though, or I shall have to do it for you.'

"'If you like to take the trouble off my hands you're welcome,' I said. I knew he wouldn't.

"'Not I,' he answered laughing; 'there's plenty of work for me without begging for it. Good-night to you.'

"And that was the only chance of detection we ran whilst going home. When we arrived there I took good care Evans shouldn't recover his senses too quickly. I had plenty of beer in the house, and brandy and snuff; and between them all I kept on plying him with hocused liquor till he was as insensible as a log. Then I made my plans with Bill, and saw that he thoroughly understood them. There was more than one ship lying in the docks, ready to start in the course of a few hours for New York. I got Bill to go aboard one of them with the first dawn of light, taking George with him (still all but insensible), and representing themselves as two brothers (one nearly sick to death) going out to find work in America. I taught him how to go on plying Evans with liquor till they should get well out to sea, and when he recovered, how to make him believe that in a fit of intoxication he had come to high words and blows with Anson, who had been found dead; and that I, finding that suspicion directed against him, had got him shipped off from Liverpool under a feigned name in order to save his life. The plan succeeded entirely. The young man left Liverpool, and by the time that the accident came to light, there was no trace left of anyone but George Evans having been seen with Mr. Anson. I felt safe, too; for I knew that, even did George Evans venture to return and brave a trial for his supposed offence, it was not in his power to fix the guilt upon Bill or myself, supposing he were sensible enough to remember we had been there. But he never came back, and five years afterwards poor Bill turned up, with the little sense he had been born with completely knocked out of him. Whether it was the fright of that night, or the terror of discovery, or the weight of the secret, I can't say; but he was brought home by a chance acquaintance, unable to recognize anybody except his sister Rebecca, or to do more than speak his own name; so what happened with regard to himself and George Evans after they left England I never heard. I expect, as likely as not, though, he died in America; and I hope he may have done so, and will never come back to worry my poor daughter, who has had trouble enough on his account, heaven knows. I sent away all the money I took from the till with Bill and George, so that nothing suspicious could be found upon my person; and I had worked for the firm for so many years, and borne so respectable a character, that it would have been strange if they had doubted me. On the contrary, Mr. Henry Evans took the bastard child my daughter had borne to his brother and adopted it as his own, as some sort of amends, I suppose, for the wrong that had been done to poor Becky. For some years I was very well contented that all should have turned out as it did (for no one could have helped the accident that occurred to poor Anson); but now that I feel I am not the man I was, and the doctors tell me I am breaking up, I think it is as well to write out this statement, in case George Evans should come back to England after I'm dead and gone, and get into trouble for want of it. I shall leave it to the care of my daughter Rebecca, with strict injunctions not to read it till ten years after my death; and when she does I hope she'll try to think as little hardly of her father as she can, and remember that what he did he did for her sake, and in the desire to avenge the injury that had been done her."

Here the confession ended.

– CHAPTER 31 –

THE FULFILMENT OF THE OATH

Leona read the confession through from the first word to the last, with trembling, eager haste, and when she had finished it she bowed her head upon her knees and cried bitterly. "Think as little harshly of him as you can," said Madame Antoine, imploringly. "He repented before he died; I am sure of it, or he would never have left this statement to ruin his character after death."

"Of what avail was his repentance," replied Leona, as she lifted her tear-stained face from the shelter of her hands, "since he refused to do justice to the living? Has it prevented *my* father from dragging out a life of purgatory in exile, and sinking at last into a suicide's grave? Hear *my* story now, Madame Antoine, and judge if it be possible for me to say from my heart that I forgive your father even in another world."

Her Father's Name

With all the powers of her elocutionary and dramatic art, Leona then proceeded to unfold her history to the ears of Madame Antoine, who listened, and wept, and lamented over the unhappy life and miserable death of her lost lover. But as Leona proceeded to describe her own resolution to avenge her father's wrongs and clear his name from an undeserved infamy, and to tell of the various disguises she had assumed, and the journeys she had taken to that end, her companion's grief was swallowed up in amazement, and she could only congratulate herself that Leona's ingenuity had led her to her abode before it was too late to assist her.

"I have never felt such peace since George disappeared as I do now," said Madame Antoine, as Leona's narrative concluded. "I am going rapidly. In a few days at the outside, all the cares of this world will be ended for me, and I shall meet him again where there is no misunderstanding and false accusations, and be able to tell him that I was the means of comforting his daughter's heart, and rewarding her courage, before I died."

"You have comforted me beyond measure," cried Leona, enthusiastically. "All the trouble of the past years seems as nothing now, and all the blankness of the future obliterated. My father's name will be purified again, and he will sleep quietly in his unknown grave. You have been his good angel and mine."

"Yet had it not been for me all this misery would never have occurred."

"But you loved him, madame, and could not foresee the end. Love covers a multitude of sins."

"You speak feelingly, my child. You have a lover of your own," said Madame Antoine with a look of scrutiny.

Leona blushed scarlet.

"Indeed I have not, nor do I know what it is to love in that way. My dear father has been my sole thought both before and after his death."

"And you have no friends?"

"Very few."

"Ah! that I might have lived to be your friend and mother."

"You have been my best friend, madame."

"And you mine. What would these poor starving little wretches have done without your help to-day? How little I ever thought I should live to receive charity at the hands of George Evans' daughter!"

"You are not hurt at so receiving it, I hope. Think that I am my father's messenger, and that his spirit sent me here to you. I owe everything to you. The oath to which my life was dedicated has been accomplished through your assistance. My heavy task is ended, and I can return to my own occupation with a peaceful mind. Why, when I am so much your debtor, should you shrink from sharing the little I possess so long as we both have need of it?"

"If you really are my debtor," cried the dying woman, as she grasped her hand, "free yourself from the claim by one act of charity."

"What is that?"

"Let me see my daughter once more—bring my Lucilla to my bedside that I may kiss her before I die."

The tone of entreaty in which this request was made, was so urgent that Leona had not the heart to combat it, though at the same time she had no idea how, with Mr. Evans' prejudices, the deed was ever to be accomplished.

"You are silent," said Madame Antoine, "you will not do it for me. Oh! think how strong a mother's claim is! How small a recompense a few minutes' interview is for a life of silence and separation!"

"I remember it all, and my greatest wish at present is to afford you this gratification. I am only thinking how to accomplish it. You must not forget that I am in Mr. Evans' household in the capacity of a servant, and have no voice in any of the actions of his adopted daughter. Lucilla believes that I am the niece of the old lady to whose care she was confided at Willowside. So do her aunt and uncle; and my supposed knowledge of her parentage and the family disgrace are the only claims I possess upon their patronage or protection."

"But you will not keep up this disguise for ever? Surely a day will come when you will disclose your identity to Mr. Evans as you have done to me?"

"I will disclose it to-morrow, upon one condition."

"And that is—?"

"That I may place this confession in his hands, to prove to him that my father was not a murderer."

"Oh, not before I am gone!" exclaimed Madame Antoine, shrinking from the shame of exposure. "Let me go in peace, it cannot be long first, and then tell them what you choose."

"Then I see no means of bringing Lucilla and you together. I can have but one plea to make to my uncle on your behalf—that your courage has cleared the honour of his dead brother. Give me leave to make this statement public, and I will engage to bring my sister to your side."

"I agree," said Madame Antoine, faintly, "to anything—to everything—only let me see my child again."

As Leona drove rapidly from Madame Antoine's lodging to the house in Hyde Park Gardens, she forgot everything except her long-looked-for success. She was no more the Leona of Brazil—the actress of New York; she was ready to rush into her uncle's presence with the precious document she held in her hand, and proclaim in one breath her own identity and her father's innocence. She lost sight of her disguise and the necessity for not relinquishing it too suddenly; she only remembered that she was herself, and her hot generous blood would inevitably have led her into some most awkward predicament, had she not been rudely recalled to a sense of her position by one of her supposed fellow-servants. She had been so oblivious of the flight of time during her visit to Madame Antoine, that it was evening before she reached the Evans' house. Dinner was evidently over, and the moving figures of the men-servants in the dining-room, seen clearly through the open window, showed that they were clearing the table. One of them came to the door in answer to Leona's knock.

"*You'll* catch it," he remarked, ominously, as she entered the hall. (Perhaps, had he known what a young and pretty woman he was addressing, he might have worded his warning more politely.) "Why, there's been a dinner party here tonight, and the whole house has been turned upside down looking for you to dress Miss Lucilla. I shouldn't wonder if you get warning tomorrow for being absent without leave."

"A dinner-party! I quite forgot it," cried Leona.

And with the remembrance came upon her the thought of her

disguise, and the character she must still assume.

"The orders was that you was to go to the drawing-room as soon as ever you came in," continued the man.

"Very well," replied Leona, preparing to go upstairs.

"And I'd sooner be I than you," said James as a parting shot, as he returned to the dining-room. This little colloquy had recalled our heroine to herself. *This* was not the moment to make her discovery known. With a room full of strangers, and without previous warning, she would have great difficulty in making her story understood, yet she chafed at the delay. She felt as if she could not keep the truth to herself another moment. She wrenched the prim gray front that covered her thick chestnut curls (now grown to a tolerable length again) from side to side impatiently, and twisted the bows of the cap that surmounted it out of all shape and decency. She renovated her wrinkles and crow's-feet with a vigour that made them caricatures, and replaced her spectacles, without so much as a second glance to see if she looked natural or not. As she entered the drawing-room, Mrs. Evans and several of the ladies present looked up at her with surprise. The paint and powder on her face were so apparent that her mistress thought at first that she must have been indulging in a drop too much. But unabashed and indifferent to general opinion, Leona made her way up to Lucilla's couch. The guests were not astonished to see her enter, for Miss Evans' chronic weakness was so well known that it was usual to see her maid in attendance on her.

"So you have come at last?" remarked Mrs. Evans, in a significant tone, as the supposed Miss Gibson approached her daughter's side.

"Yes. I am sorry I forgot the dinner-party, but I have been detained," was Leona's cool reply. Mrs. Evans felt indignant.

Les nouveaux riches are always more ready to take umbrage at anything like inattention on the part of their servants, than those who have been accustomed to be waited on all their lives, but even she felt this was not the place or time to make her anger apparent.

"You had better see if Miss Lucilla requires anything, now you have come," she rejoined, sternly, as she moved away amongst her guests. Leona drew nearer to Lucilla's couch; the, girl was occupied, and did not perceive her. But one person did; and that one was

Christobal Valera. Leona's eye had singled his figure out directly she entered the room; and as the door opened to admit Miss Gibson, he had known that it was she, and each heart had trembled and turned faint beneath the knowledge of the presence of each other.

Christobal was seated by Lucilla's couch, apparently occupied in destroying her fan. He had not spoken to Leona since the last conversation related to have taken place between them, but had confined his attentions whilst in her presence entirely to Miss Evans, greatly to the annoyance of Dr. Hastings, who hovered about his patient and her new cavalier with perturbed and jealous countenance.

Leona stood some little way apart, and watched them. Christobal saw that she was watching, and redoubled his efforts to appear absorbed in the conversation he was carrying on with Lucilla. This was his method of punishing Leona for her disregard of his wishes; it has been a favourite mode of punishment with lovers for many centuries past, but it has not lost its power, nor perhaps ever will. You may argue, and reason with, and persuade a woman as much as lies in your power, and find her obstinate; but once let her see you turn your attention to another, let her imagine her influence weakened, her attractions failing, her kingdom threatened, and, whether she love you or whether she love you not, she will use her keenest weapons with which to win you back to her side. A woman with a worshipper is a dog in the manger. She may not choose to take him herself, but she will not let another have him; and this propensity, born of selfishness and vanity, has too often led the sex into serious error; for, sooner than lose a subject, they will accept a ruler, and the change is more sudden than they care for afterwards.

Leona was no exception to the rest of womankind. From her childhood she had been accustomed to the adoration of Christobal Valera, and not a thought had ever entered her head that it would be withdrawn from her. She had rejected his proffered love again and again, simply because she believed that it would be always at her disposal. She had heard him swear times out of mind that she was and ever would be the only woman in the world for him, and her feminine vanity found no difficulty whatever in crediting the statement. She had been playing with the young Spaniard's heart for years, as an angler plays with his line, but she had never seriously contemplated the possibility of a life passed without him, at all events in the capacity of a friend or a brother, as she loved to call him. And that he should attempt even to dally with another woman appeared to her incomprehensible, unnatural, unjust.

Yet now she had to stand in her assumed capacity of servant, and listen to the half-whispered nonsense he was breathing into her employer's ear. And not only to listen, but to fall so completely into the snare as to believe that it was real. What will not a woman believe to torture herself withal when her fears and her jealousy are once aroused? She drew as near to the sofa as she dared, so as to intercept the compliments which were bringing so bright a flush to Lucilla's pale cheeks, and causing her to stammer and hesitate in her replies. She seized every opportunity that offered of addressing her young mistress, and asking if she felt too warm, if her cushions were comfortable, if she should fetch her something to drink? And Lucilla, unwilling to have her conversation with the handsome Spaniard interrupted, answered with short impatient negatives, that made Valera glance up at Leona with a look as though she were intruding. The girl's blood boiled. She felt as though it were impossible to stand by and endure it any longer—this monopolisation of her one friend by the daughter of Rebecca Levitt. But then all that that daughter represented as the adopted child and heiress of Henry Evans flashed across her mind; and she acknowledged, with a sort of desperate pang, that since his proposals of marriage had been rejected by his first love, Lucilla would prove no unenviable match for the ambitious but impecunious Valera. His birth was unexceptionable, and his identity undisputed; and, as in her own case, Mr. Evans might tell him that his daughter's happiness was the first consideration, and she had money enough for them both.

A great ball rose in Leona's throat—she felt as if she were choking.

"The evening begins to feel chilly, Miss Lucilla," she said presently, anxious to break, if only for a moment, that whispered conference, which her jealous heart was translating with the most absurd exaggerations; "had I not better put this shawl about your shoulders?"

"Oh no! I'm as warm as possible," rejoined the girl. "I don't want anything, Gibson. You can go." And then, after a moment's pause, seeing that her suggestion had not been complied with, she turned round and reiterated the words.

"Did you not hear me tell you to go, Gibson? There is no occasion for you to remain here. I'll ring if I want anything."

And Leona had no alternative but to turn round and quit the drawing-room, leaving Christobal Valera seated in an attitude of adoration at the feet of Lucilla Evans. She did not see the look of longing his dark eyes cast after her—she did not hear the sigh that broke from him as she disappeared from view. She only knew she had left him there, and the thought made her desperate. She felt like a tigress about to be robbed of her whelps, and the golden light gleamed fitfully in her eyes and made them dangerous. She ran upstairs with the agility of twenty. It was well for her that no one met her on the way, though she had become indifferent to what people might think or say, as was proved by her next actions. As soon as she had reached the privacy of her own room, she locked the door, and pulling off her dress and apron, cap, wig, spectacles, and all the minutiae that constituted her disguise, she washed off the paint and powder that disfigured her beautiful face, brushed back the thick curls from her forehead, and arrayed herself in the attire in which she had gone down to Brighton. Then she stood before the mirrors, fresh, youthful, and glowing, with the deep crimson flush still mantling on her cheek that had been called up by Christobal's apparent desertion. She was not thinking now of her father's innocence, or her own identity. She was only bent upon discovering herself for the sake of laying an open claim to Valera's friendship and sympathy, and to divert his attention from her half-sister. She no longer stayed to consider the inexpediency of the place as the occasion. Had royalty itself been present, it would not have deterred her from her purpose. Impulsive, energetic, and determined as these pages have ever represented her to be, and kindling with the new passion awakened in her breast, Leona would have walked through fire to attain her object. As soon as she had once more transformed herself from the prim old-maidish Miss Gibson to the glorious creature heaven had made her, she went deliberately downstairs again. Her intention had been to go into the dining-room and thence summon a servant to usher her amongst the company; but as she reached the landing, she encountered one of the footmen engaged in clearing away the remains of some light refreshment.

"Announce me to your mistress," she said imperiously.

The man stared at seeing a stranger descend from the upper storey, but he had no idea of her identity, and no right to question the order given him.

"By what name, miss?" he demanded in surprise.

"Miss Leona Evans," she answered steadily, and accordingly the drawing-room door was thrown open, and "Miss Leona Evans" was shouted in that peculiar tone adopted by the London footman who desires to make himself heard above the clamour of a chattering crowd. The mere entrance of an unexpected guest at that hour would have created a commotion, but as the owners of the house heard the sound of their own name, and turned to watch the advent of this beautiful, stately, and foreign-looking stranger, their astonishment knew no bounds.

Mr. Evans advanced towards her bowing, with a formal questioning smile that told its own story, but Leona prevented the need of explanation by going straight to the point.

"Good evening, uncle," she said, holding out her hand, "I am your niece, Leona Evans, the daughter of your brother George."

Had a hand-grenade been suddenly cast in the midst of the company it could not have caused more consternation. The rumour about "Brother George" was known to most of the guests, and the mere mention of his name had a visible effect upon both Mr. and Mrs. Evans.

"My brother George," stammered her uncle. "We have not heard of him for many years. We supposed that he was dead."

"He *is* dead," replied Leona, solemnly. "But he has left *me* behind him to be a living witness of the purity of his life, and the falsehood of the cruel slanders that caused his death. And if you do not believe my word, uncle, ask Don Christobal Valera, who has known me from my birth, and knew my dear father for many years, if what I have spoken is not the truth. Tobal, you will not desert me in this extremity."

As she turned her beseeching face towards him, Valera, who had sprang to his feet directly she had entered the room, came towards her.

"Desert you, Leona," he said, reproachfully. "How can you wrong me by putting the question? Mr. Evans, what this lady has told you is correct. She was born and brought up in the same part of the Brazils as myself, and she is the daughter of your dead brother, George Evans."

"But how long have you been in England? If this is the case, why did you not come to see us before," demanded Mr. Evans, still incredulous.

"I *have* been to see you before, uncle," replied Leona archly (she had fast hold of Valera's hand by this time, and could afford to be playful). "Have you forgotten the boy who called himself Christobal Valera, and disappeared so mysteriously from your house; and Miss Gibson, who waited on your adopted daughter, Lucilla?"

"Don Christobal—Miss Gibson—what have they to do with you?" said Mr. Evans, still more mystified.

"I am the false Don Valera—I am Miss Gibson," replied Leona. "I assumed those disguises for the purpose of entering your house. Forgive me, uncle! I know it was not a worthy part to play, but I had a purpose which trampled down every other consideration before it."

"What purpose?"

"The clearance of my dead father's name from the foul charge of a murder which he never committed. Uncle, he lived and died under that suspicion, but I knew him to be innocent, and I swore an oath over his dead body that I would prove him so."

"And you have done it, Leona?"

"I have done it! I hold in my hand the written confession of Richard Levitt, the real murderer, and as soon as I obtained it, I resolved to make myself known to you. I ought, perhaps, to apologise to this company," continued Leona, her native courtesy returning to her as the chief load was lifted from her mind, and she looked at the wondering faces that surrounded her, "for having broken up their intercourse by the introduction of my own affairs; but they will forgive a daughter's anxiety to clear away the foul stain that rests upon the memory of a beloved parent. And since the wrong done to my father was a public wrong, the reparation should be made public also."

"*George innocent!*" exclaimed Mr. Evans, in a bewildered, wondering manner. "My *dear* brother's name cleared from guilt! And you are his child? I see it now—his likeness in every feature. Leona, let me embrace you for his sake." And then the heroic daughter received the first instalment of her reward in finding herself folded in her uncle's arms.

"You forgive me for all my deception, uncle," she whispered.

"*Forgive you*, dear child! I bless you for adopting any means by which to arrive at this most happy conclusion. Oh Leona! I loved him very, very dearly. I have never got over our cruel separation. But this is a subject of which I cannot speak to you now."

The guests began to find out it was time they should return home, and no one had the duplicity to ask them to remain. Family explanations and reconciliations are best carried on in private, and in a few minutes the large rooms, were cleared of all but those who were residing in the house. Then Leona felt she might give the reins to her tongue, and her recital was as efficient as it was rapid.

"Here is the proof, uncle," she said in conclusions as she placed Levitt's confession in his hand. "I leave it with you, I know that you will take all means to make it public."

"And from whom did you procure it, Leona?"

"From Rebecca Levitt—now Rebecca Antoine."

"She is still living then?"

"She is still alive, but her days will be very few; and she has one great and earnest desire to be fulfilled before she dies, uncle."

"And that is—?"

"To be able to see her daughter—my father's child, once more!"

Mr. Evans glanced uneasily at Lucilla, who was standing near with her somewhat weak glance fixed wonderingly upon her new cousin, as she supposed Leona to be. It was evident that she had never been informed of the secret of her parentage.

"Do you think it would increase the happiness of Rebecca Levitt's child to be made acquainted with her mother?"

"Uncle! that is for you to decide. I only promised to use my influence with you to procure the dying woman this last pleasure, in return for the service she has done my father's memory."

"We will speak on the subject further tomorrow, Leona," replied Mr. Evans. "Meanwhile, let me assure you how happy it makes me to acknowledge you as my niece. The world little knows how deeply I have mourned my beloved brother's loss. I have hoped against hope that he might be restored to us, or some news heard of him or his descendants, but I little thought the fulfilment of it was so near at hand. To prove to you that what I say is true, I have never touched the principal of that portion of my fortune which should have been George's, and came, instead, to me; but have laid it up carefully against the possibility of his return, and left it in my will, to any one of his legitimate posterity that might be forthcoming to claim it. This money will be yours, Leona, not at my death, but now. I look upon you as a second daughter. You shall not be worse dowered than Lucilla."

"Oh, uncle, how I have misjudged you!" exclaimed Leona, as she again embraced him."

"And so this gentleman has known you from your childhood?" remarked Mr. Evans presently, as he directed his attention to Christobal; "and was the friend and pupil of my dear brother. Let me welcome you over again, and with double measure for that reason, Don Valera. And what relation do you call yourself to my niece here? Brother, eh, or bosom friend?"

Leona glanced up shyly at Christobal. His dark eyes rested upon hers, glowing with passion, and imploring her to name the relationship between them. She could not misunderstand their language nor resist it, and her heart prompted her to reward him at last for all his patient, faithful love to her.

"Don Christobal Valera is my affianced husband, uncle," she answered simply, as she stretched forth her hand and felt it clasped as in a vice between his own.

"If I permit Lucilla to visit Madame Antoine, will you engage that the fact of her being her mother is not revealed to her, Leona?" said Mr. Evans, the next morning as they sat together in the study discussing all the wonderful disclosures of the night before.

"I should think Madame Antoine would be ready to agree to the terms, uncle, and I can but go into the room first and see," replied Leona.

"On these conditions she may go, but I think it most advisable that the secret of her birth should not be revealed to her. She is not strong, physically or mentally, and I cannot anticipate what effect such a revelation might have on her. Added to which, I may tell you, Leona, that Dr. Hastings, who has been a friend of our family for many years, and is a man in whom I have implicit confidence, has proposed to me for Lucilla—(ah, you rogue! I little thought the reason you fought so shy of the honour of taking her in this very study a few weeks ago!)—and I think he has every chance of succeeding in his suit. He is thoroughly fond of the girl, and understands the management of her health, so he is by far the best husband she could have. I have told him, of course, whose child she really is, and he has no objection to her on that score, but agrees with me that she had better be left in ignorance of the fact. Still, if it will give this poor dying woman any comfort to see Lucilla, it is one we have no right to deny her."

"I think not, uncle, and I have no doubt Madame Antoine will see the matter in a proper light also."

But here she sighed.

"You are disappointed yourself," said Mr. Evans. "You would doubtless have been glad to welcome a sister in my dear girl."

"No, uncle, I did not sigh for that. I can show Lucilla quite as much affection as a cousin as I could as a sister; and I shall be with her but a little while, after all."

"What! Will not Don Valera and you take up your residence in England?"

"Oh no, uncle; at least not yet. Do not forget that I have been brought up in the free woods, or the atmosphere of the stage, and the close air and cramped manners of your great city stifle me. I feel as if I could not breathe in London, nor move, nor speak. Tobal and I will visit Spain first, and then return to New York, and pursue our former avocations. We should not be happy else."

"I am disappointed," said Mr. Evans. I hoped to keep you by my side."

"By-and-by, perhaps, uncle; in a few years, when we have grown older and more sedate; but for the present let us have our way.

And you have Lucilla, remember, to be with you always."

* * * * * *

That afternoon, the carriage conveyed Leona, Lucilla, and Dr. Hastings to the abode of Madame Antoine.

Mr. Evans had thought it better they should go alone. He had no wish himself to see Rebecca Levitt again and thought that the sight of himself might revive recollections in her breast that would militate against the reserve he was desirous she should maintain before her daughter. Lucilla had been told nothing more than than a poor woman, who had been her nurse when a baby, was dying, and wished to see her once again. She had opened her pale blue eyes in surprise at the announcement, but had not thought it necessary to make any further inquiries on the subject; and her gratified reception of Dr Hastings' attention whilst on the way there, showed how little she thought of the importance of the expedition. Leona watched her with amazement and a little disgust, and felt relieved to remember that it was not considered advisable she should claim her as a sister. With Lucilla Evans, any man who paid court to her was the right man; and she would be as happy in the future with Dr. Hastings as she would have been with anybody else. She was a phase of womanhood that made Leona anything but proud of belonging to the sex. But Tom Hastings was content, so no one had a right to be otherwise.

They arrived at the dilapidated-looking row of houses in due time, Lucilla making many a remark at the strangeness of papa's behaviour in sending her on such an errand. Leona, according to pre-arrangement, ascended the stairs first alone.

She reached the door, she stopped at it, and receiving no answer, went in. On the floor sat the dirty children, playing at such games as took their fancy; at the table sat the eldest girl with some woman, a neighbour summoned on the occasion; on the bed lay a figure, covered with the sheet on which it had lain.

Rebecca Levitt could never now disclose the relationship she bore to the young lady, dressed in silks and laces, flirting with Dr. Hastings in the carriage below.

She was dead, taken out of this sphere of misery and

disappointment, to one where, it is to be hoped, a true heart counts for more than many a marriage-ring.

THE END

Appendix A - Extract from Maria Edgeworth's *Belinda*

"The same kind friends who showed her my epigram, repeated to me her observation upon it. Harriet Freke was at my elbow, and offered to take any *message* I might think proper to Mrs. Luttridge. I scarcely thought her in earnest, till she added, that the only way left, nowadays, for a woman to distinguish herself, was by spirit; as every thing else was grown 'cheap and vulgar in the eyes of men.' That she knew one of the cleverest young men in England, and a man of fashion into the bargain, who was just going to publish a treatise 'upon the Propriety and Necessity of Female Duelling,' and that he had demonstrated, beyond a possibility of doubt, that civilized society could not exist half a century longer without this necessary improvement. I had prodigious deference for the masculine superiority, as I thought it, of Harriet's understanding. She was a philosopher, and a fine lady—I was only a fine lady—I had never fired a pistol in my life; and I was a little inclined to cowardice; but Harriet offered to bet any wager upon the steadiness of my hand, and assured me that I should charm all beholders in male attire. In short, as my second, if I would furnish her with proper credentials, she swore she would undertake to furnish me with clothes, and pistols, and courage, and every thing I wanted. I sat down to pen my challenge. When I was writing it, my hand did not tremble *much*–not more than my lord Delacour's always does. The challenge was very prettily worded I believe I can repeat it.

"'Lady Delacour presents her compliments to Mrs Luttridge–she is informed that Mrs L—— wishes she were a man, that she might be qualified to take *proper* notice of lady D——'s conduct. Lady Delacour begs leave to assure Mrs Luttridge, that though she has the misfortune to be a woman, she is willing to account for her conduct, in any manner Mrs L—— may think proper—and at any hour and place she may appoint. Lady D—— leaves the choice of the weapons to Mrs L——. Mrs H. Freke, who has the honour of presenting this note, is lady Delacour's *friend* upon this occasion.'

"I cannot repeat Mrs Luttridge's answer; all I know is, it was not half as neatly worded as my note; but the essential part of it was, that she accepted my challenge *with pleasure*, and should do herself the honour of meeting me at six o'clock the next morning —that miss Honour O'Grady would be her *friend* upon the occasion—and that pistols were the weapons she preferred. The place of appointment was behind an old barn, about two miles from the town of ———. The hour was fixed to be early in the morning, to prevent all probability of interruption. In the evening, Harriet and I rode to the ground. There were several bullets sticking in the posts of the barn: this was the place where Mrs Luttridge had been accustomed to exercise herself in firing at a mark. I own my courage 'oozed out' a little at this sight. The duke de la Rochefoucault, I believe, said truly, that 'many would be cowards if they dared.' There seemed to me to be no physical, and less moral necessity for my fighting this duel, but I did not venture to reason on a point of honour with my spirited second. I bravadoed to Harriet most magnanimously, but at night, when Marriott was undressing me, I could not forbear giving her a hint, which I thought might tend to preserve the king's peace, and the peace of the county. I went to the ground in the morning, in good spirits and with a safe conscience. Harriet was in admiration of my 'lion-port:' to do her justice, she conducted herself with great coolness upon the occasion; but then it may be observed, that it was I who was to stand fire, and not she. I thought of poor Lawless a billion of times, at least, as we were going to the ground; and I had my presentiments, and my confused notions of poetic justice—but poetic justice, and all other sorts of justice, went clear out of my head, when I saw my antagonist and her friend actually pistol in hand, waiting for us: they were both in men's clothes. I secretly called upon the name of Marriott with fervency, and I looked round with more anxiety than ever Bluebeard's wife, or 'Anne, sister Anne!' looked to see if any body was coming: nothing was to be seen, but the grass blown by the wind. No Marriott to throw herself *toute éplorée* between the combatants—no peace-officers to bind us over to our good behaviour—no deliverance at hand—and Mrs Luttridge, by all the laws of honour, as challenged, was to have the first shot. O, those laws of honour! I was upon the point of making an apology, in spite of them all, when, to my inexpressible joy, I was relieved from the dreadful alternative of being shot through the head, or of becoming a laughing-stock for life, by an incident, less heroic, I'll grant you, than opportune. But you shall have the whole scene, as well as I can recollect it—*as well*—for those who, for the first time, go into a field of battle, do not, as I am credibly informed, and internally persuaded, always find the clearness of their memories improved by the novelty of their situation. Mrs Luttridge, when we came up, was leaning, with a truly martial negligence, against the wall of the barn, with her pistol, as I told you, in her hand. She spoke not a word—but her second, miss Honour O'Grady, advanced towards us immediately, and, taking off her hat very manfully, addressed herself to my second. 'Mistress Harriet Freke, I presume, if I mistake not.' Harriet bowed slightly, and answered, 'Miss Honour O'Grady, I presume, if I mistake not.' 'The same, at your service,' replied miss Honour. 'I have a few words to suggest, that may save a great deal of noise, and bloodshed, and ill will.' 'As to noise,' said Harriet, 'it is a thing in which I delight, therefore I beg that mayn't be spared on my account; as to bloodshed, I beg that may not be spared on lady Delacour's account, for her honour, I am sure, is dearer to her than her blood; and as to ill will, I should be concerned to have that saved on Mrs Luttridge's account, as we all know it is a thing in which she delights, even more than I do in noise, or lady Delacour in blood—but pray proceed, miss Honour O'Grady; you have a few words to suggest.' 'Yes, I would willingly observe, as it is my duty to my *principal*,' said Honour, 'that one, who is compelled to fire her pistol with her left hand, though ever so good a shot *naturally*, is by no means on a footing with one who has the advantage of her right hand.' Harriet rubbed my pistol with the sleeve of her coat, and I, recovering my wit with my hopes of being witty with impunity, answered, 'Unquestionably:—left-handed wisdom and left-handed courage are neither of them the very best of their kinds, but we must content ourselves with them *if* we can have no other.' 'That *if*,' cried Honour O'Grady, 'is not, like most of the family of the *ifs*, a peace-maker. My lady Delacour, I was going to observe, that my principal has met with an unfortunate accident, in the shape of a whitlow on the fore-finger of her right hand, which incapacitates her from drawing a trigger; but I am at your service, ladies, either of you, that can't put up with a disappointment with good humour.' I never, during the whole course of my existence, was more disposed to bear a disappointment with good humour, to prove that I was incapable of bearing malice; and to oblige the seconds, for form's sake, I agreed that we should take our ground, and fire our pistols into the air. Mrs Luttridge, with her left-handed wisdom, fired first—and I, with great magnanimity, followed her example. I must do my adversary's second, miss Honour O'Grady, the justice to observe, that in this whole affair she conducted herself not only with the spirit, but with the good-nature and generosity characteristic of her nation. We met enemies, and parted friends.

"Life is a tragicomedy! Though the critics will allow of no such thing in their books, it is a true representation of what passes in the world; and of all lives, mine has been the most grotesque mixture, or alternation, I should say, of tragedy and comedy. All this is apropos to something I have not told you yet. This comic duel ended tragically for me. 'How?' you say. Why, 'tis clear that I was not shot through the head; but it would have been better, a hundred times better for me, if I had; I should have been spared, in this life at least, the torments of the damned. I was not used to priming and loading—my pistol was overcharged—when I fired, it recoiled, and I received a blow on my breast, the consequences of which you have seen—or are to see.

"The pain was nothing at the moment compared with what I have since experienced. But I will not complain till I cannot avoid it. I had not, at the time I received the blow, much leisure for lamentation; for I had scarcely discharged my pistol, when we heard a loud shout on the other side of the barn, and a crowd of town's people, country people, and hay makers, came pouring down the lane towards us with rakes and pitch forks in their hands. An English mob is really a formidable thing. Marriott had mismanaged her business most strangely—she had, indeed, spread a report of a duel—a female duel—but the untutored sense of propriety amongst these rusticks was so shocked at the idea of a duel fought by women *in men's clothes*, that I verily believe they would have thrown us into the river with all their hearts. Stupid blockheads! I am convinced that they would not have been half so much scandalized if we had boxed in petticoats. The want of these petticoats had nearly proved our destruction, or at least our disgrace—a peeress, after being ducked, could never have held her head above water again with any grace. The mob had just closed round us, crying, 'Shame! shame! shame!—duck 'em, duck 'em—gentle or simple—duck 'em—duck 'em'.

(Oxford: Oxford World's Classics, 1998), pp. 54-58.

Appendix B - Extract from Sarah Grand's *The Heavenly Twins*

Angelica considered a little, and then she answered, hesitating as if she were choosing each word: "I see where the mistake has been all along. There was no latitude allowed for my individuality. I was a girl, and therefore I was not supposed to have any bent. I found a big groove ready waiting for me when I grew up, and in that I was expected to live whether it suited me or not. It did not suit me. It was deep and narrow, and gave me no room to move. You see, I loved to make music. Art! That was it. There is in my own mind an imperative monitor which urges me on always into competition with other minds. I wanted to *do* as well as to *be*, and I knew I wanted to do; but when the time came for me to begin, my friends armed themselves with the whole social system as it obtains in our state of life, and came out to oppose me. They used to lecture me and give me good advice, as if they were able to judge, and it made me rage. I had none of the domestic virtues, and yet they would insist upon domesticating me; and the funny part of it was that, side by side with my natural aspirations was an innate tendency to conform to their ideas while carrying out my own. I believe I could have satisfied *them*—my friends—if only they had not thwarted me. But that was the mistake. I had the ability to be something more than a young lady, fiddling away her time on useless trifles, but I was not allowed to apply it systematically, and ability is like steam—a great power when properly applied, a great danger otherwise. Let it escape recklessly and the chances are someone will be scalded; bottle it up and there will be an explosion. In my case both happened. The steam was allowed to escape at first instead of being applied to help me on in

Appendix B

a definite career, and a good deal of scalding ensued; and then, to remedy that mistake, the dangerous experiment of bottling it up was tried, and only too successfully. I helped a little in the bottling myself, I suppose, and then came the explosion. This is the explosion,"—glancing round the disordered room, and then looking down at her masculine attire. "I see it all now," she proceeded in a spiritless way, looking fixedly into the fire, as if she were trying to describe something she saw there. "I had the feeling, never actually formulated in words, but quite easy to interpret now, that if I broke down conventional obstacles—broke the hampering laws of society, I should have a chance—"

"It is a common mistake," the Tenor observed, filling up the pause.

"But I did not know how," she pursued, "or where to begin, or what particular law to break—until one evening. I was sitting alone at an open window in the dark, and I was tired of doing nothing and very sorry for myself, and I wanted an object in life more than ever, and then a great longing seized me. I thought it an aspiration. I wanted to go out there and then. I wanted to be free to go and come as I would. I felt a galling sense of restraint all at once, and I determined to break the law that imposed it; and that alone was a satisfaction—the finding of one law that I could break. I didn't suppose I could learn much—there wasn't much left to learn,"—this was said bitterly, as if she attached the blame of it to somebody else—"but I should be amused, and that was something; and I should see the world as men see it, which would be from a new point of view for me, and that would be interesting. It is curious, isn't it?" she reflected, "that what men call 'life' they always go out at night to see; and what they mean by 'life' is generally something disgraceful?" It was to the fire that she made this observation, and then she resumed: "It is astonishing how importunate some ideas become—one now and then of all the numbers that occur to you; how it takes possession of you, and how it insists upon being carried into effect. This one gave me no peace. I knew from the first I should do it, although I didn't want to, and I didn't intend to, if you can understand such a thing. But my dress was an obstacle. As a woman, I could not expect to be treated by men with as much respect as they show to each other. I know the value of men's cant about protecting the 'weaker' sex! Because I was a woman I knew I should be insulted, or at all events hindered, however inoffensive my conduct; and so I prepared this disguise. And I began to be amused at once. It amused me to devise it. I saw a tailor's advertisement, with instructions how to measure yourself; and I measured myself and sent to London for the clothes—these thin ones are padded to make me look square like a boy. And then, with some difficulty, I got a wig of the right colour. It fitted exactly—covered all my own hair, you know, and was so beautifully made that it was impossible for any unsuspicious person to detect it without touching it; and the light shade of it, too, accounted for the fairness of my skin, which would have looked suspiciously clear and delicate with darker hair. The great difficulty was my hands and feet; but the different shape of a boy's shoes made my feet pass; and I crumpled my hands up and kept them out of sight as much as possible. But they are not of a degenerated smallness," she added, looking at them critically; "it is more their shape. However, when I dressed myself and put on that long ulster, I saw the disguise would pass and felt pretty safe. But isn't it surprising the difference dress makes? I should hardly have thought it possible to convert a substantial young woman into such a slender, delicate-looking boy as I make. But it just shows how important dress is."

The Tenor groaned. "Didn't you know the risk you were running?" he asked.

"Oh, yes!" she answered coolly. "I knew I was breaking a law of the land. I knew I should be taken before a police magistrate if I were caught masquerading, and that added excitement to the pleasure—the charm of danger. But then you see it was danger without danger for me, because I knew I should be mistaken for my brother. Our own parents do not know us apart when we are dressed alike."

"Oh, then there *are* two of you?" the Tenor said.

"Yes. I told you. They call us the Heavenly Twins," said Angelica.

"Yes, you told me," the Tenor repeated thoughtfully. "But then you told me so many things."

"Well, I told you nothing that was not absolutely true,"

Angelica answered—"from Diavolo's point of view. I assumed his manner and habits when I put these things on, imitated him in everything, tried to think his thoughts, and looked at myself from his point of view; in fact my difficulty was to remember that I was not him. I used to forget sometimes—and think I was. But I confess that I never was such a gentleman as Diavolo is always under all circumstances. Poor dear Diavolo!" she added regretfully; "how he would have enjoyed those fried potatoes!"

The Tenor slightly changed his position. He only glanced at her now and then when he spoke to her, and for the rest he sat as she did, with his calm deep eyes fixed on the fire, and an expression of patient sadness upon his face that wrung her heart. Perhaps it was to stifle the pain of it that she began to talk garrulously. "Oh, I am sorry for the trick I have played you!" she exclaimed with real feeling. "I have been sorry all along since I knew your worth, and I came to-night to tell you, to confess and to apologize. When I first knew you all my *loving consciousness* was dormant, if you know what that is; I mean the love in us for our fellow-creatures which makes it pain to ourselves to injure them. But you re-aroused that feeling, and strengthened and added to it until it had become predominant, so that, since I have known you as you are, I have hated to deceive you. This is the first uncomfortable feeling of that kind I have ever had. But for the rest I did not care. I was bored. I was always bored: and I resented the serene unconcern of my friends. Their indifference to my aspirations, and the way they took it for granted that I had everything I ought to want, and could therefore be happy if I chose, exasperated me. To be bored seems a slight thing, but a world of suffering is contained in the experience; and do you know, Israfil, I think it dangerous to leave an energetic woman without a single strong interest or object in life. Trouble is sure to come of it sooner or later—which sounds like a truism now that I have said it, and truisms are things which we habitually neglect to act upon. In my case nothing of this kind would have happened"— —and again her glance round the room expressed a comprehensive view of her present situation—"if I had been allowed to support a charity hospital with my violin—or something; made to feel responsible, you know."

"But surely you must recognize the grave responsibility which attaches to all women—"

"In the abstract," Angelica interposed. "I know if things go wrong they are blamed for it; if they go right the Church takes the credit. The value attached to the influence of women is purely fictitious, as individuals usually find when they come to demand a recognition of their personal power. I should have been held to have done my duty if I had spent the rest of my life in dressing well, and saying the proper thing; no one would consider the waste of power which is involved in such an existence. You often hear it said of a girl that she should have been a boy, which being interpreted means that she has superior abilities; but because she is a woman it is not thought necessary to give her a chance of making a career for herself. I hope to live, however, to see it allowed that a woman has no more right to bury her talents than a man has; in which days the man without brains will be taught to cook and clean, while the clever woman will be doing the work of the world well which is now being so shamefully scamped. But I was going to say that I am sure all my vagaries have arisen out of the dread of having nothing better to do from now until the day of my death—as I once said to an uncle of mine—but to get up and go to bed, after spending the interval in the elegant and useless way ladies do—a ride, a drive, a dinner, a dance, a little music— trifling all the time to no purpose, not even amusing one's self, for when amusement begins to be a business, it ceases to be a pleasure. This has not mended matters, I know," she acknowledged drearily; "but it has been a distraction, and that was something while it lasted. Monotony, however luxurious, is not less irksome because it is easy. A hardworking woman would have rest to look forward to, but I hadn't even that, although I was always wearied to death—as tired of my idleness or purposeless occupations as anybody could possibly be by work. I think if you will put yourself in my place, you will not wonder at me, nor at any woman under the circumstances who, secure of herself and her position, varies the monotony of her life with an occasional escapade as one puts sauce into soup to relieve the insipidity. Deplore it if you will, but don't wonder at it; it is the natural consequence of an unnatural state of things; and there will be more of it still, or I am much mistaken."

Again the Tenor changed his position. "I cannot, *cannot* comprehend how you could have risked your reputation in such a way," he said, shaking his head with grave concern.

"No risk to my reputation," she answered with the insolence of rank. "Everybody knows who I am, and, if I remember rightly, 'That in the captain's but a choleric word which in the soldier is rank blasphemy.' What would be an unpardonable offence if committed by another woman less highly placed than myself is merely an amusing eccentricity in me, so—for *my* benefit-conveniently snobbish is society. Since I grew up, however, I find that I am not one of those who can say flippantly, 'You can't have everything, and if people have talents they are not to be expected to have characters as well.' Great talent should be held to be a guarantee for good character; the loss of the one makes the possession of the other dangerous. But what I do maintain is that I have done nothing by which I ought in justice to be held to have jeopardised my character. I have broken no commandment, nor should I under any circumstances. It is only the idea of the thing that shocks your prejudices. You cannot bear to see me decently dressed as a boy, but you would think nothing of it if you saw me half undressed for a ball, as I often am; yet if the one can be done with a modest mind, and you must know that it can, so can the other, I suppose."

The Tenor was sitting sideways on his chair, his elbow resting on the back, his head on his hand, his legs crossed, half turned from her and listening without looking at her; and there was something in the way she made this last remark that set a familiar chord vibrating not unpleasantly. Perhaps, after the revelation, he had expected her to turn into a totally different person; at all events he was somewhat surprised, but not disagreeably, to perceive how like the Boy she was. This was the Boy again, exactly, in a bad mood, and the Tenor sought at once, as was his wont, to distract him rather than argue him out of it. This was the force of habit, and it was also due to the fact that his mind was rapidly adapting itself to a strange position and becoming easier in the new attitude. The woman he had been idolizing was lost irretrievably, but the charm which had been the Boy's remained to him, and he had already begun to reconcile himself to the idea of a wrong-headed girl who must be helped and worked for, instead of a wrong-headed boy.

(Michigan: Ann Arbor, University of Michigan Press, 1992), pp. 450-455.

Appendix C - Hysteria   Louise Benson-James.

All symptoms of hysteria have their prototype in those vital actions by which grief, terror, disappointment, and other painful emotions and affections are manifested under ordinary circumstances and which become signs of hysteria as soon as they attain a certain degree of intensity... The nature of the peculiar constitution predisposing to hysteria has to this day been a matter of controversy.

The truth is, that there is no such thing as a peculiar constitution of the body pre-disposing to hysteria. It is rather the mental constitution which exercises an all-powerful influence in the production of this disease.

Women whose sensibility is blunt never become hysterical, ... hysteria may occur, and actually does occur, in women of all ranks and orders. It is frequent in the higher classes of society, in ladies who lead an artificial life, who do nothing, who are very apt to go into hysterics at the slightest provocation.

Julius Althus, 'Lecture on the Pathology and Treatment of Hysteria: Delivered at the Royal Infirmary for Diseases of the Chest' *British Medical Journal* 10 March 1866, pp. 245-248.

There are perhaps few terms so difficult to define as spinal irritation, for the gradations from hysteria to this state are extremely easy; and, indeed, it will have been seen that in the foregoing chapter most of the patients complained of pain in the spine, and that there was more or less functional disturbance in all of them. The term is also used so freely and vaguely that great caution is necessary in attempting to explain its meaning. Dr Handfield Jones's term, 'Spinal Paresis' seems to me an excellent one; by it he means 'a state in which, without demonstrable organic change, there is greater or less enfeeblement of the functional power' of the spinal cord. The sensory or motor power may be affected, but rarely both together.

The cause of spinal irritation, or paresis, may be defined in one word—'debility,' this debility is always, or almost always being due to inhibitory irritation.

This state of things may give rise to wide and varied disorders, all the symptoms of which are asthenic in their character, and all of which are marked by extreme nervous prostration.

Without doubt, for all authors agree on this point, one of the most prominent causes is peripheral irritation of the pudic nerve, producing undue exhaustion.

It is difficult to say how this is produced, but most probably it is that, owing to the intimate commissoral connections between the lumbar enlargement of the cord where the pudic nerves are implanted (they themselves being small and remote in their origin from the brain), and the superior and nobler nervous centres, the intense excitation of even a small and remote centre is communicated to the others, which, as this subsides, fall as much below, as they have previously been stimulated above par. The depression is proportional to the previous excitement.

The cases I shall have to relate which may fairly be called cases of spinal irritation are few in number, for the reason I have stated, that they are but a continuation of hysteria, and, indeed, but a state of things of which epileptiform and epileptic fits are the direct sequence.

It is, however, well to draw attention to the fact that it is in cases of spinal irritation that we observe functional derangements, which are very likely to pass into actual organic diseases; and it is in this class of cases, which are essentially of a chronic character, that very long and persistent perseverance must be pursued. I would, therefore, advise all who meet with them to warn their patients beforehand that they must not be weary and faint-hearted if recovery do not come as soon as hoped for.

Case XVII Spinal irritation, loss of use of right leg—five years' illness – operation[1] – cure.

---

[1] This 'operation' was clitoridectomy. Isaac Baker Brown achieved notoriety in

Appendix C

M.B., age 30, single; admitted to the London Surgical Home November 15, 1861.

History: Five years ago first began to suffer pain in the right leg, which was ascribed to sciatica. Fourteen months since this pain became so bad that she could not walk, and she lost all use of her right leg, at the same time felt great weakness and pain in the back, preventing her sitting. For eight months has been confined to a 'spinal couch'. Is a spare, anaemic woman, dark hair and eyes, dilated pupils, very restless and nervous in her movements.

November 26, 1861 usual operation performed.

December 27., she has gradually improved in health and temper since the operation and is now quite able to walk about her room without help.

She was a long time before her nerve tone was thoroughly restored, but she ultimately got quite strong and continues well.

Isaac Baker Brown, *On the Curability of Certain Forms of Insanity, Epilepsy, Catalepsy and Hysteria in Females* (London: Robert Hardwicke, 1866), pp. 32-35

---

the mid 1860s for promoting the operation of clitoridectomy in women diagnosed with hysteria, believing that hysteria was a result of 'peripheral irritation'–whilst Brown was hesitant about using the word 'masturbation' he was very quick to diagnose this habit as being widespread amongst women. His book, of which the above is a very short extract, is full of case histories where he has diagnosed 'peripheral irritation' as the cause of any number of nervous disorders. The subsequent 'operation' which was performed on his patients was, it seems, met with unequivocal success.

Appendix D - Reviews

When we found, in the first chapter of Mrs. Ross Church's last novel, a reference to 'Titian's Fonarina' (sic), a statement on the part of one of the characters that he was 'the lineal descendant of an hidalgo, and had the right to use the title of 'Don' before his name,' we began to doubt whether a story containing such unusual views of art, and language, could possibly have been composed with sufficient attention to probability to make it worth reading. However, we went on conscientiously, and though we found other eccentricities of the same kind ('Señor,' or 'Senor,' as the authoress prefers, and 'Don' are freely interchanged, and the heroine begins a sentence with 'Caramba' and ends with 'Allons,' and so on), nevertheless, we can congratulate Mrs. Ross Church on a somewhat healthier style of fiction than we have been used to from her. The story is not very well composed, and the motives, in many cases, inadequate. The heroine finds out that her father has been accused of murder, and contrives to get, under a false name, into the family of his brother in England, whom she quite gratuitously suspects of having been the real murderer. The reader is also led to suspect this, and the various incidents are so combined as to foster the suspicion, which turns out quite suddenly to be unfounded. So the story has not even the merit which belongs to the ordinary 'detective' novel. Indeed, for all that conduces to the *dénouement* the greater part of the second and third volumes might have been omitted, unless it was needful to show how well the young lady could disguise herself. This kind of 'Tricoche et Cacolet' business is amusing enough on the stage, when the spectator shares, to some extent, in the deception; but in a book, where the excellence of the acting has to be taken, as it were, on trust, it is less interesting. There is a trifle too much promiscuous kissing at one or two points; and a woman of bad reputation is quite unnecessarily introduced. Otherwise, we have no fault to find with *'Her Father's Name'* on the score of morality; and as for taste, that is a matter which does not admit of discussion.

Unsigned review, *The Athenaeum*, No 2563, Dec. 9, '76.

Appendix D

Mrs. Ross Church has gone to Brazil for the opening scenes of her new book, and a very elaborate picture of Brazilian scenery she presents us with, a picture which serves as background to a young woman of fabulous beauty, who is attended by a goat, like Esmeralda, by a 'rhamphastos' (so called by Mrs. Ross Church, and by gods doubtless, but by men usually denominated a toucan), and by an old mule. It is rather odd that, after all this elaborate scene-painting in the beginning, we are never treated again to a single piece of description, or indeed, of careful writing of any kind. Miss, Mademoiselle, or Senhora Leona Lacoste (for she is really English, thinks herself French, and had a Brazilian mother) is a very energetic young lady who in order to rescue 'her father's name' from ignominy goes through a series of detective enquiries and transformations, which a little resemble those of Magdalen Vanstone in *No Name*. But Mrs. Ross Church has not the ingenious patience with which Mr. Wilkie Collins embroils his mysteries and plagues his characters. On the contrary, everybody tells Leona everything she wishes to know in a charmingly obliging and communicative manner. The steps, indeed, are so simple and so clear that the only wonder is why the damsel's uncle, who is represented as equally anxious to clear his brother's name, did not take them himself. In the way of probability the book will hardly stand examination. One of Leona's tricks is that she steals the letters of introduction of a long-suffering Spaniard, Don Christobal Valera (whom she teases, loves, and finally marries), and passes herself off upon an English mercantile house as commissioned by the New York correspondents. How she could have maintained this deception, which her ignorance of business must have immediately exposed, Mrs. Ross Church does not trouble herself to explain. However, the reader of easy faith and unfastidious taste will perhaps be able to pass his hour with *Her Father's Name* as well as with most of its companions. The least attractive part is the interior and society of Mr Evans' (the London merchant's) house. There are a captain and a doctor who are the stickiest of sticks; a Miss Lizzie Vereker, whose one guiding ambition seems to be that everybody should kiss her; and certain other persons not commendable for interest or novelty. But ordinary English society is a *crux* for other novelists besides Mrs. Ross Church.

Signed review by George Saintsbury, *The Academy,* 11 (1877: Jan/June), p. 6.

Victorian Secrets

www.victoriansecrets.co.uk

Victorian Secrets revives the works of neglected nineteenth-century writers and makes them available to the modern reader.

New titles are under development all the time. An up-to-date catalogue can be found on the website.

If you would like to suggest a title for publication, please contact us at suggestions@victoriansecrets.co.uk

Should you find any major errors in this book, please let us know at feedback@victoriansecrets.co.uk

Printed in Great Britain
by Amazon